# A Nasty Business

## THE JOURNEY BEGINS

*A.R. Goldsmith*

**BANATZOE PRESS**
Ellicott City, Maryland

Publisher: Banatzoe Press, Ellicott City, Maryland
Banatzoepress.com
For info: ARGoldsmith@banatzoepress.com

Library of Congress Control Number: 2022930446

―――――――――――

*This is a work of fiction.*
*Names, characters, business, events and incidents*
*are the products of the author's imagination.*
*Any resemblance to actual persons, living or dead,*
*or actual events is purely coincidental.*

*To My Wonderful Wife Pauline.*

*Special thanks to...*
*Elizabeth, Sharon, Adam, Danny,*
*Nathan, Zoe, Bailey, Allison, Donnie,*
*Vicky, Jessica and Kathy.*

# Table of Contents

# A Nasty Business

## THE JOURNEY BEGINS

*Andy Goldsmith*

# The Match

*Damn rain! Damn English weather!* Nicollette's socks were thoroughly soaked. Her cleats were muddy, her legs wet and heavy. Her breath was clearly visible as a small white cloud this cold and damp December day. Typical! What a day for field hockey, especially playing for the Midlands Club Championship.

Nicollette Beverley had joined the Evesham Ladies Field Hockey team after she first tried out nearly eight years earlier when she was just twelve years old. She had grown and matured with the team, becoming co-captain when she was just sixteen. Her natural leadership abilities were noticed by more than a few outside the coaching staff.

Nicollette took a deep breath as she looked at the Warwickshire players across the field, their opponents for the championship today. They looked sharp in their matching uniforms, bright green tops with a white stripe running diagonally across the front, and tan skirts with long white socks. *They must have paid a lot of money for their kits, but they're the rich kids,* she thought. Nicollette looked down at her old, faded uniform. Her blue top and matching skirt were a couple of seasons past due to be replaced, but there never seemed to be enough money. She shook her head. Nicollette did not know if she felt angry, jealous, or deprived. She had to work hard, taking on babysitting jobs, just to save enough money for her cleats. She remembered something her coach had once said, "Nice uniforms don't make the player. Players don't need to look good, they need to play exceptionally, with skill, determination, and heart. Let your play on the field make a statement." Nicollette felt a surge of adrenaline as she jogged towards her teammates. *I am going to make a statement today!*

This match meant more to Nicollette then just the championship, it was also a matter of pride. She wanted to win, not only for her team, but also for her village and all the kids that lived in Council Housing that had to wear "hand me down" uniforms. Nicollette wanted to convert her emotions to strength and energy. She knew that today was going to be a tough match and would require a huge effort from her and her team.

Evesham's coach was Barbara Thompson. Coach T, as she was called by members of the team, had played field hockey at university. She finished her schooling and was now a Physical Education teacher at Evesham High School. Her coaching style was simple: make the players work hard in practice, build up stamina, and focus on fundamentals. Coach T asked three things from her players—teamwork, good sportsmanship, and team loyalty. She would do everything in her power to guide them to a championship.

The referee blew the whistle, indicating five minutes until the start of the game. The Evesham team finished their pre-game stretches and drills. Coach T called the team to gather around for some final instructions. As the players circled up, the excitement grew, and the adrenaline began to flow. Nicollette drew a deep breath and stood tall. She knew she was about to deliver the most important pregame talk she had ever made.

"Ladies, we have come a long way this season. No one has worked as hard as we've had to to get to this game. We have earned the right to play today for the County Club Championship. Don't let the posh uniforms or uppity attitude scare you. Think of the player you want to be and can be! Think of your little sisters and brothers watching you! Think of how much this Championship means to you and your village! Draw on your pride! Dig deep, ladies! That team on the other side of the field is the only obstacle to our Championship."

Nicollette took a deep breath of air and looked directly into the eyes of her teammates. She could feel the energy rising in her voice. She was holding nothing back and took another moment to keep herself from becoming too emotional.

"I know this may be the last game for some of us and I, for one, want to go out on top. I want to remember this last match not for what we thought we could do, but for what we did—win the Championship!"

The referee's whistle blew, and the eleven starting Evesham players ran onto the field to their respective positions. There was some publicity in the local paper, *The Evesham Journal*, and despite the weather, more than a few on hand to watch the match.

Nicollette took a quick glance at the people watching

and saw her parents waving and shouting encouragement to her. She waved back and gave them a big smile
and thought how lucky she was to have such supportive
parents. As she turned towards the field, Nicollette spotted the well-dressed man in the suit and tan overcoat who
seemed to come to every match. He always wore a brown-
brimmed hat and sunglasses, even in the rain. She could
never get close enough to see his face. *He always dresses
so peculiarly,* she thought, *and no one seems to know him.
I wonder why he comes!*

The referee waved to the players to start the match.
The whistle was blown, the ball dropped, and there
was the first sound of wooden sticks slapping against
each other. Carol Becker, Evesham's starting center,
won the opening draw and advanced the ball down the
center of the field. On her left wing, Carol had Ashley
Tran. Ashley and her family had come to England from
Vietnam just a couple of years ago. Her father had been
in England serving as the Vietnamese trade attaché. As
the situation in Vietnam deteriorated, the family settled in
the Cotswolds where her father found employment
representing Carling Brewery. He recently left the
brewery to purchase a small pub, the "Tired Traveler"
along the main Stratford Road in Brockwirth. Carol
Becker's family had been in the Cotswolds since World
War II. Originally from London, the Beckers had come to
Evesham to escape the "blitz" and work in the munitions
factory just outside of town. After the war, Carol's father
bought a petrol station and now owned three. Carol and
Nicollette had grown up together and were fast friends.

Ashley had joined the two and now the three of them had become inseparable. "The Three Musketeers," they joked.

Carol spotted Ashley about five meters ahead, wide open, and made a quick pass that was easily handled by the winger. Carol sprinted towards the goal. With a quick flick of the wrist, Ashley made a pass to the front of the goal mouth just as Carol approached. The ball crashed off Carol's stick and into the netting at the back of the goal. *Goal!* Evesham 1, Warwickshire 0.

The rain continued to fall, turning the field into a stream of mud. Those Warwickshire uniforms that Nicollette despised were almost indistinguishable from hers. The hockey sticks were caked with mud and the handles were increasingly slippery.

Nicollette was covered in mud and damp to the bone. The heaviness of the wet brought on a feeling of fatigue, but this game meant a lot to her. This was her last game, and she wanted to finish a winner. From somewhere inside her, deep down, an inner strength rose to the surface. She shrugged off the tiredness and continued to play brilliantly, adeptly using her stick and instincts to keep her opponents from gaining any advantage. Nicollette blocked multiple shots and assisted on defending several others.

During the half-time break, as she was coming off the field, Nicollette looked towards the sidelines. It was now a sea of color created by all the umbrellas. She could see her parents under her father's large blue golf umbrella. She knew they would stay for her until the end.

The well-dressed man in the trench coat was still there as well. He stood there getting soaked, not even using a brolly! *Like a statue! Really odd!* Nicollette thought as she ran back on the field.

The second half began, and the ball was becoming harder and harder to move on the soaked field. The bare spots on the playing surface were like small muddy ponds and the grass, what little was left, was now covered with brown streaks of mud. Even still, the two teams playing for the County Club Championship trudged on, neither side letting the opponent gain any advantage. Both clubs seemed to know that this was still anyone's match to win. The field conditions worsened, passing became ever more difficult, the ball moving as if through heavy syrup. With just a few minutes left in the game, a Warwickshire mid-fielder intercepted a short pass and began to charge down the field. A quick pass and the ball was on the stick of one of the best shooters in the county.

The Warwickshire forward set up to let her shot go. Evesham's goalie charged towards the ball, her goalie stick facing down, cutting the angle of any incoming shot. Unfortunately, this left the other side of the goal mouth wide open. As the shot sped towards the open goal mouth, Nicollette reached with every ounce of energy she had to get her stick into some sort of block-ing position. She stretched as far as she could. All the while she could feel herself losing her footing. She came crashing down in the mud just as her stick reached the maximum distance from her body. Click. Nicollette felt the ball bounce off the end of her stick. Laying full out in the mud, she had managed to deflect the ball just enough to send it away from the mouth of the goal. The ball traveled harmlessly outside the goal mouth and was quickly picked up and advanced up the field. Nicollette picked herself out of the mud. She was soaking wet and caked with mud. Her clothes made her feel like she was carrying a 100-pound weight. She stood up and tried to wipe the mud off her skirt and leggings.

The goalie walked over. "Super play, Nicky! You sure saved me and the team. That just may be the play of the game!"

That statement would soon prove prophetic. Nicollette used her dry palm to wipe a chunk of mud off her face and then hustled back to her defensive position. The rain continued to fall, and the hockey ball felt like a rock against the wooden hockey sticks. Fatigue was mounting as twenty-two mud-soaked players trudged back and forth across the field. Nicollette felt like she was running in deep sand, but somewhere deep down, she found an adrenaline reserve. She knew that a great personal prize was almost hers, just a few minutes away.

The referee announced a two-minute warning. Nicollette looked over the mud pit that once was a field. A steady cloud of white vapor coming from the mouths of the players. The rain continued to fall relentlessly, and the afternoon chill was descending. She looked at her teammates and towards her coach. The realization crossed her mind that this was the last time she would be with the team. Memories of her time with her team, the friends she made, the good times, and the hard times. How much she had grown. How much she would miss all of it. She felt unable to move, too tired to be emotional, too tired to react. Nicollette knew she was leaving her best on the field and for that, she was very proud of herself.

The long shriek of the referee's whistle brought Nicollette out of her thoughts. Game over! They had won the Championship! All at once, Nicollette could no longer feel the weight of her uniform as a flood of joyous emotion rushed over her. She rushed to be with her teammates in the center of the field. Gloves flying, helmets dropping, arms raised and hands waving in the air as seventeen soaking wet and mud-covered Evesham women field hockey players celebrated in a joyously loud circle.

Coach T entered the fray, surrounded by the group of wildly excited players. The yelling and screaming seemed to go on forever. Nicollette was enjoying the triumph thoroughly, her voice hoarse with excitement.

Coach T, in the center of the circle of celebration, raised her hands to calm everyone down and gather composure. "Ladies, we still have one thing left to do. Let's line up and congratulate Warwickshire on a good season and a great game. Good sports!" Nicollette's parents met her as she walked back to the sideline. "Well played, Nicky," her father exclaimed. "We are so proud!" her mum said as they had a very wet embrace. As they walked to the car, Nicollette noticed the man with the brown hat and tan trench coat getting into his car. He was alone. *So peculiar!* She stopped to look but was unable to see his face. *Never mind,* she thought as she rolled into the rear seat.

# Celebration

Nicollette could not wait to get out of her damp dirty uniform. She practically undressed in front of the small coal fire in the living room before climbing the narrow staircase to the bathroom. The water was hot as she stepped into the tub. The stiffness she felt in her muscles seemed to melt away in the hot water. She closed her eyes and savored the events of the past afternoon.

As she was getting dressed for the celebration party, Nicollette looked at herself in the mirror, hazel eyes staring back at her. She had short dark curly hair accentuating her "peaches and cream" English complexion. Although she did not consider herself pretty, Nicollette thought she was somewhat attractive. She was fit and had a good figure and the new pair of jeans she was wearing for the party fit her rather well. She smiled at her reflection. *Not too bad if I do say so myself.*

"Carol is here, Nicky," her mum yelled up the stairs.

Nicollette rushed down the stairs and grabbed her house key. "Goodnight, Mum."

"Have a good time, Nicky."

Ashley's parents had set up a separate area in the pub for the team party. There were tables of food and decorations of balloons, crepe paper, and Asian floats. Someone pushed a pint into Nicollette's hands. "Cheers!"

That first sip always tasted so good.

Coach T arrived with her husband, Charles Thompson. It was one of the few times she saw him up close as he did not attend many of the matches. He always was away or something, the coach would say. As she looked at Mr. Thompson, Nicollette thought there was something familiar about him, like she had seen him recently, but she couldn't quite put it together.

Someone handed the Thompsons a pint. Coach T raised her glass. "Let the party begin!"

It was 9 o'clock when Charles Thompson stood up and asked for everyone's attention. "Ladies, what a day you had today! Let's hear it for Coach T!"

A loud crescendo of clapping and cheering went up as the coach stood up to say a few words.

"Thank you, ladies. First off, let's say thank you to Ashley's parents for hosting this wonderful party! Now a few words about the Evesham Women's Field Hockey Club, the Midlands Champions."

At the word "champions," a loud crescendo of excited voices echoed throughout the pub, bouncing off the walls and shaking the glasses on the table. *I bet they can hear us all the way back to Brockwirth*, Nicollette thought.

Coach T broadly smiled as she continued, "This team has worked very hard this season and we deserve today!"

Charles Thompson brought a big box forward and placed it on a table. Coach T continued, "And here is your prize!!"

Mr. Thompson lifted the box to reveal a large gold and silver trophy. Coach T went on. "It is a great day for us as a team, but sad as well. This is the last time that some of us will be together as a team. I want to recognize Carol, Ashley, and Nicollette."

A standing ovation.

"The team got together and wanted to recognize the three of you with a little token. Will the three of you please come over?"

Coach T gave each of them a hug while handing Nicollette, Ashley, and Carol small, wrapped boxes. The three opened the boxes to reveal a gold-plated hockey stick pendant with the Evesham City shield affixed to it.

Coach T continued, "I am very proud of every one of you. You have made coaching fun and very rewarding."

She pointed to the trophy.

"I want to thank my husband, Charles, for his support, patience and understanding. Coaching takes up a great deal of time and he has had his share of cold suppers. But this night belongs to you, the team. So, enjoy yourselves and no practice on Monday!"

Nicollette looked at the pendant. It was beautiful, a treasure she would cherish for a long time. Then, all at once it hit her again. After eight years with the club, she was too old to play with them again. Tears welled up in her eyes and there was a lump in her throat. Yes, the team had won the championship, but she wouldn't be on the field with them again. A bittersweet thought.

Ashley handed her a pint. "I thought you might need this, Nicky."

"Thank you, Ashley," Nicollette whispered back to her with an embarrassed chuckle. "I'll be alright."

"Get that pint down you and let's get some food."

Someone turned on the boombox that was kept behind the bar. A few of the girls started to dance and were soon joined by some boys. Even though she wasn't a big fan of dancing, Nicollette found herself caught up in the frenzy of swinging arms and moving hips. She was enjoying herself thoroughly, her earlier sad reflective moment melting away amidst the excitement of the party.

The house was dark when Nicollette arrived home. Quietly, she went up the narrow staircase and got ready for bed. Just before she fell asleep, Nicollette thought how lucky she was. It had been a terrific day and a wonderful evening. There was the fantastic party, the gift from her teammates, recognition from her coach and, best of all, winning the Midlands Club Championship. *What a day!*

Fatigue taking over, Nicollette closed her eyes and fell fast asleep.

# The Letter

The sunshine was streaming through the sheers when Nicollette awoke. She normally was not a late sleeper, but after all the excitement yesterday, her parents had let her sleep. Now it was nearly ten, half the morning gone. Nicollette dressed and went downstairs to find her mum and dad sharing a cup of coffee.

"Fresh pot, Nicky, get yourself a cup."

"Thanks, Dad, the coffee smells great."

"How about a bit of breakfast?" her mum asked. "I'll whip up some scrambled eggs and make some toast. You need to get some food inside you."

"You had some day yesterday, how are you feeling this morning?" her father asked.

"A little sore and maybe a little tired, not too bad, I'd say," Nicollette responded.

"Well both your mum and I are very proud of you. You played very well and did your team proud. I'd say that it was your best game of the year. The whole village is talking about it."

"Wow! News sure travels fast in Brockwirth!"

Her father went back to his paper as her mum brought the scrambled eggs and toast to the table. Nicollette realized she was hungrier than she thought.

"Hey, there is a nice article about the game in the *Journal*. You are mentioned as making a solid defense."

Her father passed the paper to Nicollette to read the article.

"We are going to Cheltenham for a shop, are you interested?" Mum asked.

During the holiday time of year most of the shops would be open on a Sunday. Nicollette decided to join them. She enjoyed shopping in Cheltenham during the holidays. The shops would be decorated, and the holiday lights would color the streets.

The ride to Cheltenham was very relaxing. No traffic, just some equestrians on horseback alongside the road. Nicollette sat in the back enjoying the bright sunshine this December day. *Quite a difference from the miserable weather yesterday. But that's England,* she thought. Her father drove as her mum had never learned how to drive. In Brockwirth, most conveniences were only a short walk away from the house, so there wasn't much need for a second driver. Her Dad, James Beverley, was originally from London and had served with the Tank Corps in Europe during the war. James was a big man, agile and athletic. He had reached the rank of sergeant during his service. During his training, it was noticed that he was quite a good fighter, very good with his fists. Growing up in a working-class neighborhood in London, one learned to fight rather quickly, and James was no exception. It was decided that he would join a troupe of boxers that would travel among the regiments and box in matches set up to entertain the troops. He became quite popular, winning most of his matches. At one point, he had thoughts about becoming a professional, but a bit of shrapnel from a German grenade ended that. While recuperating in London, he met Alice, a nurse in the recovery ward. They started to date after he was discharged from the army. The romance blossomed and the two were married after the war. A year later, their son Edward was born. Alice was from Brockwirth, a small village in the Cotswolds, a country girl. With all the returning troops competing for jobs, prospects were limited in London, so Alice's father arranged an apprenticeship for James at the Gordon Russell Furniture Factory in Broadway. The young family packed up and moved to Brockwirth. Nicollette arrived four years later. James enjoyed working with his hands and completed his apprenticeship. The young family moved into a small Council house. The Beverleys became part of the community, joining the local cricket club, coffee circles, and schools. Life in Brockwirth was pleasant and secure. As James grew in his job, the family started to travel. Spain was the family favorite vacation destination. Nicollette enjoyed the Spanish seaside, culture and warm climate. While there, Nicollette started to use her high school Spanish. With each trip, her vocabulary expanded, and she became more confident in speaking with the locals. She enjoyed communicating in the local language. The vacations and travel sparked another of her interests, Geography. Nicollette enjoyed Geography studies in school. Her studies reinforced her awareness of the enormity of the world. Even when she was little, she would enjoy using maps to find the cities in Europe where her father was traveling while he was on business trips.

She was comfortable with her life in Brockwirth, but as Nicollette entered young adulthood, her interest in travel and exploring the world grew.

Twenty years old, here Nicollette was, a small Cotswold village girl. She had worked hard in her schooling, finishing her "A" levels at Evesham High School. After graduation, Nicollette took a clerical job at Gordon Russell's and attended Evesham College at night, where she had courses in Math's and Administration. Her instructors were impressed with her mathematical deftness and her superb organizational skills.

James now pulled into the car park. The high street was busy with early holiday shopping. The lamps were already lit as it was getting dark earlier these days. The three of them spent the afternoon in and out of shops. Nicollette found some new jeans and her mum bought a new winter coat. They ended up at the local Pizza Hut in the late afternoon. Sunday night supper was covered with pepperoni.

"Cricket club tonight, ladies?" James asked. "The club will be open for a couple of hours tonight."

"Absolutely, sounds good," Nicollette and her mum responded.

The local cricket club was the center of the social world in Brockwirth. It was a place where friends would meet and share a pint. Some people would bring food and snacks or maybe they would bring in fish and chips. There might be bingo or a quiz. There was a pool table and a dart board. Friday night was men's night. Saturday nights and the rare Sunday evenings were family nights. Nicollette always enjoyed the cricket club. There were many friends there, always someone to talk to and plenty of young men to socialize with. In fact, many romances started at the cricket club. Subjects from local gossip to national politics were part of the many lively discussions going on. On occasion, one of the club's members might bring a guest from overseas. Typically, the guest would be from the United States or Europe.

Nicollette would listen in to the conversation with the "foreigner." She was fascinated with hearing about what life was like living abroad. She would ask about the people, the places, the land, and lifestyles, further piquing her interest in traveling. Nicollette would listen intently as the guests talked about places like Berlin, Paris, and Washington D.C. When she was seventeen, her brother Edward left home to join the Hong Kong police force. He would call home every week. Nicollette enjoyed their phone conversations about his experiences in such an interesting place. It seemed there was always something new to talk about. The family was excited that Edward and his family would be coming home to Brockwirth this Christmas.

James was now waiting at the bottom of the stairs.

"Let's go," he yelled up the stairs. "It's only open till 8:30."

"We're coming, Dad!" Nicollette yelled back.

As Nicollette and her mum started down the stairs, James noticed an envelope on the floor. "This must have been pushed through the mail slot while we were out," as he picked it up off the floor. It was an official looking envelope, complete with the government crest in the upper right-hand corner.

"What's that, Dad?" Nicollette asked as she reached the landing at the bottom of the stairs.

"A letter from the government. Must be important as it was delivered by special post on a Sunday." Her dad paused to catch his breath. "And it's addressed to you, Nicky."

"What, to me? I'm not expecting anything from the government!"

As the three of them stood at the bottom of the stairs, James handed the envelope to Nicollette, his hand noticeably shaking as she took the envelope from him.

"Go ahead, open it."

Normally, mail from the government was about taxes or passports and the like, but never delivered on a Sunday. *What could this letter be about? What have I done?* Nicollette thought as she walked into the sitting room and sat on the chair. Her hands were moist as she pulled two pages from the envelope. She slowly unfolded the letter and read it silently to herself.

"What is it, Nicky? What does it say?"

Nicollette's throat was dry from the excitement. She swallowed and read,

"Dear Miss Nicollette Beverley, we have reviewed your application and would be interested in speaking with you. We would like to meet with you on Tuesday, December 16th at 13:00 hours (1:00 p.m.). We have enclosed a list of items for you to bring. Please confirm our meeting by ringing the number below and asking for extension 267 by 12:00 hours (12:00 p.m.) on Monday, December 15th. Due to the sensitivity of this meeting, we ask you to use due discretion. We look forward to meeting with you. Thank you."

There was a Ministry of Defense symbol on the top of the page. The letter was signed by Colonel Nigel Baron, Sectional Commander. Nicollette slumped back into the chair. She looked up at her parents. The two of them had blank expressions on their now pale faces.

Her father turned slowly to her mum. "I think we should sit down for this."

In a quiet, trembling voice, as if she was struggling for air, her mum asked, "What's this all about, Nicollette? What does this mean?"

Nicollette looked at her parents sitting on the couch. Her father was holding her mum's hand. There was an uneasiness in their manner. There was tension in the room.

Nicollette took a deep breath.

"I don't remember applying for any government jobs. I know I have looked at some possibilities, but I never actually applied. I was going to wait until I finished my work at Evesham College before I did my applications. I thought having college certificates would improve my chances."

A thought crossed her mind.

"There is one possibility though. Do you remember the forms that Coach T gave me back in September? There was a lot of paperwork to complete and documents to collect. You remember helping me with that, Mum?"

Alice continued to look intensely at her daughter. After some hesitation, she replied, "Yes, I remember now. It was a lot of work, I thought, and you really didn't know what it was about. We only knew that your field hockey coach gave the applications to you."

"I do remember Coach T telling me something about traveling and work. It's been almost three months since I returned it to her, and I hadn't heard anything about it. Really, I almost forgot about it. I wonder if this letter is about all those forms I gave her?"

Her dad, visibly shaken, cleared his throat. "I guess it's possible."

"If it's true, I had no idea that application would amount to anything like this," Nicollette responded. "A letter from a colonel wanting to speak to me. Me!"

Earlier in the summer, after a long practice, Coach T had asked Nicollette to stay behind. There was something she wanted to talk to her about. Coach T was curious about what Nicollette might want to do when the field hockey season ended. She knew Nicollette was working and attending classes at night. Nicollette was very comfortable with Coach T. They had developed a relationship beyond the field hockey pitch. They had become more like sisters. Nicollette said she dreamt about a future that would include new experiences and travel, perhaps even living abroad. She talked about her brother, parents, and friends. She talked about Brockwirth, what the village meant to her and her love of England. They spoke for several hours and ended with a light supper in a nearby pub. Nicollette normally had a quiet and reserved disposition, but on that day, she opened to Coach T like she had never done with anyone before. To Nicollette, it was wonderful to talk to an adult other than her parents, who listened and was genuinely interested in her. The words and emotions seemed to flow easily. After the next practice, Coach T gave Nicollette a large manila envelope.

"What's all this?"

"Nicollette, I enjoyed our chat the other day. I've recently been made aware of a new program coming about that I thought you might be interested in. Take this home and read about it. If you are interested, fill out the forms inside and bring the package back to me."

"I'll do it tonight. Thanks."

That night, in front of the small coal fireplace in the sitting room, Nicollette opened the envelope. Inside, there was a letter describing a new program with the government. A special agency was seeking a limited number of young women to fill staff positions. Assignments with the agency could require travel and potentially include appointments overseas. Upon final acceptance, the applicant would commit to an intense period of training. The letter concluded with a statement about the need for an expedient response and the need for confidentiality, as this opportunity was not available to the general public. Nicollette's first reaction was that this sounded like an application for the military, and she wasn't interested in joining the military, but there was no military reference. The letter did sound intriguing to Nicollette, though she did have questions. *I guess I won't find answers until after I fill this application out and give it back to Coach T*, Nicollette thought. She trusted Coach T and returned the completed applications and forms as requested by the letter. That was the last Nicollette heard about the application until today's letter arrived.

"What do you think, Dad? Mum?"

Her Mum and Dad were silent. They looked at each other and then back at Nicollette. Finally, after what seemed like an eternity, her father cleared his throat.

"Well, Nicky, I think you should call Monday morning and confirm your meeting. We still don't have any idea of what this is all about other than it sounds very important, but until then, I would keep this to just your mum and me. Do you still want to go to the cricket club? I could sure use some air."

"Just a quick visit," her mum responded. "We've had a lot of excitement tonight, remember, we keep this letter to ourselves."

It was a busy Monday morning in the office for Nicollette. The end of the year stocks had to be taken and there was a mountain of paperwork and accounts to get through. Throughout the morning, Nicollette kept sneaking a look at the letter, trying to gather the courage to dial the phone. Just before lunch, the office emptied, and Nicollette was alone. She took one final look at the letter and, with a deep breath, dialed.

Two quick rings, then a woman's voice.

"Section 56 administration office, Sergeant Durbin speaking, how may I help you?"

"My name is Nicollette Beverley, and I received a

letter from Colonel Nigel Baron yesterday."

"Please hold, Miss Beverley."

The phone went quiet for maybe a minute. Finally, another woman's voice. "Good morning, Miss Beverley, my name is Lieutenant Blankin, Senior Admin to Colonel Baron. Thank you for calling."

Nicollette repeated herself. "I received a letter from Colonel Baron yesterday."

"Yes, we know, Miss Beverley, and we are glad you called us. I am sure you have a lot of questions and so do we. Are you able to make a Tuesday, 1 p.m. appointment?"

Nicollette hesitated for a couple of seconds. Now everything was becoming real. She took a deep breath and responded affirmatively.

"We are located not too far from Brockwirth in RAF Brize-Norton, about an hour away from you. You will need to come to the main gate on the Carterton Road. From there you will be escorted to our building. Please bring a form of identification for the guards at the gate. Also, please come by yourself as this is a secure area. We shall see you on Tuesday."

"I will be there, thank you. Goodbye."

Nicollette put down the phone and took another deep breath. All her prior angst seemed to disappear. A last deep breath and a sigh. Nicollette was proud of herself. She did it!

Her mum met Nicollette and her father at the door when they arrived home from work. "How did it go with the phone call, dear?"

"Not too bad, Mum. It was almost like they were

expecting my call. I confirmed my appointment to meet them on Tuesday at 1 p.m. I need to get to Brize-Norton. I should probably plan to be there by 12:30 or so."

"Are you sure you don't want me to take you?"

"I'm positive, Dad. They were very clear that I should come alone. Thanks anyway. I know it's because you and mum both care about me, but I will be fine."

Nicollette had a hard time sleeping that night. She couldn't get the next day's appointment out of her head. What would they ask her? What would they want her to do? Would she accept the position if they offered it to her? Was the dress ensemble she picked out appropriate for the interview? She thought about her parents and their reaction when the letter arrived. Finally, out of exhaustion, she fell asleep.

Tuesday morning, after breakfast, Nicollette went upstairs to get dressed, she thought the dress she picked out last night looked great on her. She looked hard at the mirror. The person looking back at her was confident, poised, and secure, clearly hiding the underlying angst flowing in her body. Keys in hand and a kiss from her mum for good luck and Nicollette went off to work.

It was an easy drive to the employee car park and Nicollette was at her desk by 8:15.

*Fifteen minutes early today,* she thought.

The morning was uneventful but busy. The stack of papers on her desk seemed to grow larger. She found herself sneaking glances at the clock on the wall. 9:05. 9:22. 9:51. 10:15, tea break. It felt good to stand up from her desk and stretch her legs. Someone had brought a tin of biscuits into the office and Nicollette politely took one to eat with her tea.

"You look nice today, Nicollette, all dressed up. What's the occasion?" one of the older coworkers inquired.

Nicollette had thought this question might come about.

"I have an appointment at school, and I wanted to look nice," she responded.

"Well, good luck on your appointment," the coworker responded as she walked away.

Nicollette wasn't comfortable telling stories as a practice to anyone let alone a coworker and she wasn't sure how believable the story was. Still, it wasn't anyone else's business about her interview and there was no need to start any rumors.

Her father came into Nicollette's office area just before noon.

"Time to leave, Nicky. Grab your things and I'll walk you to the car."

At the car, James opened the door and looked into Nicollette's eyes. He whispered to her in a soft but shaking voice. "Whatever happens this afternoon, I want you to know how proud your mum and I are of you! You are quite the young lady now. Ask questions and listen. You will do just fine."

Nicollette reached for her father, and they hugged tightly.

# The Interview

The drive was easy and uneventful, just as her father said it would be. After about an hour, Nicollette made the turn onto the Carterton Road and saw the massive complex of RAF Brize-Norton. She turned into the entryway and proceeded to the guard house. There were barricades and military vehicles all along the side of the road. Nicollette stopped her car at the gate by the guard house. Two uniformed soldiers came out from the booth.

"Good afternoon, miss. What is your business here?"

"I have a one o'clock appointment with Lieutenant Blankin."

"Wait here, Miss," the first soldier responded as the second soldier went into the guard house and retrieved a rather large clipboard.

"And your name please, Miss?"

"Nicollette Beverley."

The soldier looked through papers on the clipboard. He stopped and looked at Nicollette. "Yes Miss, here you are. May I see your ID, please?"

Nicollette handed the soldier her driver's license.

"Thank you, Miss."

The first soldier went into the booth and dialed the phone. The second soldier walked around the car, eyeing her car very intensely, making a visual inspection. After about a minute or so, the first guard returned to the car and handed the driver's license back.

"All is in order, Miss. Please follow the private through the barricade to the waiting area." Nicollette noticed the private had a holstered gun by his side as he led Nicollette through the barricade and into a small car park area off the road. He approached the driver's side window.

"Miss, please wait here for your transport. I will stay with you until it arrives. I will need your keys and I will meet you here upon your return."

About two minutes later, a military Jeep drove into the waiting area. Two soldiers wearing red berets approached Nicollette's car. "We are here to collect you, Miss."

Nicollette gathered her things and handed the private her keys. The driver assisted her into the back seat. She was both excited and nervous. *Who am I to get such attention?* she thought. The Jeep traveled past several very large buildings. *Those buildings must be airplane hangars. They are gigantic,* Nicollette thought as the Jeep turned and started down a road parallel to a long runway. She could see fighter planes on the tarmac, all lined up in an orderly fashion. The road seemed to go on for miles. Finally, they reached a cluster of small buildings and turned right onto a slip road. About a minute later, they pulled in front of a very non-descript two story building. One of the soldiers assisted Nicollette out of the Jeep and escorted her through the front door. They stopped at a reception desk.

"Here we are, Miss."

"Thank you, sir," Nicollette responded, not too sure of

military protocol regarding the use of the word "sir."

A woman behind the desk looked up at Nicollette. "Yes?"

"I'm Miss Nicollette Beverley here to see Lieutenant Blankin."

The woman picked up the phone. "Miss Nicollette Beverley is here. Yes ma'am."

The woman hung up the phone and motioned to a soldier who was waiting across the room. "She is to go to room 157."

The soldier pointed his arm down a long hallway. "Please, Miss."

The two of them walked down the hallway. It seemed endless. As they were walking, Nicollette noticed how perfectly clean everything was. She also noticed that there was nobody else in the hallway and how quiet everything was. They finally stopped in front of a nondescript door. Nicollette noticed the "Room 157" plate to the right of the door. Her escort soldier knocked twice on the door. "Enter," came from inside. The soldier opened the door to reveal a small waiting area with a desk near a door that was off to the side.

"Miss Nicollette Beverley here," the escort said.

The woman behind the desk who was also dressed in green military fatigues responded. "Thank you. That will be all." She turned to Nicollette. "Good afternoon, Miss Beverley, and welcome to Section 56. My name is Sergeant Durban. We spoke on the phone. Lieutenant Blankin will be out momentarily. Please have a seat."

Nicollette sat down on a small sofa against the wall.

A million thoughts were going through her mind. *What had she gotten herself into?* Part of her was scared and overwhelmed, telling her to call it quits and just get up and leave. Another part of her was very excited, anticipating what was about to happen.

Just then, the rear door opened.

"Good afternoon, Miss Beverley. Thank you for coming. I'm Lieutenant Blankin, please come through."

Nicollette stood from the sofa and walked through the door to a large, well-lit office. At the rear of the room, there were two windows. *Not much of a view*, Nicollette thought, as all she could see was another building from the windows. On one side of the room, there were several bookcases filled with books. Nicollette noticed a small door in the corner that was mostly hidden by a bookcase. The wall on the far side of the room was covered with photographs and plaques. There was a Union Jack in the corner and in the center of the room, a large imposing wooden desk with two green leather chairs.

"Please have a seat, Miss Beverley."

Nicollette sat down in one of the green chairs. *This is certainly more comfortable than the backseat of that Jeep*, she thought.

"Well, good afternoon again, Miss Beverley. I hope all this is not too overwhelming."

"Glad to meet you, and yes, I am a little overwhelmed."

Lieutenant Blankin reached across the desk to shake Nicollette's hand. Nicollette was hoping her palms weren't too wet with nerves as they shook hands.

Nicollette guessed Lieutenant Blankin was in her

mid-thirties. She was attractive, with jet black hair tied up in a bun behind her head. The lieutenant had piercing brown eyes and Nicollette knew she was physically strong by her firm grip when they shook hands. She had all the appearances of an assertive, in-charge woman. Sergeant Durban came through the door with a tray of tea and biscuits. She placed the tray on a small table by the desk and left the room.

"With or without, Miss Beverley?" she asked.

"With please."

"I guess we should get started, Miss Beverley. I know you must have many questions."

Lieutenant Blankin then pressed a blue button on her desk. Within a matter of seconds, the small side door opened. Nicollette nearly fell out of her seat when she turned and saw Charles Thompson, Coach T's husband, come through the door.

"Hello, thank you for coming, Nicollette."

Nicollette did not know what to say. She finally found her voice as they shook hands.

"Mr. Thompson, this is a surprise!"

"I bet it is! You didn't expect to see me, I'm sure. You will understand more in a short while. In the meantime, I think we should get started."

Charles Thompson sat down in the chair next to Nicollette and turned towards her.

"First of all, Nicollette, I hope you had a pleasant journey and haven't become too intimidated by your surroundings. What we are about to discuss is very sensitive, so I need you to be aware that you are responsible for keeping our discussions to yourself. If you are uncomfortable with this, you may leave now." He paused. "I hope you stay."

Something about Charles Thompson's voice had a calming effect on Nicollette. She felt much more at ease now.

"Yes, Mr. Thompson, I understand. This meeting is to be kept a secret."

"Splendid, let's proceed. You live in Brockwirth, not too far from Cheltenham. Have you heard or do you know what goes on there?"

"Not really, Mr. Thompson. I know the government has quite a few buildings there, but I really don't know what happens there."

"Well, let me explain. Simply, Cheltenham is a government facility where we communicate with our international allies and listen to our adversaries. We employ many people with many different skills to help us accomplish this. Skills such as mathematicians, cyphers, cryptographers, engineers and linguists to name a few. We listen and communicate twenty-four hours a day, seven days a week, three hundred sixty-five days a year. We listen all over the world. We monitor communications in Europe, the Middle East, Africa, South America, Asia, everywhere. We take these messages, break them down, determine the content and communicate the information with our allies. We do this to keep our country and our allies safe from foreign threats. These actions are vital to England and our allies' securities. We have a very close relationship with the Americans. You may have noticed at times, in Brockwirth, a few American 'tourists.' These are more than likely Americans who have come to Cheltenham to work with us. We do the same thing, sending some of our folks 'over the pond' to work with them. It's a very serious, delicate, and complicated business, but very important and necessary. But before I go on, are you following me, or do you have any questions?"

"No, Mr. Thompson."

"Good, let's continue. During World War II, our Intelligence service grew rapidly. You probably learned about the breaking of German codes and the enigma machine in school. No doubt, you may have also heard about the work at Bletchley Park as well. The activities there played a significant role in our victory. After the war, there was a need to continue this service, but due to domestic and European rebuilding priorities, funds were hard to obtain. The government was only able to maintain a smaller operation. However, as the realities in Europe and Asia began to become more concrete, the Cold War, the government awarded more funding and operations expanded both domestically and throughout the world. Many of the people who worked with the service during the Second World War were recruited back to work. Without giving a history lesson, our service has been vital to our country during the Korean War, the Suez Campaign, and even helping the Americans during the Cuban Missile Crisis. All this time we have kept a close eye on our 'friends' in the Soviet Union and Asia. Now given all this background, where does Nicollette

Beverley fit in and why are you here?"

*Now comes some answers,* Nicollette thought as she gripped the arm of the chair tightly and stared wide-eyed at Mr. Thompson.

Mr. Thompson paused. He took a sip of tea and continued.

"Just recently, the Ministry of Defense concluded an accounting of our service. Much time and effort were given to researching the efficiencies and effectiveness of our operations. The Ministry wanted to be sure that as the world changes and threats to our country come from many new adversaries, we should be ready to meet these challenges quickly and effectively."

Charles Thompson stood up from his chair and walked towards the windows.

"The Ministry understands the important and vital work we do and wants us to be sure that we have the energy and resources to maintain our high level. The final report, presented to the Prime Minister by the Minister of Defense, was a thorough and comprehensive look into our activities. Without boring you further, Nicollette, the report contained some suggestions about our operations and the need for additional funds. The report did show some concerning information that requires more immediate attention. First off, a significant number of our special operations people are older than the general population and are nearing retirement age. Some of these people have been with us since the end of the war. The Prime Minister suggests we should focus on the recruitment of more young people. He feels that this would bring in new ideas and help keep our group current with the information and ideas that are 'on the street' so to speak. Secondly, the report pointed out a distinct shortage of women in our agency and particularly in our special operations network."

Charles Thompson turned away from the window and looked directly at Nicollette. She could feel his intense stare.

"Are you starting to see the big picture, Nicollette?"

He paused.

Nicollette's head was spinning. She had just heard information she had no idea existed. There was a lot to gather in. She took a quick glance at Lieutenant Blankin and then turned to Charles Thompson. Her mouth was dry. She took a quick sip of the now cold tea in her cup.

"I think so, Mr. Thompson," she responded, her heart beating hard in her chest.

"Good, now we can get to the point of this interview and why Miss Nicollette Beverley of Brockwirth is here. The Minister of Defense has issued a directive to actively find and recruit young women to fill in areas of need. This would accomplish immediate areas of concern as put forward in the report. Therefore, we are actively searching the Midlands area for young women who we believe would fit into our special group and be successful in our agency."

Charles Thompson paused and walked over to where Nicollette was seated. He leaned in towards her. In a calm soft voice, he spoke. "Nicollette, I believe you are a prime candidate for this program."

Charles Thompson then sat down in his chair, all the while looking at Nicollette. Nicollette could feel the tension in the room. This was very serious. She took a moment, trying to avoid Mr. Thompson's eyes. She looked at Lieutenant Blankin. The Lieutenant's eyes looked right back at her.

*Breathe, Nicollette, breathe,* she told herself.

She quickly revisited the information she just heard, and it suddenly came to her. She was being recruited for a position in a special group within the Ministry of Defense. That explained Brize-Norton, the red bereted soldiers escorting her to the building, and all the secrecy surrounding the meeting.

Charles Thompson broke the deafening silence. "What do you think, Nicollette? Are you interested?"

Nicollette thought about how she should respond. The opportunity sounded exciting but thinking about the Ministry of Defense gave her some pause.

"Well, Mr. Thompson, I am flattered and thank you for thinking of me. This all sounds very exciting and," Nicollette paused, took a breath, "yes, I am very interested. I would like to talk this over with my parents and just think a little bit about it, but yes and yes again, I'm interested."

"That certainly is good news and of course you should discuss this with your parents, however, you must remember that this afternoon's conversation is to be kept among us and kept quiet to anyone else."

"What should I tell them, Mr. Thompson?"

"I would tell them that this is a clerical position with

the government that could require travel and days away from home and leave it at that."

Charles Thompson now reached over to the tea and biscuits and poured a fresh cup of tea for himself.

"Nicollette, how about a fresh cup? It's still hot."

Another cup of tea sounded good to Nicollette. Her mouth was still a bit dry.

"And you, Lieutenant Blankin?"

"Yes, please."

When he finished pouring, Mr. Thompson took a biscuit and sat back in the chair, crossed his legs and continued. "Now Lieutenant Blankin will explain in more detail the practical aspects of the position."

Lieutenant Blankin pulled some papers from the top drawer of her desk. She looked across the desk at Nicollette.

"Well, Miss Beverley, let us talk about the position. As a recruit, you will first have to pass both physical and mental tests. These tests will involve quick thinking, endurance, and creativity under stress. We will also test your abilities to remember and transfer information as well as completing assigned tasks. Sounds like a tall order, doesn't it?"

Nicollette shook her head, feeling like she was in a dream, in awe that she was selected to be here, in this room, listening to an adult other than her parents talk about her future and being brave enough to say yes.

"It will be very challenging, Miss Beverley. We are looking for the elite. The position demands peak performance both in mind and body, total concentration, twenty-four hours a day, seven days a week, three hundred sixty-five days a year. After you accept the position, the testing will commence on January 5th. Once you pass the tests, and I am sure you will, you will begin four weeks of on-site intensive training. The training will bring you to optimal performance in body and mind. After you complete the training course, you may be assigned to a peer to learn more of the intricacies of our group, or you may be assigned to assist with the next group of recruits. Our initial recruiting class will be twenty young women just like you. We expect to have maybe twelve or thirteen at the end of the course. Those that graduate will be the elite, the best trained, best equipped, and most talented of the group."

Lieutenant Blankin paused for a moment as she leaned back in her chair. She forced a smile at Nicollette.

"Miss Beverley, this is an opportunity to have a challenging, rewarding career and at the same time, serve the England we all love. As for income, we will pay you seventy-five pounds a week during training."

*That's almost my monthly salary now!* Nicollette thought.

"Upon graduation, your salary will be reviewed. Your training will be conducted at a government facility and there will be minimal contact with your family."

She paused and with a stern expression, continued, "Well, Miss Beverley, we know this is a lot to take in and you may have some questions?"

Nicollette thought for a moment. So much was going through her head that it was hard to digest it all. She had questions, but first she had to get through the combination of excitement and fear she was feeling. She thought it might be better to take a step back before asking any questions, part out of fear of looking silly and part out of fear of the answers.

"No, Lieutenant Blankin. I think I understand, but I may have questions later."

Sergeant Durban knocked on the door.

"Yes," Lieutenant Blankin responded.

"There's been a phone call for Mr. Thompson. He is wanted in building seven. They asked for him to come right away. I brought your hat and coat, sir."

Sergeant Durbin handed Mr. Thompson his coat and hat. He reached out to shake Nicollette's hand.

"Thank you for coming, Nicollette. Give this some thought. I think you are a good fit. Have a good night."

Charles Thompson put on his coat. It was a tan trench coat. Nicollette noticed streaks of mud on the back. Then she saw his hat. Brown. Everything looked familiar, the coat, the hat, the mud spots. She quickly put it all together as Mr. Thompson left the room.

*It's him! The overdressed man at the matches. It's Charles Thompson! Coach T's husband! Fancy that! But why wouldn't Coach T say something or point him out?*

"Any thoughts, Miss Beverley?" Lieutenant Blankin asked rather casually as she sat back down.

Nicollette looked at Lieutenant Blankin, thinking how to respond. The position sounded very exciting to her, certainly better than working full time at Gordon Russell's for the rest of her life. She knew that her response to Lieutenant Blankin's question was very important, despite how casually it was asked.

*What would the lieutenant think of her response? I don't want to be overexcited on the one side, yet I don't want to be too smug either,* Nicollette thought. She took a breath and cleared her throat.

"Well Lieutenant Blankin, first off, I'm chuffed that you've considered me for this position. There was a lot to take in this afternoon. A tremendous amount of information."

She changed to a more serious expression and looked directly at the lieutenant's eyes.

"Yes, I'm very interested. As Mr. Thompson was describing the position, it felt as if someone had reached into my head and pulled some personal thoughts as to what I might want to do for a career."

Nicollette paused for a moment. A weak grin appeared on Lieutenant Blankin's normally stoic face. "I'm glad to hear that, Miss Beverley. We believe you will do very well in the position."

"Like I asked Mr. Thompson, I would like to talk this over with my parents."

"Certainly, Miss Beverley. I think sharing your thoughts with your parents is a splendid idea, however, even with your parents, you must use discretion."

"Two more questions come to mind, please."

"Certainly."

"When do you need my final decision and what about my current job at Gordon Russell's?"

Lieutenant Blankin leaned forward. "Miss Beverley,

there is a need for an expedient answer to our offer as you can understand, practicalities and such, so we would want to hear from you by tomorrow 16:00 hours, 4 p.m. civilian time. Your formal training would start the fifth of January, so almost three weeks away. I have prepared a package for you to take home with some basic information, but I must remind you again that this interview must remain between us and your parents. Sergeant Durban will give you the package when you leave. Now, as for your employer, we have prepared a resignation letter for you and included it in your packet. Should a problem arise, please let us know."

Nicollette glanced at the clock on the wall. It was nearly four. She could see through the window that it was getting dark outside. The interview had lasted almost three hours. She was feeling a bit fatigued from the intensity of the afternoon.

Lieutenant Blankin leaned back in her chair. "Would you like another cup of tea before you leave?" she asked in a more relaxed voice.

"Thank you, but I'd better not. I think I should be heading home."

"I understand. You have a lot to think and talk about tonight."

Lieutenant Blankin pressed a button on her phone. "Miss Beverley will be leaving now, thank you."

The Lieutenant stood from her chair and escorted Nicollette to the front area.

"It was good meeting you, Miss Beverley. We look forward to hearing from you tomorrow."

"Thank you, Lieutenant Blankin. It was good to meet with you and Mr. Thompson as well. I shall give this all of my attention and ring you tomorrow."

"Good afternoon, Miss Beverley. Drive safe."

"I will. Good afternoon, Lieutenant Blankin."

Two soldiers wearing red berets were waiting for Nicollette as Sergeant Durban handed her a large manila envelope.

"Read this carefully."

"I will, thank you, Sergeant Durban."

The two soldiers escorted Nicollette down the hallway, past the security desk at the entrance of the building and helped her into the waiting Jeep. It was now dark, and an evening chill was setting in. The ride to the main entrance didn't seem to take as long as her earlier ride. She held the manila envelope tightly in her hand. Her thoughts kept revisiting the last three hours. Every so often, she would glance down at the envelope. *What more information might be in here? What is this all about? Do I really want to go through this training? Is this something I really want to do or am I just excited about being offered a position?* Her mind spun with the enormity of what was happening to her and how the next few days could change her life. This would most certainly be the biggest decision she had ever had to make. It was an awful lot for a twenty-year-old young lady to absorb. As the Jeep pulled next to her car, Nicollette gathered herself together. The driver helped her out from the back of the Jeep and handed her the keys to her car.

"Good afternoon, Miss. Have a safe ride home."

"Thank you and you have a good rest of the day."

Nicollette drove to the security booth at the entrance where there was a quick check of her identity. She turned onto the Carterton Road and headed home.

# The Decision

It was dark when Nicollette arrived back in Brockwirth. Her mum and dad were just sitting down to tea as she walked into the house.

"How did it go, Nicky? We want to hear all about it."

"Let me wash up and I'll be right down to tell you."

Nicollette went up the narrow staircase to her room where she quickly changed out of her dress into a pair of jeans. She washed up in the small hall bathroom. The cool water felt good on her face. After drying her face, Nicollette stared at the image in the mirror. *You can do it, Nicollette. You can do it!* Her mum had saved a Cornish pasty from lunch, and it was just coming out of the oven when Nicollette sat down. It smelled wonderful. She did not realize just how hungry she was. The first bite of the pasty tasted so good.

"Well?" her dad asked. "Let's hear all about it."

Nicollette took a sip from her cup of tea. She had to be careful. "The interview was very interesting. It was a lot to take in. I was in a nice office, and they brought in tea and biscuits. The office belonged to a woman named Lieutenant Blankin and she was very nice. A man came in and talked about the position."

Nicollette was careful not to mention Charles Thompson by name.

"He spoke for a good amount of time about the

position and then the lieutenant described where I might fit in. It is a government administrative job that involves a good deal of training and could include some overseas travel. If I take the position, they want me to start training on the 5th of January. I will be in training for four weeks. I will be staying at a training facility, but I may be able to come home on some weekends."

Nicollette wasn't quite sure about the visiting part, but it seemed to flow from her naturally in response to the look of concern on her parents' faces.

"They will pay me 75 pounds a week. They are bringing in twenty of us to start the testing and training process and they expect to have some dropouts during the program. I have until tomorrow to give an answer. They gave me a package of information on my way out. Let's look at it after tea."

As she was eating, Nicollette kept looking at her parents' expressions. She could tell by their faces that they understood that this was no ordinary government job, despite the title "administrative position." The post being offered to their daughter was much more serious than working in an office. Nicollette could see worry, fear, and angst in their eyes, an emotion she had never seen before from either of them. Normally, there would be small talk at the table, maybe about work or a laugh or some gossip, but tonight the table was quiet, only the sounds of forks and knives slowly touching the plates. The silence was deafening. After what seemed like an eternity of quiet, her father asked in a quiet voice, "What do you think, Nicky?"

Nicollette looked again at her parents. Their faces were flushed. All at once, they looked older, more aged, to her. Her father's hair was thinning and there were wrinkles under her mum's eyes. Nicollette paused. *When did this happen? Did I do that?* There really was not much more to tell her parents, but she had to talk about the afternoon. She needed to be cautious and deliberate with her answer.

Nicollette took a sip of water.

"I don't want to disappoint either of you, but I can't see my future in an office at Gordon Russell's. I know they have been good to this family, but I want more, and I know there's more out there for me than a desk job here in Brockwirth. This just might be just what I want, what I've been waiting for all these months. A chance to do something unique and interesting plus the possibility to travel."

As she was answering her father's broad question, Nicollette's words were flowing easily. A deep underlying emotion was taking hold in her mind, convincing herself that this was the perfect opportunity. Her mum, who had been very quiet, looked hard at her daughter, making direct eye contact. There was tension in her voice as she spoke.

"Nicollette, I think it all sounds very exciting. Do you think you would like the job?"

The look of deep concern on their faces had not gone away. They both waited for Nicollette to answer.

"Yes, Mum, I think I would. I think this is the opportunity for me."

"Well then, let's clear the table and take a look at that information you brought home."

Nicollette retrieved the manila envelope, opened it, and pulled out the contents. There were many forms all paperclipped together and two additional smaller envelopes, a light green one and a blue one. The instructions on the front of the light green envelope said that it should be given directly to Nicollette's doctor. A small note attached to the envelope asked that Nicollette have a check-up in the next few days. If there was any trouble scheduling, there were instructions to call the number at the bottom of the note. The blue envelope was addressed to Nicollette with instructions not to share the contents with anyone. Nicollette quickly folded that envelope up and put it in the back pocket of her jeans. There were forms requesting information regarding the family. There were spaces to be filled out about her parents, siblings, and immediate relatives. There was a form about James's job and another form asking about Alice's work status and still another asking about the working status of each of her grandparents. One form wanted more information about Nicollette's education. As she looked over the paper, she noticed that a few of the answers had already been typed in, including her school's name and her "A" level status. At first, she thought this to be a bit odd, but then remembered what Mr. Thompson had said earlier about recruiting and it started to make sense. They had been investigating her, doing background work, making sure she would be a good candidate for the group. Nicollette had a quick feeling about her privacy but that soon left her mind. *Nothing to hide,* she thought.

"Mum, we will have to call Dr. Howard to make an appointment. I need to give him this envelope."

"We will do that first thing tomorrow," her mum responded while she was busy doing paperwork.

At the bottom of the pile was one final form. It contained instructions for the disposition of all the forms in the package and specific instructions for Nicollette regarding everything she had experienced during her interview including people, places, and things. These instructions were to be followed if she were to choose not to accept the position. Nicollette took this paper, folded it and placed it in her back pocket along with the blue envelope.

Later that evening as they were filling out forms, Nicollette could feel her father's eyes on her and looked up at him from the paper she was completing. The two sets of eyes locked in at each other. No words were spoken. James looked into his daughter's eyes, he saw the intensity and maturity she was displaying in dealing with what was taking place. He was very proud of Nicollette and at the same time, apprehensive and concerned about the position being offered to her. Alice brought coffee into the front room. Nicollette could see her mum's hands shaking as she handed her a cup. In a forced whisper, Alice asked the question.

"Nicky, we have done a lot of work tonight. Are you going to take this job?"

Nicollette had always found it easy to talk with her parents, but now she had to draw up the courage to let them know her feelings. She looked at her mum and then back at her dad. She had made up her mind. This was her chance. She took a deep breath.

"Yes, I'm going to call tomorrow and accept the job. There is still the testing I must pass, and I know it is going to be a tough challenge. But, yes, I am going for it."

A sense of relief flowed through her. There was a silence in the room, only the crackle from the small coal fire broke the quiet. Her parents looked at each other and then at their daughter.

"It is a big decision and if that's what you want, we will support you all the way. We are very proud of you, Nicollette. We love you very much," her mum responded, "and both your father and I know you will be up to the challenge."

Nicollette wasn't convinced her parents were that comfortable with her decision. She could still detect the uneasiness in their manner, but she had made up her mind.

"I love you both and I will make you proud."

Later in bed, Nicollette remembered the blue envelope from her jeans pocket. She opened it. The envelope contained a single page letter. As she was reading the letter, she thought about how everything was very exciting and at the same time, so very serious. She fell into a deep sleep.

The next morning, it was quiet during the ride to work with her father. As James parked the car, he turned to his daughter.

"Big day today, Nicky," her father stated. "When are

you going to make your call?"

"I thought I would call at morning tea break. The office is usually empty then, so I will have some privacy."

"How about your resignation letter? When will you do that?"

Nicollette knew that resigning would be tough to do, but she knew it would have to be done. "I thought after lunch might be the time."

Nicollette looked at her father.

"I feel bad about giving such short notice, especially at this time of the year with stock taking and all."

"And with the Christmas plant shut down, next week," her father added.

"Well, maybe my boss and I can work something out."

She looked at her dad. "I hope this won't affect you, Dad."

"Not to worry, Nicky. We should be heading in," he responded.

The stock reporting was moving along smoothly. The receipts and invoices were lining up rather well this morning. *Lucky day*, Nicollette thought to herself. At 10:30, the tea cart came around and Nicollette was left alone in the office. Nicollette nervously pulled a piece of paper from her pocket. She double checked to make sure she was alone. *Courage, Nicky, courage.* She slowly dialed the number, taking a deep breath as the phone started to ring on the other end. Another ring, another deep breath. Sweaty palms. An answer.

"Section 56 Administration Office, Sergeant Durban

speaking, how can I help you?"

"Good morning, Sergeant Durban. This is Nicollette Beverley calling. Is Lieutenant Blankin available?"

"Hello, Miss Beverley. Please hold whilst I check for you."

Silence. A minute went by, then another. The enormity of this decision was coming to bear on her. *Any moment now*, she thought to herself. *You can do it.* Finally, a voice on the other end.

"Good morning, Miss Beverley. This is Lieutenant Blankin. How are you this morning?"

"A little nervous and at the same time very excited."

Nicollette paused to take a breath. *Here it comes, Nicky, your moment.*

"I've given it a great deal of thought and have discussed it with my parents, and I have decided to accept the offer and join your team!"

As soon as she heard herself say the words, a wave of confidence came over her. The earlier nervousness was gone and replaced by a feeling of strength. It was like her inner self reassuring her brain that this was a good decision, one she would not regret.

"That's splendid, Miss Beverley. I know this was a big decision for you. Have you made an appointment with your GP?"

"My mum's organizing that this morning."

"Have you spoken to your boss? Given him your letter?"

"I was going to do that after lunch."

"Good. Did you read the letter in the blue envelope we gave you?"

Nicollette recalled the letter from the blue envelope she read the night before. The letter was written in blue ink on government stationery with the Department of Defense symbol at the top. Nicollette thought the letter was a bit unusual in that it was handwritten, almost casual in a sense, not really what one would expect from the government. The opening of the letter was about the confidence and character needed to be successful in any career. One must accept challenges and meet them head on with vigor and strength. The most impossible questions require just a bit more thought and creativity of mind. The next paragraph talked about how the training would test her mentally and physically. There would be successes and failures, but if she, Nicollette, completed and passed the course, the experiences she encountered and the skills she obtained would bring rewards that she would carry for the rest of her life. The concluding paragraph talked about her specifically. The words described how she, Nicollette, had been under observation for a period prior to her interview and remotely during the interview. There was the utmost confidence that she would do well with the training and be a great asset to the group. The letter was signed personally by Colonel Nigel Baron. There was a typed postscript to the letter, that upon acceptance into the program, a package would be delivered to Nicollette within forty-eight hours.

Nicollette sighed. "Yes, I read it before going to bed last night."

"Good. We will get the package to you by Saturday. Please call me when it arrives. I will provide the contact number in the package. In the meantime, Miss Beverley, take a deep breath and relax. We will talk again shortly. Good morning, Miss Beverley."

"Good morning, Lieutenant."

As Nicollette hung up the phone, she thought about how this simple call could change her life. Deep inside, she knew that this was a great day for her. She would never forget "the call." She was excited and anxious to get started. One more obstacle she needed to clear today though, her resignation.

It was noon and the office was clearing out for lunch. Nicollette preferred to bring her lunch to work. Her mum always packed a nice sandwich or two and on her small salary, bringing lunch was more prudent. Nicollette prided herself on being practical. As she was opening her lunch bag, the desk phone rang.

"Hello. Nicollette Beverley speaking."

"Nicky, it's Mum. I spoke to Dr. Howard's office, and you are all set for tomorrow at 9:15. Did you make your call?"

"Yes, Mum. It went well. I'm now committed. We'll talk about it at tea."

"Very proud of you, Nicky. Have you spoken with your boss yet?"

"After lunch, I thought. About one."

"I have a little secret for you. Your father called me earlier. He knows your boss very well and he may have planted an idea with him."

There was silence on the phone. After a couple of seconds, her mum continued.

"Please don't be angry with him. He just wants to make

things easier for you because he loves you."

"I know, Mum. I'm not angry and I'll keep our secret. Thanks, Mum. See you later. Goodbye."

As she was hanging up the phone, Nicollette thought about the conversation. She was happy for her mum to arrange her doctor's appointment and understood what her father was trying to do for her at work, but she was twenty years old now and she was feeling like she should be more responsible for her life. Nicollette loved her parents deeply and they loved her very much, that was obvious, but maybe because she was their only daughter or maybe because she was the last child at home, either way, it was time for her to be more in control. A smile crossed her face as she was thinking. *I started being an adult today. I made an adult decision and made the call. Now I'm going to my boss's office and resigning. I'm going to be strong and confident. Watch out world, Nicollette Beverley has arrived!*

# The Story

Nicollette awoke naturally the next morning from a deep sleep. It was still dark outside. Her bedside clock said it was nearly eight o'clock. A sudden panic came to her as it was a Friday and not the weekend. *Did I over-sleep?* Then Nicollette remembered that her mum had arranged an appointment with Dr. Howard at 9:15. She sat up in her bed and revisited the events of yesterday afternoon. She remembered knocking on her boss's door, sitting across from him and talking about her plans. He was very receptive and although he was disappointed to lose a good worker, her boss was very supportive of her decision to move on to a government job. The end-of-year stock taking, and accounting was nearly finished, but there was still work to be done. It was arranged that Nicollette would work a couple of days during the Christmas holiday shutdown. As she was leaving his office, he reminded her about the holiday luncheon tomorrow. She walked back to her desk and thought, *That was almost too easy, why was I so worried? Well done, girl!*

She arrived at Dr. Howard's office and was greeted by the receptionist.

"Good morning, Nicollette. Your mum called and said you needed to see the doctor, everything alright?"

"Yes, everything is fine, just need to see Dr. Howard

about a form."

"The doctor should be finished in about ten minutes, then I will come for you."

Nicollette sat down in a chair across from the door leading to the doctor's office. She thought about what the contents of the light green envelope might be. Then a bit of fear came over her. *What if I fail a test here or something isn't right? I won't be able to go any further for the position and I have already resigned from my job!* The more she thought about it, the more nervous she became. She took a deep breath. *What's to worry about, I feel good. I'll be fine.*

"Dr. Howard will see you now, Nicollette, follow me."

Nicollette walked through the door into the doctor's office and sat down across the desk from Dr. Howard.

"Good morning, Nicollette. How are your parents? What brings you to my office this morning? Feeling alright?"

Dr. Howard had been the village physician for as long as Nicollette could remember. Brockwirth was a very small town and so a tenured doctor would get to know his patients very well, in fact, to most of his patients, Dr. Howard was like a member of the family.

"Everyone is fine, Dr. Howard, in fact, my brother and his family are coming here for Christmas. The reason I'm here is that I had an interview for a job with the government and was asked to make an appointment with you. They gave me this envelope to give you."

Nicollette handed Dr. Howard the envelope.

"Let's see what we have here, shall we?"

Dr. Howard opened the envelope and pulled out a single page. He read the letter to himself.

"Well, that seems simple enough."

Nicollette looked at Dr. Howard nervously. Her curiosity aroused.

"What does it say?"

"They are asking for your medical records and some information from me. Not to worry, Nicollette. What kind of job is this?"

Nicollette knew she had to be vague, even with Dr. Howard.

"It's an administrative position that may involve traveling overseas."

Dr. Howard removed his glasses and looked directly at Nicollette. His normal mild manner turned into a serious expression. In a soft but commanding voice, he asked, "Do you want the position they are offering you, Nicollette?"

Nicollette realized that whatever was written in the letter must have been very important. She had never seen this type of expression on Dr. Howard's face before. She took a breath. "I've given this a lot of thought. I've talked it over with my parents." Nicollette paused and looked directly into the doctor's eyes. "Yes, Dr. Howard, I'm very excited about this job."

Dr. Howard put his glasses back on and stood from his chair. His voice returned to the familiar tone.

"Fine, Nicollette, let's get to it."

Dr. Howard proceeded to give Nicollette a complete physical. He checked her vital signs, all the while making small talk about the village and her family. He casually asked about the job offer as well and Nicollette was careful with her replies. When they were finished, Dr. Howard asked Nicollette to remain in the waiting area. She sat on the same worn couch she had sat on many times before. She never really paid much attention to the waiting area before, but as she looked around the room, she realized that nothing had changed for as long as she could remember. The pictures on the wall, the furniture, even the posted office hours. *Just like Broadway*, she thought, *you could leave here for years, but when you return, all will be the same. Nothing seems to change here.*

After about fifteen minutes or so, Dr. Howard emerged from his office with a large manila envelope. Nicollette could tell it was rather full when Dr. Howard handed it to her. It was thick and heavy. *Much more than a couple of pages*, she thought. She could see the doctor's embossed seals surrounding the taped over clasp.

"Thank you, Dr. Howard."

"You're welcome, Nicollette. My instructions are to give this envelope to you sealed. It is only to be opened by your future employers. Please give my best to your parents and good luck in the new job!"

Nicollette was back at work by 11:30 and it seemed as though the holiday party had already started. A coworker had brought a record player into the office and holiday music was wafting throughout the building. There was a small Christmas tree in the corner, decorated and lit up by strings of miniature lights. There were plates of cookies and mince pies on one of the desks and a couple of carafes of warm cider on another. Someone handed Nicollette a cup of the warm cider. She took a sip. It was smooth as it went down her throat and there definitely was more than a little alcohol added. It was obvious that little or no work was going to happen today.

The luncheon was held in one of the empty store areas. Everyone from the company was there. Managers, shop workers, and administrators all came together to enjoy a wonderful buffet meal. There were the usual speeches by the owners thanking everyone for a good year. There was recognition for several employees and the announcement of retirements and new hires. The festivities ended with a Christmas and New Year's toast. The plant was now closed. People were shaking hands and passing holiday greetings. Nicollette walked back into her office area and sat down at her desk. Most of her co-workers had already taken advantage of the early closing and were gone. One of the more senior staff members was putting on her coat and going out the door as she turned to Nicollette.

"Don't forget the envelope on your desk, Nicollette. Have a great holiday. See you next year!"

"Thank you!" Nicollette responded. "You too."

The office was quiet now. The record player and the treats were gone and so were her co-workers. A sudden sinking feeling overcame Nicollette as she realized that this was the last time she would be working in this office. No goodbyes. When the plant reopened on Monday, January 5th, she would not be here. Just her empty desk. Fighting back a few tears, Nicollette noticed the white envelope underneath her phone. She sat at her desk and slowly opened it. There was a letter to her from her boss thanking Nicollette for her time at Gordon Russell's and asking her to help close out the year by working on Monday morning and the morning after Boxing Day. There was a number for her to ring so she could be let in. There was a second letter from one of the owners, again thanking her for her service and wishes for the best of luck in the future. Attached to the back of the letter was a check for fifty pounds, nearly two weeks' salary. A note paper clipped to the check stated, "For your hard work and dedication. Thank you."

Nicollette laid the letters down, looked around the room. Her emotions taking over, she could not hold back the tears any longer.

A knock on the door brought Nicollette back to reality.

"What's all this?" her father asked as Nicollette wiped her eyes with a tissue.

"Nothing really, Dad. Just me being a bit silly about leaving here, I guess."

James reached for his daughter. "There's nothing silly here, Nicky. Leaving is torn between two emotions. One is sadness of leaving your co-workers and a familiar situation and the other is the excitement of a new adventure and all the promise it holds. Now wipe those eyes and let's head home. There's lots of work to be done before your brother arrives."

It was still dark outside when Nicollette opened her

eyes. She had planned to run this morning; it had been over a week since she last exercised, and this was a good chance to have some alone time. She quietly dressed and headed downstairs. At the front door, she put on her new Nike Elite running shoes. She loved her Nike Elites. They were light blue with the trademark yellow swoosh, a pretty shoe as well as being very comfortable to run in. She had spent over thirty pounds to buy them, but it was well worth it. Nicollette did some stretches and started her run, slowly at first, but reaching her pace after a couple of blocks. The sun was just rising in the sky lighting up the village. Today's run was no different than the many runs she had made before. As she started her run, the cold air bouncing off her face felt invigorating. Her senses awakened and her thought process stimulated. Nicollette felt the run was doing her good, she could feel a kind of serenity and calmness as she took in the morning air. As she was running, the thought crossed her mind about how many more of these runs she would have. If she passed the testing, would her new career take her away from Brockwirth for long periods of time? Would she ever come back here? How much would she miss the small village she grew up in? Would she lose that sense of belonging? Of her roots? Tough questions for a young lady, but for now, it was all about the run.

As Nicollette continued up the village towards home, she came across the War Memorial on the village square. She had passed it a thousand times before but never stopped to really see it. Something inside her caused her to pause from her run. It was as if something inside the

Memorial was reaching out to her, inviting her to stay and visit. The statue was just there, standing alone in the small grassy area. Inscribed on the base were the names of all the local soldiers who had served in the armed forces and perished in their service for England. *What courage and sacrifice these people had made. Strength. Conviction. Sense of purpose.* Nicollette thought about this as she reached out with her hand and ran it across the individual names permanently immortalized in the graying stone. *Would she, could she, be able to make the same commitment as these brave warriors?*

Her parents were just sitting down for breakfast when Nicollette arrived home. She went to her room, had a quick clean, and dressed for the day. As she was walking down the stairs, Nicollette could hear the front door shut.

"What is it, Mum?"

"It's a package for you, Nicky."

"That must be the package from Lieutenant Blankin. She told me it would arrive today."

Nicollette took the letter sized square box package into the sitting room. She looked at her father.

"Open it, Nicky," James said anxiously.

Nicollette sat on the chair and opened the box. She pulled out the contents. There was a stack of papers and a sealed brown envelope. The paper on top of the stack was a letter from Lieutenant Blankin. Nicollette glanced over the letter.

"What does it say?" her mum asked as she sat down on the couch.

"It's a welcome letter of sorts. Let me read it to you."

Her father joined her mum on the couch. Nicollette glanced at them before she started to read. She still could see some angst in their expressions although not quite as pronounced as before. *They must be coming around to the fact that this is really happening to me,* she thought then began to read.

*Good morning, Miss Beverley.*

*Welcome to the training program for Section 56, Operations Group 228. We have received all your necessary paperwork and your initial information file is complete. As we discussed, this is your entrance package. Please follow the instructions carefully. This is a four-week training course and we have included a list of supplies you will need to bring. You will find 100 pounds to cover your expenses in the brown envelope. You will need to arrive at the main gate at RAF Brize-Norton at 01:00 hours on Monday, January 5th, 1976. This is the same gate you entered for your interview. Please show the guard your identity badge (enclosed). The guard will direct you to the drop off area where you will have ten minutes to say your good-byes. Please note that you will have very little communication with your family during your training. You will be picked up at the drop off area and brought to the staging center for further instructions. We have coordinated a plan to explain your whereabouts during the training period. The information you need is on the yellow papers in the package. Please become very familiar with your "trip" and you may start using the information immediately. I remind you that you need to be extremely discreet about this information and the program. Limit specific information to your very immediate family only. This is of the utmost importance.*

*Nicollette, we are excited to see you Monday, January 5th as a participant in our training program and we have the highest expectations for your success! Please contact me at extension 267 by 12:00 hours Monday, December 22nd to confirm receipt of this package.*

*Sincerely,*

*Lieutenant Cheryl Blankin*

*Section 56*

*Operations Group 228*

*RAF Brize-Norton.*


Nicollette laid down the letter and looked again at her silent parents. She sighed and exclaimed, "Wow, just think, a week ago I was celebrating my team's championship and now, I'm signed up to receive training for a position with a government agency. How one's life can change in such a short period of time, although I wonder if this is moving too fast."

"Perhaps they want it that way, Nicky," her mum responded. "Maybe they want to see how good you are at making quick, important decisions."

"Maybe, maybe." Nicollette looked at her father. "Do we have time to get into this?"

"I think we should, Nicky."

Nicollette removed the contents of the box and spread them across the floor. She found the brown envelope and opened it to find fifteen ten-pound notes. There was a security badge with her name and picture on it.

"I don't remember having my picture taken by anyone. I guess it was taken without me knowing during my interview. I can tell because that's the dress I wore that day."

There was a paper explaining her drop off instructions again and another three pages stapled together with the list of supplies to bring. Finally, there was a bundle of papers held together by a large clip. On top of the first page, written in big bold letters, was the word "INSTRUCTIONS."

Underneath the heading were two sentences.

*"This information can only be shared with immediate family members on a need-to-know basis. Please become thoroughly knowledgeable with the enclosed contents."*

Nicollette removed the clip holding the papers together and removed the top page. She started to read the instructions.

"What does it say?" her mum asked anxiously. "Can you share it with Dad and me?"

"Certainly, I can. You are my parents and I think you should know what's going on."

Nicollette relayed the written instructions to her parents. "These are the instructions and cover story I am to use to explain my absence while in training. The cover story is that I am going to America on January 5th to do a course at Grinnell College in Iowa. The course is about sports physical therapy and the latest advancements on stretching, exercise, and recovery techniques. There will also be courses and 'hands on training' in dealing with on field issues such as sprains and concussions. This course is offered to certain English Counties each year as part of a bilateral agreement between women's sport agencies here in the UK and the NCAA program in America. It is completely funded by the NCAA. There was a last-minute opening for the course in America. Coach T was approached to find a candidate. She asked me if I would be interested. Of course, I agreed to go."

Nicollette handed her mum an index card.

"Here's the address where I'll be and an emergency contact phone number. The letter continues by saying we are not to deviate from this story, and we must remain consistent with our explanations. It goes on by saying that the government has gone to great measures to be thorough, yet simple in the story. It must be made believable. Any questions asked of you should be answered in simple and vague terms. As an example, answer: 'I'm so excited about going to America, the details have slipped my mind.' The letter concludes that no one other than the training group, me and my immediate family, and Coach T and her husband, will have knowledge of the cover story."

Nicollette laid the paper down and looked up at her very quiet parents and exclaimed, "Now it all makes sense. That's the connection! It was Coach T's husband, Charles, the man in the trench coat and hat, who nominated me for the post. He is the one responsible!"

With a puzzled look, James asked, "Who's responsible? For what?"

Nicollette gathered her thoughts and explained to her parents.

"Did you two see a well-dressed man at the championship match? He was wearing a trench coat and a brown hat with a suit underneath?"

"I think I did, Nicky," Alice answered. "I remember thinking how peculiar this man was dressed to attend a rainy field hockey match. Everything down to his shoes was odd for that day."

"Well, that's Charles Thompson, Coach T's husband! He was at my interview and when he got up to leave, he put on the same color trench coat and hat as the man at the match. There were dried mud stains along the lower back of the coat. I recognized the coat because this man was at a lot of our matches, and he always wore the same trench coat and hat. The team used to have a giggle about him. He would always leave our games early and was too far away for me to make out his face, but the stains on his coat convinced me that he was the well-dressed man at our matches! When I saw Mr. Thompson when we got our trophy, I could not recognize him to be the overdressed man. Even though Coach T would make excuses for her husband's absences at our matches, he was there the whole time. Now it all makes sense!"

Nicollette paused and caught her breath. Her expression changed from one of excited revelation to one of question and concern. *Was he watching me in secret! Me??!!*

Nicollette looked at the next pages. There were tickets for British Air flight 846 from Heathrow Airport to Chicago O'Hare Airport and from O'Hare to Des Moines, Iowa. There were preprinted boarding passes for each flight as well. A small note at the bottom of the ticket page stated that her return flight information would be delivered to her in America. Finally, the travel document indicated that Nicollette would be met in Des Moines by a representative of the program and escorted to a shuttle that would take her to Grinnell College.

There was a moment of silence in the sitting room.

"Someone has gone to a great deal of trouble for you, Nicky!" James exclaimed nervously. "I think it's very important that we all become very familiar with this story. In the Army, they used to tell us, 'The less said, the better,' and I think this is a good time to put that to use."

Alice walked the contact card into the kitchen and placed it on the small refrigerator.

"What's on the last page?" her father asked.

"It's a letter explaining my instructions if I do not complete the training. My excuse for coming home from America will be an illness and that I am to remain in the house for two days with no visitors. I will be contacted for a debriefing after the two-day period. I am reminded that by agreeing to enter the program, I am also agreeing to abide by the Official Secrets Act and remain diligent and private about the program. There could be severe penalties if any of us were to violate or fail to adhere to these instructions."

"What's on the shopping list?" Alice asked as she walked back from the kitchen, changing to a more light-hearted subject.

Nicollette pulled a small stack of stapled papers from the floor. "It looks like the usual, Mum. Toiletries and personal items to last me a month for a start. A couple of pairs of jeans and two black knee length skirts. One blue and two white blouses. A couple of dresses and four dressy tops. That's just the start, the list is long, even down to hose and underwear. They must have pre-shopped the list at Marks and Spencer's. Here, take a look, Mum."

Nicollette handed her mum the list. Alice put on her glasses and peered over the papers.

"I think you're right, Nicky. Beside each listing is an item number. This must have taken a lot of work, but it does make our job easier. Even the prices are listed."

"I believe you should follow that list very closely," James added. "We can make a start on it today if we leave now."

"Let's go!" Nicollette exclaimed.

Nicollette had plans to meet up with her friends, Carol and Ashley, later that night at the Traveler pub. She saw Ashley by the bar.

"Hello, Ashley. Nice crowd tonight."

"It's going to be more crowded later. The music goes on at nine. Whatcha having?"

"I'll have a half lager for now."

Nicollette wanted to pace herself. She never was a big drinker, and she knew she needed to have all her resources to contain her news. The two of them shared small talk. The pub was getting crowded. Carol walked into the pub and saw the two of them at the bar.

"How's it going, you two? Sorry I'm a bit late, last-minute chores and the lot."

"You haven't missed anything. My folks are about to put on the music. What's your poison?" Ashley asked.

"I'll have a pint of bitter, please, I've got to loosen up my dancing shoes if you know what I mean!"

The music started and a few couples got up to dance. Despite the crowd, the Trans always made room for dancing. Nicollette, Ashley, and Carol stood at the bar enjoying their drinks and singing along to "Bye Bye Baby" by the Bay City Rollers. The song got the pub rolling. Everyone was singing and dancing and having a good time. Nicollette had a second half pint. She was feeling relaxed, enjoying the music and the company of her friends. Far from her mind was the future, tonight was about having a good time.

The music continued. The hit song "The Bump" played and the three girls "bumped" at the bar. They were laughing and cheering "The Bump" as they downed their glasses. Nicollette felt a tap on her shoulder. She turned to see it was George Knight.

"How about a dance, Nicollette?"

"Sure, why not."

The two of them waded through the crowd and found a spot. The "Hustle" was playing, and they danced. Nicollette was a good dancer and she pushed George along. George was a couple of years older than Nicollette. He had grown up in the village and was now working in his father's painting business. George loved Cricket and he was a useful enough player that he played on the first eleven. For some time now, Nicollette had the feeling that he liked her. He would seek her out at the cricket club or at the pub and buy her drinks and snacks. There were even a couple of casual dates at one of the local bistros. Nicollette could tell that George was a little shy around a crowd and sometimes had to force the conversation. Still, he was just a friend, harmless but nice to her.

They shared a couple of dances and then went back to the table for another round and some small talk. Carol and Ashley had found dance partners as well. The evening was flying by, and it was getting late. Ashley's father announced the last song of the night. "Stairway to Heaven" seemed an appropriate finishing song to a wonderful evening. George held out his hand for Nicollette as the music started. The pub floor was crowded with dancers, but that was no distraction as the two came together in a slow dance. The song ended and to Nicollette's surprise, George leaned into her, and they kissed.

It was after eight when her mum knocked on the door.

"Wakey wakey, Nicky! Going to be a busy day! Lots to do!"

Nicollette crawled out of bed. Sunday was normally a "lie in" morning, but there was a lot going on today. Her packages had to be organized and there was Edward and family arriving Tuesday morning.

Nicollette's older brother, Edward, had signed up to join the Hong Kong police force just over five years ago. Growing up, he had always talked about becoming a policeman, and even his favorite shows on the tele were police programs. He worked hard in school and after graduation, an opportunity became available to join a police officer recruiting class that would be sent to Hong Kong. The training was rigorous and there were many dropouts, but Edward excelled and even became comfortable with Cantonese. His superiors liked his energy and enthusiasm and moved him up the ranks quickly. He had recently been promoted to detective. Ed married a local woman in Hong Kong, Sying, and they had two girls. Sue was three, as she was proud to point out, and Mae was twenty months. And now, they would be here for Christmas!

Monday, Nicollette had a quick run into town for some last-minute supplies. By the time she got home, the sky had become dark, and it had turned quite cold. A few snow flurries were falling as she unloaded the car and piled the shopping bags in the living room. Her mum went to start the fire in the fireplace. The coals were stubborn at first, but eventually, they emitted a warm glow. Soon the room was warm. James had already started to separate everything into a neat arrangement, presents, supplies and food. Nicollette was in the kitchen "putting the kettle on."

"Nice cup of tea coming," she announced to her parents from the kitchen door.

"Hey, Nicky, I think you should make your call now before it gets too late."

Nicollette brought her package down from her bedroom and pulled out the letter with the phone number on it. She dialed the number and sat down at the kitchen table as the phone call was connecting.

"Good afternoon, Section 267, Sergeant Durban speaking."

"Good afternoon, Sergeant Durban. This is Nicollette Beverley calling. I have received my package and I'm calling as instructed."

"Thank you, Miss Beverley. Do you have any questions about your instructions?"

"No."

"How about your supply list?"

"All finished."

"Excellent and I see here that you've had your doctor's visit."

"Yes, on Friday."

"Sounds like all is in order. We will see you on January 5th. Have a wonderful Christmas and a happy New Year, Miss Beverley."

"You too as well, Sergeant Durban. Goodbye."

"Goodbye."

Nicollette hung up the phone and went into the family room. She saw the sealed folder that Dr. Howard had given her on the buffet chest. Nicollette looked at her parents.

"I made the call and now I'm all set. Interesting thing though. Sergeant Durban, that is my contact today, said that they already have my medical report. I just saw Dr. Howard Friday morning and he gave me this envelope to bring with me on January 5th. Interesting."

Monday night routinely was "tele" night and tonight was no exception. "*Are You Being Served*" was airing their Christmas special as well as "*Man About the House*" and

"*The Two Ronnies.*" Alice brought in the sandwiches as the family got comfortable for the evening. Nicollette looked around the room and at her parents, comfortable and relaxed on the sofa albeit emotionally drained from the week's events and the anticipation of their son's arrival tomorrow. The warmth from the coal fire seemed to melt the angst and tension away. A brief respite.

It was nearly ten when Nicollette looked over at her parents and saw their eyes were closed, her mum's head resting comfortably on her father's shoulder despite his muted snore. Nicollette thought about her future and how different her life could become. She took another look at her parents. A shiver shot up her back. *Would this be the last time she shared the Monday night routine with her parents? How many more little events would change? How many more last times?* She closed the door to the front room and headed upstairs, the picture of her parents sleeping by the fading fire permanently etched in her mind. As she lay in bed later, the excitement of the upcoming day started to swell within her. *Just think, Nicky, Edward and family are already on a flight from Hong Kong to England. How excited his wife and their two little girls must be to visit us for the first time.* Nicollette's eyes started to get heavy as she realized how much she missed her older brother. He was her mentor and friend, always looking out for her as they grew up. She missed him.

In the early morning, Nicollette put on her running shoes and headed down the village. The air was crisp, and it was gloomy overhead. Not much sun today. *Probably some rain or snow later,* she thought. The village was not too crowded, although there were some tourists milling about. *Christmas Eve in Brockwirth. How lovely the village looks this morning,* she thought as she followed her usual path up to Brockwirth Tower. She stopped at the tower and looked down on the village as she must have done hundreds of times before. Her favorite spot. Her favorite view of the village. Brockwirth. Her home.

The phone rang in the kitchen.

"Edward is here, they are leaving Heathrow now," James announced to Alice and Nicollette. Alice was pacing the sitting room and every so often would check the window to see if her family had arrived. Finally, she spotted the car coming around the corner and rushed to open the front door. Edward pulled into the driveway and parked the car. He opened the rear door of the car, and two little girls held their father's hand as they walked towards the front door to meet their grandmother for the first time. Unable to contain her excitement, Alice ran towards Edward and the two little girls.

"Hello, Edward."

"Hello, Mum." The two of them embraced.

Alice reached out for her granddaughters who quickly hid behind their father.

"You must be Sue and you must be Mae."

Edward nudged the two shy toddlers from behind his back.

"This is your grandmother, girls. Don't be shy."

Slowly, the two little ones took steps towards their grandmother.

"That's it, girls. Say hello to your grandmother."

"Hello, Grandma," they said in unison.

Alice again reached out to the little girls and this time was rewarded with a loving embrace. James and Nicollette walked over to Sying.

"Welcome, Sying. We are so happy to finally meet you and welcome you to our family. Let's get you lot inside and get acquainted."

Later, as they were finishing tea, Edward turned towards Nicollette.

"We heard about the championship. Dad told me you played very well and made the play of the game."

"I don't know about that, but it sure was exciting! It was also a little bit sad though, because I realized that it was my last match with the team."

"But you went out in style! Well done, Nicky. So, what else is happening with you? Still working at Russell's and going to night classes?"

"Well, there is something actually, big brother." Nicollette paused for a breath before her big announcement. "I am going to America in a couple of weeks."

"Wow, that sure sounds exciting, tell us about it."

"I'm going to take a course in sports medicine and team management at Grinnell College in Iowa. My field hockey coach was informed of an opening for this course. It is sponsored by the N C double A in America for women athletes, and they partner with certain counties to include British women in the program as well. Barbara, I mean Coach T, recommended me and now

I'm going to America! My itinerary card is on the fridge. Good news though, I've made a start on getting ready so I can spend more time with you and Sying and my two beautiful nieces!"

With that, both girls jumped on their aunt's lap and chatted away about their favorite colors and animals. This year, Christmas Eve was very special in the Beverley home.

"How about a quick bath and a good night's sleep for you two? Big day tomorrow. I heard Santa is making a special trip here for you two, but only if you are good," Edward told his daughters.

"How about Grandma helping Mummy get you ready for bed? Would you like that?"

The two little girls yelled out a resounding "yea" and ran up the stairs, followed by Sying and Alice. Soon the water could be heard filling the bathtub. Edward sat down on the floor in the sitting room between his father and sister. The inquisitive part of his brain taking over, he looked at Nicollette and asked, "Is your coach Barbara Thompson the same Barbara Thompson that was there when I was in school?"

Nicollette nodded her head in the affirmative. Edward continued, "Isn't she married to a man named Charles?"

Again, Nicollette nodded yes.

"What's this all about, Edward?" James asked his son.

"If I remember, Charles had some kind of government job that made him travel a lot. I remember some of my friends saying that Barbara would be worried about him traveling all the time and not being at home more often.

I think he had one of those hush-hush jobs."

Nicollette looked at her father and James looked back at her. Nicollette broke the stare. "You know I could never hide anything from you, Ed. The letter did say close family only and my big brother is a policeman."

"What letter? What's this all about?" Edward asked.

"It's alright, Nicky. Go ahead and tell him. But son, what Nicky tells you is only for us, the only other person who knows is your mum," James replied.

"Now I'm really curious, Nicky. What's happening?"

"Alright, Ed, let me start from the beginning. A while back, I filled out an application for a government job. Somehow, Charles, I mean Mr. Thompson got wind of it and put out feelers on me and the family. Just last week, I received an official letter from a Colonel inviting me to an interview at Brize-Norton. I agreed to the interview, and I must admit, I was very nervous. They talked about the job and what was expected from me. The more I listened, the more interesting the job sounded. I started to see myself in the position and by the end of the interview, I all but agreed to come on board, pending talking to Mum and Dad first of course." Nicollette paused and took a breath, letting the information settle with her brother, then continued, "I will be leaving on the fifth for four weeks of testing and training. They made me see Dr. Howard and even sent me money for supplies. They provided a detailed list of clothing to bring, and very importantly, they sent a set of instructions about my cover story and the specific women's training in the states. We were given instructions about who to tell what to. So just Dad and Mum and now you know the truth."

There was silence in the room, only the muffled sound of the small coal fire permeated the room. With a blank look on his face, Edward stared at his sister. His mind revisiting images of a very young Nicky always tagging along with him, taking the last biscuit and fighting over the bathroom. Now he looked over at her, all grown up, no longer a little sister but a young lady about to embark into the adult world. *Where did the time go*, he thought, *where did the time go?* Edward took a deep breath and stood to stretch his legs. He broke the quiet and with a grin on his face exclaimed, "Wow, Nicky, they want to make a spy out of you!"

Nicollette gasped and took a pause. This was the first time she had heard the word "spy" associated with herself.

Ed went on, "Do you remember Ian McKenzie?"

"Wasn't he on your junior cricket team in school?" James asked.

"Same one, Dad. We've been friends a long time," Edward continued. "Ian went into the army, and they selected him for the Intelligence Services. They sent him away for specialized training and now he works overseas. I caught up with him, in, of all places, Hong Kong. He looked me up and we had a drink together. He did not talk much about his work, but I kind of gathered what he was doing. Anyway, your story sounds like Ian's. My sister, the spy. Crickey!"

There was a pause. James looked at his son and

daughter. There was emotion and angst in his face as he addressed his two children.

"Ed, I must admit that your mother and I are still having a hard time with this, much like when you left for Hong Kong. Like your job, this one could be dangerous for Nicky. These are serious people in a serious business. A lot of effort has been made to get to this point and your sister still has a way to go, so let's make sure we are clear about what to say and to whom we say it to."

"Well, little sister, your secret is safe with me, and I wish you the best in your training. I know you will do well."

Nicollette looked up at her brother. She was still thinking about how he had used the word "spy." *Me, a spy!?*

"Thank you, Ed. I'll work hard." She looked at her father who still had the fearful expression on his face. Nicollette went to him and kissed his cheek. "Don't worry, Dad, I'll be fine. You taught me well."

# Christmas 1975

Christmas morning in the Beverley household was sheer pandemonium! Two excited little girls turned the front room into a mountain of ripped wrapping paper and ribbons. All the presents so carefully wrapped, now revealed to happy smiling faces. After an early Christmas lunch, James looked at the clock on the mantel and turned on the tele.

"Time for the Queen's speech."

Everyone stared at the tele as the Queen spoke. It was like the whole country just stopped to listen to the Queen's Christmas speech. *Such elegance and grace,* Nicollette thought, *it's as if the Queen is speaking to us individually and as a nation at the same time. We are indeed fortunate to have Queen Elizabeth.*

James poured a celebratory brandy, and the glasses raised.

"To the Queen!"

"Cheers!"

"Maybe we should start to clean up?" Alice announced as she winked an eye towards James.

"I think there might be one more present somewhere." He pulled a box from behind the buffet. "Nicky, this is for you."

"Me?"

"Go ahead and open it," Edward said.

Nicollette carefully removed the wrapping paper to reveal a white cardboard box. She slowly opened the box and pulled out a black leather soft carryall. It had brass clasps and brass rings that held the shoulder strap in place.

"It's beautiful! I love it! Look, it even has my initials engraved in gold lettering! I will use this with pride! Thank you! Thank you!"

"We thought you might be able to use it in your new career."

"I will use it every day," Nicollette replied, gazing at the soft leather.

Nicollette handed the case over to her young niece to see. Sue rubbed her hands over the soft leather and touched the gold initials.

"This is so soft and pretty, just like you, Auntie Nicky," she exclaimed in her toddler voice.

*A wonderful and perfect Christmas*, Nicollette thought to herself as she looked around the sitting room. How much she enjoyed this day and this moment, the laughter, the warmth, and all the love. Family. How this was so important to her and how much she hoped her new career would not get in the way of Christmases in the future. A grin crossed her face as the words of her niece resonated in her brain. *A soft and pretty case and a spy as well*, Nicollette thought.

The phone rang at Nicollette's desk. Nicollette had come into work the day after boxing day to finish up the stock taking, just as she promised her boss. It was hard to get up and come to work, she was enjoying her brother's family and those two nieces kept her busy all the time, but a promise was a promise. It was her mum, calling to see how she was doing and to see how long she would be.

"Not too much longer," Nicollette responded.

Nicollette placed the completed work on her boss's desk. She looked around one last time as she put on her coat. As she left the building, Nicollette watched the big door close behind her. She heard the click as the door shut and the lock engaged. *How apropos.* She remembered the saying, "When one door shuts, another one opens." As she walked away, something inside her made her stop and look back at the door. *How many times have I come through that door and didn't even think about it and now, well...?*

Nicollette turned towards home. She wiped a tear from her eye.

Wednesday, James and Alice volunteered to watch their grandchildren so the "kids" could have a night out. The pub was rather full when Nicollette, Edward, and Sying arrived. Ashley had "reserved" a table for the five of them. Carol was already there sitting down. Ashley brought five pints to the table.

"I have about ten minutes before they want me back at the bar," Ashley said as she laid the pint glasses on the table.

"How about a quick Christmas toast?"

The five of them raised their glasses and cheered the holiday.

"To good friends," Carol exclaimed.

"Yes, and to a wonderful holiday and the warmth of the season," Nicollette added.

As if in unison, all the glasses met together in the air with the expected "clink" and the toast was completed with the first taste of beer.

"We have another toast," Ashley exclaimed.

"Welcome home, Edward, and welcome to Brockwirth, Sying!"

As he looked around the pub, Edward commented, "The place looks great, Ashley. You've done the pub up nice. I like the decorations and the tree; I even like the wreaths attached to the walls. Very festive." Edward pointed to the mistletoe hanging over the bar.

"I wonder how much action that mistletoe will see to-night?" he added smugly.

Nicollette looked at her friends, Carol and Ashley. She then took a quick glance at her brother Ed. His eyes caught hers and he responded with a wink. It's like he can read my mind! Nicollette thought. I guess now is as good a time as ever! She took a breath.

"I do have some news to share," Nicollette announced.

"Do tell, Nicky, what have you got?" Ashley asked.

"Well, you two are my best friends, so I want you to be the first to know."

"Go on," Carol insisted.

"I am going off to America in January!"

"What?" Ashley and Carol shouted in unison.

"It's true," Nicollette continued. "It seems that there is a joint program with the Brits and the Americans in the

States for training in sports medicine and management. Coach T nominated me. I talked it over with my family and accepted, and so I will be off to Iowa after the first."

"Wow!" Ashley exclaimed. "How long have you known? It seems so sudden."

"I only found out about a week ago, and there was so much to do. I had to do the paperwork, had to see the doctor, all that with Ed coming as well. So, I wanted to tell you when we were all together, and now seemed like a good opportunity!"

"How long will you be away?" Carol asked.

"Four weeks or so. I will miss you guys!"

"This calls for another round," Ashley said as she went over to the bar.

Carol leaned in towards Nicollette. "Are you going to tell George?"

"I guess I have to. I am not looking forward to that."

The evening rolled on. The holiday music was changed to the "top hits of the year countdown" on Radio 2.

"Look who just came in!" Carol exclaimed.

Ashley pointed over to George who was making his way over to the table.

"Are you going to tell him, Nicky?" Ashley asked.

"I guess I should but let me do it my way and you two behave. No prompting!" Nicollette knew her friends. They could be quite mischievous if they wanted to be.

"Ok, we'll be good." Carol smiled as she responded.

George approached and laid his glass on the table.

"Hello, ladies. Did everyone have a good Christmas?"

The three responded "yes" almost in unison.

"And you, George?" Carol asked.

"Ours was quiet but very nice, thank you."

"Do you mind if I sit?" George asked as he pulled a chair from the adjoining table and sat down next to Nicollette.

"Sure, but you buy the next round! George, this is my brother Ed and my sister-in-law Sying," Nicollette replied, not too sure if she was already too drunk.

George returned with drinks. "Cheers!" Then: "Anything new, Nicky? I haven't seen you for a week and you didn't call me back?"

Nicollette thought for a moment. *When did he call me? Did I get the message? Did Mum forget to give it to me?* Then she thought this might be the opportunity to tell him about her "trip." She pushed her drink aside and gathered her thoughts. *No slips, Nicky. Take your time!*

"I'm sorry for not calling you back, but this has been a very hectic week for me, what with Edward and family coming from Hong Kong and everything, but I do have some news I need to tell you."

"Do tell, I'm all ears." George leaned in towards Nicollette.

"George, I'm going to the States in January."

George fell back in his chair, his mouth open and eyes not blinking.

"What....When....How?"

He could not get his questions out fast enough to complete his thoughts. Nicollette looked him in the eyes and grabbed his hand.

"Calm down and let me explain. Now take a deep breath." George nodded. Carol and Ashley watched as

Nicollette explained the details of her trip.

George, still in a small state of shock, looked into Nicky's eyes. "I will miss you."

"I know."

# New Year's 1975

The New Year's party was held at the local cricket club. This was one of the only places in Brockwirth that could accommodate the 150 or so people attending. The plan was for everyone to bring a dish and champagne was provided by the earnings of the weekly 50/50 drawings held at the club since spring. The affair would start at around 6 p.m. so that families could bring their children to the party.

The Beverley family arrived at around seven, with five adults and two children in tow. Despite the chilly temperature, there were many outside the Cricket pavilion with bottles and glasses in hand. Someone had brought a large radio and music was blasting loudly away. After greeting the outside crowd, the Beverley family went inside to tables of food and beverages. Nicollette walked to the side door of the building, like she had hundreds of times before. But this time was different. The cricket club had been such a big part of her life. A strange feeling came across her. *How long till I come here again? Could this be the last time I come here? Is this my last New Year's party here? Another last?* Nicollette sighed as she led her nieces inside. James unpacked two bottles of his "Brockwirth Brew," a mixture of whiskey, ginger ale, and a few other "secret ingredients"—a true family recipe. Alice unpacked a load of cookies while Edward and Lin brought large bags of crisps. The family settled at a table in the corner. Nicollette bought the first round, saving her father's brew for later.

Once the family settled, Nicollette excused herself so she could circulate. She knew her friends Carol and Ashley would be arriving soon. And then there was George coming later. She grabbed her beer and headed back outside through the side door.

"Happy New Year!" Carol said as she saw Nicollette.

"Ashley called and said she will try and sneak away later," Carol told Nicollette,

"The pub is full, and her parents want her to stay and help. She invited us to come over later for a toast if we could. So, what's going on? Are you getting excited for Monday?"

"Nervous and excited. But that's Monday. Tonight, we party!"

Carol noticed a group of people she knew from her tennis club standing on the side of the building.

"Come on, Nicky, I think I recognize some people over there."

"Hey, Colin!" Carol shouted.

"Come and join us!" Colin responded.

"Nicky, meet Colin, Peter, Garrett, and this is Martin. They're in my tennis club."

Carol's family belonged to a sports club in Evesham. There were four indoor tennis courts as well as badminton and handball courts, plus an indoor swimming pool and a workout room. It was expensive to join, so it was mostly a rich person's club. Nicollette had been invited there by Carol, so she was familiar with the facility. The club was impressive, but not some of the members Nicollette had met there. The rich seemed to have their own language and set of rules. Except for Carol and a few others, they all appeared snobbish and aloof. Definitely a class-driven club. Nicollette's family was of more modest means, so there was little chance of membership, even if she wanted to join. But this was New Year's Eve and Carol seemed to know this group. Carol also knew how Nicollette felt about "the rich kids" so maybe these friends were different, plus George was nowhere around, so with drink in hand and a little courage, she joined the conversation.

"So, you're Carol's friend from school," Garrett asked, "is she as 'cheeky' around the hockey team as she is at the club?"

Nicollette noticed right away that the party had already started for Garrett. He was a bit unsteady on his feet and rather loud. His breath smelled of alcohol.

"Well, I don't know about 'cheeky,' but I do know she is a terrific hockey player and a good friend," Nicollette responded defensively, placing her arm around Carol.

"That's right, you two just won the county field hockey championship, right?" Garrett continued. "Men, we are in the presence of two champions! We must toast to their success! Here's to Carol and Nicollette, our two champions!"

The bottles were raised and clinked together. "Cheers!"

"So Nicollette," Martin chipped in. "Where do you live?"

"Just up the road in Brockwirth. I've lived here all my life."

"I'm sorry we haven't met before. You seem nice...and

pardon me for saying, you are kinda cute. Do you have a boyfriend?"

Nicollette thought for a moment before she responded. *Was Martin being a bit forward or just making conversation?*

"Sort of. We have been friends for a while." Nicollette was satisfied with her response. She was flattered by the compliment, but not too comfortable where the conversation might be heading. Carol sensed this and changed the subject. Nicollette wanted to get back inside. It was getting cold, and she was feeling a bit uncomfortable.

"Nice meeting you, gentlemen. I am going to head in. Carol?"

"I will see you in a bit," Carol responded.

Nicollette noticed that Peter had shifted closer to Carol and now had his arm around her back. *Peter and Carol?* Nicollette thought. She had never mentioned him before. Of the four young men, he was the quietest and seemed to be the most pleasant.

Nicollette started to walk around the building towards the side door. She had gone about twenty steps when she felt a strong arm on her shoulder. She turned around to see Garrett. Unsure of what was happening and knowing the state he was in, she asked Garrett to take his hands off her and go back to his friends. He did not respond. She asked again and his grip got tighter.

"I'd rather be with you," Garrett responded. "You're cute, and it's New Year's!"

"Garrett, you are hurting me. You are drunk and you don't know what you are doing! Now take your hands off me!"

Nicollette's words were falling on deaf ears. This was not going to be good. She tried to break free of his grip.

"Let go of me now!" Nicollette screamed but to no avail.

The music was too loud for anyone to hear her. With that, Garrett pushed Nicollette into a small alcove by a shaded window outside of the building. She struggled, but Garrett was bigger, and drunk. She started to yell but he placed his hand over her mouth.

"You are pretty and need a man," he whispered to her. "And its New Year's, celebrate!"

He shoved up tight against her with his hand still covering her mouth. Using his body as leverage, he had her pinned against the wall, her legs useless in defense. His left hand went down the small of her back. She was fighting as best she could, but she was unable to break free. Garrett bent his face inward and whispered.

"You are pretty, so, so pretty."

His hand had now reached her bottom as he began to kiss her neck. Nicollette was struggling with everything she had. Garrett continued to kiss her neck at the same time as his hand was rubbing and squeezing her backside. With all her strength, she was fighting. She was drawing on energy she did not know she had. She bit his hand that was covering her mouth.

"Ouch, you wench. You bit me! Now I am really going to enjoy this!"

Garrett resumed his attack. His left hand was now on her thigh and moving upward. His mouth on her face. He moved his right hand to land a kiss on her mouth. At that moment, Nicollette screamed with what energy she had left. He moved his mouth to hers. She could feel his breath on her cheek. His other hand was roaming higher on her thigh. She was fighting. Fighting. She closed her eyes, unable to look at his face. Fighting. Fighting. She gritted her teeth. And just when she expected the worst, his hands were gone. There was no breath on her face. No pressure on her body.

She opened her eyes to see Edward. He had Garrett in a headlock with his arm bent up his back. Garrett's nose was bloodied, and he was gasping for air.

"You are being a very naughty boy to my sister, sir. I ought to break your arm for what you did! And don't think I won't! I think you need to apologize to this young lady! And I mean now!"

A small crowd was gathering to see what all the commotion was about. Carol ran to her friend.

"What happened?" she screamed.

"He was assaulting me. It was terrible, Carol!" Nicollette responded, her body shaking and her emotions clearly visible as tears fell from her eyes.

Nicollette gathered herself together as best as she could. Edward forced Garretts's head towards his sister.

"That apology, sir!"

Garrett seemed to become instantly sober.

"I am terribly sorry, Nicollette, please forgive me."

Before Nicollette could respond, Edward threw Garrett to the ground. "Nothing to see here, folks, just a little New Year's fun."

The small crowd dispersed. Carol had her arm tightly around her friend. Nicollette was still shaking but slowly regaining her composure. Edward looked down at Garrett on the ground.

"And you! Let me make this very clear: If I ever see you near my sister or in this club again and you are not on your best behavior, that bloody nose you have will seem tame! Now take yourself and your friends out of here, NOW!"

Garrett scrambled to his feet. Martin tried to assist, but Garrett threw his arms off.

"I don't need your bloody help, thanks."

"I'm sorry, Nicollette," Pete whispered. "I do hope we meet again under better circumstances. See you soon, Carol."

The four young men walked around the building and into a car. Edward watched from the corner of the building as they drove off. He came back for his sister.

"You ok, Nicky?"

"Better now, thank you, Edward. I tried to fight as best I could, but he was bigger and stronger."

"You did good."

"Your timing was excellent. How did you find me?"

"It was getting a bit stuffy inside, so I came out for a fag. I was walking around the corner, and I saw what I thought was a couple making out in the alcove. It was dark, but I could see this was not a passionate embrace. Then I heard a muffled scream and saw a glimpse of your face in the moonlight. My brother and police instinct took over."

Nicollette, still shaking, gave her brother a big hug.

"Thank you, Edward, I will never give you a hard time about smoking again."

Edward reached over and kissed his sister on the cheek.

They smiled at each other.

"Carol, why don't you head in? I want to talk with Nicky."

"Right. Alright, Nicky? See you two inside."

"Thanks, Carol...and Carol, let's not make a big deal about this. I think it would be for the better, ok?"

"I promise, Edward. See you inside."

Edward turned to Nicollette as Carol went around the corner. "Are you sure you're, ok?"

"Yes," Nicollette whispered, still shaking, "much better now, thank you."

"I want to explain why I didn't get the police involved even though we could prosecute an assault charge. You are leaving Monday for a great adventure. The last thing we need is to get you tangled up with the courts and all and I suspect he's learned his lesson. You were very brave, and I am very proud of you."

The two of them headed back into the cricket club.

"A drink would surely taste good about now and I bet you could use one yourself, Nicky."

Nicollette looked at her brother and nodded in the affirmative. He handed her his handkerchief, and she wiped her face deliberately so as to not rub off her light makeup. As she walked to the club entrance with her brother, she began to think. She realized that she had never been in such a serious situation before. Scary thoughts kept crossing her mind. What if her brother hadn't shown up? What if she couldn't break away? What if....What if? Her mind worked hard to wrap around all the "what ifs." As they were about to re-enter the cricket club, Nicollette stopped for a quick second while her brother held the door open for her. She turned and looked up into the starry sky. At that point she made a commitment and a promise to herself. There would be no "what ifs" in her life. She would be in control and able to deal with situations. She would be independent and strong. She would be in control!! No "what ifs!"

Nicollette slept in on New Year's Day, she was not awakened by her two energetic nieces or the noises coming from upstairs. Today, she was aroused by a gentle hand on her shoulder. Nicollette opened her eyes to her father's face.

"Good morning, Nicky. Time to get started. Lots to do today."

Nicollette gathered her things and headed upstairs to straighten up. She decided to take a quick bath. While soaking, she recalled the events of the last evening. She revisited the event at the cricket club. She remembered leaving just after midnight with Carol to see Ashley at the Pub and she remembered the strained conversation between her and her best friend over what had happened. She remembered the toasts at the pub, and she remembered not seeing George. She wondered if she had chased him away by telling him about her trip to America. Most of all, she remembered the commitment she had made to herself, to be strong and in control.

She saw Edward in his room, and he motioned for her to come in. "Did you sleep alright last night? Quite an eventful evening, wasn't it?"

Nicollette's expression turned serious. Her smile changed to a stoic grin. "Ed, I can't thank you enough for what you did last night. I don't know what would have happened. I felt helpless. I felt very scared. I felt ashamed."

"You needn't feel that way. You did nothing wrong. But Nicky, it's a big world out there and not every place is like Brockwirth; sunshine, unicorns, and the lot."

Edward paused and placed his hand over his sister's hand.

"They taught us in the police force to always pay attention. Stay alert. Be aware. Nicky, you are about to embark on a new experience. Remember what I've said. Take it to heart."

Edward lovingly squeezed Nicollette's hand. "You will be fine, Nicky, learn from your training. Pay attention. Ask questions. Take it all in. And when you are finished with your training, keep learning. I know we have some big things coming from you. You are my sister and I love you."

The big day, January fifth, seemed to arrive all too soon. As Nicollette was getting ready, her mum sat down on the edge of the bed and whispered into her daughter's ear, "I am ever so proud of you. I know you are strong and brave. Whatever challenges you are given, you will handle them with strength. I believe you are destined for big things, and this is the first step. I know you will make us proud. I know it's only for a short time, but I will miss you terribly and no matter what happens, remember, we love you."

Nicollette looked into her mum's eyes. She realized

how lucky she was to be surrounded by such a loving family. Small tears formed in her eyes as she embraced her mum.

Nicollette dressed in the outfit that Lieutenant Blankin had proscribed, a black skirt with a white blouse and two-inch heels. She looked around her bedroom and into the mirror. *Well, this is it, Nicky! You're a big girl now!*

"Good morning, Nicky," her father said as she came into the kitchen. "You look very sharp and very professional."

"Wow! My little sister is so grown up. You look great, Nicky," Edward exclaimed as Nicollette took a seat.

Alice brought over a plate of scrambled eggs and sausages. There was hot toast and a pot of coffee on the table. Nicollette suddenly felt very hungry. *Nothing like a good "English" breakfast,* she thought. There were stirring noises from upstairs and soon two little girls were running into the kitchen and jumping on their father's lap.

"Good morning, Daddy!"

"Good morning, you two!"

"Is Auntie Nicky leaving today?"

"Yes, I am, and I'm really going to miss you two. Now come give me a big hug!" Giggles, kisses, and big hugs.

Sying followed the children into the room and sat down next to Edward.

"Good morning, everyone. How are you doing this morning, Nicky?"

"A little nervous, a little scared, and very excited."

"Well, it's a big day."

"Speaking of big days, I think we should start getting

a move on. Time's getting on," James announced. "There may be traffic."

It was nearly 8:30. Nicollette ran upstairs for a final freshening. When she returned, she was greeted at the bottom of the stairs by her mum. Barely able to suppress her emotions, Alice whispered into Nicollette's ear. "Good luck, Nicollette. I know you will do fine and make us very proud."

Nicollette could see the tears forming in her mum's eyes and the tension in her body as she hugged her. Two little girls broke the moment, grabbing her legs.

"Bye, Auntie Nicky, see you soon!"

Nicollette bent down to receive two wet kisses from her nieces.

"Bye, Nicollette, and good luck, we'll be in touch. Be strong," Sying said as she hugged her sister-in-law.

"Come on, Nicky, it's getting late!" James yelled from the car.

Nicollette said one last goodbye as her mum slipped her the special pass that came in the package. "Don't want to forget this, Nicky." Alice held out the carryall that Nicollette received for Christmas.

"Thanks, Mum," she said as she entered the back of the car.

The weather was favorable for the drive. Sunny sky and dry conditions. Not too cold. About four degrees outside. The car was warm. The drive was uneventful, just like when Nicollette had driven it not long ago.

"It's a beautiful country we live in, isn't it," Nicollette

said, trying to make conversation to hide her anxiousness.

"It certainly is, "James responded, "and definitely not as crowded as Hong Kong, that's for sure. I guess I never paid much attention to it, as I am usually driving, but yes, it is beautiful."

They arrived at the main gate of RAF Brize-Norton at about 9:50 a.m. On time. They turned onto the main entrance road, past the array of barricades and military vehicles and approached the guard house and the lowered gate. Just like Nicollette's first visit, the vehicle was approached by two guards. One went to the passenger side and the other asked James to roll down his window.

"Good morning, sir. What's your business here?"

"I'm here dropping off my daughter."

Nicollette handed her pass to the guard through her dad's window. The guard looked at the pass. "One minute, miss."

He asked for her father's license then went back into the guardhouse. About a minute later, the guard came back to James's window.

"Ok miss, they are expecting you. Please, sir, follow the private here to the waiting area."

He returned James's license and handed Nicollette's pass back through the window.

The gate was raised and the private led them to the waiting area. He then approached the car and motioned Nicollette to roll down her window.

"They will be here for you shortly, miss, I will stay here with you till they arrive."

"I guess this is it," Nicollette announced, breaking

the silence and trying to sound calm. A military jeep pulled alongside the car. The corporal tapped on James's window and motioned for them to get out of the car. James went to the trunk and retrieved the cases. Nicollette grabbed her carryall, small bag, and the instruction envelope. The soldier took the cases from James and placed them in the Jeep.

"Ok folks, say your goodbyes," he instructed.

Nicollette turned to Edward and gave her brother a firm hug.

"Be strong and have courage," Edward whispered in her ear, "and remember what I said, Nicky."

"I will, Ed. Thank you. I will miss you and the family. I love you," she whispered back.

Nicollette turned to her father, tears flowing down her cheeks. The two entered a firm embrace. "I love you, Dad. I will miss you and Mum very much. Thanks for bringing me."

"I know you will do your best, Nicky. We are very proud of you," James whispered in his daughter's ear. He kissed her on the cheek.

"What's all this?" he asked as he saw the tears rolling down Nicollette's face. "We can't have all this going into the base."

He handed her a tissue from his pocket. Nicollette wiped her tears.

"I think you may need one as well," she said with a smile as she saw her father's watery eyes.

They hugged once again. The corporal assisted Nicollette onto the waiting Jeep. Nicollette turned and waved to her father and brother. "I love you."

James and Edward watched as the vehicle carrying Nicollette drove away. The private motioned for the two of them to get back into their car and pointed the way out. As the two of them made a right turn to head back home, James turned to his son.

"Our Nicky is off on an adventure that will change her life. She will return to us as a professional young lady. I know she will do great things."

Edward smiled at his father. "You know, Dad, I think you're right."

# Welcome to Brize

Nicollette recognized the route the Jeep was taking from her visit three weeks earlier. They drove past the large hangers and the array of fighters on the tarmac. Again, the runway seemed to go on for miles. At the small cluster of buildings, the Jeep turned right and stopped in front of the two-story building, just like last time. The soldier sitting in the passenger seat got out, came to Nicollette's door and opened it for her.

"We're here, miss."

Nicollette grabbed her handbag and exited the Jeep, but unlike last time, Sergeant Durban was there to greet her.

"Hello, Miss Beverley, and welcome to the program."

Nicollette was not used to the formality of the greeting, but she guessed this was the way it was going to be under the training.

"Thank you, Sergeant Durbin, good to see you again."

Sergeant Durban turned to the driver of the Jeep. "Thank you, that will be all."

The Jeep drove away as the two of them entered the building. Nicollette followed Sergeant Durban past the small desk, this time without stopping. They stopped at a nondescript green door. Sergeant Durban opened the door to reveal a stairway. She walked up the single flight of stairs and Nicollette followed. At the top of the stairs,

Sergeant Durban opened the door to what appeared like a very large classroom. There were chairs set up and a movie screen in front of the room. To Nicollette's left was a long table with three uniformed soldiers, two women and one man. At the other end of the room, Nicollette could make out Lieutenant Cheryl Blankin talking with two other young women. There were another ten or so young ladies milling about. There was a table set up with refreshments at the side of the room.

"Let's get you signed in, Miss Beverley," Sergeant Durban stated as she directed Nicollette to the long table. The first soldier, a woman, greeted her.

"Good morning, miss, your name please?" she asked.

"My name is Nicollette Beverley."

"Let's check our information." The soldier looked at her clipboard. "From Brockwirth, Worcestershire?"

"Yes, that's me."

The soldier turned the clipboard around to Nicollette.

"Please check all the information to make sure it is correct and then sign on the bottom." Nicollette checked the information. Her full name, date of birth, and address were correct. She noticed her dad's and mum's names were listed as well as her brother's and sister-in-law's.

"It's all correct."

She picked up a pen from the table and signed the appropriate spot. The soldier behind the desk handed Nicollette a name badge, the same badge style that the soldiers wore, only it was in blue with white lettering instead of the standard black badge with white lettering. It said only Beverley.

"Please put on your identity badge, miss, and go to the next station. Good morning."

Nicollette applied the badge to her blouse. It was a different type of badge, held on by magnets, not pins, so no holes in her blouse. She walked down the table to the next soldier, also a woman.

"Good morning, Miss Beverley."

"Good morning," Nicollette responded.

The soldier then reached under the table and pulled out a large box. She reached into it.

"Let's see; Beverley, here it is." She handed Nicollette a large zippered brown portfolio. Nicollette noticed it had her last name printed on it.

"This is your information packet. Do not look through it until you are told to. There is a lot of information inside it. Keep it with you for now. Please sign here that you have received the portfolio."

The soldier then slid a clipboard and a pen to Nicollette for her signature. She signed the form.

"Good morning, Miss Beverley. You may now go to the last station."

Nicollette moved along the table to the last station. She stood in front of a male uniformed soldier sitting across the table.

"Good morning, Miss Beverley. My name is Captain McWilliams, and I am one of the coordinators of your training. Welcome."

Nicollette recognized his accent as Scottish brogue. He appeared to be sterner and more businesslike than the other two soldiers, but he was also the only one who introduced himself.

"I see you have your portfolio. Good. Do you have the envelope from your doctor?"

"Yes sir."

Nicollette handed the captain the sealed envelope, her hands trembling just slightly.

"Thank you, Miss Beverley, and please relax. Take a deep breath."

*He must have seen my hand shaking. Calm down, Nicky!*

"That's better, miss."

Captain McWilliams reached below the table and pulled a file from the file cabinet underneath. "Let's see what we have here."

He opened the file and started to read aloud.

"Nicollette Beverley, born August 28th, 1955, that makes you twenty years old. Achieved 'A' levels in mathematics and Spanish. Some studies in geography and a keen interest in home economics. Good grades. You are athletic and a member of a local field hockey team. Your team must be quite good. It says here that your team just won the Midlands championship. That's how you know Barbara Thompson. You were referred to this program by her husband Charles Thompson. Did you know that, Miss Beverley?"

"Yes sir, I thought there might be a connection."

Captain McWilliams looked up briefly at Nicollette then went back to the pile of papers in the portfolio. He pulled another paper out and started to read aloud again.

"Parents are James and Alice Beverley, married over twenty-five years. Your father works at Russell's in

Brockwirth, and your mum is a housewife. You have a brother, Edward, serving in the Hong Kong Police force. It appears you come from a stable family."

*They sure know a lot about me!* Nicollette thought nervously. *I wonder what else they found!*

He flipped another page. "Your medical report says you are healthy and up to date in your immunizations." He flipped another page and then another. He then looked up at Nicollette. "All appears to be in order. Now just a few pieces of housekeeping, Miss Beverley."

Captain McWilliams reached under the table again and pulled some papers from his briefcase. He laid three documents in front of Nicollette.

"I need you to read and sign each of these documents. Take your time and read them carefully."

Nicollette picked up the first paper. She read it thoroughly. The paper basically said that she was specifically chosen for the training and that she entered the program voluntarily and under her own free will. The paper further read that not every candidate will pass the course, however, every effort will be made to ensure the successful completion of the course for all candidates. Her name was typed in on the bottom of the page. Above her name was a space for her signature. Nicollette noticed that her name was spelled wrong. Her last name was Beverley with an "e" between the "l" and "y," but the "Beverley" on the paper below her signature line did not have the "e" in it. *Do I say something or just put it down to a typographical error? On one hand, I just arrived here, and I don't want to make any trouble, but on the other hand, this is an official document. What to do?*

Nicollette thought for a moment and looked at Captain McWilliams and in a soft, nervous whisper, she said, "Sir, there appears to be an error in the spelling of my name on this document. Below the signature line, my last name is spelled wrong. The 'e' is missing. I'm sure it is just an oversight or typing error, but I want to bring it to your attention before I sign it."

What happened next caught Nicollette by surprise. Captain McWilliams got up from the chair and with a stern expression, looked directly back at her. His stare was becoming more unbearable with each passing second. His stern expression never changed. His look brought chills up Nicollette's body, and a sudden fear went through her brain. *Did I do something wrong? Was I wrong in challenging something so insignificant as the missing "e" in my last name? Did I break a rule about complaining?* Several seconds passed when finally, Captain McWilliams spoke directly to Nicollette, his stern expression never leaving his face.

"Miss Beverley." He paused for a breath. Then in a firm voice, "Thank you for pointing out the error to me. You followed my instructions, and it appears you have a good eye for detail, no matter how insignificant or harmless they may appear to be. Plus, you had the courage to speak out, even to someone of higher authority, such as myself. When there is something out of place, question it, no matter what. In our line of work, this is a trait that is vitally important and, in some cases, even a matter of life and death! Never dismiss even the smallest details.

Never be afraid to question. Take the extra time to be sure. The answer could be in the details."

With that, Captain McWilliams sat down in his chair. He continued, "Miss Beverley, I congratulate you. This was a test. There are errors on each of the three documents. Some simple, some not so simple. We are using the same test on all the candidates. Those that stop at page one, like you did, pass immediately. Those that stop at pages two or three are on probation and those that signed the errored documents without any question are being sent home. We have sent four home so far and we have a few more candidates yet to arrive."

Nicollette took a quick glance over her left shoulder to the entrance to the room. There were three more young ladies being escorted in. She then looked back at Captain McWilliams. He pulled another set of papers from his briefcase and handed them to her.

"These are the corrected documents. Again, take your time reading them and sign the appropriate spots. Remember the details."

With that, he motioned to a soldier who was standing nearby.

"Please bring this young lady a chair."

Nicollette sat down across from the captain. She could see he was making notes on a piece of paper, not paying any attention to her. She began to read the first document again. Catching her by surprise, Captain McWilliams spoke.

"Miss Beverley, just for curiosity, a moment ago when you looked over to the entrance, how many candidates did you see?"

"Three, sir."

"That's right." He gave her a half smile and went back to his notes. "Don't worry, not a test, just curious."

Nicollette took a deep breath. *The captain does not miss anything,* she thought, *I better be on my toes all the time during training, that's for sure.* Nicollette took the captain's words to heart. *Details.*

Nicollette slowly and deliberately reviewed each of the documents. The first document was identical to the one that had the misspelling of her name. She noticed it had been corrected. All seemed to be in order, so she signed the document. The second paper was basically a review of the information that Captain McWilliams had read to her earlier, her personal and biographical information as well as the results of her medical examination. Nicollette again took her time and looked it over very carefully. All seemed to be in order, spelling and numbers included, so she signed it. The last document had more of a serious nature, the Defense Department insignia embossed on the top of the page. The page read that the training program required the utmost participation from the candidates. Every course and activity required one hundred percent commitment and one hundred percent attendance. There might be some physical challenges and that every precaution for safety will be observed. There might be some travel. All efforts would be made to assure success and fulfillment of the course objectives. There was a paragraph about what to expect upon completion of the course and that more details would be forthcoming later. The last paragraph contained a reminder as to the seriousness of the program. "All participants are to remain silent about their participation in the course. All training, techniques, and information received during the program are to be classified under the 'Official Secrets Act' for a period of ten years. Any violation of this provision could result in legal actions and could result in imprisonment. Your endorsement on this page shows your agreement to comply with and carry through all the above listed stipulations."

Nicollette read the page again and again. She double checked for accuracy. There were no errors. She signed her name in the appropriate spot. Nicollette then took a deep breath and looked at Captain McWilliams.

"I'm finished, sir."

Captain McWilliams looked at her and then held his hand out for the documents. He took a glance through them and then looked back at Nicollette.

"Well done, Miss Beverley. Our meeting will start in about thirty minutes. In the meantime, please help yourself to some refreshments. They're located over in the corner."

He stood up from his chair and held out his hand. Nicollette extended hers and they shook hands. He had a very strong grip.

"Thank you, Miss Beverley, I'm sure we'll be seeing a lot of each other."

# New Friends

Nicollette picked up her coat and portfolio and walked across the room to the refreshment table, her heart still racing from the interview with Captain McWilliams. She was feeling a bit "cotton mouthed" and in need of something to drink.

As she headed towards the refreshment table, she glanced around the room, but didn't recognize anyone. However, she did spot Lieutenant Blankin standing next to the refreshments table talking to two young ladies. *At least there will be one person I know.*

"Hello, Lieutenant Blankin," Nicollette announced herself.

"Well, hello, Miss Beverley. Glad you are here. I see you made it through the paperwork alright. Let me introduce you to Miss Davies and Miss Wilson."

Nicollette held out her hand and the three of them shook hands.

"Nice to meet you."

"And you as well."

"How about some refreshment?" Lieutenant Blankin asked Nicollette.

"Thank you. I'm a bit parched."

Nicollette helped herself to some ice water; the cold liquid hitting the back of her throat seemed to settle her anxiousness.

"Well, what do you think so far?" Miss Wilson asked. "It's all so serious and formal."

"Well, it doesn't have to be among us. My name is Valerie Davies, but my friends call me Val."

"My name is Margaret Wilson. My friends call me Peg."

"Well, my name is Nicollette Beverley, and my friends call me Nicky!"

The three of them had a chuckle. They shook hands again amidst smiles.

"That fruit looks nice. I think I'll have some," Nicollette said as she picked up a paper bowl.

"Already had some but help yourself. Don't eat too much though as I understand we're going to have lunch soon," Val said.

Nicollette filled her bowl about halfway. She took a forkful and turned to her new friends.

"So, tell me about yourself, Peg."

Peg was a taller girl with curly black hair. Her eyes were a deep brown. She was lean with long arms and legs. There was a beauty mark on her left cheek.

"Well, I'm from Alton in East Hampshire. Three weeks ago, I was in Alton College finishing my studies in mathematics and physics. I like to swim and play tennis when I'm not studying. My father works at Worldham golf course. He's one of the golf pros there. I have two younger brothers. My mum stays home."

Nicollette could tell Peg had an assertive personality and was from a privileged background as evidenced by her "posh" accent. *One of those rich kids*, she thought. Her mind recalled the pretty Worcestershire uniforms that she despised and what Garret did to her on New Year's Eve. She paused and realized she was now at Brize and would have to try and make an effort. She forced a smile at Peg and asked, "I'm curious, how did you get involved with all this?"

"Several months ago, I made a general application with the government. Then about three weeks ago, I received a post from the government and when I opened it, there was an invitation to meet someone at RAF Odiham about a government job. I went to the appointment. Evidently, I was nominated for the interview by someone who plays golf at Worldham, a retired Air Force Colonel. He had seen me working with my father on weekends. He began to ask my father a few questions about me, schooling, activities, just general stuff. At first, both my father and I thought it was a bit odd with all the questions, but we just let it go thinking he was just being friendly. Anyways, I received a letter and went to the interview. It was a long afternoon; I can tell you. They talked at length about the position, and it appeared very interesting to me. There could be travel and you know I do like to travel. They gave me two days to decide, so after some serious thinking, I accepted and now here I am."

"How about you, Val?"

Nicollette thought Val was a pretty girl. She had thick shoulder length black hair accentuating her hazel-colored eyes. She and Nicollette were about the same height and build.

"My story is pretty much the same. I'm from Brandon, a small village in Suffolk. I like to run with the Suffolk

Striders. I also applied for a government job last summer as there's not much going on in Brandon. My letter came about three weeks ago as well. My interview was at RAF Lakenheath and like yours, Peg, mine was also a long interview. My sponsor was a man that also runs with the Striders. Anyway, like I said, there's not a lot in Brandon so here I am. How about you, Nicollette?"

Nicollette thought that Val's story was very similar to hers. They were both from small villages and had a desire to "get away."

Just as Nicollette was about to tell her experience, Lieutenant Blankin's voice came over the loudspeaker.

"If I could have your attention, ladies, please take a seat so we can get started."

Nicollette took a quick glance at her watch; it was exactly noon. She, Peg, and Val walked over to the seats in front of the screen. There were twenty seats, two rows of ten, neatly arranged, but only twelve other girls. Lieutenant Blankin was standing at a podium just to the side of the screen. There were five chairs next to the podium. Sergeant Durban was seated at the last seat.

Lieutenant Blankin started. "Good afternoon, ladies, and welcome to RAF Brize-Norton. I had a chance to meet most of you at your interviews, but just in case, my name is Lieutenant Cheryl Blankin, and I am the logistical director of this program. I want to take this moment to congratulate and thank you for your decision to participate in this very special government program. You have taken the first step towards working in a profession that is vital for our country. You have declared your loyalty, dedication and commitment to the preservation of our freedoms and way of life. Again, I thank you. I know there are some questions you may have. There will be time for questions and answers a little later. But first, let us look at this short film."

Lieutenant Blankin took a seat as the lights in the room were turned off. The film opened with a picture of the British flag and the Department of Defense insignia. Then a woman in a military uniform introduced herself as Royal Air Force Major Elizabeth Hartwell. The major narrated the film, introducing the history of intelligence and information gathering. There were early photos of espionage activities in India, South Africa, and Arabia. Then activities during the First World War were shown with actual footage of agents in the air and on the ground. There was discussion and archival footage of the Gallipoli Campaign, noting how poor intelligence can be disastrous. She reminded the viewers that over 70,000 British and Irish troops were killed or wounded in that battle. There was an in-depth discussion as to the critical role the Intelligence Services played during World War II and the importance of gathering and dissemination of critical information. Major Hartwell continued the narration of the film with an introduction to the Intelligence Services at Bletchley Park and the work of breaking the German secret codes using the enigma machine. She made a point that all the information is useless unless it can be given to the people who can act upon it and referred to this as *Mission Critical.* The Major noted the best, brightest, and most innovative were employed in this critical arena and that women played a vital role in a male-dominated service. Then a segment on post-war Europe, colonial nationalism, the Suez campaign and the Cold War. The film concluded with the need of Intelligence Services, with the many more global challenges facing the country, to continue to grow and expand. Major Hartwell then appeared on screen with a summary, explaining the current acute shortage of qualified personnel due to attrition and retirements and the need to continually attract qualified people to serve in the Intelligence Services. The film ended and the lights came on.

Lieutenant Blankin came back to the podium. "Ladies, I hope this film gives you a good backdrop to what is going on here. Now, it is my honor to introduce you to the officer in charge of the program here at RAF Brize-Norton. She works directly for Colonel Nigel Baron and has been appointed to this position by the cabinet minister for Defense and approved by the Prime Minister, the narrator of the film. Please welcome Major Irene Hartwell."

Major Hartwell came to the podium. She was a stout woman of average height, with her jet-black hair tightly wound in a bun underneath her hat. She had a powerful jutting jaw surrounded by a complexion accentuated by makeup. Nicollette guessed her age around the mid-forties range.

She cleared her throat and began to speak. "Thank you, Lieutenant Blankin. I want to personally thank each of you for joining this very special program. A great deal of time and resources have been used to create the training you are about to receive. You will be exposed to many situations and challenges, mental and physical. There will be times of stress and exhaustion. Other times of fatigue and even boredom. You will be tested and retested and then tested some more. You will be pushed to extremes. You will draw upon energies and resourcefulness that you did not know you had. There will be times when you may feel like 'just packing it in,' and some of you may. We hope you don't, but we understand this. We will do everything possible for your journey here to be a success. We will be strict but fair. We will be available for you. The success of this program is a joint effort, you and us together, and this will pave the way for future specialists and assure that our nation has the brightest and the best, ready and trained, to meet the challenges of the future."

Major Hartwell stepped away from the microphone and walked in front of the podium. She looked directly at each of the young women sitting in front of her. Nicollette could feel the major's eyes penetrating her mind with almost a hypnotic effect. Major Hartwell started to speak, at first in a soft tone, then gradually rising into an oratory crescendo.

"If you have the courage, the strength, the stamina and the will and you are committed to what we are doing, then surely all this effort will be worth it! You will have a unique opportunity to serve your country in a special way that is reserved for just a very few. Mission Critical!" Major Hartwell paused to let her words sink in, then continued, "A great deal of work and time has gone into your selection. We know you have what it takes to achieve success with your training. My personal challenge to each of you is simple: do your best, work hard, and complete your training. Now who is ready to take on the challenge?"

There was a spirited response and a resounding chorus of yeses and I ams and fifteen hands raised in the air. Nicollette felt as if the major was speaking directly to her, pushing and motivating her to achieve and become part of something bigger than herself. A surge of energy poured through her body as Nicollette held up her hand and said, "I am."

Major Hartwell then concluded by raising her hand. "I am too!"

Major Hartwell left the podium and sat in the chair next to Sergeant Durban. Lieutenant Blankin walked back to the podium.

"Thank you, Major Hartwell. Well, ladies, what do you think? Sounds interesting? Exciting? Challenging?"

Lieutenant Blankin knew these were rhetorical questions, but she wanted to extend the emotional wave of enthusiasm for the next speakers.

"Now ladies, it gives me great pleasure to introduce another very important member of our group. He is our civilian liaison to the Department of Defense, Mr. Charles Thompson."

Nicollette turned to her newfound friends, excited.

"I know him. That's my field hockey coach's husband. He's the one who referred me!"

Val and Peg nodded their heads in acknowledgement of Nicollette.

"Good afternoon, ladies, and welcome. As Lieutenant

Blankin said, my name is Charles Thompson, and I am a civilian Senior Intelligence Officer. I have served in this position for several years and was asked to assist in the development and execution of this program. Through the years, I have gained invaluable experience and knowledge that I hope to share. As a civilian, I will act as a liaison between you and your military instructors."

Charles Thompson paused for effect, leaned forward on the podium as if to address the young women individually.

"Ladies, you are here for a very special assignment. You have been individually selected because we believe you are best qualified to be trained and retained as professional Intelligence Officers for the Department of Defense's special activities division. There is a whole big bad world out there that we need to monitor, decipher, and act upon to safeguard our country. The ladies who graduate will join a special activities division which we will now refer to as Group 228. Your training will be tough and intense. You will be encouraged to 'push the envelope and think outside of the box' with your mind. You may be surprised as to what you can really accomplish. So, again, welcome. Now I would like to re-introduce you to Captain George McWilliams."

Captain McWilliams approached the podium from behind the row of chairs and began to speak as Charles Thompson took a seat next to Major Hartwell.

"Good afternoon. As you know, I am Captain McWilliams and I have had the pleasure of meeting all of you when you first arrived. To all of you here, congratulations on passing the first of what will be many tests. I oversee the physical part of the training and your overall evaluation. Yes, ladies, you are going to sweat! There will be regular exercises as well as courses in self-defense and you may even shoot a gun or two. We want you to not only be able to do the tasks at hand mentally, but physically as well. We want you to have endurance and stamina so that you are on your 'best game' all the time. I am sure we will get to know one another quite well over the next several weeks. Now Sergeant Rene Durban who will go over the logistics for the program. Sergeant Durban."

Nicollette thought nervously as the words from Captain McWilliams resonated in her mind. *Physical challenges, physical challenges! Whatever did he mean by that? Should I worry? I think I'm in good form but who knows what they expect!*

Sergeant Durban approached the podium and adjusted the microphone. She was a stocky, solid woman on the short side. Her blond hair was neatly tied up in a bun behind her head. Nicollette could see that the Sergeant was all business and took her position very seriously, quite a change from when they first met. Her facial expression never changed.

"Good afternoon, ladies. I am Sergeant Durban, and I oversee the day-to-day logistical aspects of your training. We will get to know each other very well I expect. When you signed in, you received a portfolio. Please open it and pull out the first page."

Nicollette followed the instructions. Sergeant Durban

continued.

"The page should have your name on the header."

She looked out at the group.

"Anybody with the wrong portfolio?"

There was no response from any of the ladies.

"Good, all-in order then. The page you have is a schedule for today's and tomorrow's activities as well as your room assignment. Your cases have already been taken to your rooms. Take a minute to look it over. Please remember this is a military base and military time is used."

Nicollette looked over her page. The day's itinerary included lunch and a tour of the facilities followed by a skills test. Then off to her room to settle in and take a break. There would be tea and an evening activity. Tomorrow, physical training in the gymnasium is at 06:30 followed by breakfast at 09:00. There would be a morning activity at 09:45 hours to 12:00 hours, then a break and lunch. The rest of the day would be announced at lunch. At the bottom of the page was the name of her roommate.

Nicollette turned to Valerie, excited. "You are my roommate."

Valerie looked at Nicollette and smiled.

Sergeant Durban started again. "Alright, ladies, has everyone had a chance to look the itinerary over? Any questions? None? Excellent. Now a couple of important pieces of information. First, we are in a military base, so it is vitally important for you to wear your name badges all the time. This will identify you as someone who is allowed to be here. Secondly, you are only allowed to be in the areas we identify. Do not wander or roam. Make sure you are where you are supposed to be. If you find yourself separated or lost, find the nearest green phone and dial 228. The green phones are in most halls and rooms. These phones are internal use only, so sorry, you can't use them to call home." Sergeant Durban cracked a rare smile with that comment. "Thirdly, there is to be no intermingling or socializing with any other military personnel or civilians on base other than those assigned to our group. And finally, under no circumstances are any aspects of your training or any information you receive to be shared with anyone other than this group. Ladies, these rules are 'hard and fast.' There will be severe repercussions for any violation. So, pay attention to your responsibilities and listen to your instructors and all will be well. Now, put the papers back in your portfolios. Are there any questions? None? Good."

At dismissal, Nicollette, like the rest of the group, followed Sergeant Durban through the door and down the main corridor to the other side of the building. They entered the mess hall. It was a large room, much bigger than the orientation room. It was filled with soldiers and civilians alike. At the far end of the room was a buffet line. Sergeant Durban directed the group to an area that was sectioned off from the main dining area. There were four large tables in the section. When everyone was seated, Sergeant Durban explained how the dining worked.

"Ladies, please place your portfolios on the table, then go and help yourselves to lunch."

Val, Peg and Nicollette sat with each other. Peg turned to Val.

"So, who's your roommate?"

"Believe it or not, it's Nicky. Who's yours?"

"Sarah Green. I saw her sitting behind us. She seems nice. We should invite her over to our table."

Peg turned to the table behind her. "Sarah, Sarah Green?"

A red-headed young lady responded. "I'm Sarah Green."

"I'm Margaret, your roommate, you can call me Peg. Come join us."

Sarah gathered her portfolio and sat down next to Peg.

Sarah was a petite young lady with red shoulder-length thin hair parted in the middle of her forehead. She had a fair, rather pale complexion, and wore round rimmed glasses. She appeared to Nicollette to be on the shy side. *This may be a first impression, but this is going to be an interesting pairing*, Nicollette thought to herself. *Peg is assertive and posh, and Sarah is quiet and just the opposite.*

Sarah held out her hand to shake Peg's. "Glad to meet you, Peg."

"Glad to meet you as well. Let me introduce you to my new friends. This is Valerie, she goes by Val, and this is Nicollette, and she goes by Nicky." There was a chuckle.

"Well, pleased to meet you, Val and Nicky, I'm Sarah Green."

"Now that we are all acquainted, let's go eat. I'm famished!" Val exclaimed.

The four of them headed towards the food line. Everything from salads to sandwiches and hot foods. There was shepherd's pie and roasted chicken, not to mention all the sweets. The four of them filled their plates and sat down at the table.

Peg turned to Sarah. "So, tell me, Sarah, I detect a Yorkshire accent. Is that where you are from?"

"Yes, I'm from Pickering in Yorkshire."

"How did you get involved with all this?" Val asked.

"I was a graduate student at Selby College. I earned my advanced degree in physics and chemistry. You may say I'm a bit of a brain."

The group let out a chuckle. Sarah continued. "I was trying to decide between going further with my education or starting a career or some combination of both. There is scientific work with the government at Harrogate, so I submitted my application. I heard nothing. Then about four weeks ago, I was asked to interview at RAF Fylingdales and now here I am."

"Did you find out who sponsored you?" Val asked.

"Not too sure but I suspect it was through my father. He works at Harrogate with Americans on some hush hush things. Anyways, one Sunday, we went to his boss's house for a meal. My mum and sister stayed home. I thought it a bit unusual for it to be just the two of us. At dinner, my father's boss asked me a lot of questions, almost as if he was interviewing me. On the way home, my father said that his boss was very impressed with me. About a month later, the letter arrived."

Val turned to Nicky.

"You're the quiet one, Nicky. You know about us, but we still don't know anything about you. How about it, tell us your story."

Both Sarah and Peg followed.

"Yes, do tell, we're all ears!"

"Well, my story isn't as exciting as yours, but here goes."

Nicollette told them her story. About Brockwirth and small village life. She smiled proudly as she talked about her field hockey team's championship.

"And there you have it!"

"Well, ladies, we sure make an interesting group," Val exclaimed.

They continued with small talk over the rest of the lunch, mostly about school, food and the program. When the conversation turned to boys, Nicollette became quiet. The painful memory of New Year's Eve was still fresh on her mind. She smiled and pretended to listen, nodding her head occasionally, acknowledging the conversation. Nicollette then remembered her promise she made to herself. *I will be in control, and I will be strong!*

# The Tour

Sergeant Durban walked around the lunch tables speaking with the recruits. She announced they would be starting the tour in fifteen minutes. She reminded the group not to forget their portfolios. Exactly fifteen minutes later, showing her military precision, Sergeant Durban announced it was time for the afternoon tour. She asked the ladies to pull out the map of the building complex from their portfolios. With her map in hand, Nicollette and her new friends, Val, Peg, and Sarah were first to line up.

Sergeant Durban pointed out that all the rooms on the second floor began with the letter "B," the first floor was "A" and the third floor a "C." The group went down the stairs to the first floor. They walked past the security desk and outside the building, stopping only to put coats on. Sergeant Durban walked the group to the building next door. They entered the building and walked past the security desk. They came to a double door. Sergeant Durban opened the double doors and the group walked into a huge gymnasium. It was at least twice as big as the one at Evesham High School.

"This is the fitness building," Sergeant Durban announced sternly. "This is where you need to be tomorrow morning at 06:30."

There was a stack of tumbling mats in one corner and two volleyball nets against the wall in the other corner.

The basketball backboards were hoisted up towards the ceiling.

Val turned to Nicollette. "It's a large gym for sure. It even smells like a gym."

The group left the gym and Sergeant Durban pointed out the weight and exercise room. It was a large room filled with free weights and exercise equipment. The back wall was covered with mirrors. They continued past the security desk and back outside. The next building looked like an apartment building in the city. It was five stories high and was painted in a red brick color. The group entered the building, but this time stopped at the security desk. Sergeant Durban identified herself to the two soldiers behind the security desk. The sergeant behind the desk looked at the group. A phone call was made for verification. While waiting for clearance, the group was asked to pull out their room assignments and "buddy up" with their roommate. Nicollette pulled her room assignment from the portfolio. She and Val were assigned to E11, and Peg and Sarah were assigned to the adjoining room E9.

"We must be on the fifth floor, ladies," Peg announced to her friends.

The phone rang. "Yes sir," the soldier sitting behind the desk said into the phone. He then turned to Sergeant Durban. "They all have to sign into this book."

The soldier turned his chair around and reached into the middle file of the file cabinet behind him and pulled out a red binder. The binder was labeled "Group 228." He turned back around, facing Sergeant Durban and the group. The security sergeant placed the red binder on the desk and opened it to a prepared page. He stood up and announced the check in and out procedures.

"Ladies, this is a secure area, and this desk is occupied twenty-four hours a day. This is military housing so there are rules that must be followed. First, you must check in whenever you enter or leave this building. You must have some sort of identification when you are at this desk. I see you have your identity badges on. They will work as identification. Make sure you have them on or on your person. There are not to be any outside visitors in this building without prior permission and passes from your supervisors. There are many people in this building. Some of our residents work unusual shifts and sleep at unusual times. Please be considerate of them and keep the noise down in your rooms. All bags and packages are subject to inspection. We expect 100 percent cooperation with the rules and regulations of this residency building. Follow the rules and there will be no problems. I see you are all on the fifth floor. I hope you find the accommodations comfortable. Sergeant, you need to sign in first."

Sergeant Durban asked the ladies to form a line with their bunk buddies. Nicollette's turn came to sign the book. Her name and room assignment were already printed on the page. The top of the page said, "Group 228" and next to her name was her room assignment, E11. Below her name, Val's name was listed indicating a shared room. Nicollette signed her name in the appropriate space and Val did the same. In a short time, half the group was traveling up in the elevator to the fifth floor. Two trips for the elevator. Out of the elevator, Sergeant Durban directed the group to a common area. The common room was furnished with sofas, chairs, and tables. There were three desks against the rear wall and a refrigerator and sink in the corner. There were more desks underneath a row of windows.

Once all were present, Sergeant Durban announced, "Ok ladies, let's find your rooms."

She first stopped at room E1.

"Ladies, this is my room. I will be bunking with you. I will be here if you need me. Now let's get you ladies organized. When you find your room, you will have twenty minutes to get organized, then we will meet back in front of my room. Twenty minutes, ladies."

The rooms were assigned in numerical order. Peg, Sarah, Val and Nicollette walked down the hallway counting out the door numbers as they went. E3. E5. E7. E9.

"This is us," Peg and Sarah opened the door to their room and went in.

"This is our room, Val," Nicollette exclaimed.

Nicollette and Val opened the door and walked into a spacious room with a big window at the end. There were twin beds on either side as well as a closet for each of them. There was a chest of drawers with a mirror attached and carpeting on the floor. They each had a desk as well and a bathroom attached. Their baggage was at the base of the beds.

"This is a nice room, Nicky! It reminds me more of a hotel room than a dormitory room!"

"It sure does, Val! It's way bigger than my room at

home! Quite nice. Remember, we only have twenty minutes to unpack and organize, so we better get cracking."

The two of them set about unpacking. There was plenty of room for everything they brought. The time went quickly. They could hear Sergeant Durban from outside their room.

"Two minutes, ladies. Finish up, please. Don't forget your keys to the room and your name badge."

Nicollette found the door keys on her nightstand. She gave one to Val. Both still had their name tags on, so no problem there. They grabbed their portfolios and headed to Sergeant Durban's room. Val stopped to lock the door. Sarah and Peg were already there.

"What do you think of your accommodations, ladies?" Val asked.

"They'll just have to do. I will miss my butler, though," Peg responded in her posh voice.

Nicollette looked at Peg, not knowing if she was kidding or telling the truth about the rooms, but she laughed at the comment along with Val.

# The Test

"Ladies, we are headed back to the main building. Let's stay together please," Sergeant Durban commanded.

It was getting colder as the winter sun was beginning to set. Fortunately, it was not a long walk. The group entered the main building and again approached the security desk. Once again, name badges were shown, and the list was signed. The group was led to room A3. Inside, the room was a classroom complete with student's desks and a blackboard at the front.

"Ladies, please take a seat."

Sergeant Durban walked to the front of the room and began, "Ladies, you are now going to be taking a skills test. We want to test your thinking abilities and how you are at problem solving. Assisting us with the test is Sergeant Hale."

Sergeant Hale had been standing in the back of the classroom. He walked to the front and stood next to Sergeant Durban.

"We will now hand out the test packages. When I call your name, come forward and receive yours. We will give you two pencils. When you are finished, please bring the packets back to me. Now I know that you are used to school tests, but these tests are different. They have been individually prepared for your individual skill set. We will use them for evaluation only. Now place your portfolios under your desks. You will have two hours to complete the assignment."

Sergeant Hale began to call out names.

"Adams. Beverley."

Sergeant Hale handed Nicollette a manila envelope and two pencils. Nicollette saw "Beverley, Nicollette" written in bold lettering at the top of the folder, as Sergeant Hale called out three more names. "Brown. Chester. Davies."

Val went to the front to get her package.

"George. Green."

Now it was Sarah's turn to get her package. Sergeant Hale continued until the last name was called.

"Wilson."

Peg went to get her package whispering "last again" to Nicollette and Val as she walked past them.

"Alright, ladies. Please open your packages and begin," Sergeant Hale directed.

"Remember, this is an evaluation, so please do your best. I will be here if there are any questions. You may begin."

Sergeant Hale took a seat in the front of the class-room and stared out at the assembled ladies. Sergeant Durban left the room. Nicollette opened her package. There were ten pages, two each of a different color. Red, pink, yellow, green and blue. She started on the red pages. Maths. *What a way to start,* Nicollette. She looked over the pages. There were some simple arithmetic equa-tions as well as some geometry, algebra and calculus. There were word problems and graph questions as well. Nicollette took a deep breath, grabbed one of the pencils, and started the test. The first problems were solved rather easily as her math skills returned to her. The problems became increasingly harder the further along she progressed. More time. More thought. Finished. Thirty minutes gone, ninety minutes left.

Green test next. Geography. Nicollette opened the packet. There were a series of maps with countries and cities to identify plus other geographic points to mark. There appeared to be a trick question on one map as she was asked to identify Grinnell College on the map of America. *Devious,* she thought. This test was easier, taking her only twenty minutes. Next was the pink package. Spanish. Nicollette opened the package. The entire test was written in Spanish. *All those vacations to Spain are going to pay off now,* she thought. Nicollette looked over the test. The first part was more conversational, mostly fundamentals, simple sentences and responses. This went smoothly for her. The next section was more advanced with harder phrases and responses. *More like a conversation with an engineer or scientist,* Nicollette thought. Difficulties. The last section was four paragraphs in English to be rewritten in Spanish. It was a short bit about ships and the weather on the ocean. *Not too bad,* she thought to herself. Three down, two to go. She glanced at the clock. Forty-five minutes left. Next was the yellow packet. This was an essay. The topic was "Keeping England Safe in a Dangerous World." The instructions were relatively simple. "If you were the Prime Minister, what activities, programs, and actions would you use to keep the country safe?" There was a limit of 300 words. Nicollette thought for a moment. *If I were the Prime Minister. Hmmmmmm. What would I do?*

She started to write, slowly at first, then faster as thoughts evolved into words on the page.

*I would begin by maintaining a strong military, Army, Air Force and Navy. As Prime Minister, I would install a strong Diplomatic Corps and work to keep healthy alliances with friendly countries and make sure to take advantage of the full resources of the Commonwealth.* Nicollette continued her essay, writing about pursuing actions to "cool down" the situation in Northern Ireland, and concluded her essay with a brief discussion of economics and growth for the country. Her final sentences read: *A strong country must be strong at home first. Her citizens must be free and motivated to protect and defend their way of life and educated to take on the challenges of the future.* Nicollette took a deep breath. Essay done. A quick look at the clock. Fifteen minutes left. *The blue package is still left.*

She opened the package and was surprised to find only one page inside. It was a word search puzzle. Cool. A great way to finish. The instructions were easy. Find as many words as possible, minimum three letters. Each word would have a point value. The more letters, the more points. The grid was one hundred by one hundred. Ten thousand letters. Nicollette went right to it. She had worked these puzzles many times before, but never on this scale. Finding words were easy at first, mostly three- and four-letter ones. Her list grew. She found the word "specialist," ten letters. Then the words "diplomatic, substitution, relinquishing, and specialization." The word list grew along with the length of the words she was finding. Nicollette was deep into the assignment when she heard Sergeant Hale say there were two minutes to go. Nicollette found the words remuneration, generations, aeronautics, and operations.

"That's time, ladies. Please put your pencils down."

Nicollette looked at her word list. The count was sixty-three words. Sergeant Hale looked around the room.

"Ladies, please place your tests back into your packages. Sergeant Durban will be by to collect the packages."

He paused as the packages were collected. Once Sergeant Durban had placed all the packages on his desk, he continued, "That wasn't too bad now, was it?" He smiled, mocking. "I want to thank you for your participation in the testing. We will evaluate your answers and have a review with each of you tomorrow."

Sergeant Hale gathered the packages and left the room.

Sergeant Durban then addressed the class. She drew an exaggerated deep breath.

"Well done, ladies! I know that testing can be tough and draining, but this was very important. So now, everyone stand up and let's stretch it out."

Sergeant Durban extended her arms forward and then raised them upwards, indicating to the seated women to stand up. Fifteen ladies stood up behind their desks.

"Ok ladies, let's stretch it out!"

Sergeant Durban then led the class with several stretches.

"Arms overhead and reach for the sky! Higher, higher. That's it. Keep reaching! Now, let's do some arm rotations."

Sergeant Durban then demonstrated the stretch by extending her arms straight out from her sides and moving them in a circular motion.

"That's it, ladies! Loosen up those shoulders! Now let's bend down and touch those toes. Down, down. Come on, you can do it! Reach! Ok, now stand upright and place your hands on your hips. Now turn right. Hold it, hold it! Now full rotation the other way. Hold it, hold it! Now back to normal. Deep breath! Exhale! Now ladies, back to the dormitory and meet up in the common room. There are a few things I need to go over with you," Sergeant Durban directed.

It was past five and dark outside as the group headed out of the building. The cold air hit Nicollette in the face with a jolt. The recruits entered the dorm building and went through the sign in process, up the elevator and into the common room. Sergeant Durban spoke to the group.

"Listen up, ladies. I want to quickly review your schedules for the remainder of tonight and tomorrow. After tomorrow, you will have a new schedule for each day. For tomorrow, there will be early exercises at 06:30 in the gym. Dress appropriately. Breakfast will be at 09:00. This will give you time to clean up. The rest of the morning will be classroom activities beginning at 10:00 hours. As for tonight, we will leave for tea in thirty minutes. After tea, we have some entertainment planned. You should be back in your rooms by 22:00 hours. I suggest a good night's sleep. Tomorrow will be a busy day. The dress for tonight's activity is casual, comfortable. Same for class tomorrow. Now, off to your rooms. See you back here at 17:45."

Nicollette, Val, Sarah and Peg walked down the hallway to their respective rooms.

"What did you think of those tests, Val?" Sarah asked.

"They weren't too bad. I did manage to finish them all with some time to spare. How about you three?"

"I just managed to finish," Nicollette responded. "Some of the questions were hard, especially the maths. But that's over now."

"Did you have five tests?" Sarah asked.

"Yes, five," Nicollette answered.

"I only had four tests," Sarah continued. "How about you two?

"I had five as well," Val responded.

"I guess I won the prize, ladies, I had six!" Peg exclaimed.

"See you in a few," Sarah announced as the four of them went into their respective rooms.

Thirty minutes later, they were headed back to the dining hall. They found seats together. The buffet was an assortment of meats, salads, vegetables and soups. At the end of the line was the dessert section. Cakes, pies, jellies and biscuits. There was coffee, tea, water and a soda dispenser.

"I could get used to this," Val said to her friends as they were loading their trays.

Nicollette did not realize how hungry she was until she sat down to eat with her friends. The conversation was light, small talk about the day's activities and the tests. The time seemed to fly by. Sergeant Durban came over to the table.

"Ladies, let's finish up, we have about ten minutes."

It was half past seven when Sergeant Durban raised her hand for the group to leave. Sergeant Durban called the group together outside the dining hall.

"Now for the rest of the evening, you have two options. First, we have been invited to attend a talent show at one of the base pubs. The show is being put on by some of the RAF people. Secondly, you can go back to your rooms or use the common room. Now remember, we are guests here and you know the rules. We will head back from the show at around 21:30 hours. You may go back earlier if you wish. Don't forget the early start tomorrow, so please keep that in mind tonight. The pub is located downstairs, and we have set a section aside for us."

"I'm not much of a drinker," Sarah announced as she turned to Nicollette and Val.

"Don't be a spoilsport, Sarah," Peg responded rather forcefully.

"I'm sure they have soft drinks. Sarah, please join us. We'll all get to know each other better," Val said softly.

"Ok, I'm in," Sarah answered, "but not late, please."

*What a pair those two are! Posh Peg and Shy Sarah! I hope they can get along!* Nicollette thought as they followed Sergeant Durban into the pub.

Back from the pub, the group dispersed into their rooms. Nicollette, Val, Sarah and Peg agreed they would meet at the elevator at 6:20 in the morning.

"Oh, you mean 06:20!" Peg chuckled.

Later, as Val was turning off the light by her bed, she turned to Nicollette. "Today was an interesting day, not too tough, not too bad."

"I think today was a tease. They were being nice to us today, but I think it will get tougher tomorrow and even harder as we go on," Nicollette responded sleepily.

Little did she know how right she would be.

# Evaluation

The alarm clock's loud ring shattered the silence of the early morning.

"How come 5:45 comes so early in the morning?" Val whispered to Nicollette as she climbed out of her bed. "Is the sun even up yet?"

"It's probably still asleep," Nicollette responded sleepily as she stood up from her bed and raised the shade to look out the window. It was still dark outside, with only the streetlamps illuminating the road below from the chilly darkness. "How'd you sleep?"

"Ok, I guess," Val responded, "and you?"

"When I fully wake up, I'll tell you."

It was 6:15 as the two of them left the room. The elevator was filled as they descended to the main lobby. Identification. Sign outs. Into the cold. A short walk to the building with the gymnasium. At exactly 6:30, Sergeant Durban walked in with Captain McWilliams and a third person. All three were dressed in military workout gear.

"Good morning, ladies! I hope you all slept well," Captain McWilliams opened. "Now we know that each of you are familiar with fitness training because your physical activities were part of our selection process. Now we are going to kick it up a notch and get those bodies in tip-top shape. We will be having calisthenics every morning at 06:30 hours for a start. To help us with this endeavor, let me introduce Sergeant Emily Harris. Sergeant Harris is a fifteen-year veteran and a physical education specialist. She has a black belt in Karate and is a master in self-defense. She competes in the Royal Air Force's women's triathlon yearly. She has years of experience training raw recruits as well as seasoned veterans. I too have attended Sergeant Harris's training program and she will have you working very hard indeed. So please pay attention."

Captain McWilliams then turned his head towards Sergeant Harris.

"Sergeant Harris."

To Nicollette, Sergeant Harris looked like a soldier's soldier. She was tall with a stocky, almost masculine, muscular build. Her facial skin was tight, revealing a protruding jaw line. She kept her hair short and had a rather thick neck.

*Oh no! Here it comes! I hope I can keep up! And so early in the morning!* Sergeant Harris sure looks like a tough one! Nicollette thought as Sergeant Harris addressed the recruits.

"Good morning and welcome to your first session of morning calisthenics. We'll start out each morning with a series of stretches and exercises to get your blood flowing. Then we will finish the session with a light physical activity to cool down. As Captain McWilliams said earlier, we will be having morning exercises each day at 06:30 and we will finish by 07:30. I will also be leading your self-defense classes. We will be introducing you to a new program called Krav Maga. You will learn more about that later. Today, we will work on some lighter stretches and exercises just to get the blood moving. Let's get started."

Nicollette's earlier suspicions of toughness were only reinforced by the Sergeant's deep booming, expressionless voice. Sergeant Harris commanded the recruits to line up in two rows of eight, two arms lengths apart. Once organized, she led the group through bending and stretching exercises followed by jumping jacks, deep knee bends and push-ups. The clock on the wall showed 07:15. Sergeant Harris led the class on a sprint five times around the gym then twice around in a paced jog to cool down.

"See you tomorrow morning. You are dismissed," she announced.

Nicollette gathered her coat and walked out with Val, Peg and Sarah. "Well, what did you think?" she asked Val. "I mean if this is a light day?"

"I get the feeling that Sergeant Harris is a no-nonsense kind of woman and today was just an easy introduction."

"I agree," Peg piped in. "Sergeant Harris is going to be tough! So, I guess we should expect our 6:30 sessions to be most enjoyable!"

"Sarcasm, ladies? It's a bit early for that," Nicollette added with a chuckle and continued, "Sarah, you haven't said much. What about you?"

"I'm a bit knackered to be honest with you. Today's physical training really got the best of me. I'm not used to this early routine and I'm also afraid this is just the preliminary to a lot of hard work, so I guess we better get used to it."

Back in the room, Nicollette noticed envelopes waiting for her and Val on their nightstands. Nicollette saw her name on one of the envelopes and quickly opened it.

"What is it?" Val asked as she picked up her envelope.

"It's a note with instructions for me to come to a meeting in room A56 in the main building at 09:00 hundred hours. The note says I should wear my black skirt and white blouse. What does your letter say?"

Val opened her letter and turned to Nicollette.

"My note has the same instructions. I have to report to room A42 at 09:00. We'd better get cracking, Nicky, we still have to eat breakfast."

"I don't know about you, ladies, but I'm famished," Peg announced as the four of them walked into the dining hall. "Let's see what's up."

In line, Nicollette could see the big variety of food available. There were cereals, fruits, eggs, breads, hot foods and meats as well as pastries and yogurts.

"This is great!" Sarah exclaimed as she sat down with a loaded plate. "I hope I don't put on any weight!"

"Not if Sergeant Harris has anything to do about it!" Nicollette responded.

At 8:45, the four of them left the dining room and headed to the staircase. Sarah was going to A12 and Peg to A22. Down the stairs and through the double doors that opened into a small foyer area, there were three large hallways heading out from the foyer. Nicollette looked down each hallway. They seem to extend further than the length of the building above, she thought. All the assigned rooms were on the East hallway and in numerical order. The hallways were quiet except for a few other recruits looking for their assigned rooms. The four of them headed down the hallway to their respective rooms. The doors to the rooms were very nondescript with only the room number at the side. It was a very sterile hallway, pale green walls and a white ceiling, the doors painted light gray. Nicollette was the last to reach her assigned room. As she opened the door to the room, she glanced down the rest of the length of the hallway. It seemed endless. Nicollette walked into the office and the door automatically shut behind her. The room, like the hallway, was very plain. There was a single steel desk in the center of the room, light blue walls and a single chair underneath a portrait of the Queen. There were no windows, only a small single door behind the desk.

The door opened and a woman dressed in military attire walked through. "Please have a seat, Miss Beverley, the captain will be with you shortly."

Nicollette sat down on a chair in front of the desk. She looked at the soldier sitting behind the desk and noticed the rank on her shoulder. She appeared to be a corporal. Two minutes passed and Nicollette began to feel a little nervous. She kept thinking about her tests and this meeting. *What if I didn't do as well as I thought? What if I failed to meet the standards for the job? What if I must go home? What would she say to her family and friends? How would she handle the disappointment?* Her palms were sweaty, and she couldn't sit still. Another two minutes passed. The time was dragging on. Her nervousness increased. *Why are they making me wait? Surely something is wrong.*

Nicollette's hands were shaking as she discreetly wiped them on her skirt. The silence was shattered as the phone rang. Nicollette nearly jumped from her seat. The corporal answered.

"Yes, sir."

She hung up the phone and turned to Nicollette.

"The captain is ready for you now."

The corporal opened the small door behind the desk.

"This way, miss."

Nicollette stood from her chair and walked around the desk and through the door. She thanked the corporal as the door was shut behind her.

"Come in, Miss Beverley."

Nicollette was surprised to see Captain McWilliams standing behind the desk.

"Good morning, sir," she said as she shook his extended hand.

"Good morning, Miss Beverley, please have a seat."

"Thank you, sir."

As she was sitting down, Nicollette took a quick glance around the room. It was much larger than the entry room. There were bookcases on either side, a file cabinet, and a small table holding a typewriter. On the top of the captain's desk was a phone and a small stack of papers. Behind the desk was another portrait of the Queen.

"I guess you might be a bit surprised to see me," Captain McWilliams said as he sat down.

"A little bit, sir," Nicollette responded, trying very hard to appear calm.

"Let me explain. During our little introduction

yesterday, I had a chance to observe you. Now to be clear, I observed all the recruits, but something about you caught my eye. The way you carried yourself with confidence and determination in a strange environment. You were unafraid to challenge a 'wrong,' like the spelling of your surname. Your attentiveness to council, detail, and direction. I saw these traits not only in your actions, but also in your eyes. Now admittedly, I wasn't totally in favor of this initiative from the start, but our orders were very clear; find the right candidates and be successful. Yesterday, after I first met you, I asked myself if my intuition was right, were you the right candidate? Did you have what it takes? Would you be successful?"

Captain McWilliams paused, leaned forward, and looked directly into Nicollette's eyes. His expression turned very serious; his eyebrows motionless above those piercing eyes.

"Let's look at your scores, shall we?"

Nicollette did not know how to respond to his question or even if a response was necessary. She nodded her head affirmatively. *Here it comes*, she thought, *the answer.* Her palms started to sweat again and now her leg twitched as well.

Captain McWilliams leaned back in his chair as he picked up some of the papers on his desk, his expression unchanging.

"Despite my reservations about this initiative and questions about the trainability of young women for this job, you may, I repeat may, be just the type of candidate we're looking for."

All at once it hit her, a combination of feeling relief that she would continue in the training and the fear of what was going to be expected of her to stay. Her mouth very dry, all Nicollette could do was respond softly, "Yes sir, thank you."

The next words he spoke took Nicollette by surprise. His expression softening and in a gentler, less firm voice he said, "Miss Beverley, I want you to take a deep breath or two and try to relax. I know you are a bit anxious. You may ask how I know?"

Again, a rhetorical question. This time, however, Nicollette responded. "How do you know, sir?"

"Two ways actually, first, most people are naturally anxious when entering an unknown or strange environment and secondly, your palms were a bit wet when we shook hands. These are just two of the many individual characteristics of people you will learn about. Now let's continue with your tests from yesterday, shall we?"

He looked at the top page and put it face down on the desk.

"We'll deal with that one later," he continued. "Your first test was in mathematics. In our line of work, maths and logical reasoning are essential. The abilities to construct and dissect formulas and equations as well as problem solving, are essential in this type of work. You may wonder how your scores compare to the other recruits?"

Captain McWilliams paused purposely for effect, a slight grin crossing his otherwise stoic face. He continued. "Top five in the class. Well done. Your second test was about geography. Obviously, with all the interests we have in the world, our recruits better be proficient in knowing where places are as well as their relative strategic importance. How did you do? Top three in the class. Again, excellent. Your third test was about Spanish. Having a good understanding of a second language is a big plus in our business and the ability to communicate, even with just a basic understanding in another 'tongue' can be most useful in certain circumstances. How did you do? Let us just say you need some improvement. We will make additional instructions available to you to bring you up to snuff, in the meantime, I have to make a note on your record that we've had this discussion and that improvement is expected."

*I knew my Spanish was a little rusty but didn't realize it was that bad. I could have failed out of this program!* Nicollette thought nervously.

"Test four was the essay," he went on. "We thought it might be interesting to see what ideas and values our candidates have with regards to England and the world. I must tell you; we've had some very interesting essays. I have read them all and have concluded this is a very bright group of recruits. I particularly liked your inclusion of diplomacy and a strong military, plus a strong economy. Very good, very good indeed. Finally, the word search. Another interesting idea we came up with during the preparation meetings. Have you ever heard of cryptanalysis, Miss Beverley?"

Nicollette paused before she replied, still thinking of her poor results in Spanish.

"No sir, not really."

"I'm sure you've heard of secret codes though."

This time, Nicollette replied affirmatively, "You mean like Bletchley Park and all that during World War II?"

"Now you've got it," Captain McWilliams replied and continued. "Coding and deciphering are the most integral part of secret communications. I don't have to tell you how important the work at Bletchley was during the war. But communications are a two-way street. The decoding of others' secret messages is important, but so are communications between allies and their forces. This was discussed in your initial interview. The word puzzle in your testing is a form of elementary cryptanalysis if you think about it, and you, Miss Beverley, have a keen sense of discovery. Top score in the class."

He paused while looking at Nicollette, his grin turning into a little smile. There was a quiet tap on the door.

"May I come in?"

"Yes sir," Captain McWilliams replied while rising from his seat.

Nicollette stood up and turned towards the doorway. An older gentleman in an officer's uniform walked in and extended his hand to her.

"My name is Colonel Nigel Baron."

*Omigosh, what's he doing here? The man in charge of the whole program is with me in this office! Whatever does this mean?* The nervousness she had felt earlier now returned. She swallowed hard as she held out her hand to receive his, hoping her palms hadn't become wet yet.

"Pleased to meet you, Miss Beverley."

Nicollette swallowed again. "Pleased to meet you too sir," she replied, trying hard not to show her anxiety.

The corporal brought a chair in from the front room and shut the door as he left the room. The three of them sat down with the Colonel sitting next to Nicollette. The Colonel cleared his throat.

"I have regards to you from Mr. Charles Thompson."

Not knowing what to say, Nicollette just nodded her head in acknowledgement.

"So, Miss Beverley, how's your meeting going with Captain McWilliams? Any questions or thoughts?"

Again, not knowing how to respond and still trying to calm herself, Nicollette replied in a soft steady voice, "Very well, I guess. Thank you."

"Splendid. Please continue."

"Thank you, sir. We were just discussing the final exam and basic cryptanalysis. Now I am going to summarize the tests for Miss Beverley."

Captain McWilliams received a head nod of approval from the Colonel. The captain then turned to Nicollette and looked directly at her. The grin and smile he displayed earlier had disappeared. *Probably coinciding with the presence of Colonel Baron, I suspect*, Nicollette thought to herself.

"Miss Beverley, as we have discussed, you performed well on each of the tests except Spanish. You showed a natural ability to locate and identify. You have more than a passing knowledge of the world, but we will need to improve your grasp on Spanish."

There was a pause. Colonel Baron broke the silence.

"May I continue, Captain?"

"Certainly, sir, please do."

"Miss Beverley, Nicollette, we believe you will be an asset to group 228. These tests, however, are just the first step. From today forward, your training will be very intense and demanding. You will learn new skills and discover just how strong you are. This program is tough. There may be times you may want to quit and times of sheer exhaustion. But, in the end, the reward will be worth it."

The Colonel stood from his chair.

"I have to leave now," he announced.

Nicollette and Captain McWilliams followed suit and rose from their chairs.

"Before I leave, Miss Beverley, I want to ask you a question."

Colonel Baron paused and with a stern expression looked right into Nicollette's eyes. Nicollette could feel the intensity of his eyes on hers.

"Are you on board? Are you willing to take up the challenge? Are you ready?"

There was silence as his eyes continued to peer at hers. Nicollette reached deep inside herself to respond. She tried to speak but it was as if all the air was taken out of her lungs. After what seemed like an eternity, and with the colonel still sternly staring at her, Nicollette finally found enough air to respond.

"Yes sir! I'm ready!"

"Splendid, Miss Beverley," the colonel responded, his stern expression changing to a softer grin. "I know you will do well in your training. Now if you will excuse me, I have other people to see. Captain McWilliams will review the schedule with you. I'm sure we will be seeing each other again. Good morning, Miss Beverley. Captain."

The colonel left the room, shutting the door behind him. Nicollette turned around to see Captain McWilliams already seated behind his desk.

"Please have a seat, Miss Beverley, and we'll continue."

Nicollette did as instructed, rubbing her hands together to see if they were wet from nervousness.

"Now we just have a short time till lunch so let's make a start on your schedule."

Nicollette noticed the clock on Captain McWilliam's desk showed 11:30 and realized how fast the morning had gone. Captain McWilliams handed her two pieces of paper. The front page had her name on top and underneath her name was "Group 228."

"Let's look at the schedule sheet, Miss Beverley, shall we?"

Captain McWilliams reviewed the schedule with Nicollette. The paper showed course work every day starting at 09:00 hours and finishing at 20:30 hours. There was a break for lunch at 11:30 hours with courses resuming at 13:00 hours. There was a thirty-minute break at 15:00 and course work continued till tea at 17:30, then a short evening course from 19:00 till 20:30 hours.

At the bottom of the page, there was a listing of the courses she would be attending. Cryptanalysis, Observation, Surveillance and Analysis were listed as well as Information Integration, Mission Preparation and

Self Defense, plus advanced Spanish. Guest Speakers were also listed.

"As you can see, Miss Beverley, you have a very busy schedule, and we haven't included the additional Spanish tutoring yet."

Nicollette glanced up from the schedule sheet in acknowledgement to Captain McWilliams. *I'm going to be a very busy young lady*, Nicollette thought, *when do I sleep?*

Captain McWilliams paused as he leaned back in his chair, then continued. "We have left the weekends open for planned activities. You may have classes in evasive driving or small arms instruction or maybe just time to study or relax. Each evening, a schedule for the next day will be posted in the common area of your dormitory meeting room and another copy will be left in your room. We will also provide your schedule to Sergeant Durban." He paused again. "Any questions, Miss Beverley?"

Nicollette looked up from the sheets of paper she was holding, still trying to absorb it all. *Evasive driving? Small arms instruction? I'm going to shoot a gun!* These thoughts were running through Nicollette's head as she looked at Captain McWilliams.

"No sir, no questions."

"Splendid! However, if a question should arise, there will always be help for you. Just find a green phone and dial 228. Now, Miss Beverley, it's lunch time. May I accompany you?"

Nicollette looked at Captain McWilliams, her brain spinning from all the information of the meeting. As if her voice was on automatic, she answered, "Yes sir."

Captain McWilliams came from behind the desk and helped her from the chair.

"Good, I'm hungry," he said as he opened the door from his office.

"We're going to lunch Corporal, be back at 13:00."

"Sir," the Corporal responded.

Captain McWilliams held the door leading into the hallway open for Nicollette. The hallway was crowded with people moving about. Nicollette suddenly felt special being accompanied by the captain as they walked down the hallway and into the cafeteria.

The cafeteria was buzzing with people. Captain McWilliams pointed out the three tables in reserve for the group and pointed Nicollette in that direction as he headed off to the officer's area. Val and Peg were already sitting down as she approached the table.

"We've saved you and Sarah a space," Peg said as she pointed to an empty chair.

Nicollette sat down and took a breath. "That was an interesting morning, how about you two?"

Val was about to respond when Sarah arrived at the table. "This seat for me?"

Peg nodded her head in the affirmative.

"Thanks, ladies," Sarah said as she sat down. "What a morning! My head is spinning! How about you three?"

"It has certainly been a morning, that's for sure!" Val responded. "Let's get some food first then we can share our morning, besides, I'm famished."

"Good idea, girls, I have to be in room A10 by one, sorry, I mean 13:00 hours," Peg said as she stood up from the table.

"Did you say a class in room A10 at 13:00?" Nicollette asked as she turned to Peg. "That's my next class as well."

"Me too," Val threw in.

"I guess we're all going to the same class this afternoon," Sarah added and continued, "Let me tell you about my meeting and then we can compare."

"Go on, do tell, Sarah."

"Well, my results were given to me by Captain Murphy. He certainly knew a lot about me even though I've never seen him before. Anyways, he reviewed each test with me in detail. He says I did very well and that I have passed into the program. Then, Colonel Baron came in and things got really serious! He gave me a brief overview of my scores and what they showed of my talents. He then got real stern and asked me about my commitment to the program. I guess that was the moment of truth, ladies. Yes or no, I said yes. He stood up and shook my hand and left the room. Then I got my schedule. Wow! Am I going to be busy! Next thing I know, it's lunch time. It sure was a great deal to take in! How about you lot?"

"My experience was like yours, Sarah, and just like you, Colonel Baron came to my meeting as well. Anyways, he said my results were good and that I passed into the program. Like you, Sarah, the Colonel asked me about my commitment; yes or no, full stop. I said yes and here I am."

Both Val and Nicollette described their interviews in much the same detail. Each had a visit from Colonel Baron and were asked the same question about committing to the program. Both answered yes. "So, I guess the four of us are stuck with each other," Val quipped.

There was a chuckle at the table.

"And Sarah, I agree with you that we are going to be really busy these next few weeks. I think 'playtime' is over, ladies."

# The Speech

It was nearly 12:50 hours as the four of them headed to their first class of the training. Room A10 appeared to be a normal size classroom with about twenty-five seats and a blackboard and desk in front. At exactly 13:00, an officer came through the door. He shut the door behind him and went to the front of the room.

"That's Captain Murphy," Sarah whispered to the other three, "he's the one who gave me my scores."

Val looked around the room and counted fifteen total students.

"Looks like we lost one already," she whispered.

Captain Murphy looked around the room and directed the recruits to move to the front rows of desks. He introduced himself and began to speak about the importance of cryptanalysis.

"The ability to send and receive secure information is vital to the Intelligence community. I will tell you up-front that this is a very intense course. In the next few weeks, you will learn to code and decipher. How to pick patterns and separate the real from the false. You will become confident in special communications and be able to work in a variety of environments. So, with all this to do, let's get started."

He produced two boxes from under the desk and placed them on top. Captain Murphy opened the boxes and pulled out a red binder.

"When I call you, please come up and get your workbook. Please do not open it until instructed to do so."

The names were called. "Adams, Beverley."

Nicollette went to the front desk and received her red binder from Captain Murphy. It was a nice binder, much nicer than the usual school ones. It seemed to be made of leather or a leather-type material. It was filled with papers and was heavy. Her name was engraved in gold lettering on the front. A sense of curiosity came over her, but she quickly remembered the instructions given by Captain Murphy. *Do not open until instructed to do so.* Temptation subsided.

"Smith, Wilson."

The last of the binders were given out. Val whispered to Nicollette, "I didn't hear O'Neil's name, did you?"

"Can't say that I did, and I don't see her either. Our first casualty."

"Ladies, now that you have your binders, let's get started. Please open them to the first page."

For the next two hours, Captain Murphy went through the first section of the binder. It was a thorough introduction of cryptanalysis and coding. Notes were taken. There were some class exercises. One exercise was to say the alphabet backwards. Nicollette was selected and stood at her chair. Despite a little shyness, she managed to say it right the first time. There were other volunteers as well, including Peg, who had to repeat every third letter and skip the fourth. At 14:30 hours, Captain Murphy stopped the class to allow for a thirty-minute break.

"Please leave your binders here and I expect you back here at 15:00."

The girls headed to the cafeteria.

"I find this interesting," Sarah turned to the group, "How about you?"

"It's a lot to take in," Peg responded. "I wonder what happened to O'Neil?"

Another one of the recruits overheard the question. It was Mary Porter.

"I was Katherine O'Neil's roommate. I saw her leaving her meeting this morning. She was very upset. When I asked her what happened, she told me that she hadn't tested very well and that she would be leaving the program. She hadn't made the grade. Katherine continued by telling me that they were going to find her a government job near her home, so for all her effort, this wasn't a total loss."

"Where was she from?"

"She's from Newcastle, you know, coal country. Shame really, she's such a nice girl and we were getting on rather well."

Mary joined in with Nicollette and the group walking to the cafeteria. The women made small talk, but inside each of them, there was the realization that Katherine's plight could still be any one of theirs as well.

The class resumed precisely at 15:00 and Captain Murphy continued with the cryptanalysis training. At 17:15 hours, he stopped and placed his materials in his satchel. Looking over the class, he thanked the class for their attention and announced a self-study assignment that would be due at tomorrow's 13:00 hour class. He added that the binders were to be the responsibility of the recruits and to take care of them accordingly.

Sergeant Durban had quietly come into the room a bit earlier. She stood and faced the class. "A few announcements, ladies. You will have till 19:00 to have tea and refresh. There will be a short meeting on our floor in the common room at 19:00. We will go over scheduling and other activities at that time, in the meantime with the captain's permission."

She paused and looked at Captain Murphy. He acknowledged her glance by nodding his head. "Class is dismissed."

As they walked into the hallway, Nicollette turned to Val.

"I thought I would be done with homework, but I guess not."

"I'm afraid this is only the beginning," Sarah responded.

"I can't wait to see what our assignment is for tonight," Peg added sarcastically.

The four of them decided to head back to the room to drop off their binders, then have their tea. As they entered the room, curiosity took over and Nicollette opened her binder to the assignment. Her eyes grew wide open.

"Oh my gosh, Val, you need to see this assignment, we have a lot of work to do tonight!"

Val brought her binder over to the small desk and glanced over the worksheet.

"Well, there goes any fun tonight! This will take hours! I guess there is some good news in that we work together on this project."

The assignment was to translate an assigned document into code. The code would have to be unique and created by the two of them. Coding would consist of a combination of logical patterns and mathematical principles. The proper deciphering guide would need to be developed to accompany the coded document. The document assigned to Nicollette and Val to be coded was a speech delivered by Sir Winston Churchill. At the bottom of the assignment sheet was a sentence that caught both girls' attention.

"We may be asked to present our project to the class, Nicky! I'm not so good in front of people," Val exclaimed.

"I'm not very good at public speaking either, but I guess now's as good a time as any to overcome that fear."

At exactly 19:00, Sergeant Durban was waiting in the common room as the young women arrived from tea. Once everyone was seated, she began. "Well, ladies, congratulations on your first day. You will soon get the hang of the routine, I promise. In the meantime, I know you have an assignment tonight. Tonight, will be like most nights. There will be homework assignments and projects. Occasionally, we may have an additional course or a special speaker. The cafe is open till 21:00 and there is tea and coffee downstairs till 23:00 hours. Did everyone see the schedule?"

Sergeant Durban pointed to the schedule sheet tacked onto the front bulletin board. "Are there any questions about the schedule?"

No replies.

"Good. You should also have a copy in your rooms."

There was a knock on the door. "May I come in?"

The door was slightly ajar, so Sergeant Durban was able to see the person wanting to come in. "Yes sir, please do."

"Thank you, Sergeant, good evening, ladies." It was Lieutenant Blankin. "So how was everyone's first day? Interesting? Different? Exciting? Maybe even exhausting?" She paused for reactions. "Anybody have any questions?" Again, pausing for reactions.

"Good, I see you are all settling in nicely and ready to get to work and that's great. Does everyone have the schedule?"

There were several yes answers and an equal number of affirmative head nods. The Lieutenant continued. "I know you have a lot of work ahead, including tonight, so I will say good night. I'm sure you will see me tomorrow."

Lieutenant Blankin turned to Sergeant Durban. "Thank you, Sergeant, please carry on."

With that, Lieutenant Blankin left the room. Sergeant Durban continued. "Ok, ladies, there you have it. The serious business of training has started. I also want to remind you that the morning exercises start at 06:30, but before we break, I want to let you know about Miss O'Neil. You may have noticed her absence. She has left the program voluntarily. We wish Katherine the best. I will see you in the morning. Good night. "

Nicollette and Val decided to go back to their room and complete the assignment. Nicollette left the door open as she and Val entered their room.

"I guess we better get started," Val stated as she grabbed her binder and flopped onto her bed.

"But that's just the problem, Val. Where do we start?" Nicollette responded. She turned on the small desk lamp and opened her red binder to the assignment. "Let's look at the assignment, Val. The instructions say we need to transfer the assigned document into code by using mathematics and logic."

Nicollette pulled Churchill's speech from the binder.

*"We shall fight on the beaches, we shall fight on the landing grounds, we shall fight in the fields and in the streets, we will fight in the hills; we shall never surrender!"*

Nicollette put the speech down and stared out of the window. There were snow flurries flying around in stark contrast to the darkness of the night. *How dark was it for this country during that time,* she thought. Nicollette turned towards Valerie. The two looked at each other.

Suddenly Nicollette exclaimed, "I have an idea!"

"I'm glad you do, because I'm lost," Val replied.

"Let's get started, Val. First, we need to create a code. Grab a sheet of paper and write the alphabet across the top."

"Got it, what's next?"

"Let's use mathematics! Under the letter 'A' write plus 1. Under 'B,' write plus 2, under 'C' write plus 3 and so forth down the alphabet. So 'A' becomes 'B' and 'B' becomes 'D.' 'C' becomes 'F' and so on."

Val proceeded through the alphabet until she reached the letter Z. When she finished, she looked up at Nicollette and exclaimed. "You're brilliant, mate! A simple, but great code. How did you think this up?"

"I kept thinking of the instructions of 'maths and logic' and this idea popped into my head. Now, let's come up with a number code. Go ahead and write one through ten on the paper. Think, my girl, how can we change these numbers to logical code? Any ideas, Val?"

Val scratched her head with the pen as she stared at the numbers on the page. Several moments passed. A smile crossed Val's face as she looked up at Nicollette. "I think I have it! Simple really. Why not substitute letters for numbers? Let's see if it works."

Val started to write on the paper. Suddenly, she let out a resounding, "Yes!"

"Let me show you how it works."

Nicollette looked over Val's shoulder.

"The code is very simple," Val explained. "We start by substituting the number zero with letter 'A.' One becomes 'B,' two becomes 'C' and so on."

Val looked up at Nicollette and handed her the paper.

"What do you think, Nicky?"

Nicollette looked at the numbers on the paper.

"By Jove, I think she's got it!' Nicollette exclaimed, mimicking Peg's posh accent.

The two of them had a laugh.

"That's a relief. Homework done!"

Val looked at her alarm clock on the bedside table. It was nearly 21:30. That took us nearly two hours. I must admit that I am 'knackered.' How about you?"

At that moment, Nicollette let out a big yawn.

"I guess that's my answer, I think we should call it a

night. Big day tomorrow."

There was a noise in the room. *Was it a dream or that damn alarm clock going off?* Nicollette thought to herself. She opened her eyes. It was the alarm clock. Damn. This time she was the one who shut it off.

"Wakey, wakey," Nicollette whispered to Val. "I'll get ready first so you can get a few extra minutes."

"You're a true friend," Val responded sleepily.

Nicollette looked out of the window. Still dark, but it looked like a little snow fell overnight. *Must be cold this morning,* she thought.

The two of them left the room and knocked on Sarah and Peg's door.

"Come on you two, it's getting late. We don't want to get stuck getting into the elevator."

"We're coming."

The door opened.

"Someone wanted to 'lie in' this morning," Sarah stated as she snickered at Peg.

"But I'm up now and ready to go," Peg responded sarcastically.

"You two make a lovely couple," Val chuckled.

They made the elevator in time and were in the gym at 06:20, changed and ready. Sergeant Harris came through the door.

"Good morning, ladies! I trust you all had a good rest. Now, let's get that blood circulating! Let's do some stretching before we exercise. Line up arm's length apart." Unlike yesterday, Sergeant Harris worked the recruits hard this session. She had them doing wind sprints and extra calisthenics. She ended the class with a mile jog around the gym.

"Ok, ladies, see you tomorrow. Dismissed!"

Nicollette was feeling hungry as she, Val, Sarah and Peg made it to the dining hall. The hot shower back in the room helped relieve some of the soreness from the early morning exercises. *I haven't sweat like that in a long time,* she thought. *Hopefully, a good breakfast and I'll be ready for the day.*

"The schedule says our first class today is on International Situations," Sarah said as the group walked into the classroom. "I wonder what that is?"

"We'll soon find out," Nicollette responded as they took their seats.

The door opened and Captain Sousa walked in.

"Good morning, ladies," he announced. "This class is about International Situations and England's role in the world. Our goal is to have you up to snuff on the current world situations, some history about how they got this way and some ideas as to where we are headed. You will also polish up on your geography."

For the next couple of hours, Captain Sousa talked about world affairs. He showed a movie about Colonial England and another short film on the British Navy. Nicollette reached over to Val who was having a hard time keeping her eyes open.

"Stay awake, Val. We're almost at lunchtime," she whispered.

As the class was ending, Captain Sousa handed out

books to the recruits. He assigned a section for the class to read for homework and announced there would be a review discussion during their next class.

"Be prepared," he directed as the class was dismissed.

"Don't forget your binder," Nicollette reminded Val as they headed to their dorm room before going to lunch.

"I sure hope we don't get called to make the presentation," Val responded as they left the room.

"I hope you didn't just 'jinx' us," Nicollette chuckled.

Peg and Sarah caught up with them at the elevator.

"Everyone has their binder?" Sarah asked.

"All here and accounted for," Val responded in military fashion.

In the elevator, Val turned to Sarah and Peg. "How'd you get on with the assignment?'

"We finally were able to put something together. It took us a while, but Sarah got an idea and we ran with it. You two?"

"Same here, Nicky had an idea and we put it together. It was a lot of work. I hope they don't call on us though. I'm a bit shy in front of people."

"You will be fine, Val. Besides, we'll be there," Sarah added.

It was 12:50 hours when the group of ladies left the cafeteria and headed to room A10. Captain Murphy was standing at his desk when the group arrived.

"Good afternoon, ladies! Come in, come in and grab a seat and we'll get started."

Once all were seated, Captain Murphy continued,

"How did you find your assignment last night? Did you find it difficult, challenging, exasperating? Or did it come easy? Either way, I can't wait to see what you've come up with. Let's do some presentations. There are seven teams working together. Six teams of two and one group of three."

"That must be Mary Porter's group," Peg whispered to Val.

Captain Murphy continued, "I have placed seven names in this cup, and I'll pull out the volunteers. He reached into the cup and pulled out a paper. "Beverley, you're up."

Nicollette looked at Val. "Just our luck."

"Confidence, mate! We can do this."

The two of them walked to the front of the room. Captain Murphy had organized an overhead projector and a large screen for the presentations. Val turned to Nicollette and whispered, "You do the letters and I'll do the numbers."

"Ok, here goes."

Nicollette turned towards her fellow classmates, placed the code decipher sheet on the projector and switched it on. Captain Murphy turned the lights off. Nicollette took a moment to gather her thoughts.

"As you know, our assignment was to create a code using maths and logic. Valerie and I wanted to keep it simple. We came up with the code you see on the screen. As you can see, the alphabet is here on the right side of the page and the corresponding letter on the left. We created this code by adding one space to each letter based on that letter's position from the letter 'A.' Hence 'A' becomes 'B' by adding one space and 'B' becomes 'D' by adding the position away from 'A,' two positions, and so forth and so on. This creates a simple code, using both maths and logic."

Nicollette took a moment to look out at her peers and to judge the reaction on their faces.

"Any questions?"

No response. No questions. *Did they get it? Did they understand the code? Was she clear in her explanation?* Nicollette took a quick glance at Captain Murphy. He acknowledged her glance with an agreeing head nod encouraging her to continue. Nicollette then changed the decipher sheet on the projector and replaced it with a sheet of the dramatic portion of Sir Winston Churchill's famous "We shall fight on the beaches" speech. Nicollette thought how fortunate she was to have memorized that speech for an assignment in primary school as she placed the coded version next to the English version already on the projector.

"Everyone here should recognize this famous speech by Sir Winston Churchill." She paused and waited for the class to look at the lines on the screen. "And here are the same lines using our code. As you can see, without a deciphering guide, it would be impossible to tell what the coded lines say."

Nicollette looked at the class again.

"Any questions?"

Silence. Again, she took a glance at Captain Murphy.

"Continue on, Miss Beverley," commanded Captain

Murphy.

"Now for the number coding, here is Valerie Davies to go over the maths portion." Nicollette removed her documents from the projector as she stepped to the side. Val came to the front and placed her first document on the projector. She looked at Nicollette. Nicky gave her a nod of encouragement.

"Deep breath," she whispered.

Val took a glance at Captain Murphy. He motioned with his hand to proceed. Val took a deep breath. She started.

"For the maths portion of our assignment, we modeled our code like the one we used for the alphabet. We kept the code simple and logical and here is how it works. We merely substitute letters for numbers. Simple really."

She then placed the coding sheet on the projector.

"We start with the number zero, and we substitute it with the letter 'A.' The letter 'B' becomes one and 'C' becomes two and so on. "

Val then placed another sheet on the projector with a simple addition problem written on it.

"As you can see on the screen, we take for example the arithmetic of adding 467 to 385 with the answer 852. The same problem, using our code, looks like this: EGH plus DIF equals IFC. No numbers, only letters. Simple, yet effective."

Val looked out to the class. "Any questions?"

Silence. She then looked at Captain Murphy. He stood up from his chair and turned on the classroom lights.

"Thank you, Miss Beverley and Miss Davies."

Captain Murphy motioned for the two women to go

back to their seats. Nicollette and Val gathered their project material and went to their respective seats. He turned and addressed the class.

"I believe we have time for one more presentation."

He pulled the cup from his desk and drew a card.

"And the winners are, Miss George and Miss Norris. Please make your way forward."

Nicollette watched as the two women went to the front of the room. She had met Helen George in passing but had yet to introduce herself to Colleen Norris. Curiosity was praying on Nicollette's mind as the two women began their presentation. How would their project compare to hers and Val's? Did she and Val do a good job or just a passing one? Nicollette quickly put the thoughts out of her mind as the presentation proceeded. This was not a competition, merely an assignment and she should view it as such.

About an hour later, Helen and Colleen had finished. Captain Murphy acknowledged Helen and Colleen's hard work as the two returned to their seats.

"Thank you, Miss George and Miss Norris." He then turned to the assembled young ladies. "Well, ladies, so far so good on the assignment, but please remember, this is a very elementary assignment. Real cryptanalysis, however, is a very difficult and serious business. It is the mode of communicating very sensitive and private information with codes and deciphers that are changing by the second. Yes, that fast! Of course, very little of this is done by hand anymore, we are now using computers to handle the burden. This is something we are going to discuss later. We are going to make each and every one of you proficient in cryptanalysis in a very short time."

Captain Murphy took a quick glance at the clock on the wall. It was 15:00 hours.

"It's time for a short break, but before you leave, I have an announcement for this afternoon's schedule. We want you to reassemble in this room at 15:45. We have a rather fun activity planned for you that will require you to change into more casual clothes. Class dismissed."

The class emptied into the hallway. Nicollette turned to Val as Peg and Sarah joined them walking down the hallway.

"How do you think we did?"

"I think we did ok; I mean we did the assignment and explained it well, I think. Peg? Sarah?"

"Well, you two, I think you did fine, and thank you for going first," Sarah responded.

Peg harped in.

"I think Captain Murphy made us do this exercise to reveal the complexities of coding. I don't think he was looking at this assignment to get us to think."

"You are too smart, Peg!' Val quipped. "But perhaps he wanted us to do both."

*Yes, both,* Nicollette thought.

# Bang Bang

It was 15:40 hours when the four of them returned to the classroom. There were already six other recruits there. Nicollette, Val, Peg and Sarah grabbed four seats together as the remaining ladies entered the room. At 15:45, Captain Murphy walked into the room followed by three camouflage-dressed soldiers. He went to the front as the soldiers stood at the side with their hands behind their backs.

"Good afternoon, ladies. This afternoon, we are going to take a little field trip. Don't worry, we are not leaving the base." He paused and gave a smile, something he rarely had done in the training. "We are headed to the armory where you will start weapons training."

There was a bit of chatter in the room as the announcement was made.

"Now settle down, ladies," Captain Murphy continued.

"Let me introduce Sergeant Richards. He will spell out the logistics. Sergeant Richards please."

The first of the three soldiers walked to the front of the room. He looked at Captain Murphy. "Sir," Captain Murphy acknowledged him. "Proceed."

"I'm Sergeant Richards. Gather your belongings and we will proceed to the rear of the building where transport is waiting. When we arrive at the armory, you will follow me to the designated area. Once we receive permission, we will then head to the range. Corporals Stanley and Vance will be accompanying us." He pointed to the two other soldiers. "All right, ladies, the vehicles are ready. Let's proceed."

It was about a ten-minute ride to the armory where they were led through a side door into a small waiting area.

"Before we proceed, I need to check our list." He pulled out a paper and started to read the names. Nicollette responded "here" when Beverley was called.

"All present," Sergeant Richards announced after receiving an affirmative from the last name on the list, Wilson.

The group left the small room and went down a long descending hallway. Nicollette guessed that they must have walked nearly a quarter of a mile when they came to a double steel door. Corporals Stanley and Vance opened the doors. The group entered the shooting range. It was a large room that resembled a bowling alley. There were multiple shooting lanes and a counter where weapons were displayed. The group was ushered to an open area off to the right where tables and chairs were set up.

Everyone sat down as Sergeant Richards started to speak. "How many of you have shot a weapon before?"

No hands raised.

"We are going to change that this afternoon. Corporals Vance and Stanley are going to pass out a weapon for each of you. They are not loaded, so do not be nervous. Today, we are going to learn about the Browning Hi Power FN-6P35 Pistol. This is the standard issue weapon in the service. It is a single action semi-automatic pistol that is lightweight and easy to use. Why don't you take a quick minute and look it over?"

Nicollette picked up the weapon and studied it. For the next hour, Sergeant Richards gave a thorough briefing about the pistol. He had each recruit disassemble and reassemble the weapon, identifying each part. The ladies were instructed on properly loading and cleaning the gun and most importantly, how to use the weapon safely. The young women were then divided into three groups and led to a shooting lane by Corporals Vance and Stanley. Nicollette, Val, Peg and Sarah made up the group that was led by Sergeant Richards. At the lane, Sergeant Richards went over the safety procedures again, now including eye and ear protection.

He reviewed the loading of the pistol, turned towards the lane, and demonstrated the proper posture, hand and eye position. He fired and then fired again.

"Which one of you wants to go first?"

Nicollette felt a poke in her back. She turned around to see Sarah with a snicker on her face.

"You go, Nicky, you're the brave one."

Nicollette turned around and made eye contact with Sergeant Richards.

"How about you, Miss Beverley?"

"Sure, why not," she mumbled as she walked towards the shooting lane. Sergeant Richards handed her the protective eyewear and ear plugs. He instructed her to examine the pistol on the table in front of her. He asked her to load it and stand in the proper position and aim at the target at the end of the lane. Sergeant Richards then positioned himself behind Nicollette to adjust her posture. He pointed out to the rest of the group her posture and positioning. He then stepped away.

"Okay, Miss Beverley, hit the target."

Nicollette eyed the target and gently squeezed the trigger. Pow!

The pistol recoiled, causing her arms to raise.

"Again, Miss Beverley, please."

Nicollette aimed and squeezed the trigger. POW!

"Now Miss Beverley, there are six bullets left in the magazine, empty the chamber."

Nicollette raised the pistol, eyed the target, and gently squeezed the trigger six times.

POW! POW! POW! POW! POW! POW! When she finished, Nicollette slowly lowered the pistol. A strange feeling crept over her: a combination of amazement that she had fired a weapon and a feeling of fear that she, Nicollette, was being trained to use it.

"Let's see how well you did," Sergeant Richards spoke as he pulled on some cables that brought the target forward.

"Miss Beverley, you had eight shots and it looks as though you hit the target with almost every shot. "

He held the target up for all to see.

"Three shots on the chest, two on the waist, one on the head and two misses. Not bad, Miss Beverley. Now who's next?"

"Beginner's luck," Nicky whispered to Val as she stood in the group.

At 17:00, the weapons were brought to the arms counter in the rear of the range. Sergeant Richards gathered the women together.

"Thank you, ladies, for a successful training session. By the end of your time here, you will know how to assemble and disassemble the service pistol blindfolded. You will be asked to clean, load, and draw the weapon. And finally, you will have the skill to hit the target with precision and accuracy under many different conditions, including blindfolded. You are welcome to practice here during range hours. You will need your ID badges to enter, and transport can be arranged at the security desk at your dormitory."

Later, in the dining hall at tea, Nicollette, Val, Sarah, and Peg sat down with their trays.

"I was hungrier than I thought," Peg said as she laid her overly full tray down.

"I can see that by your tray," Sarah blurted out.

"You should talk," Val added as she pointed to Sarah's tray.

"I think we should all enjoy our tea because we're all hungry!" Nicollette laughed as Val, Sarah, and Peg joined in.

"Today was interesting enough. First, the pressure of presenting our code and then finishing with an afternoon of shooting," Val injected.

"And don't forget our homework," Nicollette added.

As they were eating, Sergeant Durban walked up to the table.

"Everyone having a good day, I trust? A quick 'heads

up' that we'll be having a short meeting in the common room in the dorm at 19:00 to go over tomorrow's schedule and plans for the weekend. See you at 19:00 hours. Enjoy your tea."

It was just shy of 19:00 hours when the four of them wandered into the common room. Most of the other women were already there. Sergeant Durban and Lieutenant Durban walked in at exactly 19:00 hours. The Sergeant addressed the room.

"Good evening, ladies. Hard to believe you've been here three days already. I hope you are settling in alright. A couple of announcements. After morning exercises tomorrow, you'll have your first Krav Maga Self-Defense course. Sergeant Harris will be teaching. There will be a light breakfast available in the gym. Please dress accordingly. After lunch, you will have a full afternoon with Captain Murphy. Then, after tea, you will have a short discussion group meeting in room A326 in the main building. As for the weekend, on Saturday, we will assemble here at 09:00 hours for a special trip to London."

There was a "buzz" in the room. Lieutenant Durban continued. "It will be a busy day Saturday, so you will need a good rest Friday night. Oh, and one other announcement, if you want to write home, we will collect your letters as we board transport Saturday morning. We will take care of the postage. Any questions? No questions? Good. There is writing stationary on the table behind me. I must remind you, there is to be no mention of where you are or what you are doing. Remember, your story is that you are in America taking a sports medicine and management course. You may talk about the weather, the food, the teachers, but I repeat, nothing about where you are or aspects of the training. There are some sample letters on the table, please use them."

Nicollette picked up a few sample letters. She hadn't thought much about home, after all, it was only her third day away. There hadn't been much time to think about anything else but the training. But now, thoughts crossed her mind wondering how her parents were doing. She thought about Edward and his family getting ready to fly back to Hong Kong, about Carol and Ashley and maybe just a little about George.

"We're going to London!" Val turned excitedly to Nicollette, bringing her back from her thoughts. "I wonder what's planned for us?"

"I can't even begin to guess, but you know it's going to be something special! Between now and then though, we've got a lot to do including a stack of homework that's waiting for us!"

"You had to mention homework, Nicky. And we have Sergeant Harris all morning!" Val added.

# Self-Defense

The group was met in the gym by Sergeant Harris for the early morning exercises. The usual warmups, stretching, and calisthenics. Sergeant Harris led the group to the far end of the gym where mats had been placed on the floor. At the edge of the mats were fourteen armless mannequin torsos mounted to hard platforms by heavy duty springs.

"Today, ladies, we will be beginning our training in Krav Maga. Krav Maga was developed by the Israeli Defense Forces as a contemporary means of self-defense. We will have twelve sessions and by the time we finish, you will be confident in your abilities to handle yourselves in threatening situations."

As Sergeant Harris was describing the course, a man dressed in all black walked into the gym from a door behind her. He was a big man over six feet tall and was being very deliberate as he approached Sergeant Harris from behind. He raised his finger to his lips asking for quiet. He moved stealthily behind the Sergeant and suddenly grabbed her in a choke hold. Sergeant Harris struggled briefly and then, as if by magic, made some quick moves. The attacker ended up on the floor, face to the mat with Sergeant Harris holding him in an arm lock position. She released him and turned to the group.

"And that, ladies, is how it's done!"

There was a round of applause.

"Now let me introduce you to the victim, Sergeant Peters."

He stood up from the mat.

"Good morning, ladies."

Sergeant Harris continued, "Sergeant Peters will be assisting our training group as well as Sergeant Allen."

Sergeant Allen walked through the door.

"Good morning, ladies."

"Both Sergeants Peters and Allen have mastered the art of Krav Maga and are experienced trainers. Now you ladies were selected for this program not only for your brains, but also for your athleticism and durability as well. You may feel uncomfortable in some of what you are going to learn or even the notion of hitting and hurting another human being, but this is a dangerous world we are in, and you must be prepared to handle yourself when it is necessary. A show of hands if any of you have been in a situation that you wish you were better able to handle physically?"

Nicollette's memory was still fresh with the events on New Year's Eve. She remembered the commitment she made to herself that night and when she entered the training program. Self-defense education would allow her to follow through on part of that promise. Nicollette shyly raised her hand and looked around to see three other hands raised. She took little comfort that over a quarter of her peers were also hand raisers. Nicollette wondered what happened to them. *Was their situation like mine, or maybe worse?*

The recruits were paired off in three groups. Nicollette, Val, Peg and Sarah were one group, and they would work with Sergeant Harris. *Now I know this is going to be tough, but worth it in the end I'm sure,* Nicollette thought, determined to learn. For the next three hours, the recruits were introduced to the basics of Krav Maga self-defense. Holds, throws, blows and avoidance. They practiced with the mannequins and each other. It was nearing 11:00 hours when Sergeant Harris called the groups to finish and gather around her.

"I hope you learned something today. Krav Maga takes a combination of strength, awareness, reaction and preparation. Today was a good start and as we go through the course, you will become more confident and prepared. Now I know you have a class this afternoon and a big day tomorrow, so we'll break now to give you time to refresh before lunch. Also, Sergeant Durban asked me to remind you about your letters home. I will see you tomorrow. Make sure you get something to drink before you leave. You are dismissed."

Nicollette walked over to the refreshment table with Val and grabbed some water.

"That was really some workout, Nicky," Val said between drinks of water. "I'm knackered."

"Me too," Nicollette responded, "and I know I'm going to be sore later."

Sarah joined in.

"That's the first time in my life I ever was physical. I've never had to defend myself. My father did tell me about hitting a boy below the belt though," Sarah said with a chuckle.

"I'm like you lot," Peg joined, "I've never had to get physical in my life nor was I ever in a situation that would call for me to defend myself. But I found this lesson to be empowering, not that I want to ever want to use it, mind you, but still—empowering."

*Yes, empowering,* thought Nicollette, *empowering indeed!*

"I saw you raise your hand about a situation, Nicky, anything you want to talk about?" Val asked.

"I'd really rather not." Nicollette responded in a soft voice sounding as if she was holding back her emotions. "Maybe someday, but not now."

The afternoon class was taught again by Captain Murphy. More in-depth cryptanalysis and secret communications work. Two more presentations. Captain Murphy used the last hour of the class to present examples of actual communications to the group. Nicollette was finding the subject more and more interesting.

The clock on the wall showed 16:30 hours. Captain Murphy announced the evening, after tea session, would be led by Captain Sousa and start at 17:30 hours, then the group meeting at 19:00 hours. He handed out a reading assignment and reminded the group about their letters home and then dismissed the class.

As Nicollette stood up to leave, she could feel the stiffness in her body. All the physical activity earlier that morning was now coming back to prey on her, plus, sitting in the class for several hours certainly didn't help.

She was tired and fatigued, worse than any field hockey practice she'd ever had. Nicollette was not alone. Val, Sarah, and Peg also felt the same as they left the classroom. It was decided to have tea now then head back to the dorm to write their letters and attend the evening meeting.

"What a day!" Nicollette looked at the other three. "I'm tired, sore, and famished."

"I guess we all are a little tired," Sarah responded. "And we still have to write something home and go to a meeting. And homework!"

"But tomorrow should be fun all over again," Peg added with a sarcastic smile.

The meeting started at 19:00 hours with Sergeant Durban and Lieutenant Blankin.

"Did you have a good day, ladies?"

There were several head nods and a few quiet yeses from the assembled. *I guess we're all kind of tired,* Nicollette thought.

"Good, I'm glad everything is moving along smoothly. Tomorrow's schedule will be a full one. You will have your usual early exercises and International Situations course at 09:00 hours followed by lunch at 12:00 hours. At 13:00 hours, you have Cryptanalysis and at 15:30 hours, you will have a course on Observation, Surveillance and Analysis. After tea, we will have a meeting here at 19:00 hours. All this is on your schedule sheet. May I suggest an early night and don't forget your letters. Good evening, ladies."

*Great idea about the early night,* Nicollette thought as the lieutenant left the room.

"I think I'm just going to grab a cup of tea and head back

to the room. How about you lot?" Nicollette asked as she turned to her friends.

"I'm too tired to get up," Sarah responded.

"Early night for sure, ladies," Peg added as she poked Val who had already closed her eyes.

"Where's my bed?" she responded, half-asleep.

# Friday

The alarm clock bellowed at 05:45. Nicollette stretched heavily as she turned on the light next to her bed. She was still in her bathrobe when she climbed out of bed. The last thing she remembered about the night before was her hot shower and lying down on her bed afterwards. *I must have crashed*, she thought to herself, *I don't even think I made it to ten o'clock!* Nicollette looked over towards Val. She was gone and her bed was made. *What's going on? Where's Val?* The door opened and Val, already dressed and ready, walked in with two cups of tea.

"I thought I would repay you for those lie-ins you gave me. How'd you sleep? You were out by nine-thirty, Nicky."

"As I remember, you were out as well and good morning, Val."

"At least we finished our assignments and our letters home."

"And now we get to start our day with Sergeant Harris," Nicollette continued. "Happy Friday!"

Sergeant Harris was waiting as the recruits staggered in.

"Good morning, ladies! I trust you enjoyed yesterday's session." she said sarcastically.

"Let's get to it."

*So much for an easy morning*, Nicollette thought, still feeling the effects of yesterday's session.

Stretches, exercises, and wind sprints as per the usual routine. Nicollette's soreness began to melt away. The workout made her body feel good and she could sense her strength and stamina increasing. She felt stronger.

Captain Sousa was waiting as Nicollette, Val, Sarah and Peg arrived at their morning class. With military precision, the class started at 09:00 hours. Captain Sousa started the lecture with a conversation about the homework assignment on Global Reach. He then opened the class for discussion. They talked about Eastern Europe, the Soviet Union, and China. Nicollette found the subject interesting and, despite her shyness, was an active participant. She had always enjoyed reading the *Sunday Times* International News Section, which tied right in with her interest in travel. She was a little surprised at how much she knew about the world compared to her fellow recruits. Still, there was much more to learn.

"Interesting class this morning," Nicollette said to her friends as they headed off to lunch.

"I'm glad we did our homework, that's for sure," Val responded.

"I wonder what we are going to do in London," Sarah asked as the four of them sat down for lunch.

"It must be important to take us away from Brize," Nicollette responded.

"Did you finish your letters home, ladies?"

"Strictly by the book," Sarah responded.

"I wonder what my parents must be thinking?" Val added.

FRIDAY

*I do wonder what my parents are thinking,* Nicollette thought, *and this is the day Edward and family head back to Hong Kong as well!*

Captain Murphy was ready as the recruits entered the afternoon class.

"We have two more projects to review today. Let's get started."

He called the last two groups to present their codes. Nicollette watched as each group made their presentations. One group used figures and signs for each letter and the other group used a substitution letter for dashes and dots code. *Like Morse coding,* Nicollette thought, *I still think Val's and mine were the best.*

"All the projects were good," Captain Murphy exclaimed. "I think you are getting the basics. But now comes the hard work. Please pull out your red binders."

*That's it! Nothing more on the projects. All that hard work and all we get is a "good." I guess that's the way it's going to be,* Nicollette thought rather disappointed.

The break couldn't have come at a better time. Cryptanalysis training was getting very intense in Captain Murphy's class. He had reviewed several pages in the red binder and assigned homework for the weekend. He dismissed the class at 15:30, leaving just enough time for a quick cup of tea before the next class.

Captain Sousa was waiting at the door as the recruits walked in for the late afternoon class. *This must be protocol for all the instructors,* Nicollette thought. *They are always waiting for us.* Captain Sousa handed out notebooks to the recruits. He started his lecture on surveillance techniques and then showed a film used by Scotland Yard for training undercover observations. Nicollette found the film quite interesting. *Patience,* she thought to herself, surveillance requires patience. Captain Sousa ended the class with some actual satellite photographs. He pinpointed buildings and equipment to the class. Nicollette was amazed at the detail and clarity of pictures taken from space. *It's like watching Dr. Who with all that technology,* she thought as the class was dismissed.

"What did you think of that class?" Sarah asked as the four of them headed to the dining hall.

"I found it really interesting," Nicollette responded. "Believe it or not, I'm actually looking forward to learning more from Captain Sousa."

"Wait till after you do your homework, Nicky! It's only one hundred pages of reading over the weekend," Val added sarcastically.

"And, we're going to London tomorrow, ladies," Sarah added.

# London

The meeting in the common room started promptly at 19:00 hours. Sergeant Durban closed the door and addressed the recruits. "Good evening, ladies. What did you think of your first week? Tired? Overwhelmed? Or maybe you feel more interested, more involved. Maybe you feel physically stronger, I do know Sergeant Harris after all."

That comment seemed to grab the ladies' attention as a rattle of laughter flowed through the room. Sergeant Durban continued, "You have just completed five days, but there is much more to do. Tomorrow, we are off to London. As we talked about last night, we will meet downstairs at 08:00. I suggest you have an early breakfast. We request that you wear your white blouses and black skirts and don't forget your overcoats as it will be chilly tomorrow. Finally, don't forget your letters home and please, ladies, remember the guidelines for your letters. As for tonight, Lieutenant Blankin has thought you may need a little break. So, the options are the pub, the base movie theatre where *The Man with the Golden Gun* will be playing, or you could just relax here and do your homework. I understand that badminton courts are set up in the gym as well. So several choices. If you are headed to the pub or theater, transport will be leaving in twenty minutes. Otherwise, I will see you all at 08:00 tomorrow. Oh ladies, not too late tonight as tomorrow is going to be a long day."

Sergeant Durban dismissed the group.

Nicollette turned to Val as they were leaving the room. "What do you want to do?"

"I vote the pub. We deserve a pint! How about you lot?"

Peg turned to Sarah, shrugged her shoulders. Sarah looked at the group, shrugged her shoulders back.

"You know I don't drink much, but I do like lemonade."

"I guess it's a pub visit then. I'm glad we did our letters earlier, ladies!"

The four of them met early the next morning by the elevator as planned. An early breakfast then off to meet the coach. They eyed each other up and down. They looked sharp in their white blouses and black skirts.

"We look a right bunch," Val exclaimed.

"I haven't worn stockings in a long time," Sarah mused.

"I don't think any of us have," Val chortled as they headed down the elevator.

"Letters?" Nicollette asked as she held up hers for all to see.

One by one, each of them produced their letters.

"By the book as well," Peg added as she showed the letter in her hand.

There was a crowd waiting at the front door. The coach was visible through the security window. Lieutenant Blankin and Sergeant Durban appeared from the elevator. Lieutenant Blankin addressed the crowd.

"Good morning, ladies. It is 07:55 hours and we will be boarding the bus in five minutes. If you have your letters,

Sergeant Durban will be collecting them now."

Sergeant Durban walked through the crowd and collected the letters.

"We will now start boarding." Lieutenant Durban made her way to the front door. As the women approached her, she checked their names against her list and motioned them to board the bus. As Nicollette went through the door, she noticed two soldiers on either side of the sidewalk and that the bus had very dark tinted windows. She stepped up into the bus and immediately noticed it was one of those luxury coaches, spacious and comfortable. As she made her way to an empty seat, she was surprised to see who was sitting in the back of the bus. Charles Thompson was sitting next to Captain McWilliams and Colonel Baron was sitting with Major Hartwell. Sitting behind them was Captain Murphy, Captain Sousa, Captain Rheims and Sergeant Harris. It seemed that anyone affiliated with group **228** was going to London.

"What a great surprise! It's good to see you, Mr. Thompson," Nicollette exclaimed as she held out her hand for a handshake. *I hope I didn't break any protocols,* Nicollette thought to herself after offering her hand.

She was relieved when Charles Thompson responded. "Good to see you as well, Nicollette. How's it going?"

Nicollette noticed a seat nearby.

"I'd say very well. I am learning a lot and I feel great physically."

Charles Thompson turned to Colonel Baron. "This is Miss Beverley. I don't believe you've met."

"We have, actually," Colonel Baron responded. "We

met in Captain McWilliams' office. I was impressed with her tests, and I wanted to meet her. You did say you're coming along well, didn't you, Miss Beverley?"

"Yes sir, thank you. I am and this trip sounds very exciting!"

"Splendid. We will talk more later."

The coach was filling up now. Val saw Nicollette and sat next to her. "Don't look now, but there are some powerful people sitting behind us."

"I know," Nicollette responded. "I just had a chat with Mr. Thompson and the colonel."

"Oh, hobnobbing with the brass I see," Val said as she mimicked drinking an imaginary cup of tea with her pinky finger extended.

The two of them smiled as they watched Sergeants Durban and Richards board as well as Corporals Vance and Stanley. There were three other uniformed personnel boarding, two men and one woman that Nicollette did not recognize. Lieutenant Blankin was the last to board and announced it was about a two-hour ride. The door closed and the coach pulled away. Peg and Sarah had found seats in front of Nicollette and Val. The bus was filled with small talk. Peg and Sarah looked over their seats at Nicollette and Val.

"Where do you think we're going?" Sarah asked.

"It's kind of a mystery to me," Val replied.

"One thing's for sure," Peg added. "There's a lot of important people on this coach. We must be headed to someplace special."

Nicollette looked out of the window. *Peg's right. We're*

*all dressed up and traveling with the people in charge of
our group. Something tells me this is going to be a very special day.*

As they approached downtown London, Lieutenant
Blankin stood in front and addressed the passengers.

"Attention please!" she commanded. "We are almost at
our destination. So, some last-minute instructions. First,
please leave the coach and enter the foyer area of the
building in an orderly fashion. No talking or stopping. We
want to get inside as quickly as possible, so all eyes forward and remain in line."

Nicollette could see Big Ben as the coach turned onto
King Charles Street. She had been in this area before when
her father brought the family to London, probably passing
this exact building. A feeling rushed inside her that this
visit could be some sort of "destiny moment" and that this
trip and in fact this day was going to have a profound impact on her.

"Alright, ladies, you will be leaving the coach first.
Remember, exit in an orderly fashion and head directly
into the building."

Lieutenant Blankin stood at the front as the women left
the coach. It was raining lightly, and the air was chilly as
Nicollette stepped off the coach onto the sidewalk. She
noticed several trenchcoated men on either side of the
pathway into the building. Val was right behind, followed
by Sarah and Peg. The entryway was closed immediately
after the last of the group entered the building.

Colonel Baron addressed the group. "Ladies and
guests, this is indeed a very special day, and it is my

pleasure to welcome you to the War Cabinet Rooms. As you know, these rooms were used during World War II by Sir Winston Churchill, his cabinet and military, to conduct operations. We are indeed fortunate today to have Admiral Sir Deric Holland-Martin, Chairman of the Board of the Imperial War Museum, to greet us this morning."

Admiral Sir Deric Holland-Martin greeted the group.

"Good morning to our special guests. Today you will be among the first few to experience these war cabinet rooms as they are not opened to the public yet. You will find that the rooms have been left in the same condition as they were almost thirty-five years ago. Everything you see is as it was during the last days of use in 1945. We ask you not to touch any objects or furniture and to be careful walking through. Please enjoy your tour."

The guides were introduced, and the guests were divided into three groups. The first group set off down the corridor, followed a few minutes later by groups two and three. As they toured the rooms, Nicollette was struck in awe as to how small the work areas were in comparison to how big the war was. As she walked through the rooms, Nicollette closed her eyes several times and imagined Sir Winston walking around the area, she could almost smell his cigar in the air. As the tour continued, Nicollette became very moved and could feel her deep-rooted love and loyalty to England coming to her foremost senses. *Just think what these men and women achieved in these very rooms with such little resources. They must have had a great deal of grit and determination and love for this country.*

All too soon, the group was re-boarding the coach. Lieutenant Blankin announced the next destination was Whitehall to attend a special luncheon. It was just a short ride from the War Cabinets Rooms to Parliament. The rain was coming down heavier as the coach stopped in front of another nondescript building. This time, umbrellas were available as they exited the coach. Nicollette and Val shared an umbrella as they left the coach and walked into the building. Once inside, they were directed to an elevator then down a long hall to a set of open double doors. The doors were opened to reveal a dining area. There were four round tables with eight seats and one long table at the front. Nicollette noticed how formal the room was. All the tables were all set with placemats and silverware. There were water pitchers at every other seat and large floral arrangements as centerpieces. Sarah and Peg caught up with Nicollette and Val. Seated at the table next to them were Sergeant Durbin and the other enlisted soldiers. All the officers were seated at the head table. Lieutenant Blankin, Captains Murphy and McWilliams, Major Hartwell and Colonel Baron. The only civilian at the table was Charles Thompson. The center three seats were left empty.

Colonel Baron rose from his chair and addressed the room. "Good afternoon, ladies and gentlemen. I hope you enjoyed the War Cabinet Rooms. We were indeed fortunate to be able to visit there and a special thank you to Major Hartwell for organizing the trip. Thank you."

A polite applause followed.

The Colonel continued, "It was certainly an interesting

visit. I hope you take away some memories and thoughts from this morning. One personal thought I'd like to share with you. As I was exiting the War Cabinet Rooms, it became clear to me how important those few square meters were to England at a time of unparalleled crisis. Those few square meters were the 'brain center' of operations. Those few square meters housed the Prime Minister, Sir Winston Churchill, and all his top military and domestic advisors. I then thought about the men and women who supported their effort. It is those men and women who day in and day out provided the intelligence and information to their superiors. These men and women in those few square meters became the backbone of operations. I can imagine the buzz of activity in the rooms undeterred by the bombs falling above them and the ground shaking beneath them. These men and women continued to deliver crucial information without fail. That importance, that dedication, that spirit in those few meters, well, that's the right stuff!!"

A pause, then applause.

"Thank you! Now it is indeed my pleasure to introduce our hosts. First, from the Ministry of Defense, Colonel Paul Tremont."

Colonel Tremont walked to his seat and stood behind it. He was followed by another Colonel from the Ministry of Defense, Colonel Peter Halls.

"Now our special host, Sir John Barraclough, former Air Secretary and currently serving as Commandant of the Royal College of Defense Studies." Sir John walked to his seat passing the now standing guests at the head table. He was an older gentleman of average height, Nicollette observed, with perfect posture, upright and straight. He took his officer's cap off to reveal a head of jet white hair. He raised his hands in appreciation and motioned for all to be seated.

"Good afternoon. I hear you had an interesting morning. The War Cabinet rooms are truly inspiring, and your visit later today to Bletchley Park should prove to be interesting as well. When I was asked by my good friend and colleague Colonel Baron to address group 228, I asked him what was group 228? About thirty minutes later," he paused and there was a little laughter from the attendees. Sir John continued, "I agreed to speak to you this afternoon. I must say I am impressed with how much you have achieved in just a short time and equally impressive is how determined you are to complete this program. We live in dangerous times. Our adversaries are constantly updating their abilities and challenging our interests. Add to this the proliferation of advanced and nuclear weapons combined with the ability to deliver them and the danger becomes even more terrifying. We face these realities every day. So, what can we do?" He paused. "There are many answers to this question. Simply put, we can update our military resources and tactics. We can strengthen our regional and global alliances. We can improve and update our technologies, and to tie it all together, we need to advance our communications and intelligence systems to be the best in the world."

Sir John paused for a breath.

"To work towards achieving this goal, we need an influx of new ideas, new thoughts, new energy and, importantly, new people. This is where group 228 fits in. I know this group is small and seemingly insignificant, but do not underestimate your importance. You are the trailblazers of this new program and by looking out at all of you here, I am confident you have the will and desire to make this important contribution. I thank you for your efforts and wish you the best of luck. Thank you."

Lunch was served. Nicollette turned towards Val and whispered, "I know where our next stop is."

"The Colonel mentioned Bletchley Park. Isn't that about the enigma machine and all that coding during World War II?"

"It should be very interesting," Sarah added.

"Not to change the subject, but the food is fantastic," Peg offered as she put a fork full into her mouth. "Just like at home."

About an hour later, Lieutenant Durban announced that transport was ready. She repeated her earlier instructions and soon all were aboard the coach. The ride was about ninety minutes and Nicollette took advantage of this time to have a short nap. Closing her eyes, she was still absorbing the tour of the War Cabinet Rooms and the luncheon, especially Sir John's comments and the lingering imaginative smell of Churchill's cigar.

Nicollette awoke as the coach was pulling up to a large mansion with beautiful grounds and an adjoining small lake. Lieutenant Blankin stood at the front of the coach and reminded the group about decorum. Nicollette looked out of the window and took a moment to take in the architecture of the building. The front entrance was a magnificent archway guarded by two gargoyles with wings at either side. Once through, the group was met by three uniformed tour guides.

"Good afternoon. My name is Captain St. Reitz and I want to welcome you to Bletchley Park. I believe you know how important Bletchley was to the war effort. In fact, many say that World War II was won right here at Bletchley. Recently, work that was performed here has been declassified and you are among the first to visit these buildings that housed our country's largest secrets. As you tour, please be alert as many areas are in poor condition and under renovation. Restorations are underway and you may come across working areas. Please exercise caution. Tours will be given by Lieutenants Pike, Reed, Mead, and myself. We will meet back here at 18:30 hours, approximately three hours from now. Let's break into groups of five. Enjoy your tour."

Nicollette, Val, Sarah, Peg and Helen George lined up with Lieutenant Reed. Val looked over and saw Colonel Baron and the rest of the officers as well as Charles Thompson being escorted on the tour with Captain St. Reitz. The lights in and around the complex were already lit as the January sun began to set. The late afternoon chill felt almost invigorating as the group walked out of the back of the mansion towards a row of brick buildings and nondescript huts. There was construction equipment everywhere and building materials stored neatly in several places. As Nicollette walked through the tour, it seemed as though she was in a time warp. The furniture, the wall hangings, the rudimentary machinery, all brought back to life a time over thirty years ago. Nicollette again was in awe as the group went from building to building. Lieutenant Reed was giving a detailed and thorough explanation of what a day was like at Bletchley. He stopped at a rundown building.

"This is what remains of Hut 8," he announced. "There were about eight thousand women who worked here at Bletchley. Most were in clerical positions, only one, Joan Clarke, was allowed to use 'Banburismus.' Banburismus is a cryptanalytic process developed by Alan Turing, who some credit as being the 'Father of modern computing.' Clarke started at Bletchley as a clerk but soon her mathematical skills were recognized, and she was promoted. She worked directly with Alan Turing to decipher the German Enigma Code. Clarke was actually engaged to Turing but they never married. This is the building where she worked."

As the group walked away, Nicollette stood alone for a moment. *Joan Clarke must have been quite a woman. Imagine, one woman working side by side with all those men. What scrutiny she must have faced and barriers she had to break through. And yet with all the publicity and history of Bletchley Park, I'd never heard of Joan Clarke till today. Shame.*

The coach pulled away and Nicollette took a last look at Bletchley through the window. She promised herself that she would return one day to visit again. The hum of the engine and the darkness outside made it easy for her to take a short kip. The coach was getting close to Brize when

Lieutenant Blankin addressed the group.

"Quite a day today. I hope you take something away from our visits and keep it as a memory of what can be accomplished when we work as a team and use our ingenuity and skills to achieve a common goal." She continued, "Let's show our appreciation to Colonel Baron and his staff for arranging such an interesting and informative day."

It was 20:30 hours when the coach pulled up to the main training building at Brize. It was raining when Nicollette exited. The cold moist air hit her face hard as she walked from the coach to the main building. *January in England.*

"Quite invigorating this rain, eh, Nicky?" Val asked as they walked together into the main building. "I hope they've made something hot for us in the dining hall, I'm hungry and this weather. I could just dive into a stew!"

"Me too," Nicollette responded as the two of them headed through the door.

Sarah and Peg caught up with Nicollette and Val at the cafeteria line. Sarah's red hair was matted down by the rain and her glasses were wet.

"See, I told you to bring a brolly or at least a hat," Peg scolded a wet Sarah.

"At least I'm not still wearing that silly hat, Peg," Sarah responded.

Peg had almost forgotten about the shiny pink hat she was wearing. She quickly pulled it off and stuffed it into her pocket.

"Now girls!" Nicollette mockingly scolded. "Let's eat!"

"May I join you?" A voice came from behind. The ladies looked up and saw Lieutenant Blankin, holding a tray, standing over an empty seat.

"Sure, please do," Val responded. Lieutenant Blankin sat down and placed a napkin over her lap.

"What've you ladies been talking about?" she asked.

"Nothing really, just about the day," Peg replied.

"It was quite a day at that," Lieutenant Blankin replied.

Nicollette realized that this was the first time that Lieutenant Blankin was having any social interaction with the girls. No instructions. No directions. No business. Just a conversation among the ladies. The small talk continued. *She's really trying to be one of us*, Nicollette *thought, it's actually quite nice. But remember, she is still in charge.*

At 22:00, Sergeant Durban approached the chair where Lieutenant Blankin was seated and motioned to her that it was meeting time. Lieutenant Blankin nodded back in acknowledgement and motioned for her to gather the rest of the recruits to have seats at adjoining tables. Lieutenant Blankin took a quick glance around and grabbed a napkin to wipe her mouth. She then took a deep breath, smiled at the ladies seated, and stood to address the women. She looked around at the adjoining tables and asked for all to bring their chairs closer.

"I hope you all enjoyed today's activities. There is a lot to be learned. We wanted you to experience history firsthand and by listening to your reactions, I believe we have succeeded. Your first week of training is now nearly over. We are very proud of your progress. We started with fifteen young ladies, and we now have fourteen young women, working hard every day, learning every day, and becoming stronger every day. But now the training will intensify, and you will be challenged to your limits. These next few weeks will be very difficult, and you will be taxed to the extreme. There might be times you want to quit, leave and be dismissed from the program; however, we are confident you will pull through and persevere to the end of the training. You are strong and capable. Continue your hard work."

Lieutenant Blankin paused for effect, took a breath and continued.

"Tomorrow is Sunday. The cafeteria will be open till 01:00 hours, allowing for a more leisurely breakfast. Laundry will be picked up at 09:00, outside your door, so have yourself organized by then. There will be two classes tomorrow. Your exercise class will begin at 09:00 hours. At 13:00, you will be picked up outside the dorm to attend a class I think you will find very interesting, but we will leave it at that. Then after tea, there will be a meeting. So now, you have the rest of the night to yourselves. I will see you tomorrow. Good night."

Lieutenant Blankin picked up her tea and left the table. *A quick reminder that she is back in charge*, Nicollette thought.

It was nearly 09:00 when Nicollette and Val left their room the next morning. They walked into the gym to find Peg and Sarah already there.

"Sorry we're late. Time just got away from us."

"This one had a hard time getting out of bed," Nicollette

joked, pointing at Val.

"Good morning, ladies!" Sergeant Harris announced as she walked into the gym. "We need to make up for yesterday's off day. So, let's get to it!"

It was a long session, stretches, exercises, capped off by several long wind sprints.

"Sergeant Harris really worked us hard this morning," Nicollette commented as they walked into the dining hall.

"I think she was upset about missing yesterday's work-out," Val said. "All I know is that the shower felt great this morning. I ache all over."

"May we join you two ladies?" Val asked in a mock posh voice imitating Peg as they approached the table where Sarah and Peg were sitting.

"Why certainly," Sarah responded in the same tone.

"I wonder what this afternoon's activity is all about?" Nicollette asked.

"Who knows, but I think we are in for lots of surprises," Peg replied.

The group, along with Sergeant Durban, assembled in the lobby waiting for transport. It was 13:00 when a gray coach arrived. The sun was prominent against a clear blue sky and all the evidence from the rain yesterday was gone. It was unusually warm for a mid-January day. There was an air of excitement about the possibilities for the afternoon.

"I wonder where we are going?" Peg asked.

"I don't know, but we're about to find out," Sarah added.

"Look."

The four of them stared out the window as the bus entered a very large building. "Ladies, we are going into an airplane hangar," Nicollette observed.

The coach unloaded the passengers inside the massive structure. Sergeant Durban motioned the women to an area where seats were arranged in a semicircle. There were five black Ford Cortinas parked in front of the chairs.

"My father has one of those," Sarah exclaimed.

The Cortina was a bigger car in comparison to other British models and the vehicle of choice for the government. It was a comfortable four door automobile, solid and dependable. Sergeant Durban walked to the front of the group.

"Ladies, this afternoon you are in for a treat. We know you all have driver's certificates and have experience driving English country roads."

There was a slight chuckle and Sergeant Durban even cracked a smile then continued,

"However, you may be in situations which require more than just experienced driving. How about having to drive to save your life?" She paused. "Yes, ladies, driving to stay alive. Do not be shocked. You are going to be trained to be proactive and prepared for these types of situations and that education starts this afternoon. Let me introduce you to Captain Swanson and his staff."

There were two men and two women accompanying Captain Swanson as he addressed the ladies.

"Good afternoon, my name is Captain Swanson and with me are Lieutenants Brown, Frye, Rand and Nye. We will spend the next several hours training you on how to drive. Not your normal civilian commute, but how to drive to stay alive. This will be the first of at least several sessions. When we are finished, you should have the confidence and instinct to handle a serious situation. All we ask is to trust us and listen to what we are instructing. Now let's go drive!"

The group was divided into groups of three recruits plus one instructor. Nicollette went with Val and Peg while Sarah went with another group. One of the cars was driven through the course to show the route. It was obvious that a highly skilled driver was effortlessly maneuvering the Cortina. *Am I really going to be able to drive like that?* Nicollette thought to herself as she nervously volunteered to be the first to drive. Lieutenant Brown sat in the front passenger seat with Val and Peg in the back.

"Now just relax, miss. Take a deep breath. When you are ready, we'll go."

At first, Nicollette was gentle and a bit reserved as she drove through the course. Suddenly, Lieutenant Brown barked instructions to stop the car. He turned to Nicollette. "If you drive like this when you are in a situation, you are going to have difficulties for sure. Now I want you to put this car through its paces. There are no traffic 'bobbies' or MPs here. Now drive like you really mean it! And you two in the back, buckle up and hang on."

The lieutenant looked at Nicollette.

"Now show me how to drive the way I showed you, as if your life depended on it!"

Nicollette started the car and put the car in gear. She

entered the course. She could feel a rush of adrenaline flowing through her veins as she increased her speed. The wheels made a loud screeching sound as she rounded the curves. Her nervousness and all the earlier driving inhibitions she had seemed to go away as the speed increased on the straight portion of the course. The Cortina felt as if it would roll over as it weaved through the cones at a high speed and then through the hard turns. Finally, a hard brake and a controlled spin before she pulled to a stop.

"Wow, Nicky, that was some driving," Val offered.

"I'm still catching my wind," Peg added.

"Me too!" Nicollette added as she wiped her sweaty palms on her pants.

"Not bad for a start, miss," Lieutenant Brown said. "But you will do much better by the time we are done. Now, who's next?"

The afternoon went by very quickly and it was getting dark. Everyone had a chance to drive with varying levels of success. The group was taken back to the hangar for some light refreshments. A movie screen had been set up in the front of the chairs and everyone was asked to sit down. Lieutenant Brown addressed the women.

"Ladies, this afternoon you've had your first experience in situational driving and my observations are that most of you did fairly well. Those that did not will have plenty of time to catch up. We would now like to show you a short film on situational driving and then transport is waiting to take you to tea. I would also like to remind you that this type of driving is not recommended for the motorway under normal conditions. The police may not take kindly to it."

A pause and a few snickers.

"Anyways, the film."

The coach was waiting as the group exited the hangar. The weather had changed as the sun went down. It was now chilly and there was a mist of rain in the air when they arrived at the main building. Sergeant Durban addressed the women.

"Ladies, that was quite an interesting afternoon, wasn't it? The time is nearly 18:00 hours, so I suggest everyone have tea now. There will be a meeting in the common room at 19:30 hours. I will see you then."

It was 19:30 hours when Nicollette, Val, Sarah and Peg joined the group in the meeting room. Sergeant Durban and Lieutenant Blankin were already in the room as Nicollette took a seat. There was also another woman standing with them. It was Major Hartwell. She was dressed in her Royal Air Force attire. There were rows of multi-colored ribbons adorning the perfectly fitting uniform. Pert and proper. After all were seated, Lieutenant Blankin spoke.

"Ladies, your first week is now complete. Well done to each of you. Let me reiterate what I said last night. The training will now become much more intense, so be prepared. Your routine will become more consistent and far more exhausting. There will be a short meeting every night in this room promptly at 19:00. Mandatory attendance. Now Major Hartwell would like to say a few words.

"Good evening, ladies. As you know, I have a vested interest in you and this program. I was a strong advocate for this type of program, and I worked closely with Colonel Baron and others to organize and create group 228. This took a great deal of time and effort and we, that is you and all of us, are working hard to make it succeed. And it will. Throughout the rest of your training, I will be observing, listening and taking notes. Please do not be intimidated. You will be stressed, and you will be exhausted, but you will succeed. I look forward to personally meeting each of you and getting to know you. Now, it is nearly 20:00 hours, a little late for going to activities or the pub, so we thought it would be nice to bring the pub to you."

At that point, soldiers brought in bottles of beer and wine as well as sodas, chips and finger foods. Major Hartwell asked for quiet in the now noisy room.

"Ladies, your attention, please. There are two celebrations tonight. First, congratulations on the completion of your first week and secondly," she paused for effect, "we are going to celebrate Sergeant Durban's birthday!"

As if it was rehearsed, in unison, "Happy Birthday" was sung. Sergeant Durban stood up, working hard as she could to hide her emotions, and thanked the group. A birthday cake was wheeled in and a party ensued. Fun and angst, Nicollette was feeling both. The party was wonderful and a great release from the stress of the day, but the angst became more real as she and Val went back to their room. *It was great to see the major, Lieutenant Blankin and Sergeant Durban try to be at one with the recruits and celebrate our first week, but I think that is*

—211—

*only temporary, I believe we are in for a much harder time starting tomorrow,* Nicollette thought. Would she be up to the challenge?

# To The Limits

Monday morning started early as they always seemed to do. Exercises. Breakfast. Classes. Lunch. More Classes. Tea. Meetings. Evening activities. Monday flowed into Tuesday and then into Wednesday and Thursday. There was homework on top of homework. I barely have time to breathe, Nicollette thought to herself. The social aspect of the training was all but gone. *Thank goodness I have Val, Sarah, and Peg.* The week flew by. There was little time to feel tired. Krav Maga. Gun Range. Driving course. More meetings. More classes. Cryptanalysis. Memorization activities. Puzzle solving. Self-study and the additional work on Spanish. The stress mounting, physically and emotionally. Pushed to the limits. *Everything hurts, from my body to my brain,* Nicollette thought. Sheer exhaustion. Sunday, finally, a lighter day. Sleeping till 09:00, then a leisurely breakfast and finishing homework till an afternoon activity at 13:00. As was planned the night before, Peg and Sarah joined Nicollette and Val at the elevator to go to breakfast.

"I really needed that lie in," Val stated.

"I must admit, I needed it as well," Peg responded.

"I think we all are better for it," Nicollette added. "I hope they take it a little easier on us today. My head felt like it was going to explode!".

"What day is it?" Sarah injected sleepily.

Imagine their surprise when at the security desk waiting for them was Major Hartwell in civilian clothing. She was wearing a business attire dress and her hair out of the military style bun. It was nearly shoulder length in a "page boy" type cut. Nicollette had seen the major around throughout the week. Major Hartwell smiled at the group.

"Good morning, ladies. Would you mind if I joined you for breakfast? It will give us a chance to get to know each other."

*This must be something special*, Nicollette thought as she answered, "Yes, please do."

"Splendid and thank you, but please, be relaxed and be yourselves. This morning, I am one of the group and you can call me Major."

The five of them walked to the main building and into the dining hall. There was small talk around the table. The Major asked each of the women about themselves, almost as in an interview. Nicollette quickly noticed that when the conversation turned towards anything about the major's personal life, she would quickly steer the conversation to another subject. Now, Major Hartwell steered the conversation towards the training. There was seriousness in her voice.

"Well, ladies, how do you think it is going? Talk to me, I need your input."

There was silence at the table. The girls looked at each other and back at Major. "Come on, talk to me," Major repeated.

Another silence.

Finally, with an encouraging kick under the table from

Val, Nicollette spoke up.

"Well, Major, the first week was interesting. I think I can say for all of us that it was a great experience. We were exposed to many new things both mentally and physically. I personally liked the gun range and the driving course. The trip to London was very interesting and I learned a great deal. The War Cabinet Rooms and Bletchley Park were fantastic and a real treat. I felt very special being there. Now, honestly, though, this week has been a challenge. It's been very tough! We seem to be going at a quick pace with very little time to breathe! For me at least, it's an awful lot to take in all at once, especially since we are all committed to complete, even excel, this training. I must admit, I was looking forward to today as at least a small chance to catch my breath."

"Thank you, Nicollette, for being so frank. Does everyone else feel the same way?"

The Major looked around the table and one by one, each of them acknowledged in the affirmative. The Major put her hands on the table and leaned in with her head. She spoke in a soft voice forcing the group to lean in to hear.

"Ladies, I am glad you feel challenged and fatigued. That is the idea. In the future when you are working and everyone and everything is coming at you all at once, you need to be on your game, making the right decisions, perhaps even impacting lives." She paused and leaned back in her chair then continued, "I appreciate what you are going through, and I want to let you in on a little secret." The Major leaned in again and spoke in the same soft voice again. "You four are doing very well. Not only have I noticed but so have others, many of whom you have never seen. I am proud of you. Now, the bad news, the training is going to get even harder, but I know you all will do well and be very successful."

Again, the major sat back in her chair. She appeared to relax as she casually asked, "How would you like to join me at the Officers' Mess for tea tonight? A sort of reward for the hard work you have put in this week. Of course, you will have to dress. Your black skirts and white tops will do. What do you think?"

*Tea with the major! This is special!* Nicollette thought as a sense of pride and accomplishment swept over her. *But why all the attention to the four of us? I wonder what is going on? Still, tea with the major!*

"Thank you, Major, it would be an honor," Val spoke enthusiastically.

The rest quickly followed with positive responses and big smiles.

The major rose from the table and she turned to the group and leaned in for a third time.

"Ladies, I do appreciate your discretion as I have only invited the four of you, so let's keep this among us, please."

"Yes Major," Peg responded as the others nodded their heads in the affirmative.

"Splendid, I will meet you in the lobby at 18:00 hours. Have a good afternoon."

The major walked away, and the ladies looked at each other almost in disbelief.

"Wow, what a treat to be invited to tea with the major,"

Sarah said. "And we get to dress up and eat with officers and the like."

"And we get to behave like proper young ladies," Val added as she held out her hand as if holding a cup of tea in a posh fashion with her pinky finger extended.

"Now you lot behave yourselves," Nicollette added in a mock scolding voice.

"Speaking of behavior, ladies, I think we need to get a move on as it's nearly 13:00 hours!" Peg interjected.

The afternoon class seemed to drag on. Cryptanalysis. Decoding. Coding. Radio frequencies. Continuity. Tap tap tap. Multiply and divide. Tables and more tables. Complete messages. Information. Memorize and recall. Finally, 16:30 hours. Class dismissed. Back to the dorm to get ready for the special evening. As the group passed the security desk and entered the elevator, Nicollette turned to her friends.

"Ladies, that was some afternoon! My brain worked overtime today. I think we earned tonight's treat in just this afternoon's work! I'm really going to enjoy tonight!"

As planned, Nicollette, Val, Peg and Sarah all met at the elevator at 5:45. Waiting for them in the lobby was Major Hartwell's driver. He assisted as the ladies put on their coats and left the building. Waiting for them was a large black sedan. Inside was Major Hartwell and Lieutenant Blankin.

"Good evening, ladies," the major welcomed them. "I've asked Lieutenant Blankin to join us."

The vehicle was warm, and the seats were very comfortable. Nicollette had never ridden in such a luxurious automobile. *I could quite easily fall asleep here,* she thought.

"We have about a thirty-minute ride, ladies, so sit back and relax." The major paused, then asked, "What did you think of today's class?"

Nicollette, maybe feeling more comfortable than the others in the presence of the two officers, spoke first. "It was a lot to take in. The information kept coming at us. The pace was very fast. I must admit that I was very tired at the end. Plus, it's been a very long week!"

"I must admit I was exhausted as well. But it was a different type of tired." Val added, "I was and still feel tired, yet somehow, I feel fulfilled, like when I was at school and finally completed a difficult task. A sort of satisfied tiredness."

"I think both Sarah and I would agree," Peg included as Sarah nodded her head in acknowledgement.

"I must add, Major, and I'm sure I speak for all of us, that we thank you for this wonderful evening. It's truly a wonderful reward for the week's hard work," Nicollette added.

The car pulled up to the front of the officers' club and the door was opened for the passengers to exit. The six of them, led by Major Hartwell, were led to a reserved table. The club was rather full. There was a small band playing jazz dinner music in the corner. They reached the table, and all were seated. Nicollette felt rather special at the table. There were real cotton napkins and crystal water glasses, a large basket of rolls, fancy silverware and a real floral centerpiece. Very elegant. Very posh. The Major ordered two bottles of wine for the table. Red and white.

"Ladies, we are off duty tonight," the major announced

as she turned towards Lieutenant Blankin. "And that includes you, Cheryl!" There was a chuckle.

The menu was like no other one Nicollette had ever seen before. There were no prices next to the items listed. Nicollette ordered the filet mignon and a jacket potato. Val and Peg ordered the lamb and Sarah ordered salmon. There was small talk over the glasses of wine. Salads were brought to the table.

"I think we should make a toast to our host and thank her for this lovely evening," Val rose from her seat. The rest of them stood.

"To the major."

"Here, here!"

The clink of wine glasses.

"Thank you, ladies," the major spoke as all were seated. "It is indeed my pleasure for this evening, but I must admit there is something Lieutenant Blankin, I mean Cheryl and I, need to discuss with you later."

*Here it comes.* Nicollette's earlier suspicions revisited her. Deep down, Nicollette could feel as if something very serious was about to happen, that they were being set up for something. She tried to put those fears behind her as the major continued.

"Nothing to be concerned about, actually rather exciting. We'll talk later."

As the salads were finished, the main courses arrived. The major quickly pointed out the geography lesson on the table. "Argentinian beef, Australian Lamb, American Salmon, British Chicken, French wine and Irish potatoes and local vegetables. You see, ladies, the world is a very connected place even at this table. This makes the world a more exciting and more dangerous place at the same time. Just a short lesson. Now, let's tuck in, shall we?"

Small casual talk. A second glass of wine. Nicollette started to feel very comfortable. At first, Lieutenant Blankin appeared to be intimidated about participating in the small talk with the major at the table. When asked about her family though, she soon loosened up and spoke more comfortably. It was a special dinner. The food. The wine. The conversation. The setting. Little did Nicollette, Val, Peg and Sarah know just how memorable the evening would really be.

The dinner dishes were cleared.

"Dessert, coffee?"

"Why not?" the major replied.

Nicollette was eyeing the ice cream sundae on the menu. *How much more exercise will it take to burn that off?* she thought. *Sergeant Harris will see to that!* Soon, dessert was finished, and a second cup of coffee was served. Then, the major surprised everyone when she ordered a brandy for the table. She poured the brandy. Even Sarah joined with a glass. Nicollette noticed the club was emptying out a bit. She looked at her watch. It was nearly 20:30 hours, they had missed tonight's meeting! *I guess Lieutenant Blankin will take care of that!*

"Ladies, it has been a great evening, I hope you enjoyed the meal. Now it's time for some business. We asked Lieutenant Blankin to observe group 228 from a slight distance over the past two weeks. You may have noticed that most of your directions have come from Sergeant Durban, and you have had only little direct contact with Lieutenant Blankin. Lieutenant Blankin was asked to look for certain characteristics and tendencies among group 228. I will let her explain."

Lieutenant Blankin took over the conversation.

"I was asked to look for how the recruits molded, subgroups, leaders, strong and weak links. Diversity and similarities. Personalities. Companionships and dividers. And other traits. This was no small task given the elite group of young women in the training program. This was going to be a challenge."

She paused and looked at each of the four young women then continued, "Sergeant Durban noticed how the four of you had developed into a subgroup within 228. We asked her to intensify her observations and report to me. I became more involved, behind the scenes, almost invisible to 228, but I was watching, observing, and learning. I reported to the major that we thought we had found that small subset we were looking for in you four. The major did some of her own observations and came to the same conclusion. Nicollette Beverley, Valerie Davies, Sarah Green and you, Margaret 'Peg' Wilson, you are that subset. Four young women from different backgrounds and families. Each bringing their own skills and talents to the table, so to speak. Diversity, yet unity and cohesiveness. The four of you have developed into a team. Nurturing and supporting each other but not closed off to the rest. Flexibility yet core strength."

Lieutenant Blankin paused, looked at the four again, took a breath and continued, "Now, what's next? Major

Hartwell will give the details."

"Ladies, next week will be the start of your third week. We want you to continue your training with the rest of the group. This is by no means permission to slack off from your work, in fact it is quite the opposite. What I'm going to tell you now requires your absolute discretion. Next Saturday, we want you to be packed and ready to go by 07:30. You will be given a list of items to pack for your transfer to the temporary location. We will just leave that little detail private for the time being. As your training enters a new phase, there is the small issue of your cover for being away from home. I believe we used the cover of sports medicine and management training in the states. Is that correct?"

The Major looked at the four. Nicollette responded in the affirmative and mentioned Grinnell College in Iowa. Peg, Sarah, and Val all confirmed the same story. The Major continued.

"Good, we have that arranged as well. Starting Wednesday after tea, you will have a class on sports medicine and management. You will have classes on Thursday and Friday nights as well. This will give you some basic background on the subject should any issues arise."

The Major paused, took a deep breath.

"Miss Beverley, Miss Davis, Miss Green and Miss Wilson, I know this is going to be a tough week, but I'm confident in your abilities and determination. If there are any questions?" Again, the major paused. No questions. "Splendid, should any arise though, you may ask Sergeant Durban to reach out for Lieutenant Blankin. Now, it's getting late, and you have a busy schedule next week. And ladies, I would ask for your utmost discretion on this matter."

As Nicollette and Val walked down the quiet hall to their rooms, Nicollette invited Sarah and Peg to join them in her room.

"Omigosh, omigosh, ladies! What just happened?" Val exclaimed as she shut the door.

"I'm not too sure, but I think we've been promoted," Sarah added while landing on the bed. "I mean they've been observing us this whole time and now this special dinner with the major!"

"And we have to pack up and leave here on Friday because we're going to 'who knows where,'" Peg said, "and do who knows what!"

"Ladies, I still have chills up my spine just thinking about it," Nicollette added, trying not to be too excited. "We're pretty smart, but I think it may be counterproductive for us to try and figure this one out. One thing is for sure, we have been singled out for something very special and it will be a waste of time for us to dwell on it. We should just continue what we are doing and let everything happen as it will. Plus, I think we should take what the major said very seriously, no mention of this to anyone!"

"You are very sensible, Nicky, but I can't stop thinking about it."

"Me either."

Nicollette walked over and put her hands on Val's and Peg's shoulders simultaneously.

"All this excitement has made me tired! I think we

should try and get some rest if we can for two reasons. First, this upcoming week is going to be very taxing and secondly and more to the point, it's late and Sergeant Harris won't like it if we are tired and late!"

"Remember, ladies, due discretion!" Val reminded everyone as she shut the door.

# Week Three

"Of all the great things that have been invented, why did man have to invent Mondays?" Val blurted out as the alarm rang.

"I think he must have been asleep, and did it when he was unconscious," Nicollette responded as she rolled out of bed. "This is going to be a hard week, Val, but at least it should go fast, and speaking of fast, we better get a move on as it's getting late and the last thing I need is to face an angry Sergeant Harris!"

The routine all over again: Exercise. Krav Maga. Classes. Observation skills. Cryptanalysis. Computers. World affairs. Analysis. Satellite pictures. Evaluations. Pencils and paper. Monday night gun range. Meetings. Tuesday night driving skills. Sleep. Wake up. Soreness and fatigue.

It was Wednesday tea time. Nicollette, Val, Peg and Sarah dragged themselves into the dining hall for something to eat and to enjoy a short respite from the day's hard work.

"I'm knackered, ladies," Val announced as they sat down.

"I think we all are," Peg responded. "I'm more tired now than I was at the end of last week!"

"But we're getting through it, you lot! Just a couple more days. We can do it," Nicollette added as she gave a large yawn.

"Ditto," Sarah included as she worked hard to keep her eyes open. "And don't forget we have our first Sports Medicine class tonight."

"Splendid," Val responded in a posh voice. "At least we're excused from tonight's meeting!"

As they were finishing their meal and enjoying the break from the hectic schedule, Nicollette glanced at Peg. The past weeks had changed her. It seemed as though Peg no longer had that posh privileged attitude and was now blending into the group; even her upper-class accent was fading, albeit just slightly. Knowing how she felt inside about "those rich kids," Nicollette pondered, *Is Peg really adapting to the group or am I just getting used to her? Am I changing or is she, or are we meeting in the middle? Am I ready to fully invest in her?*

The Sports Medicine class started at 19:00. Inside the room, there were mannequins and two large posters of human body muscles, one of the front and one of the rear. A large mat was on the floor in the rear of the room and a projector screen against the rear wall. The four of them found seats and sat down. Five minutes went by. *Did everyone forget about the class? What were they to do?* Five more minutes. Val looked at Peg.

"What do you think?"

"Let's give it another five."

There was a knock on the classroom door and in walked Sergeant Harris.

"Sorry, ladies. Last minute instructions."

Sergeant Harris placed her briefcase on the desk and

turned to the four.

"Great!" Val whispered to Nicollette. "We've got her twice today!"

"Lovely."

For the next two and a half hours, Nicollette and the group received their first introduction into sports medicine. Because of the small group, there was a more casual pace, but Sergeant Harris was very thorough in her instruction about breaks and sprains, bandages and splints. Each of the young women were given manuals for study.

"Tomorrow night, we will do even more," Sergeant Harris announced as the four of them stumbled out of the room. It was 21:30 hours. Her stomach growling, Nicollette suggested they go to the canteen for a quick coffee and sandwich.

"This has been a tough three days," Nicollette said as she nursed her coffee.

"Same here," Sarah added. "The major wasn't kidding about being tired."

"But ladies, this is what we signed up for and we'll get through this."

"I'm asleep," Val yawned.

There was a note waiting for Nicollette and Val under the door of their dorm room.

"They want our laundry by tomorrow morning, Nicky. It seems they want everything that's being packed to be clean. They have also given us the required dress. Casual for the trip. Jeans and tops. Blouses and skirts for our destination."

Val looked up from the list and turned towards Nicollette. "That's easy enough, just pack everything."

"I guess an extra early rise tomorrow," Nicollette responded with a sarcastic smile.

The alarm sounded. Wake up. Get ready. Laundry. Sergeant Harris and exercises. Quick breakfast. Cryptanalysis. Lunch and a much-needed break. Nicollette could feel the hectic routine start to take a toll. She politely held a yawn while looking at her friends. Nicollette didn't want to let them see the fatigue creeping inside her. *A second cup of tea should get me through the afternoon,* she thought.

The afternoon classes. More cryptanalysis. Memorization. Mathematics. Signals. Respond and repeat. Self-study. 16:00 hours. Class over and a ninety-minute break till tea. It was decided among the four to go back to their rooms for a break before tea and the evening class, plus, there was homework to do. Nicollette decided to lie down for a quick rest.

"Wakey, wakey sleepy head!" Val whispered to Nicollette as she shook her arm.

"Wow, I just closed my eyes for a minute!" Nicollette replied sleepily. "How long have I been asleep?"

"Nearly an hour and look, I have my homework done!" Val answered with a boastful smile.

"I must have been really tired! I don't remember anything! How much time till we have to leave?"

"We've got about thirty minutes, so I would suggest you at least get a start on your assignment, my girl."

At tea, Nicollette could feel herself becoming more

awake; the cobwebs from her late afternoon nap were fading away and she was feeling much more alert and focused. When the four of them walked into the evening class, Sergeant Harris was already there. The chairs in the room had been pushed to the rear and a large mat was on the floor. Sergeant Harris had the group work on dressing wounds and cleaning wounds. They addressed stretches and concussions as well as dislocations and sprains. There was a lot of information flying around and Nicollette was glad that she did not choose to be a doctor. At 21:30, Sergeant Harris dismissed the class.

"In just five-and-a-half hours of intense learning, I think you ladies could pass for being sports medicine people. We will have another class though, just to fine tune what you have learned. Remember your cover story, ladies," she continued as they left the room, "remember your cover."

The alarm went off. 06:00. Up out of bed for 06:30 exercises. Sergeant Harris announced a change in schedule for today. After breakfast, the women would go to the gun range till lunch. After lunch, class would resume till 15:00. At 15:45, Krav Maga till 17:30 then tea at leisure till 19:30. The evening class would start at 19:45 hours for just an hour. After that, a free evening.

"Finally, a bit of a reprieve from this exhausting week!" Nicollette whispered to Val. "And besides, we still have to pack!"

At 20:45 hours, and precisely on schedule, Sergeant Harris ended the last class of the day. Nicollette, Val, Peg and Sarah shared their mixed emotions as they walked towards the dining hall.

"Just think, tomorrow morning we'll be on a plane going off to some unknown destination to do some unknown thing!" Val said to the group. "I'm excited, yet a bit scared! Did we learn enough? Are we prepared for what is about to happen?"

"Well, I for one will not miss the early morning exercises one bit," Sarah responded.

It was nearly 21:30 hours when they left for their rooms. Nicollette and Val had envelopes on their beds. Inside was a note reminding them what to pack and to be downstairs, ready to go by 07:15 hours. As they were organizing their cases, Nicollette looked at Val.

"It's hard to believe we have been in this room for almost two weeks. The time has flown by! I've learned so much."

Val smiled back. "Me too."

# Brussels

Nicollette was in a deep sleep when she was abruptly awakened by the bright shine of a flashlight pointing at her and someone shaking her shoulder.

"Wake up, you lot!! You have fifteen minutes!"

Nicollette's eyes focused on Sergeant Durban barking the commands at Val and herself.

"Whaaat's going on?" Nicollette asked as she forced the words through her mouth.

"No time for explanations, you two need to be downstairs in fifteen minutes. We will take your bags now. We will leave your two small bags for the rest of your belongings."

Sergeant Durban barked. "The plane's not going to wait. Now you two get cracking!"

Nicollette looked at the clock on her nightstand. The time was 02:32. She and Val had thirteen minutes.

Transportation was waiting outside when Nicollette, Val, Peg and Sarah exited from the elevator. A soldier quickly ushered them past the security desk and into the cold, dark night. A light snow was falling gently to the ground. The soldier held open the door as the group entered a large dark sedan. As soon as they were seated in the rear, the sedan took off. Nicollette was becoming more aware as the mind fog from her abrupt awakening was leaving her. There were the four of them in the back and a driver taking them to an undefined destination. Nicollette noticed that there was another passenger in the front. Curious, she leaned to the side to try and get a glimpse of who it might be.

"Good morning," Lieutenant Blankin said as she turned around from the front seat. "Hope your 'alarm' wasn't too loud this morning, ladies," she said with a smile. "We have a plane to catch so sit back and relax."

After a drive of about twenty minutes, the vehicle stopped. The doors were opened by the driver. As she exited, Nicollette could see that the vehicle had pulled next to a long set of stairs leading into a large airplane.

"Wow," exclaimed Val as she stepped out of the sedan, "talk about your door-to-door service."

The four of them were ushered into the plane by Lieutenant Blankin. The plane's cabin was like nothing Nicollette had ever seen before. All the passenger seats had been removed and the interior looked like a large sitting room in a stately home. There were sofas, chairs, and tables as well as several large poufs scattered about. The lighting was provided by several chandeliers. Nicollette noticed a door in the back of the room. The five of them were greeted on board by Sergeant Durban and three Air Force attendants, two men and a woman in their blue and white uniforms.

"Please, ladies, have a seat and buckle in. We will be leaving in about ten minutes."

Nicollette found a seat on one of the sofas. One of the female attendants asked if they were comfortable and offered them a refreshment.

"Once we are in flight, I will bring you some juice; this will help your body adjust to the time and make the flight easier."

Nicollette and Val looked at each other.

"This might be a long flight if we have to adjust for time," Val whispered.

The plane had a very smooth takeoff, and the juice was served. It was sweet and refreshing. Once everyone was finished, the attendant removed the glasses. Nicollette leaned back on the sofa and started to feel very relaxed. She looked across at Peg and Sarah. Sarah gave out a big yawn and Peg was sleeping. A warm feeling crept up on Nicollette and she could feel her eyes becoming very heavy. She glanced over at Val who was already sound asleep. Nicollette's eyes closed and she fell into a deep sleep.

A bell sounded. At first Nicollette thought it was in her dream. Then it sounded again. She opened her eyes to see Lieutenant Blankin holding a small bell. Lieutenant Blankin rang the bell for a third time.

"Alright, ladies, time to rise and shine!"

Nicollette rubbed her eyes as she slowly regained consciousness. She looked around and saw that Peg and Sarah were waking up as well. She turned to see Val looking at her watch.

"We have been asleep for six hours!" Val exclaimed.

"How about some breakfast, ladies?" the male attendant offered.

Before they could respond, a tray was placed in front of

each of them.

The plane landed and Lieutenant Blankin ushered the group off the plane, down the stairs and into a waiting large car. Nicollette stopped for a deep breath. The fresh, chilly air was invigorating. The sky was a clear blue and there was a gentle breeze. As they sat in the car, Peg turned to the group.

"I can't believe we slept for six hours; it must have been a long flight."

Sarah pointed out that the windows of the car were very dark. "I can't see anything outside. Very private."

The ride was quiet. Nicollette was anxious and yet excited. She felt as if she was in a closed box, knowing the inside, but having no idea of anything on the outside. *Where were they? What was going to happen? What was expected of them?*

Nicollette looked at her friends and they looked back at her, puzzled.

After about an hour's ride, the car slowed down, proceeded slowly, then came to a complete stop. The door opened and the group exited into a large garage. Lieutenant Blankin escorted the women through a small door at the side and down a corridor into a nondescript conference room. There was a large wooden table in the center and the walls were painted off white. There were no windows, only fluorescent bulbs to light the room. The group was asked to take a seat. Once seated, Lieutenant Blankin left the room, leaving Nicollette, Val, Peg and Sarah alone in the room.

"I wonder what's going on?" Val asked the group.

"I'm curious too," Peg said. "One thing I do know for certain, this is very serious and I'm a bit scared."

*Me too,* Nicollette thought to herself, *me too!*

Several minutes went by before Lieutenant Blankin returned to the room. Behind her were Major Hartwell, Captain McWilliams, a third uniformed officer and two civilians. Nicollette was very surprised when lastly, Charles Thompson entered the room. He shut the door and acknowledged the group. Nicollette was excited to see him. His presence brought her a sense of stability in a still uncertain situation. She gave him a slight smile and he returned a head nod in return. Charles Thompson spoke.

"Welcome, ladies. I hope your flight was comfortable. I know you may have some questions, so let us try and clarify what is happening. We have brought you here to experience firsthand an event we have been planning for some time. A great deal of time and effort has been expended to get to this point. We are almost at the culmination of this event, and we thought this was an excellent opportunity to bring you in to observe. As for this 'event,' Captain Blasingame will brief you on the details. We have prepared a dossier for each of you to follow."

One of the civilians handed each of the women a leather-bound dossier. Charles Thompson stepped away as Captain Blasingame addressed the group.

"Good morning, ladies. Let me start off by reminding you that what you are about to hear and see is classified and top secret. We expect the utmost discretion from you. This is no game."

The room fell very quiet as the captain continued.

"About two months ago, the Russians set a trap and captured one of our middle-ranked agents. His name is Alexander Perry." *Now the class on World Situations and the Cold War are coming alive,* Nicollette thought to herself as Captain Blasingame continued.

"Here is some background. Mr. Perry and his group were in East Germany posing as representatives of an American Farm Machinery manufacturer. Because the East German Communists do not want to deal directly with an American company, we in England were asked to provide support and act as a middleman if you will. England still retains a small diplomatic presence in East Germany, so this move made sense. After many contacts and negotiations, arrangements were agreed upon and we were able to get Mr. Perry and two supporting staff into East Germany. The East Germans worked with us because they are under pressure to increase their dairy production as fast as possible. Their machinery, what little they have, is antiquated and unreliable at best. The southeast area of East Germany is where most of the dairy is produced. Coincidentally, the East Germans and the Russians have two major bases in the southeast portion of East Germany, a forward airbase and a large infantry base. We have an acute interest in both bases. Satellite images showed us the Russians have a quantity of Mig 27's stationed at the airbase but of more interest to us, there is also a number of Mig 31's and the newest fighter plane, the Mig 29. These aircraft are the first we've seen of their latest interceptor aircraft. The infantry base also holds some surprises as well. There are three brigades stationed at the base, approximately 2500 troops complete with artillery and tanks. Along with a large number of T62 tanks, there is a quantity of the latest T72 tank. We have an interest in these as well. We wanted more information and closer, more detailed pictures. A unique opportunity presented itself. Preparations were started and plans were proceeding. Finally, after intense negotiations, we were able to get the East Germans to allow Alexander Perry plus two representatives and their equipment into East Berlin. The itinerary included several presentations in southeast Germany, coincidently, not too far from each of the bases. Just over six months ago, the operation was set, and Perry and his crew entered East Germany. The mission was proceeding well. Mr. Perry and his group were able to send us close up pictures and valuable information, slowly at first, but with more regularity as the mission progressed. And surprisingly enough, he sold a few pieces of farm equipment as well. The mission came to a crashing halt, unfortunately, because of one sloppy transmission. A code was not reset, and Perry was arrested. The two assistants managed to escape back to West Germany through Czechoslovakia. We were soon approached by the East Germans to arrange an exchange. We are holding one of their agents outside London and they seemed rather keen to get him back. We did not want to tip our hand, so we played it not to be as enthusiastic as they were. We certainly did not want to show them how valuable the information we received from Perry was and we did not want to admit to any wrongdoing. Their man, however, seems to be rather important. We caught him with diagrams of the London tube. Hardly any secret, but evidently, their man has high level connections. So, now, after long negotiations, we are going to exchange their agent for Perry. The exchange will take place at the Glienicke Bridge tomorrow at 16:30 hours. So, there you have it. Any questions? None. Good. Now for your itinerary, Miss Deborah Hollings will explain. Mrs. Hollings."

One of the civilians stood and addressed the group.

"Good afternoon, ladies. As Captain Blasingame said, my name is Deborah Hollings and I'm responsible for you during your visit here. Ladies, during the next twenty-four hours or so, you will see first-hand the hard background work and lengthy planning involved just to get a person across a bridge. In just a few minutes, we will introduce you to a world you never knew existed. Maybe you have seen international drama on tele, but let me assure you, this is real and very serious. You will be amazed and awed, and I wouldn't be surprised if you were even a bit terrified. You will have a seat in the 'front row' as this operation unfolds. In your portfolio you will find your identity badges. Check them for accuracy now. Please place them on and keep them always displayed and I do mean at all times! If you are found without the badge, you will be held on the spot, and it will make an awful mess plus be very embarrassing. You will stay with your group and only speak when spoken to. Your new group is assigned to section 157/228. The group consists of Misses Beverley, Davies, Green, and Wilson, Lieutenant Blankin, Captain McWilliams, Captain Blasingame, Major

Hartwell and me. Nine altogether. From here we will proceed to your section room for an update briefing. Please stay close. Our escort will be here in about fifteen minutes, so take this opportunity to stretch and refresh. I will be back in with the escorts."

Deborah Hollings left the room. Nicollette turned to her friends. Her eyes were wide open and filled with amazement.

"This is getting very interesting!" she commented.

"I have a serious case of dry mouth. How about you lot?" Val asked while trying to hide her angst over what she just heard.

She went to get a drink and Nicollette, Sarah and Peg followed. At the table, Lieutenant Blankin and Major Hartwell joined them.

"Badges on, ladies?" Lieutenant Blankin asked as she eyed the women. "It looks like all is in order."

Major Hartwell continued. "I want to remind you again, ladies, that we are here as observers. We need to be in the background, out of the way so to speak. There will be several briefings in which we will be attending with a final briefing currently planned at 15:30 hours Sunday. There will be meals and some rest time, but you will be awake most of the time. Any questions or concerns should be given to Lieutenant Blankin or myself."

Deborah Hollings returned with two-armed soldier escorts.

"Ladies, if you follow me, I will take you to your section room. Please stay close together as it is a long walk with several staircases."

The group went through a double steel door and down a very long corridor that seemed to slope downwards. They entered another double steel door and down three long staircases that led to another steel door and another long corridor. Another steel door, another long corridor and another staircase. Nicollette thought they must have walked a couple of miles when Deborah Hollings stopped in front of a wooden double door. A small card at the side of the door read "Section 157/228."

The room was of good size, easily accommodating the entire group. Again, there was a large table in the center and smaller tables against one of the side walls. There was a blackboard on the other side wall. The room did have one outstanding characteristic. The back wall of the room was made entirely of glass. Nicollette wandered over to the back wall. It was a very large window and the view caused her to pause and catch her breath. She was standing about twenty-five meters above a massive circular room.

"Val, Peg, Sarah, come here, you have got to see this," she announced, excited.

The girls wandered over and had the same reaction Nicollette did.

"Crikey!" Peg exclaimed.

"I've never seen anything like this," Sarah added.

Major Hartwell observed the group by the window and walked over to the four of them.

"What do you think, ladies?" the major asked.

"It's the biggest room I've ever seen to be sure," Val responded.

"It looks bigger than four hockey fields," Nicollette replied.

"Well, ladies, it is a big room. We refer to it as the 'eye.' It is here that all work begins and ends, you may say that it is the nervous system of the department. Everything emanates from the 'eye,'" Major Hartwell continued. "At any given time, there are many people coming and going from the 'eye' and you will have first-hand experience of the 'eye' shortly. Take a minute and just observe what is going on below."

Nicollette turned from the major and looked down at the floor below. The view reminded her of when the Americans first landed on the moon. The news showed the activity at ground control in Houston. She remembered asking her father about all the people watching their little teles.

"Is that what they do all day, Dad? If so, that job is for me!"

She remembered her dad responding. "Watch and see, Nicky. Everyone is watching different things on their little teles, but working together so the landing is successful."

Nicollette hadn't thought about that moment for a long time. She refocused on the "eye." There were rows and rows of personnel seated at desks separated by short thin walls. Like little cubes. Each desk had a monitor and appeared to have several phones. There were civilians and uniformed soldiers coming in and out of the "eye," stopping at various "cubes." Then leaving through unseen exits. It seemed choreographed and almost surreal. The group was watching for nearly ten minutes when Lieutenant Blankin summoned all to the table in the middle of the room. Everyone was seated except the major and Deborah Hollis.

Major Hartwell began, "Ladies, as you can see, we are right in the thick of things and in just a few moments, we will be going down into the 'eye.' But first, some housekeeping. We will be here for approximately forty-eight hours. As we have stated, this room is our staging area. If for some reason you get separated, proceed immediately to this room. Your ID badge will activate the electronic key mechanism allowing you entrance. The key mechanism, when activated, will alert security and Lieutenant Durban, Deborah Hollis, and I will be notified. This facility has sleeping quarters on site and arrangements have been made for your gear to be placed there. Your portfolio has a map in it, please open it."

Nicollette opened her map and placed it on the table. The shape of the facility reminded her of a circle inside of a square. The circle had hallways that reminded her of spokes in a bicycle tire. Everything was attached to the center area, the "eye."

Major Hartwell continued. "The facility should remind you of a pie cut into eight slices. Each of those slices is an area. The map shows these slices are named A through H. We are in area G as you can see by the blue dot on your map. The red boxes are staircases, and the green boxes are security stations. Your rooms are in area H, just over here." Major Hartwell pointed to the spot on Nicollette's map. "We will be taking meals in area F. Does everyone see the yellow box?" Pause for response. "That is the mess hall. You need not become too familiar with the facility as we will be escorted throughout our stay. Deborah Hollings will now take us to the 'eye,' please stay together and remain quiet."

As the group stood from the table, the major motioned for Nicollette, Val, Peg and Sarah to join her in the corner. In a soft but direct voice, she spoke to them.

"You may wonder why you are here in Brussels."

*I was wondering about that. So, we are in Brussels,* Nicollette thought. *Hang on! Belgium! Six-hour flight? What's going on?*

"Miss Beverley, Miss Davies, Miss Wilson and Miss Green," Major Hartwell continued as she looked at each of them. "As I've said, we have been brought here as guests of British Intelligence to witness not only a top-level prisoner exchange, but also to experience what happens behind the scenes, if you will, of operations. This is what we do. You four were specifically selected because after just two weeks of training, we feel you have achieved far more than our expectations. Colonel Baron requested that we bring the four of you here."

The conference room door was opened and Nicollette, Val, Peg and Sarah were led to a stairwell. Nicollette counted the steps as they descended. Every twenty-four steps there was a landing and a steel door. She counted five landings, over one hundred steps. At the fifth landing, the group was led through a double steel door, down a hallway, through another double steel door and onto the floor of the "eye." Deborah Hollings led the group down an outside aisle to a section of desks. There were eight desks in the section. Each desk had a screen and there were three phones on each desk. Every desk was occupied by a man wearing headphones. They were studying the screens intensely. One of the men took a quick glance at the group. He picked up the middle phone. "Yes," was the only word he said. Nicollette noticed that almost immediately another man walked up to the desk and the two exchanged places, first the headphones, then the seat. The man, now replaced, turned to the group.

"Good afternoon, Mrs. Hollings, what have we here?"

"This is the group you were briefed on yesterday, Mr. Caldwell."

"Well then, good afternoon to group 228 and welcome to the 'eye.' It is here that we will be monitoring the upcoming 'festivities.' Come closer and you can see what is happening."

Nicollette and the group eased forward to see the screens on three adjoining desks. Mr. Caldwell pointed out that each screen was showing a different view of the Glienicke Bridge where the exchange for Alexander Perry would be taking place.

"We have cameras at various strategic positions on our side of the bridge and the signal comes directly from those cameras to these screens. Each analyst in this section is totally familiar with their area. Look at this screen. Take a good look."

Nicollette was able to get a close view of the screen as Mr. Caldwell continued. The screen showed a building on the right side of the East German side of the bridge. At first glance, Nicollette thought the building was just an ordinary plain structure. Very nondescript. It was three stories high with about a dozen windows on each floor. There were several antennas on the roof. The steel antennas reminded Nicollette of the one her father put on the roof of their house for the tele. It was easy to recognize that the building provided a great view of the bridge.

"Just a simple building at first glance, wouldn't you agree?" Mr. Caldwell asked the group. "That's exactly what the KGB and the Stasi want it to appear as, but we know better."

Mr. Caldwell reached into his pocket for a pencil. He pointed to a window on the third floor.

"I want each of you to take a good look out of this window, what do you see?"

One at a time, each of the group took a minute to stare at the window. When everyone had a turn, Mr. Caldwell continued.

"Did anybody see anything unusual? No. Well to the untrained eye, it may not be too apparent, but let me tell you what we can see. Through that window, we see that the Stasi and KGB have placed a machine gun and a small rocket launcher. How about the roof? Looks like normal television antennas and water cisterns. That is what they want you to believe. But in reality, some are communication towers. The other 'antennas' are small rockets and still others are elevated cameras, all aimed at our side of the bridge. Oh, and on the second floor, 4th window from the right, that's where Franz Klausen, who oversees this operation for the KGB and Stasi, has his front row seat as so to speak." He paused, took a breath and continued. "And this is just one view. As you can see, we have multiple views. We have ground views, sky views and radio wave views as well. We receive new data constantly. Each station here is monitored by several analysts on a rotating basis. They can switch views at any given moment. They can amplify and redirect the view as needed. The phones on the desk each connect to a different area. The yellow phone on the left is a direct line to our folks on the frontline at the bridge and the blue phone on the right is to the Senior Director of operations for emergency use only. We'll talk about the red phone in the middle later."

He stopped a moment to let the four young women absorb the information. Mr. Caldwell then looked directly at Nicollette, Val, Sarah and Peg.

"This is intelligence, ladies, knowing your adversary's strengths and weaknesses, his moves and understanding his strategies. Like the game of chess, planning and playing to win. Checkmate."

Deborah Hollings guided the group through a side door and up one flight of stairs to a double door. A small sign on the side of the door said "Communications room." The doors were opened, and the group entered. The room was filled with desks and monitors. The sides of the room were filled with rows of large machines with spools of tape going around in circles attached to them. *It's like something from* Dr. Who, Nicollette thought as she walked in. There were clicking and clattering noises coming from the machines as well as a pervasive hum that permeated the room. As with the section room, the entire back wall was a window overlooking the "eye." Captain McWilliams motioned the group to follow him to a corner of the room. He spoke to the four women directly.

"This is one of our communication centers. Remember the lessons on cryptanalysis? Well, here is where those lessons are going to become real. There are over fifty cryptanalysis analysts working in this room and there are several rooms like this in the facility. We are going to focus on the group that is handling the communications on the agent exchange. I want you to observe the analysts and the flow of information in and out. Remember our discussion and the practice you had using the computer to help with code? Well, there are twenty-five machines in this group alone. The computer has become an integral part of the job. Watch and learn. Now let's go to the group handling the exchange."

Captain McWilliams led the four women to an area near the window. There were ten people at desks. Each desk had two screens and three phones. The analysts wore talking devices and headphones. Nicollette thought they looked more like telephone operators than analysts. The group observed the analysts for nearly fifteen minutes. Not only was there a lot of typing and clatter, but there seemed to be a lot of notes passing as well. Nicollette counted at least three messengers entering and leaving the one group.

Captain McWilliams tapped her on the shoulder and whispered to the four women. "We must leave now and head back to our section for a quick briefing."

The walk back to the section room took almost twenty minutes.

"One could really get lost in this mosaic," Val whispered to Nicollette.

"That may be the idea," she responded.

Back in the section room, Nicollette, Val, Sarah, Peg and Captain McWilliams were reunited with Deborah Hollings and the rest of the officers. Major Hartwell asked all to take a seat and she proceeded to talk about the evening's itinerary. Nicollette looked at her watch. It was nearly 17:30. The afternoon had flown by.

"Ladies, I hope you 'enjoyed' your tour this afternoon," Major Hartwell said with a seldom seen smirk. "As we said earlier, our visit here is a short one. Currently, we are in a slow time."

"I wonder what it's like when it's busy," Sarah whispered to Nicollette.

The major continued after giving Sarah a bit of a look. "This is an excellent time to get you settled and have tea. Then later, we will meet back here for updates. You will be escorted to your quarters. You will have thirty minutes to freshen up. We will then escort you to the mess hall for tea. Deborah Hollings will take you to your lodgings."

Deborah Hollings motioned for all to follow her. The doors were opened, and two uniformed soldiers joined the group as they proceeded to the living quarters. Nicollette noticed that everyone who was in the group was going to the living quarters. They must have walked and climbed and walked for nearly thirty minutes until they came to another double steel door. As they were walking, Nicollette kept revisiting the day's events. *What did I just see? I had no idea this type of activity existed beyond the tele! Have I done the right thing? Am I in over my head? What have I done?* These thoughts on top of still feeling uneasy about being drugged and knocked out for the short flight earlier in the morning. Nicollette looked around at her friends, trying not to show her increasing angst as they walked quietly down some endless hallway.

The two uniformed escorts opened the doors into what at first glance looked like a Hotel Lobby. Deborah Hollings talked with the soldiers behind the counter. After a minute or so, she asked each of the group to come to the counter one by one. First was Major Hartwell followed by Captains McWilliams and Blasingame. Then Lieutenant Blankin and finally the four young women. Nicollette was first to the counter. She was still feeling a little nervous at the counter when she was asked for her badge and thumb print. She was asked a few questions then given a card to use as the room key. When everyone had checked in, Deborah Hollings directed the group to a nearby elevator. Soon, all were in a landing area staring down a carpeted hallway with doors on either side. One by one, everyone found their room. Sarah and Peg's rooms were across from Nicollette's, and Val's room was next door. At the front of her door, Nicollette slid her key into a slot and the door unlocked. It seemed to her that this was like any other hotel she had ever seen, but that changed when she walked into the room. It was a small, cold room. The walls were a painted block material and the room was very spartan. There were no windows. The room consisted of a twin bed, a nightstand with a lamp and a chest with a small mirror. There was a phone on the nightstand. The phone had four buttons, but no dial. Nicollette also noticed there was no clock in the room. A single light fixture lit the room. There was a small bathroom and shower. Her luggage was on top of the bed. There was a note that mentioned the dress code for the evening. Black skirts and white tops. Nicollette looked at her watch. She had about twenty minutes, just enough time for a quick shower. The hot water helped relax her. There were still questions crossing her mind, *but I'm sure everything will become clearer. Just pay attention and observe, Nicky.* Twenty minutes later, there was a knock on the door. Nicollette was happy to see her friends waiting for her. The uniformed escort guided them to the mess hall, another long walk away. Walk, walk and more walking. *You can stay in great form just by just working here,* Nicollette thought.

The mess hall was like the one at Brize. Val, Peg, Sarah and Nicollette found a table. Nicollette looked at her friends. She felt reassured being with friends.

"After all we have seen and learned today, it's great to be with friends for tea. I propose a toast," Nicollette stated as she raised her water glass along with her friends. "To the future, whatever it holds, there will always be us! Cheers!"

Lieutenant Blankin and Captain Blasingame came by the table. "Good evening, ladies. I trust you are enjoying tea. May we join you?"

"Certainly, please do," Val replied.

"First let's set some ground rules," Captain Blasingame announced. "I want all of us to be 'at ease' at this table. There is a lot of pressure around and having a meal gives us a bit of normalcy. Agreed?" All nodded. "Secondly, there is no rank at the table and that especially goes for you, Lieutenant Blankin. Agreed?" Again, all nodded. "Good, now let's eat, I'm famished."

The table conversation was light and engaging. Captain Blasingame was an older woman, Nicollette guessed in her late forties. She had shorter brown hair with touches of gray blended in. Her stature wasn't as rigid as the younger officers, causing her uniform to look a little loose on her. *Captain Blasingame seems less strict than the other officers, far more engaging and open. I enjoy talking with her,* Nicollette thought. *I guess even officers are human.*

The relaxed table talk was ending as Deborah Hollings approached.

"We are wanted in the section room for a briefing."

"Ladies, I think she means it," Captain Blasingame announced.

The group left the mess hall and traveled back to the section room. Another long walk. Inside the section room, Nicollette was glad to see Charles Thompson there.

"Hope you are getting along alright, Nicollette," he said. "This is a lot to take in, but you'll pick it up just fine."

All were seated except Major Hartwell. She addressed the group. "In the last two hours, we have received communications that our friends across the bridge now want a second agent to be exchanged with the 'tube' spy and in return, we will get back one Mrs. Manning and her two children ages thirteen and ten. Evidently, the three went horseback riding for a picnic and ended up on the wrong side of the border in East Germany. The Mannings are Americans visiting here while Mr. Manning, or should I say Colonel Manning, is working in Bonn. We have agreed and the second agent to be exchanged is enroute. Now for the rest of the evening, you will be in the 'eye' with Mr. Caldwell and then in the communications room with Captain McWilliams. If all is quiet, you will return to your quarters at 23:00 hours for sleep. We will have a morning briefing at 09:00 hours. We will collect you at 08:45 hours. Throughout the evening, Captain Blasingame, Captain McWilliams, Lieutenant Blankin, Mr. Charles Thompson and myself will be unable to join you in the entirety as we have other tasks to engage. But you will see us as time permits."

Another walk down the stairs and long hallways. For the next ninety minutes, Nicollette and the group watched the screens on the desk and the large screen on the front wall. Nicollette kept thinking about the Mannings. *What must it be like to be enjoying a nice day with your young children, riding horses and having a picnic? No cares or worry. Just a wonderful time. Then out of nowhere, armed soldiers arrest you! What do you do? What do you say? The children! The children!* Nicollette took a deep breath, trying to leave her emotions behind and focusing on the screens. The big screen in front of the 'eye' brought back memories of the last movie she saw at the Evesham theatre. *Home,* she sighed, *no armed soldiers there! But never mind,* she thought, *this is an important business, the Mannings, no time to think of home.* The little screens would switch views every three minutes or so. Mr. Caldwell pointed out that each analyst had the ability to control the sequence of scenes. Freezing them. Repeating them. Magnifying and enlarging, never to miss the slightest detail. At one point, the screen focused on Franz Klausen's office. The light was on and Mr. Caldwell pointed out an image moving around in the room. There also appeared to be smoke in the room.

"That's Klausen having his evening cigar and whiskey. Every night at 09:30 hours on the dot." Mr. Caldwell gave a short chuckle.

Nicollette was amazed at the detail that was projected. It was like Caldwell and Klausen were neighbors rather than adversaries. There was a break as the analysts handed over to another shift.

"All is in order for the night," Mr. Caldwell announced. "I hope, Misses Beverley, Green, Davies and Wilson, that you received a better understanding of this part of the 'eye.' We will see you in the morning. Captain McWilliams will escort you to the communications room. Good night."

"Ladies," Captain McWilliams pointed towards the double doors.

In the communications room, Charles Thompson was examining a document.

"Good evening, ladies. We have just received confirmation that the second agent being exchanged is on his way and should arrive shortly. Our Intelligence also is getting signals that Perry has been moved to a point across the river, however, we have no intelligence on the Mannings. We are still looking, but at this time, we have no idea where they are!" He paused.

Nicollette could see a bit of concern crossing his face. *Omigosh!* Nicollette thought while trying to remain calm. *What if the exchange fails? What would happen to them? The children!*

Charles Thompson continued, "We will continue to apply all available resources to locate the Mannings. Now let me bring you over to the communications area responsible for monitoring and transmitting information regarding this upcoming exchange."

Nicollette, Val, Peg and Sarah were escorted to a group of desks.

"This is Louis Needham or as we affectionately call him, 'Listening Lou.'"

"Good evening, ladies. Let me give you an update on the latest transmissions. As Captain McWilliams mentioned, we are ready on our end, but we are concerned about the Mannings. So far, there is nothing unusual in the traffic of signals we are monitoring. Nothing to indicate any trouble or delay in the exchange. Look at this screen."

Nicollette and the group gathered around a man who looked like a telephone operator. He was typing and talking into a mouthpiece simultaneously. A clerk was walking between the operator and the computer section carrying bits of paper. Mr. Needham intercepted the clerk and read one of the papers to the ladies.

"It seems the weather in Irkutsk has become a bit colder and that the trains are running on time in Bucharest. Normal signal nonsense, but we still need to investigate each message for ulterior meanings. Oh, and you will be happy to know that the grain harvest in Hungary is projected to be better this year. Just a normal night, ladies. So, let us see how this all works."

Mr. Needham started to explain how transmissions are intercepted, deciphered and investigated. Some signals are mathematical equations while others were merely readings from popular books. There was music and news. All were investigated for relevance. Every so often though, some of the deciphered transmissions proved to be useful. Especially during war games, joint exercises, single signals from person to person and between organizations. He invited each of the women to sit at the desk. Nicollette put the headphones on and immediately heard a combination of different languages being spoken. She had heard Russian and German before, but her translation screen showed there was some Polish mixed in as well. *Fascinating.* The signal continued and the translation was a story of a Russian Prince falling for a Princess. *Typical fairy tale stuff,* Nicollette thought. But then there was static on the line, like when the tele was left on after the late show. Oddly enough, her screen showed a series of equations. They reminded her of calculus in school. Curious indeed. Then there was a news presenter giving the late news in Czech. Val, Sarah and Peg each had a go. Very interesting. After her turn, Val looked at Mr. Needham and asked if any of the analysts ever got bored or frustrated by the tedium of the work. He responded to the group citing an example of the minor mining for gold. The minor keeps mining no matter the odds or hardship. He continues to mine and remains in focus till he strikes gold.

"We are mining for gold all the time, ladies."

*The gold being the Mannings!* Nicollette thought.

Deborah Hollings tapped Val's shoulder and she motioned the others that it was time to leave. The long walk and climb to the section room. The last briefing of the day. In the section room, Major Hartwell reviewed the day's activities. She assured the group that all was going according to plan and that she was sure the Mannings would show up, safe and sound. As of this moment, the exchange was planned to go off without any obstacles at 16:30 Sunday. She asked if there were any questions. At this point, Nicollette felt a bit fatigued. The day was filled with a wide range of emotions and it was catching up to her. She turned to Val who was doing her best to hide a yawn. Peg was struggling to keep her eyes open, and Sarah was fidgeting to try and stay alert. Major Hartwell repeated the instructions for Sunday. She dismissed the group. Two uniformed soldiers escorted the group back to the lobby. There was a table with coffee, tea, and biscuits in the lobby and the group decided to grab something to take back to the room. Nicollette reached her room, swiped her card, turned to Val, Sarah and Peg.

"What a day, see you ladies in the morning. Goodnight."

# The Exchange

The phone rang, abruptly waking her from a deep sleep. Nicollette opened her eyes to see a red button on the phone flashing. The ringing was loud and incessant. She turned the light on and in a sleepy motion she picked up the receiver. The voice on the other end explained that there would be an emergency briefing in thirty minutes and that she should get ready immediately. Nicollette forced a "yes" from her dry throat. She looked at her watch. It was 5:30. She went to look outside but then remembered there were no windows. A cold shower quickly brought her back to life. There was a knock on her door, the escort was waiting for her, and soon she, Val, Peg and Sarah were in the section room.

Within minutes, everyone was present. Major Hartwell, the two Captains, Lieutenant Blankin, Deborah Hollings and Charles Thompson.

Major Hartwell asked for everyone's attention and asked all to be seated. In her hand were some papers. She looked them over and proceeded.

"Sorry for the early morning everyone, but we received a communique from the East Germans at 03:00 asking us to advance the exchange time from 16:30 hours to 10:30 hours this morning. We sent a reply to assure that this was a genuine request and not a hoax. We received confirmation at 04:30 with a warning that the exchange takes place 10:30 hours or the whole operation will be cancelled. We responded at 05:00 that we would be ready, and that established protocol will be observed. So, there you have it. We are going to be ready by 10:00 hours for the exchange. Ladies, you will observe an uptick in activity here. We are in rush mode. Now to give you more detail, Charles Thompson will say a few words."

Charles Thompson held papers in his hand as he spoke.

"There is a lot happening here. First, and good news, we found the Mannings!"

Nicollette did everything to contain her relief at the news.

Mr. Thompson continued, "It seems the younger Manning had taken ill, and he was taken to an infirmary last evening. He is feeling much better now. Secondly, we did not want to be caught short for this prisoner swap, so we took the precaution of having the necessary players ready last night. Thirdly, Intelligence has reported an uptick in chatter along the airways, but visual activity has been unchanged. This is a little irregular because when there are changes, there is usually physical movement as well, and finally, Intelligence believes that there must be a reason the Stasi and KGB want their agents back sooner rather than later, as shown by the additional prisoner demand and advanced timing."

Charles Thompson paused, placed his papers on the table, leaned in and continued, "Intelligence believes that there is something unusual in play about this exchange and I tend to agree with them. But what? Both communist agents are low key men, although 'tube' man does have some higher connections, but the other man isn't more than a blip on the radar. So, Intelligence is going back over the dossiers of the two, looking for clues that might bring us some answers. In the meantime, ladies, look sharp and get ready for your front row seat at 10:30 hours."

Major Hartwell addressed the group.

"Well, there you have it, we will keep everyone informed if there is any additional information. Captain Blasingame, Captain McWilliams, Lieutenant Blankin, Mr. Thompson and I will be leaving here shortly. In the meantime, I suggest you eat something as it may be a while before we are back in this room. Mrs. Hollings will remain here with you until your escorts arrive in the next thirty minutes, so please take care of any personal business now and be sure to eat a little something. At ease all."

It was just after 07:00 when the escorts arrived at the section room. Nicollette had just finished her second cup of tea and was hoping she would not regret that decision later. Mrs. Hollings and the escorts walked the women to the communications room where Captain McWilliams was already at Louis Needham's desk. There seemed to be more activity than the night before. The clicking and buzzing of the machines were coming at a much faster pace.

"Ah, there you ladies are," Captain McWilliams acknowledged the group. "Let me catch you up. There is a lot of chatter out there, most of it appears to be meaningless. We do have information, however, that Perry and the Manning family are in place for the exchange. Everything seems to be in order, but it is still unusual for this amount of traffic on the airways. Remember, it is Sunday morning and most are still tucked up. Perhaps it is nothing."

Nicollette, Val, Sarah and Peg were in the communication section for ninety minutes. Each of the young women had another opportunity at the desk. While Nicollette was at the desk, something unusual happened. When she first sat down, there was the normal static and corresponding nonsense on the screen, then suddenly, the static cleared and the voice of a young girl, perhaps five or six, was singing something in German. The screen showed the translation. It was a children's song, "The Farmer in the Dell." Mr. Needham, who had been looking over Nicollette's shoulder, tapped her and exchanged places. As she stepped away from the desk, Nicollette thought about what the possible meaning of this might be. *In a high stake's situation, a children's song?* A clerk brought over a paper from the computer area and gave it to Mr. Needham. The screen showed a repeat of the song, then it was played an additional two more times. There was a brief pause, and the static returned, and the screen went fuzzy again. A subordinate came over and relieved Mr. Needham. He rose from the desk and asked the women to follow him. He motioned for Captain McWilliams and two other men to follow as well. He led them to a small conference room off to the side. He closed the door.

"Any ideas, people?" Mr. Needham asked.

Nicollette looked at Val, Sarah and Peg. They all looked puzzled. *How with all this complicated coding and transmissions could this children's song be of importance? What is the significance and how is it related to the prisoner swap?* Nicollette thought. The room was silent.

"We have an idea what the meaning is, but I would like to hear from one of you, ladies," Captain McWilliams added. "A teaching moment. Think."

There was silence in the room.

"Ok, you are stumped. Let's ask one of our analysts then."

Captain McWilliams turned to one of the analysts. "Go ahead."

Just as the analyst was about to speak, Nicollette softly spoke, "I've got an idea."

"Splendid, Miss Beverley. Tell us your theory."

"Well Captain McWilliams and Mr. Needham. I remember that Mr. Perry's cover for the mission was that of a representative of a milking machine company and that one of the sentences in the song is 'Hi Ho the dairy oh, the farmers in the dell.' Could this mean that Mr. Perry is in position for the swap and that because it is a children's song, and there are two Manning children, that they are in place as well?"

Captain McWilliams looked back at the analyst. "What do you think?"

"I think she may be spot on. There is no great secret to what is about to happen so maybe a bit of levity before the swap. We do get nursery rhymes, bedtime stories, and the lot sometimes. Or it may mean nothing at all.

Just a bit of fun maybe."

"Well done, girl," Sarah whispered and patted Nicollette on the back.

*A child's song? A simple verse with all this at stake! A bit of fun!* Nicollette thought. *I was just guessing!*

It was just after 09:00 when Deborah Hollings entered the communications room to collect the four women.

"We have a little less than ninety minutes till the exchange, ladies, we are heading to the 'eye' where the action is about to start." It was a shorter walk to the 'eye' but a walk, nonetheless. Deborah Hollings brought the group to the same area as yesterday. Mr. Caldwell was busy overlooking about a dozen analysts.

"Welcome, ladies, the action is about to go into high gear."

He motioned them to four empty desks that had been set up for the group.

"Each of you will have an opportunity to experience the exchange firsthand. Watch and observe. Mrs. Hollings will be here for any questions."

Mr. Caldwell walked over to the other desks. Nicollette sat down, put on her headphones, and watched the screen. The images were moving more rapidly this morning. The first image she saw was of the two communist agents that were being exchanged in a holding cell with armed guards. Over the headphones she heard, "Prisoners in check. Movement in thirty minutes." The next scenes were of different views of the Glienicke Bridge. The bridge was entirely clear, motionless, almost surreal, Nicollette observed. As the view changed, there was a corresponding voice over the headphones. "Position A1 check. Position B4 check." This was repeated over and over. At 10:00 hours, the large screen in the front of the 'eye' split in two. One side showed the prisoners being escorted to a staging area and the other side showed a ground level view from the Allied end of the bridge right down the center of the full length of the bridge. Once the prisoners were at the staging area, one side of the large screen changed views to a "bird's eye view" of the center of the bridge. The images on Nicollette's screen continued to rotate. "B5 ready. C17 ready. G8 ready."

At 10:10 hours, all screens switched to an overall view of the bridge. Deborah Hollings announced, "Get ready, ladies, the show is about to start."

Nicollette watched the big screen. From the East German side of the bridge, a green flare was shot over the bridge. Five minutes later, a green flare was shot over the bridge from the Allied side. Deborah Hollings explained that the green flares signified all was in order and the exchange would proceed in fifteen minutes. Nicollette's screen showed the prisoners being escorted to the bridge. A yellow flare was then shot over the bridge by the Communists and a responding blue flare was shot by the Allies. Deborah Hollings explained that the yellow flare was a signal that the Mannings would be exchanged first, and that Perry would be exchanged five minutes later.

At 10:25 hours, the first Communist prisoner started to walk towards the center of the bridge. He was escorted by five Allied soldiers in complete battle gear and an unarmed officer. There were also two civilians in the escort. The Communists escorted the Mannings with the same number of personnel, armed soldiers, an officer and two civilians. The large screen image was focused on the center of the bridge. There were three demarcation lines painted on the road at the center of the bridge. Two wide white lines sandwiching a wider red line that divided the bridge's two sides. Nicollette watched intently as the two sides walked closer and closer to the middle of the bridge. Her breathing started to race and her heart started to pound, increasing even more when the Manning family came into view. The "eye" was very quiet, it seemed that everyone was holding their breath. All eyes forward. The two sides exchanged the customary salutes and the civilians shook hands. The Mannings were escorted back to the Allied side and the Communist prisoner was escorted back to the other side. A small cheer erupted as the Mannings reached the Allied end of the bridge. A smile and a sigh of relief on Nicollette's face. A collective deep breath in the "eye." From there the Mannings were escorted to the staging area. Now the exchange for Perry. The "eye" became silent again as the "tube" prisoner was escorted to the transfer point at the center of the bridge. The same Allied escort group that had just delivered the Mannings, brought the second prisoner. The Allies and the Communists met again at the transfer point. The same customary salutes and hand shaking. The exchange was made. Alexander Perry was being escorted to the Allied side of the bridge when a series of gunfire erupted from the Communist side. Nicollette watched in disbelief as the "tube" agent was shot dead just as his escorting party was reaching the Communist side. There was more gunfire. The large screen focused on the commotion. The "tube" agent was lying dead on the bridge, and it looked like one of the civilians was shot dead as well. The other civilian appeared to be wounded, the soldiers dragging him away. Another group of soldiers appeared and removed the two limp bodies. Nicollette felt her body go numb. She had never seen anything like this before. She had just witnessed a killing, a murder. A person alive just ten minutes ago, now dead. Shot. Her stomach wanted to empty, but she was too numb to react. She managed to turn to her side to see Val, Peg, and Sarah in the same state as her. Faces pale white and struggling to breathe. Deborah Hollings placed her hand on Nicollette's shoulder.

"Breathe, Nicollette. Breathe."

After what seemed to Nicollette like an eternity, but was only about ten minutes, the "eye" appeared to be back to normal. The buzz and chatter in the room resumed. Another day. Deborah Hollings escorted Nicollette, Val, Peg and Sarah back to section room 157/228. It was 11:30 hours when the group entered the room.

There were refreshments in the room, but Nicollette did not feel much like eating. She looked at her friends. "I can't believe what we just saw. It was like something on the tele."

"I am in disbelief as well," Sarah responded, her face still wet from tears.

Val just nodded her head in agreement, unable to find the words and Peg just stared at the ceiling. About twenty minutes later, Major Hartwell, accompanied by Captains McWilliams and Blasingame, Lt. Blankin and Charles Thompson, entered the room. Mr. Caldwell and Mr. Needham followed about a minute later. When all were present, Major Hartwell asked all to be seated. A large overhead view of the bridge was attached to the side wall. She motioned for Charles Thompson to address the group.

"This is a current briefing regarding the prisoner exchange for the benefit of our four intern agents."

Nicollette had never heard her position described as an "intern agent" before. Agent Nicollette sounded very professional to her, but still did not settle her stomach.

"From our perspective, the exchange went well. Everything was coordinated and proceeded as planned. We have the Manning family and Alexander Perry back on Allied soil. The Mannings are at this moment being reunited with Colonel Manning and Alexander Perry is being debriefed nearby. Again, from our end, job well done. Now for the benefit of our interns, what you experienced just a short time ago does sometimes happen. As you saw, the 'tube' agent was shot dead as he was approaching the Communist end of the bridge."

Charles Thompson pointed to the Communist end of the bridge where the shootings occurred. He continued, "Both of the civilian escorts were shot as well, one is dead on the bridge and the other looked to be severely wounded. The second prisoner was unharmed. We are currently investigating the reasons behind the shootings and how or if it affects us. We will update you at your final briefing before you head back to Brize. Again, a successful culmination to a lot of hard work. Thank you."

Major Hartwell thanked Charles Thompson as he exited the room. She turned to speak.

"By way of the exchange having been brought forward, we have made a few changes in the itinerary. Lieutenant Blankin will bring us up to date."

Lieutenant Blankin stood and addressed the group.

"We will be leaving here tomorrow after your final briefing, scheduled at 10:00 hours and our flight back to Brize will be at 12:00 hours. We are currently planning for you to attend a reception this evening with a few special guests. It has been tentatively scheduled for 18:00 hours. It is now 12:30 hours and I suspect some of you are hungry or tired or both. We will be escorted to the mess hall from here. From there you can go back to your room for a couple of hours or to the recreation area. At 15:30 hours, we will meet back here for an additional briefing. You will have some time later to get ready for the reception at 18:00 hours. We will meet in the mess hall tomorrow morning at 08:30 hours and proceed to this room for your final briefing at 10:00 hours. You will need to be packed and ready before breakfast tomorrow. Please leave your luggage on your bed. Any questions? None, good."

Lieutenant Blankin turned towards Major Hartwell. The Major motioned for all to follow her to the mess hall. Nicollette looked at Sarah, Val and Peg.

"Well, ladies, what do you want to do?"

"My stomach is still a bit uneasy and I'm also a little tired," Sarah responded.

"Me too, but a cup of tea might be nice," Peg added.

"I agree," Val included, "but I am also interested in this recreation room."

"I'm still wound up from this morning so I don't think I could nap. I also think the recreation room sounds interesting. I need to regroup myself and the recreation room might just be the ticket," Nicollette stated. *After what I just saw, I really need a diversion, although I will probably never forget it!*

Major Hartwell brought the group into the mess hall. She appropriated a large table for the nine of them. She asked all to be at ease and enjoy the break. The tea was just right for Nicollette. Her stomach had started to settle down so she added a scone to her tray. There was a hesitant conversation at the table and the major could feel it. Captain Blasingame and Captain McWilliams talked about the spring plantings that were coming up and the prospects in the upcoming cricket season. Nicollette looked at Val, Sarah and Peg. Sarah decided for a nap. Nicollette, Val and Peg would try the recreation room.

The recreation room was like a very large pub. There was a bar, a couple of billiards tables, four ping pong tables and several dart boards. On the walls, there were six large television screens. Three of them were showing Australian cricket, two race car events and one showing a newscast. They found a table and Captain Blasingame along with Deborah Hollings joined them. Nicollette decided against having a pint as it would certainly put her to sleep so Coca-Cola would be her drink for the afternoon.

At 15:00 hours, Deborah Hollings led the group back

to section room 157/228. Sarah and Captain McWilliams were already there. At 15:30 hours, Major Hartwell and Lieutenant Blankin walked into the room. Major Hartwell was carrying a dossier. Everyone was seated. The Major placed her dossier on the table, opened it and sat down. She looked directly at the group of interns, moving her eyes to each one. "Ladies, I hope you were able to get some rest this afternoon. Before we start with our next activity, I want to share with you some information Intelligence has uncovered about the shootings this morning. Remember the children's song we heard over the channels before the exchange? And we wondered about the relevance of the song? The East Germans were sending a signal about an internal operation. The second verse of the song, where the farmer takes a wife, was a signal to proceed with their internal operation. As we dive in deeper, we now know why 'tube man' was wanted by the Communists and why the second prisoner was 'thrown in.' In this case, the word in the song, 'takes,' means arrest or dispose of. This was a signal to the bridge to eliminate 'tube man' and proceed with the Manning exchange. It appears that the higher connection we thought 'tube man' might have had was valid. His connection was to a senior officer in the Stasi. While the 'tube man' was in London, his wife, who lives in Potsdam, admitted to an affair she was having with this senior officer. It also appears that 'tube man' suspected or knew of the affair as well. The Stasi, not wanting to be compromised in any way at home or having 'tube man' defect to the west, arrested the senior officer and the unfaithful wife. We have not been able to account for them so we presume they may have been shot. Knowing they were holding Perry, the East Germans sent an agent, who would become the second prisoner, to London to collect the 'tube man' and escort him back to East Germany. The second agent purposely compromised both to the British authorities. Our agents picked them up and the exchange was negotiated. Once the exchange was made at the bridge and wanting 'clean hands' of the situation, the Stasi shot the 'tube man' at the bridge. he other two agents were shot because they worked directly for the cheating senior officer and knew of the affair without reporting it. We also suspect that prisoner number two has or will be shot as well. This eliminates any connection to the affair. At least six people dead."

The major paused for thirty seconds or so as she looked very sternly at each of the four intern agents. Nicollette could feel the major's piercing eyes look right into her head, into her mind, into her psyche. A numbness crept over her body. The air at the table was thick with intensity. The thirty seconds felt like an eternity.

Finally, mercifully, the major continued. "Ladies, this is what we come up against. We are in an arena with little compassion. We deal with people who are vicious and determined. There is little room for error. Ladies." The major paused for effect. She continued, "Ladies, we are in a nasty business."

Nicollette swallowed hard at the major's words. The last twenty-four hours were like a whirlwind of emotions. Angst, anxiety, nerves and fear compounded by the unknown. Gratitude and pride in the successes. She kept revisiting the time in her mind, gaining more confidence in her decision to join the program. *I have grown more in the last few hours than I have in the last few years,* she thought to herself. A nervous smile crossed her face.

The rest of the afternoon was much quieter. There was a tour of some of the areas and visits with people working behind the scenes. Nicollette enjoyed the tour and the walk. It gave her a chance to think through what the major had said earlier. Kind of a chance to clear her mind and to reassure herself that she was really committed to this type of life. Although as hard as she would try, she could not get the major's piercing eyes out of her head.

# A Large Family

Nicollette was dressed and ready to go when the escorts came to collect her, Val, Sarah and Peg to the reception. They were led to a small ballroom about a ten-minute walk away. Nicollette saw Charles Thompson and Captain McWilliams over by one of the drinks tables. She wandered over.

"Good evening, Miss Beverley," the two men said in unison. "Would you like a drink?"

"Just a Coke for now please, thank you."

"Interesting day, Miss Beverley. What do you think?" Captain McWilliams asked.

"This morning was like something I would see on the tele. I never thought that I would have a front row seat to something like this. I must admit I was not expecting to witness shootings and real people dying. My stomach was not expecting it either."

The last comment caused a chuckle among the two men.

"Don't worry, Miss Beverley. In our line of work, nothing is ever as expected and never expect anything. All you can do is be prepared for the unexpected and act accordingly."

Charles Thompson nodded then continued. "I do hope you, Miss Davies, Miss Green and Miss Wilson have learned from this visit and continue to learn. It is of the utmost importance that you do."

There was the sound of clinking glass coming from a table at the front of the room. An officer was tapping a knife against a glass and asking all to take a seat. Nicollette found Val and Sarah and they joined Peg who had already found a seat at a table. There were ten round tables in the room, each having eight seats, Nicollette noticed. About eighty people attended the reception. Lieutenant Blankin and Major Hartwell joined the young women as well as Captain McWilliams and Charles Thompson.

"Good evening, everyone. For those who do not know me, my name is Colonel Joseph and prisoner exchanges fall under my command. Today, we completed a successful exchange. Give yourselves a round of applause." Applause. "This was truly a team effort. We had many obstacles to deal with including a last-minute change in time, but we did it. Tonight, we have some special guests who would like to show their appreciation to you. Let me first introduce Mr. Alexander Perry."

Alexander Perry walked over to the head table as the guests stood and applauded. He acknowledged the attendants with several hand waves. The Colonel continued. "Now I would like you to meet my good friend Colonel Carl Manning and his wife Pam and their two children Steven and Joy."

Colonel Manning walked over to the head table, shook Colonel Joseph's hand. He was followed by his wife and two children. Mrs. Manning stopped and gave Colonel Joseph a hug and the two children waved as they took their place at the head table. Standing ovation. Colonel Joseph used his hands to ask all to be seated. Colonel Manning stood to speak. Nicollette could tell he was an American by his accent.

"On behalf of my family and myself, I would like to thank each of you for the safe return of my family." Applause. "I know it took a lot of hard work and coordination and I'm pleased to announce mission accomplished!" He paused to gather his emotions. "I look forward to meeting you after dinner and personally thanking you."

Colonel Manning gave a salute to the attendees. Colonel Joseph stood from his seat, shook Colonel Joseph's hand and continued.

"Now, I would like you to meet Mr. Alexander Perry who risked his life to gather vital data and sell a few milking machines."

Alexander Perry stood from his seat and shook Colonel Joseph's hand as the applause became a standing ovation. He acknowledged the room with several hand waves.

"First of all, thank you for all the hard work and perseverance in making my release possible. There were many times when I was sitting in my cell in Potsdam that I thought I was forgotten by you." He paused for a breath. "I should have known better. When I joined the service, I was told we're a family, albeit rather large and with many strange behaviors, but a family, nonetheless. Today, I feel that family and I will always be grateful. Thank you!"

Alexander Perry acknowledged the room again then turned to shake Colonel Joseph's hand.

Colonel Joseph spoke.

"Alexander, we want to thank you as well for your

bravery and continued service in the organization. We have another special surprise guest, please welcome Marsha Perry, Alexander's wife."

Alexander Perry stood from his chair and the two rushed to embrace each other in front of the head table. Nicollette could feel tears flowing down her cheek. She turned to see Val and Sarah using their napkins to wipe their eyes. Peg, however, just had a stoic expression across her face.

Colonel Joseph was seated, and dinner was served. Nicollette saw the filet mignon and salmon on the plate. Before she started to eat, she thought of the many people working behind the scenes who were unable to join in the celebration, those men and women who worked tirelessly to make these victories possible. To them, she thought as she raised her water glass, to them.

As they were eating, Charles Thompson looked across the table at the four young women.

"This celebration is rather rare in our business, ladies. Normally, a bit of bubbly, a pint at the pub or most times, nothing at all. But Colonel Manning will be a general in a couple of months and he wanted to do this as a thank you. So, when these celebrations happen, enjoy and savor the moment."

After dinner, Major Hartwell summoned Nicollette and the others. "Ladies, come with me, there is someone who would like to meet you."

The major brought the group over to Colonel Manning.

He turned to the women. "Good evening, ladies. Major Hartwell tells me you are intern agents under the new British Intelligence initiative. You came from Brize. Beautiful area, been there many times. What did you think about today's festivities?"

"It was very interesting and anxious at the same time. All the work that goes into this. It's almost mind boggling," Nicollette responded.

As she was answering, Nicollette noticed how relaxed the colonel was. *How can he be so calm! His family were prisoners twenty-four hours ago! His wife! His children! How does he do it? I would be a mess!*

Val added, "It's like a show on tele except we are living it."

The colonel smiled at Val's comment. He then shook each of the young women's hands and wished them good luck.

"That was very nice of him to greet us, Major," Sarah said.

"As Alexander Perry said earlier, we are one big family. Remember that."

Nicollette, Val, Sarah and Peg were escorted to their rooms at 23:00 hours. A sense of relaxation and accomplishment was pervasive throughout the evening, almost like a collective sigh of relief. Nicollette was able to meet Alexander Perry and his wife and exchange small talk. He spoke about being captured and the unknown of each proceeding day. She also made small talk with Mr. Caldwell, Mr. Needham, and a few of the agents.

But the highlight of the evening was her conversation with Colonel Manning's wife, Pam. Mrs. Manning had visited Nicollette's village of Brockwirth many times. She enjoyed the quaint village and friendly people. It was wonderful to talk about home.

Later, as she lay in bed, Nicollette revisited the day's events in her mind. From the early wake up to the evening's celebration. Two thoughts continued to cross her mind as she drifted off to sleep, the shooting of the three Communists right in front of her eyes and her conversation with Pam Manning about Brockwirth. Quite a contrast in emotions!

The phone rang at 08:00, rousing Nicollette out of her slumber. A recorded voice gave a reminder to have her luggage ready and placed on the bed. She would be collected at 08:45 hours for breakfast. The exit briefing would be at 10:00 hours. The shower was invigorating, and she thought how nice it would be to have a real shower at home, now it was just a tube hung over the bath. Home. One more week, then home.

Val, Sarah and Peg were all called for at the same time and together with Nicollette, were escorted to the mess hall.

"How did you two sleep last night?" Val asked Sarah and Peg.

"Went right off, no problem," Sarah responded.

"Me too! Slept like a stone," Peg added.

"Wasn't yesterday 'the day'?" Nicollette asked the group. "I mean, to me, it was like living on the tele. So surreal and unbelievable. But I, I mean, we lived it."

There was a pause for reflection among the group. A quiet, more subdued walk to the mess hall. At breakfast, more small talk. Nicollette found some "eggy bread" at the buffet. She looked at her friends.

"I hate to admit it, but this 'eggy bread' reminds me of home. On Sunday mornings, my mum would make this as a treat. I have been thinking more about home recently. After all, it's been three weeks."

Val looked at Nicky and at the others. "Me too."

Lieutenant Blankin approached the table with her coffee cup. "May I sit with you for a few minutes?"

"Sure, please do," Sarah answered for the group.

"So, what are we talking about, ladies?"

"Home," Nicollette answered.

"I think all of us are getting a bit homesick," Peg added.

"You know something, ladies? Me too! I know it's been almost three weeks for you lot, but for me, it's been almost five weeks."

That last statement from Lieutenant Blankin caught the group by surprise. The Lieutenant was not too open about her private life around the training facility at Brize, but then again, it seemed that none of the officers were. A thought occurred to Nicollette as she looked at Lieutenant Blankin.

"I bet you really miss your two boys, Adam and Colin," Nicollette said, remembering the picture on the lieutenant's desk at her interview.

"Terribly and what a memory you have, Nicollette! I'm impressed."

To Sarah, Peg and Val, this was news to them. Lieutenant Blankin was a mother of two.

"Tell us about your two boys," Val asked.

Lieutenant Blankin talked about her children until it was time for them to leave for the briefing. After three weeks of intense training under strict supervision and authority from Lieutenant Blankin, a bit of humanity was coming through. She's *human*, just like us!

In the section room, at exactly 10:00 hours, Major Hartwell and Captain Blasingame arrived followed by Captain McWilliams, Charles Thompson and Deborah Hollings. All were asked to take a seat. Major Hartwell announced that Deborah Hollings had a few brief words for the group.

"I wanted to tell you ladies that we were glad to be a part of your training. This was a fast twenty-four hours and I hope you take away from this visit some serious insight as to what we do. Thank you and maybe we will see each other again. Good luck for the future."

With that Deborah Hollings left the room. Nicollette wondered if she would ever see her again. Major Hartwell stood and addressed the group.

"Ladies, this is the final briefing of your short stay here. You may have a question or two, so let me see if I can answer them in this briefing. First, let me tell you that we are located just outside of Brussels, in Mons, Belgium at an auxiliary position of SHAPE, Supreme Headquarters Allied Powers Europe. We took some liberty during your transport here to give you a little sleeping aid. We wanted you to focus on the training and not trying to guess the 'where' portion of the trip."

As the major spoke, it was becoming very clear to Nicollette about the transport, the rationale of the early flight, the deep sleep, the darkened windows of the car, and even the room with no outside view.

"I can assure you that you will be awake for the hour trip back to Brize."

The Major gave a smile then continued.

"What you experienced here was real. This happens. We did not plan for the shootings, but that happens as well. Therefore, we need to be agile and flexible. Many people are involved, working tirelessly to gain information, even down to the last detail. We must remain one step ahead of our adversaries or we fail."

She paused to let that last statement settle.

"I might also add those events like last night do not happen very often. So, do not expect them with each success. We are expected to do our job without reward, only the satisfaction of doing our job well and successfully. I want to take a minute to say how proud I was of you last night. You handled yourselves with great maturity and poise and it did not go unnoticed in our circle of work."

She paused again then passed out a schedule to the four young women.

"Now for the rest of the day, we will be escorted from here and fly back to Brize. At Brize, you will have till 15:00 hours to relax. We have planned for you to call your parents. Let me remind you that you are still in 'America,' according to your cover. At 15:00 hours, Captain McWilliams will be holding a session in your training classroom. Sunday tea is at 18:00 hours. There will be a group meeting at your dormitory common room at 19:30 hours, followed by an open activities evening. Let me remind you in communicating with your other class-mates, no questions and no answers, full stop!"

As she was boarding the plane for the short flight back to Brize, Nicollette felt a little uneasy about being "drugged" on the flight over. *Will this affect me on future travels, or can I let it go as being a part of my training? They drugged me!* Her thoughts turned to the events over the past two days as she sat back on the soft sofa. There was a lot to digest.

The plane landed and soon she, Val, Sarah and Peg were walking through security at their dorm. As they entered the elevator, another recruit walked out from the elevator.

"Hey, you lot. Where've you been? We missed you at Saturday's classes."

Nicollette smiled and replied, "Around the world, around the world."

# The Finish Line

The phone was ringing and Nicollette was anxiously waiting for someone to answer. Another two rings. Finally, a voice, "9547."

"Mum, it's me, Nicky!"

Nicollette felt a smile come across her face as she envisioned her mother in the kitchen talking to her.

"Nicky, this is a great surprise! How are you keeping? Is everything alright?"

"I'm doing fine, Mum. Everything is fine. It's very hard work, but I'm managing well. It's so wonderful to hear your voice, Mum. I must admit I'm getting a little homesick."

"Well, you will be home next week for Sunday dinner. That's not too much longer."

"I know, Mum, I can't wait. How's Dad?"

"He is at the cricket club doing some jobs. I know he will be disappointed about missing your call."

"Tell him I said hello and that I love him, oh, and Mum. If anyone asks if you have heard from me, you can say that I called from America and that I am doing fine. I must go now. See you soon, Mum. I love you and miss you. Bye."

"Bye, Nicky. Take care."

As Nicollette walked away from the phone, she felt a bit uneasy. *How many of these phone calls would she have to make in the future? Would she have the strength and the will to make these calls? Would she ever get over being homesick?*

Captain McWilliams joined the afternoon class with Captain Murphy. It was a surreal feeling to Nicollette that just a few hours ago, she and Captain McWilliams were in Belgium. Despite her absence this weekend and except for her brief encounter with the one other recruit, there weren't many questions or enquiries from her peers. Val, Sarah and Peg also commented on the lack of curiosity from their peers. It felt to them that it was as if they never went away. Never missed. *Oh well,* Nicollette thought, *less to worry about. More energy to devote to training.*

Sunday dinner was nicer than usual, and the mess hall was more crowded than usual. Nicollette noticed a lot more uniformed people in the mess. She thought she heard American accents. Fortunately, she, Val, Sarah and Peg, were able to find a table and were joined by Lieutenant Blankin.

"It seems the mess hall is crowded tonight, Lieutenant Blankin. Any ideas?" Val asked.

"Not too sure, but there's a number of Americans here. It looks like Air Force uniforms. That's about all I know." Lieutenant Blankin changed the subject. "How were your calls home this afternoon?" she asked.

"It was wonderful to speak to my mum," Nicollette replied.

"My mum as well."

"My father and mum."

"Mine as well," Peg responded.

"I was able to speak to my boys today," Lieutenant Blankin added.

At the evening meeting, Lieutenant Blankin asked for everyone's attention and introduced Captain Blasingame. Nicollette realized that apart from herself, Val, Sarah, and Peg, none of the other recruits had met the captain before.

"Ladies, I would like to introduce Captain Blasingame. She would like to say a few words about the upcoming week."

"Good evening. I'm Captain Blasingame and I am with British Intelligence. I'm here for your last week at Brize and to assist in your transition. Let me first congratulate each of you on the success you have achieved so far. At the start, we reviewed twenty-five applicants and we started with eighteen recruits. We are now at fourteen. Well done to you! Your last week here is going to be very tough and thorough. All we ask is that you work hard and remain focused and dedicated. The end is near, finish strong! Thank you."

Captain Blasingame left the room and Lieutenant Blankin handed out the week's schedule. Nicollette noticed that the week was very full. There would be the normal early exercises followed by Krav Maga on Monday, Tuesday and Wednesday. There was a lot of class time but there was also time scheduled at the gun range and driving course. At the end of the week, final individual exit meetings were scheduled on Friday. Nicollette's name was listed for 11:00 hours. At the bottom of the paper in big bold letters was an announcement for a commencement ceremony on Saturday at 11:00 hours followed by a graduation luncheon on Saturday at 12:00 hours. The class would be dismissed at 14:00 hours. Off to the side was a handwritten note stating the necessary arrangements for invitations for family guests will be made on her behalf. *Well, this is it,* Nicollette thought to herself, *one more week, five days, then home, sweet, warm home.*

The alarm went off at 05:45 as it had done every day for the past three weeks. Nicollette was first to rise. She looked over at Val who was wrapped in her blankets like a caterpillar in a cocoon.

"Wake up, Val. You know the routine. Exercises at 06:30."

Val rolled over. "Do I have to?"

"I think we both know the answer to that question," Nicollette replied. "After all, we are interns and we must keep interning."

The warmup exercises seemed to be a bit easier this Monday morning, Nicollette thought, but there was something new in the Krav Maga classes. Sergeant Harris asked the fourteen young women to pair off for some hand-to-hand self-defense exercises. She asked Sarah to join her on the mat. Sergeant Harris asked Sarah to make an attack move and just like that, Sarah found herself flat on her back.

"And that's how it's done!" Sergeant Harris announced to the class. She asked if Sarah was alright and received a mumbled "ok" in reply.

For the next hour, Nicollette and Val went at it, gently and controlled. No one was hurt and no one's ego bruised, they were friends. Later in the room freshening up for lunch, Nicollette took a good look at herself in the mirror. With the hectic schedule, she really hadn't paid too much attention to herself. But now, looking in the mirror, she could see changes. Her face was narrower, and her shoulders seemed broader. Her arms and legs were solid with none of the "jiggles." Nicollette pushed on her midsection, it was firm and taut. Her hips seemed thinner. She guessed she had lost about a stone. Getting dressed, Nicollette realized her jeans were looser and her top was draping her shoulders. *I wonder if anyone at home will recognize me*, she thought. *I may have to buy some new clothes!*

Walking with Val, Sarah and Peg to lunch, Nicollette revisited the long morning class in her mind. She remembered her first early morning exercise class and how sore and tired she was afterwards for the day. Now three weeks later, Nicollette felt very little soreness and even less fatigue after the class. Her body felt much stronger and agile. The Krav Maga training increased her confidence as she remembered the promise she had made to herself on New Year's Eve. *I am stronger both inside and outside. I have grown, Nicky, I have grown, and I feel great!*

The afternoon classes went fast, with Captain Murphy working the women on cryptanalysis and computers. That evening, after tea, it was back to the gun range. Nicollette enjoyed shooting and was getting quite adept at it. Val called her "the British Annie Oakley."

"All she needs is a horse and a ten-gallon hat," Val would say. "After all, she's got the shooting part done."

Tuesday started the same way, exercises and Krav

Maga. While in class, Nicollette noticed Captain Blasingame observing the group. Again, Sergeant Harris had the women paired off learning new skills.

Nicollette motioned to Val. "Look who's here."

Val briefly turned to see the captain.

"First we've seen her since Sunday."

With that little distraction, Val found herself on the floor.

"Cheeky, Nicollette!"

They had a quiet laugh as Nicollette helped her friend up.

The afternoon class was again about signals and cryptanalysis. Captain Murphy rolled a strange-looking machine into the room. He asked the ladies to pay attention to the monitors on the desks and to put on their headphones when he asked.

"The class today is about blocking out all distractions and acutely focusing on the signals. You will receive a signal that must be coded and resent. Turn on your monitors and get ready. You may put on your headphones."

Captain Murphy turned off the lights in the room and turned the strange-looking machine on. Messages were coming across the screen, same as they had practiced before, but the strange machine was creating a strobe effect in the room. Nicollette felt as if she was working in a bad lightning storm. Bright flashes and pounding lights in no particular sequence. Some long and some short flashes and now to make it even harder, Captain Murphy turned on loud thunderous noises. Boom. Crack. Bang. The messages kept coming and the lights and sounds became more intense. Nicollette forced herself not to become distracted. She focused on the screen and her fingers pressing the keys. It was very demanding and required tremendous concentration. After about thirty minutes, Captain Murphy turned off the machine and order was restored to the environment.

"Ladies, we must be prepared to carry on with our jobs no matter what the circumstances are. This requires a great deal of concentration and focus and will take a lot of strength. I've sent each of you the same message, let us see how well you have done."

Captain Murphy looked at his monitor for a few moments. Nicollette rubbed and blinked her eyes. To her, it felt like the moment after getting your picture taken by a flash camera. Blue spots all around. Finally, her eyes cleared. Captain Murphy looked up from his monitor,

"You all did very well, but not quite one hundred percent. We will try again tomorrow."

On the way to tea, Sarah mentioned that her stomach was a bit uneasy after the class.

"I'm a little bit dizzy as well," Peg added.

Val was quiet, still trying to recuperate from the intensity. Nicollette felt a bit guilty in that she wasn't really having any effects but felt more comfortable among her friends by just saying, "Me too."

The evening class was about international affairs and alliances. Some bookwork for a change, Nicollette thought, sarcastically remembering the additional Spanish work she had to do that evening. *I'm going to be a busy girl tonight!*

The 05:45 alarm again. Same routine. Nicollette up first. Argument from Val. Then off to exercises. Sergeant Harris gave the group their usual sets of stretches and calisthenics, however, she stopped the class a little bit earlier than most days. Nicollette thought this to be odd for the normally "by the book" Sergeant Harris, but a rest, albeit a short one, was always welcomed. At 07:30 hours, Krav Maga training. Sergeant Harris asked the women to line up on the mat, eyes forward facing her. She asked all to stand arm's length apart and watch as she showed them a new technique. All eyes watched Sergeant Harris demonstrating the new move. In an instant, Nicollette felt herself being grabbed around the neck. Without reservation or hesitation, she threw her elbow into the side of her attacker and kicked her leg against the assailant's knee. She was now broken from the stranglehold and grabbed the attacker's arm, twisted it, and forced the attacker to the mat. She spun around and was about to kick the attacker in the groin when Sergeant Harris yelled, "Stop and release!"

Nicollette released the attacker's arm. The assailant stood up and removed the mask covering his face. Her attacker was a male soldier, about six feet tall. Nicollette was breathing heavily, trying to catch her breath from the sudden exertion. She stepped away from the assailant, never losing eye contact. Sweat was pouring through her palms. Nicollette's mind was racing, *What just happened! What did I just do? How did I do it? Me, Nicollette Beverley!*

A deep masculine voice broke her trance. "You did very

well, missy," the soldier assailant stated.

Still in disbelief, Nicollette did not know what to say. She took a glance around at the other recruits then at Sergeant Harris. There was a clap then another and another. Nicollette turned to see Val and Sarah smiling as they joined the applause. Nicollette's right arm was being raised in victory by the male soldier. Her shocked white face regained color as her expression revealed a small grin.

"I'm sorry if I hurt you," she whispered.

"That's not the point, missy, don't be sorry, you did what you had to do to defend yourself and you did very well, besides, I am protected." He pointed to the padding around his body. "Oh, and yes my privates too!" He laughed.

Sergeant Harris asked the recruits to catch their breath and then she asked for volunteers to describe what they just witnessed. Nicollette heard words like awareness, prepared, confidence, instinct and unafraid to describe her reaction. Nicollette was not used to such attention and started to blush a bit. Sergeant Harris asked for Nicollette to discuss her reaction. She took a breath to gather her thoughts.

"I did what I had to do with the tools I had. My instincts took over my mind and body."

Nicollette did not want to say anything anymore. She was emotionally and physically drained. Sergeant Harris thanked Nicollette for being the victim and continued to talk with the class. From behind, an attacker was sneaking up behind the sergeant. He motioned for all to keep still, then pounced on Sergeant Harris from behind. True to form, the attacker was down in nothing flat.

"Even the teacher must remain prepared!"

Sergeant Harris announced the Krav Maga class was finished and dismissed the class. As Nicollette was walking back to her room, her thoughts returned to what happened on New Year's Eve. She remembered when Garrett tried to force himself on her and how Edward had to come to her rescue. She remembered those feelings of helplessness and fear, driving her to make a commitment to herself that night. Now, walking back to her room, she felt more confident and surer of herself, well on the way to fulfilling that promise she made to herself. She would be able to maintain control and protect herself. There would be no more "what ifs."

The afternoon schedule was rearranged to take advantage of an unusually nice day. After lunch, Nicollette and the group were taken to the large hangar for another lesson in defensive driving. An area outside of the hanger was set up as an obstacle course. As serious as this training was, Nicollette enjoyed the high speed, spins, and turns. The avoidance maneuvers and the sudden stops and starts. She felt exhilarated while driving the course. Her stomach gave her no trouble, unlike some of the others. Plus, she was outside. She hadn't seen much of the sun the last four weeks. This was a good afternoon. When they were headed back for tea, Nicollette turned to Val, Sarah, and Peg.

"I wonder if my dad will let me drive home this weekend?"

The four of them had a good laugh.

After tea, the group went to Captain Murphy's class. Again, he brought the noise and light machine. The drill was repeated. Twice. After the third time, Captain Murphy looked up from his monitor. He had a rare smile on his face.

"One hundred percent, ladies. You've done it!"

Captain Blasingame had inconspicuously walked in during the final drill and was sitting in the rear of the room. She stood up and walked to the front of the room. She looked at the fourteen young women in the room. She said two words, "Well done!"

At Thursday's exercise class, Sergeant Harris was in her usual form, barking out instructions to the routine exercises. At 07:30, when the class would normally end, Sergeant Harris gathered the group together. It was a little surprising to Nicollette because Sergeant Harris was a woman of few words.

"For the past four weeks, I have worked with you and watched you grow into physically strong young women. You have worked hard to get to this point. Remember what you have learned about self-defense. You may need it someday. Keep up exercising. Run, jog, or walk. Stretch often. Take care of your body and it will take care of you. Your jobs require not only sharp minds, but healthy and strong bodies as well. It has been my pleasure to set you down the right path." Sergeant Harris paused to gather herself, a very rare bit of emotion.

"I shall miss you lot. Thank you."

Despite the early morning routine, the barking

instructions, the physical strain and the soreness, Nicollette would miss Sergeant Harris, she would leave an indelible mark in her memory of the training.

There was a short class after breakfast. Captain Blasingame gave a talk about protocol. Nicollette felt as if it was a lesson in adult manners and diplomatic behavior. Knowing the situation and thinking before speaking. Controlling one's emotions and other practical formalities.

"I guess we are now officially grownups," Nicollette whispered to Val as the group headed off to lunch.

Captain Murphy's afternoon class. Cryptanalysis. Monitors. Radio signals. Codes. It seemed like a long afternoon. There was a lot of repetition. At the end of the class, Captain McWilliams sat on his desk and addressed the group.

"Today was your last class with me. We have gone over a lot of material, and you have learned a great deal. We have done our best to prepare you for your next journey. My advice to you is to continue to learn and stay updated. Communication techniques are very fluid and constantly changing. Those who relax will be left behind. Use your common sense, your instincts, your gut feelings and never ever forget the details, even the smallest minutia can make a big difference." He paused and leaned forward. "I have the utmost confidence in you and your success. I am sure we will be seeing more of each other. Class dismissed."

It was after 17:30 hours when they left the class.

Teatime. Nicollette, Val, Sarah and Peg found their usual table. Sergeant Durban approached and asked to join the group. "Absolutely, please do join us."

There was light conversation around the table. The subject turned to the day after the training.

"What about you, Sergeant Durban, what is the first thing you will do when you get home?" Val asked.

"Well first off, for this conversation only, call me Linda."

Nicollette thought that despite knowing Sergeant Durban for over a month, she had never mentioned her first name.

"Ok, Sergeant Durban, I mean Linda, what are you going to do?"

"I'm going to my flat near Birmingham and take a hot bath for two days."

Her comment gathered a few chuckles among the group. She continued, "I will visit my mum who lives not too far away and then I will allow my boyfriend to take me out; only if he is nice to me, mind you."

"A boyfriend? Do tell, Linda," Peg asked.

Nicollette was a bit curious as well. Sergeant Linda Durban was not much older than the girls, maybe twenty-five or twenty-six. Linda Durban told the group she joined the service when she was eighteen. *Sergeant Durban seems to be like more of one of us*, Nicollette thought as the conversation continued.

"Well, my boyfriend is an American who works in Birmingham as an engineer."

"How did you meet?" The girls were getting curious.

"Through a friend's friend."

"Dating long?"

"About a year, although with my schedule…"

Linda did not finish the sentence, but merely nodded her head. The girls understood what she was referring to.

The evening class was about reading and understanding satellite imagery. Mr. Charles Thompson led the lesson. Satellite photos, along with guides, were given to each of the women and they were asked to identify different shapes in the photos using the guides. Nicollette found this very interesting as she stared at the photos using a magnifying glass. Charles Thompson explained the importance of satellites and the imagery they provided. "The devil is in the details," he explained, "The devil is in the details."

# Graduation

Nicollette and Val dressed and headed towards their meetings in the main building. The hallways were unusually void of people. A strange silence permeated the halls in the building. Nicollette's final meeting was in the same room as her first with Captain McWilliams. She walked with Val through the double doors and down the long corridor. Val found her room first.

"Wish me luck," she said as she opened the door and entered the room.

Nicollette was assigned the same room as her first meeting almost four weeks ago. She entered and saw the same corporal as her first time.

"Miss Beverley?"

"Yes."

"Please have a seat."

The side door opened, and Captain McWilliams invited her to come in. He shut the door behind him. Nicollette was surprised to find Major Hartwell sitting behind the desk. "Please have a seat, Miss Beverley," she said.

Major Hartwell silently started to read the opened folder in front of her, every so often raising her eyes towards Nicollette. Nicollette could feel the major's eyes piercing through her head. A tense numbness crept over her body and her palms were wet. The pounding of her heart was so strong, Nicollette was afraid the major and

Captain McWilliams could hear it through the severe silence of the room. *What is she reading? What have I done? Pass or fail?* Nicollette tried to calm herself as the seconds turned to minutes and even those few minutes felt like hours. She turned towards Captain McWilliams. He was sitting, legs crossed, staring straight forward, completely emotionless.

Nicollette discreetly wiped her hands on her now shaking legs and forced a grin at the major. Her mind started screaming, *Please, Major Hartwell. Let's get to it!*

Major Hartwell looked up again from her reading. Her eyes looked directly at Nicollette's. "Good morning, Miss Beverley. I have just reviewed your report and as I suspected, you did very well in this training program. You even improved your Spanish. Both Captain McWilliams and I are very proud of you!"

As if from nowhere, Nicollette felt a huge weight being lifted from her. *I did it! I really did it!* She wanted to jump out of the chair and scream with joy. She reached out to Captain McWilliams outstretched hand for a congratulatory handshake, followed by one with Major Hartwell. An uncontrollable smile crossed her face as the major continued.

"Miss Beverley, I want to talk with you about your future. You live in Brockwirth. A charming little village, I have been there a few times myself. Anyways, are you familiar with Cheltenham?"

"Yes, Major, we go there quite often."

"What else do you know about Cheltenham?"

"I know there is a government facility there, not too

sure what goes on there, maybe something to do with satellites as there are big satellite dishes on Cleeve Hill that I can see when we arrive through Prestbury."

"Well, Cheltenham is a communication facility, rather hush hush. You will be working there. Your assignment will be working with me, Captain Blasingame, Lieutenant Blankin and Sergeant Durban. We have assigned Lieutenant Blankin to be our adjutant officer. We will be in the mission communications area. Your job will have the appearance of a normal 8 to 5 government job. But once in the building, everything will change. There may be long days and some traveling. We do not want to raise any suspicions, so do you want us to arrange housing for you? Think about it. Your cover for the last four weeks was that you have been in America attending training in sports medicine and management and even playing a little field hockey. Well, your job cover here is that you are a sports liaison with the government. Your 'job' entails passports, visas, travel arrangements, health issues and the like for athletes and teams going abroad. Your cover does not require direct contact with the teams or athletes, so no autograph hounds, if you get my point. Merely a desk job that requires a bit of travel. Should be easy enough. Now, tomorrow you will receive your dossier, not to be shared with anyone, you will be an agent of British Intelligence, sworn to the official secrets act."

She paused and looked hard at Nicollette and smiled.

"You will be pleased to know you will be working together with your friends Valerie Davies, Sarah Green, and Margaret Wilson. Eight of us to start with."

The Major leaned forward towards Nicollette,

"We are under the microscope, young lady. We are being watched by our superiors. There are a number in leadership who are not too happy with the minister's new women's initiative, so let's prove them wrong, my girl."

Major Hartwell extended her hand again and the two shook hands. Major Hartwell leaned back in the chair. She asked if Captain McWilliams had anything to add.

"Miss Beverley, we are expecting big things from you. I was impressed with you from our first encounter. You have keen senses and terrific problem-solving abilities. I think your group will be just fine. Now, a bit of 'fatherly advice,' if I may?"

Nicollette nodded.

"Take the flat in Cheltenham. You still can go home when you want to, but with the travel and the nature of our business, you may find having a flat on campus more comfortable. Again, congratulations on training; well done."

Captain McWilliams extended his hand again and the two shook hands.

"Now for logistics Nicollette," the major continued. "This afternoon, you have a wrap up class and this evening at 19:00 hours there will be a farewell banquet, so dress up. Transport will meet you at 18:30 hours at your dorm building. As you know, there will be a commencement ceremony at 11:00 hours tomorrow followed by a graduation luncheon at 12:00 hours. Any questions?"

Nicollette thought a minute, a million things going

through her mind. It was hard to formulate a response. She shook her head. "No questions for now, but I'm sure I will have some later." She looked at Major Hartwell. "I think I will take the flat."

"Good decision, we will make all the arrangements. In the meantime, make yourself comfortable. Lieutenant Blankin and Captain Blasingame will be in shortly to go over some details. Now would you like a cuppa?"

Nicollette's mouth felt as if it were full of cotton balls, very dry. The tea would just hit the spot. "Yes please."

The Corporal in the front room rolled a tray into the office. He poured then left. The tea was just the right ticket. Nicollette felt more relaxed and comfortable. *My own place and I will be working with Val, Peg, and Sarah! This is going to be great!*

Captain Blasingame and Lieutenant Blankin walked into the office. Lieutenant Blankin was carrying a large briefcase. Captain Blasingame stood behind the desk and reached for Nicollette's hand. She stood and shook hands.

"Well done, Miss Beverley. Welcome to the team. We're going to show them something, my girl!"

They sat down.

Lieutenant Blankin pulled a portfolio from the brief-case. Nicollette noticed her name across the top.

"Nicollette, let's go over the details. Your first day will be Thursday, February 5th. You will be able to move into your flat Tuesday morning, February 3rd. It is fully furnished and under twenty-four-hour surveillance. It's only a short walk to the facility, so you should be quite comfortable."

Lieutenant Blankin handed some papers to Nicollette. The top page was a map of Cheltenham showing the location and address of the flat and a highlighted route to the entrance of the building where she would be working. It looked to be about a ten-minute walk. No problem there. Nicollette knew that her father was familiar with Cheltenham, so finding the flat should be no problem.

The next page was a written dress code followed by the work schedule for her first days, Thursday and Friday. Normal hours 8 to 5. The third page dealt with finances. Her salary would be one hundred pounds a week. After the rent and taxes, she would have sixty pounds spending money a week. *A King's ransom! That's twice as much as Russell's!* She would let her dad go over the finances with her as he was her personal banker. The next page was a list of items for a "getaway bag" that Nicollette should always have ready. Lieutenant Blankin suggested that Nicollette assemble the bag after she moved to her flat, less questions at home. Lastly, Lieutenant Blankin handed her an information binder, an employee handbook and her ID badge. She explained that the ID badge would be used for entry into her flat and the work building. Nicollette looked at the stack of information she was just handed and at her ID badge. It said: Nicollette Beverley Special Liaison, International Sports, Her Majesty's Government. She repeated it in her mind, several times.

It was nearly 13:00 hours when Captain Blasingame announced it was lunch time and adjourned the meeting.

In the mess hall, Nicollette saw Val and Peg sitting at a table.

"So, how was your meeting?" Nicollette asked as she looked at her two friends.

Val looked at Nicollette and then at Peg. With a big smile, she announced excitedly, "We're working together! We're a team and we're neighbors as well!"

"It's wonderful and so exciting!" Peg added. "We'll make a great team."

Nicollette looked at Peg and smiled. *Has Peg really changed from the rich kid? Is she really excited to work with us? Or am I just more tolerant?*

Sarah approached the table. Three sets of eyes watched as she sat down.

"Well? How was your meeting?" Val asked.

Eyes staring down, Sarah responded in a soft voice. "It went very well, I guess. Looks like I'll have to move away from home though and work and live with you lot!"

The table had a laugh.

"You had us going there," Val quipped. "Cheeky girl. Let's make a toast to our future. Put 'em together, ladies! To our future, cheers!"


The afternoon review class started at 14:00 hours. Captain Murphy began the class with a cryptanalysis review. He handed out several messages to decode and resend. *Easier this time without all the distractions,* Nicollette thought. He then pulled down a world map on the front wall. Each country was shaded in a different color representing alliances, friends and foes, trouble spots and peaceful areas. Using a pointer, Captain Murphy then located a few of the major British and Allied Intelligence Centers. He went into detail about the "special relationship" between America and England and how reliant each country was on the other. Then he produced a signal that was about a month old and asked the class to decipher the message. Captain Murphy opened the floor for a discussion about what to do with the information.

"How do we solve this puzzle?" he asked.

He reminded the class about using the five W's, who, what, where, why and when and toss in the how.

"And there you have it. Solve any problem." Captain Murphy gave a small smile, a rare show of emotion for the normally stoic officer.

There was a knock on the classroom door and Charles Thompson asked to come in. Captain Murphy then told the class that Mr. Thompson would talk about civilian and military protocols in the Intelligence community. He led a practical discussion about formalities and processes. Then he talked about dealing with the world outside work. Subjects proper and useful and those to avoid. Charles Thompson then reviewed a prior class on how to think before speaking and react to various situations. How to listen, really listen not only to what was being said, but how it was said. Charles Thompson then pulled a projector screen down over the world map, darkened the light and showed a short film on body language.

"You have seen this film before but let us watch it again.

Let's see if we can pick up some new information."

Nicollette watched intently. Although she had seen it before, she did not remember the eye movements she saw this time. *Remember to look at the eyes*, she thought, *they tell a story.*

After the presentation and discussion, he addressed the class.

"I want to wish you all great success in the future. You have devoted time and energy to this process, been away from home for nearly a month, and now are ready to become integrated into British Intelligence. We have done our best to give you a solid background, but remember, never stop learning and never be afraid to think 'out of the box,' be creative or imagine. Yours and our success is not measured by the number of runs or what number we place at but knowing that we did our job to keep our freedoms and stop our adversaries from taking them away, even if it's just in a small way. For that and what we accomplish in the future, I thank you."

Nicollette could not help herself and applauded Charles Thompson. The whole class joined in. Charles Thompson waved his hand in acknowledgement and left the room. Captain Murphy shut the door behind him and turned to the class.

"Ladies, it is now 17:45 hours and I know you want to get ready for this evening, but before you leave, I would like to reemphasize what Mr. Thompson said and add a few thoughts of my own. You have done well and have set the groundwork for future training classes. Stay focused. Enjoy the work, never feel overwhelmed or defeated. You have convinced this old soldier that there is a future for women in our trade. You young women in this room are 'pioneers' for future recruits and you are part of a great team. I wish you well. I have enjoyed instructing you. Now go out and show us proud! For the final time: class dismissed!"

Captain Murphy stood by the door and shook each of the young women's hands as they left the classroom. Nicollette felt a bit of sadness as she shook Captain Murphy's hand. She had learned so much in his classes. Nicollette looked into his eyes as she said, "Thank you" and he responded by wishing her good luck.

As she was walking back to the dormitory with Val, Sarah, and Peg, the reality of finishing the training hit her.

"We did it, ladies, we're finished, we passed and now onto the future," Nicollette stated.

"Yes, we did it, girls!" Val added.

They walked back to the rooms feeling like children on the last day of the spring school term and the summer break ahead. Almost giddy.

Nicollette and Val met up with Sarah and Peg at the elevator. The lobby was filled with the fourteen young women, dressed up and ready to go at 18:45. Even Sergeant Durban dressed up. Transport arrived. Four to a car. Twenty-minute drive. The ladies were escorted into a small ballroom. There were tables, beautifully set with flower centerpieces. The small band from the officer's club was playing music in the corner and there was a bar in the rear. Nicollette looked around and it seemed like everyone connected to group 228 was here. She saw Captains Murphy, McWilliams, Sousa and Blasingame in their dress uniforms. Major Hartwell and Charles Thompson were talking by the bar. Sergeant Harris looked different dressed up and not in her usual fitness outfit. It looked to Nicollette that the officers were required to dress in their dress uniforms and the enlisted could come in civilian clothes tonight. The room was filling up as Captain Swanson and Lieutenants Brown, Frye, Rand and Nye from the driving course arrived. Nicollette saw Sergeant Richards with Corporals Stanley and Vance from the gun range. Val commented that the men looked very sharp all dressed up.

"Cheeky girl!"

At a small podium in the front, Major Hartwell asked everyone to take their seats.

"Welcome all. We are here to celebrate the conclusion of our inaugural training course under the Ministry of Defense's initiative to incorporate more women into traditional male roles. I would like to ask our fourteen graduates to stand and be recognized. Well done, ladies. "

The major led the applause. Nicollette felt a little shy as she was not used to being recognized, but she enjoyed it just the same. Major Hartwell motioned with her hand for the women to be seated.

"I now would like all the instructors and administrative staff and everyone else affiliated to rise and be recognized for your contribution in the success of the course."

Nicollette watched as over half the room stood. She did not recognize most of the administration people, but that did not keep her from enthusiastically applauding. Major Hartwell motioned again to be seated.

"Now I would like to ask everyone to rise and give yourselves recognition of a job well done!"

The whole room rose and applauded. Nicollette guessed there must be nearly eighty people in the room.

"We have some very special guests, please welcome Colonel Peter Halls and Colonel Paul Tremont from the Ministry of Defense."

The two Colonels sat at the table with Major Hartwell.

"Now, allow me to introduce Colonel Nigel Baron, who is in charge of the program. Colonel Baron was seated at the major's table.

"Finally, please welcome Sir John Barraclough, Ministry of Defense."

A standing ovation. He sat at the major's table as well. The major asked all to rise for "God Save the Queen" and then motioned for all to be seated.

"Sir John Barraclough has asked to say a few words. Sir John."

He walked to the podium, cleared his throat, and began. He had a prepared speech. He opened by congratulating the women. He reviewed the Ministry of Defense's initiative to recruit more women into the Intelligence Services and the resistance and unease it received, even from people directly involved. He would consistently hear, "Do women have the abilities to do the job? Could young, inexperienced ladies be trained and trusted to perform as well as men? Are we prepared for the risks?"

Sir John paused and continued about the reports

he received from the officers in charge of the training program. Summaries talking about the successes achieved almost every day, leading up to tonight.

"You will be scrutinized and challenged on many levels and there will always be doubters. But I have the utmost confidence in your abilities to take on these challenges 'head on' and be successful and show what you can really do!"

Sir John concluded by commending the many people involved, both civilian and military, and especially the fourteen young women graduates, thanking them as trailblazers for future trainees and setting the standards very high. He finished by saying how proud he was of each of the women and wished them all good luck.

Major Hartwell shook his hand as he went back to his seat. Colonel Baron now was at the Podium. Again, congratulations and a talk about the future and the efforts to remain one step ahead. Speeches. A few words from Colonel Paul Tremont. Now it was Major Hartwell's turn. She talked of the pride she had for all who participated in the program and singled out the fourteen brave, young women graduating. She concluded by stating that this was truly a proud moment for everyone involved, the Ministry of Defense and England. A standing ovation.

It was a wonderful evening. Nicollette felt as if she was a princess at a ball. She was talking with very important people all night. Asking and answering questions. She was surprised to know that Colonel Tremont had been to Brockwirth several times and stayed at the local bed and breakfast. The music started again. Nicollette was flattered to be chatted up by Sergeant Richards and Lieutenant Brown. She was asked to dance, but declined, wanting to remain available to socialize. Nicollette looked around for Val who was talking with Lieutenant Frye. Sarah and Peg were dancing with Corporals Vance and Stanley.

Charles Thompson walked over to Nicollette. "A long way from the field hockey team, Nicollette."

"It's been like a dream, Mr. Thompson. I am so thankful for your recommendation and confidence in me. My life will truly never be the same. I will never be the same."

"It was my pleasure, Nicollette. You know that Barbara thinks the world of you, and I really believe you will be a great asset to group 228. Now how about a drink?"

It was nearly one hundred hours when transport arrived. Nicollette rolled into her bed. She looked over at Val, who was already in dreamland. Looking at the dark ceiling, her thoughts turned to Brockwirth and home. She would be in her home, her bed later that day. She drifted off to deep sleep.

With encouragement from the 09:00 alarm, Nicollette woke from her deep sleep. She threw a pillow at Val.

"Nicky, the sky is falling!" Val responded, half asleep. "Every girl for themselves."

"Wake up, sleepy head, we graduate in less than two hours, then you get to go home and sleep for a couple of days."

Nicollette was dressed and packing up when Val got out of her bed.

"My head, why did I do that last night? I don't remember when I drank so little to feel like this."

"You must be out of practice, now you better hurry. We have to be out of here at 10:30 hours."

"I won't miss that either!"

"Damn military time!" They both laughed.

As instructed, Nicollette and Val left their cases in the meeting area by the elevator. They caught up with Sarah and Peg in the ceremony room. Chairs were set up in two rows with a podium in the front. There was tea and pastry off to the side. Nicollette noticed a black shrouded area in the rear and a table with cardboard boxes stacked on top.

"How'd you two sleep?" Nicollette asked Sarah and Peg.

"Like a stone and this one I think is still asleep." Sarah pointed at Peg.

"Good thing Val and Peg weren't roommates, they would have slept through the whole training," Nicollette chuckled.

"You're being cheeky again, Nicky!" Val chirped.

There was just enough time for a quick cup of tea. She and Val helped themselves. Colonel Baron and Major Hartwell entered the room with Captains Murphy, Blasingame, and McWilliams. Lieutenant Blankin and Sergeants Durban and Harris followed.

"Back in uniform," Nicollette whispered to her friends as the sergeants walked by.

Major Hartwell asked all to be seated. She commented that she has been asking people to be seated a lot recently. Quiet laughter.

"Good morning, ladies. I hope you had a good time last night and as I look out at you this morning, some of you may have had a better time than others." Quiet laughter again. "It's ok, you worked hard and deserved a respite." She paused, then continued, "Now for the business at hand."

Colonel Baron walked to the podium.

"Today, we graduate group 228 from the inaugural training program at Brize-Norton RAF base. It is with pride as the commanding officer in charge of group 228, to officially announce the graduation of the following women. Please stand when your name is called and remain standing." He read the names. "Sharon Adams. Nicollette Beverley. Deborah Brown. Kimberly Chester. Valerie Davies. Helen George."

He read till the last name was called, then asked everyone to be seated. Colonel Baron asked all to raise their right hand and take the Defense of the Realm Oath. He turned to Major Hartwell. They saluted. Major Hartwell motioned for all to be seated.

"Congratulations. I think you have heard enough speeches recently, so I won't be giving you any this morning." Quiet laughter again. "In a few minutes, we will collect you for your exit interview and take an ID picture for your individual work area. You may walk around if you want, but please stay away from the tables off to the left. Thank you."

Captain McWilliams approached Nicollette and escorted her to one of the tables. They sat across from each other. Captain McWilliams pulled out Nicollette's records from a small file cabinet. There were documents to sign. She had already signed the 'Official Secrets Act' paper, but there were still many papers to sign. Government documents. Employment documents. Lease agreement. Nicollette felt as if her right hand would fall off. The documents completed, Captain McWilliams escorted her to the black shrouded area. A soldier took her behind the shroud and asked her to sit down. He asked her to smile and look straight ahead. Flash. The soldier then brought over a tray. Fingerprints. She was handed a moist towel as the soldier showed her out. As she stepped from behind the shroud, Nicollette saw Val next to go in. Raising her hand, "New fingernail polish," Nicollette said as Val was escorted behind the shroud.

It was nearly 12:00 hours when all the formalities were finished. Major Hartwell called all the women to their seats one last time.

"Ladies, in just a few minutes, we will walk into the luncheon just down the hall. We will walk in in alphabetical order and proceed to your assigned table. Your parents or guardians will already be seated. We will play 'God save the Queen' and then I will say a few words. There will be a buffet lunch till 14:00 hours at which time I will dismiss the class. You and your parents will be driven to the front gate where you will retrieve your luggage and turn in your Brize security badge. Now, please line up."

Nicollette stood behind Sharon Adams as the young women organized themselves. Captain McWilliams and Lieutenant Blankin opened the cardboard boxes to reveal black leather shoulder bags. Each young woman was handed one. Nicollette saw her initials, NCB, embossed in gold lettering on the side. She now had two wonderful bags, remembering the one she received for Christmas. The women were asked to wear the bags on their right shoulder, and they followed Colonel Baron, Major Hartwell, Captains McWilliams, Blasingame and Murphy. Lieutenant Blankin was next followed by Sergeants Durban and Harris. *Quite a parade*, Nicollette thought. Her heart started beating faster as the leading officers entered the luncheon room. There was applause. Sharon Adams entered the room and as Nicollette followed, she felt as if her heart was going to come right out of her chest. She saw her parents and quickly walked and embraced them with tears.

Her father stepped back. "We're very proud of you, Nicky, and we miss you. Now let us have a look at you."

Nicollette stepped away and turned around.

"You look very fit," her mum said, tears of joy coming down her cheeks.

"Very fit indeed," her father added.

They embraced again and then sat down. Colonel Baron walked to the front of the room and asked all to rise for the playing of "God save the Queen." He introduced himself and said a few words about commitment and how proud he was of these wonderful young women. He introduced Major Hartwell who added words of personal congratulations and how wonderful it had been to get to know every one of them personally.

Major Hartwell concluded, "A month ago we welcomed

fifteen young recruits, today we graduated fourteen confident, professional women."

Charles Thompson walked over to say hello to the Beverley family. Each officer came by the tables to personally say hello to the fourteen families. Sergeants Durban and Harris also made the rounds. The time flew by and soon Major Hartwell asked for everyone's attention.

"For the last time, Group 228 is dismissed!"

Tears and hugs as the families left the room for the transport. Nicollette introduced Val, Sarah, and Peg to her parents and they to theirs.

Nicollette whispered, "See you lot on Thursday," to her friends.

More tears and hugs. At the gate, a tent was set up and the luggage was dispensed by two soldiers. Nicollette kissed her Brize ID badge before she handed it in. *For good luck.* The training would provide a great memory for the rest of her life and in no small way, she would miss it. As they went to their car, Nicollette asked her father if she could drive home.

James responded, "You haven't driven in a month."

"That's what you think, Dad," she said as she grabbed the keys and started the car. She looked at her mum and dad. "Let's go home!"

# Home

Home! Wonderful, warm home! Nicollette walked into the small living room and took a deep breath. Her mum walked into the kitchen and announced she was putting on the kettle while her father brought in the luggage. Nicollette took off her coat and walked into the kitchen. On the counter there was something ready to go into the oven.

"A surprise for later," her mum said.

Her father walked into the kitchen.

"Now Nicky, let's get a real good look at you."

Nicollette spun around.

"It looks like you've lost some weight, didn't they feed you?"

"Oh yes, very well in fact."

"I think you look very well. You look so fit and trim. I know it's only been a month, but I also think you look more grown up as well!"

The teapot was boiling. The three of them sat down.

"Now Nicky, let's hear all about it."

Nicollette had to think quickly about what she could say to her parents, even though they had been cleared and had a general feel for what was going on, she still did not want to give them any more angst or fear than they already had. Even as her father innocently asked the question, Nicollette could still see the concern in both her parent's eyes. She decided to be selective in her response, not too vague, but not too much detail either.

"Where do I start?" Nicollette asked aloud. "I guess I'll begin from when you and Edward dropped me off. As you saw, I was picked up by some soldiers and brought to a welcome area. I had to sign a bunch of forms and then there were introductory words by the officers in charge, a lot of introductory words. We were assigned our rooms and given badges. That's when I met my roommate, Val. I also met Sarah and Peg. You met them earlier today. Anyways, we got to know each other and the four of us became fast friends, practically doing everything together. We shared our stories of how we were recruited into the program. That was very interesting to say the least."

Nicollette paused then continued.

"My normal day started around six in the morning. We would have exercises before breakfast and then classes throughout the day. They taught us a lot about communications, recognition, and problem solving. We would have classes till about noon and then in the afternoon till about 17:00 hours. Oh, I forgot to mention that we were also on military time, so I apologize if I mix up the time." Nicollette chuckled before she went on.

"In the evenings, we would have bookwork to study or an assignment or even a class. They kept us very busy, we had very little free time. On Saturday and Sundays, our class schedule was more relaxed."

Nicollette purposely didn't talk about her Krav Maga training, or her defensive driving course and she certainly didn't want to mention the gun range or the trips to London and Brussels. *No point in creating more anxiety.*

Nicollette took a deliberate smell of the kitchen, trying to relax the conversation.

"Mum, whatever you are baking, it smells wonderful and speaking of food, the dining hall was open early every day and didn't close till late. The food wasn't that bad really and there were always a lot of choices, although not as good as yours, Mum, I promise!"

The last comment brought a big smile from her mum.

"We also spent some course time on sports medicine, after all, it was our 'cover' and I should know something about it. So, that about sums it up for the training aspect, but I have other news."

Her parents suspected there was more to what their daughter was telling them but did not want to dig deeper into her story.

"She'll tell us when she wants to," James whispered to Alice.

Nicollette left the table and gathered her shoulder bag from the living room. She brought it into the kitchen and placed it beside her chair.

"That's a nice bag, Nicky."

"They gave it to us before the luncheon today, now I have two special bags."

Nicollette sat down and finished her tea.

"I can see why you look so fit, Nicky, it sounds like you were exercising every day," her father commented.

"And probably watching your sweets as well," Mum added.

Nicollette poured more tea, buying some time and thinking how she was going to tell her parents about her cover job and the flat in Cheltenham. She stalled.

Nicollette was surprised that her normally quiet mum was so direct. *Curiosity? Concern? I guess this is how parents are,* Nicollette thought, *so here goes.*

"I'm very excited to say the least about the job! I will be doing several tasks in the government. My title is Sports Liaison for Her Majesty's Government. I will be involved with foreign travel arrangements for sports teams. I will be communicating with embassies throughout the world about visas, travel permits, medical requirements and the like. My position requires some travel, and I may not get much notice." Nicollette paused, took a breath, and continued. "Unfortunately, I'll have no direct contact with the teams or athletes, so no autographs from the golfers, Dad!"

Nicollette and her parents had a laugh. She knew how much her father loved to play and watch golf and how much an autograph would mean to him.

"Now for some very exciting news! My job may require some unusual hours and last-minute travel, after all, I'm dealing with people all over the world, so they've offered me a flat in Cheltenham so I can be near work! I hope you two are not unhappy about this. I am still close enough to visit and stay the night here, plus, I am a Brockwirth girl." Nicollette tried to soften the news with her last comment. She knew this was a big step for not only herself, but her parents as well. They would be alone now in the house. She looked at her parents for a reaction. Her mum drank some tea and her father sat back in his chair.

"I can't say we're too surprised by that Nicollette. We knew it would happen someday but we were not expecting it this soon," James said.

"When do you move into your flat?" Alice asked.

"It is available this Tuesday and I start work Thursday."

Nicollette opened her shoulder bag and pulled out the information on the flat and the financial information about the job.

"We can visit the flat Tuesday morning, Mum, and see what I need to get started. We can make a day out of it!"

She turned to her father.

"I do need your help, Dad. These are my financial papers."

Nicollette handed her father the documents.

"It says somewhere that my salary is one hundred pounds a week. They will automatically hold out the rent for the flat and taxes as well, but I should have about sixty pounds a week spending money left over."

James looked over the documents. He found the salary sheet.

"They are paying you well, Nicky! You will not starve!" He chuckled. "I will look at the financial papers later." Her father found the information on the flat. He showed the paper to Nicollette. "Is this where you will be living?"

"Yes," she responded.

"This is a nice area of Cheltenham, Nicky, I know where this is. There are a lot of government buildings in the area, that's for sure. I reckon you might be working in one of them?"

"Yes, I am, Dad. Here is my pass key for the flat." Nicollette reached into her shoulder bag and pulled out the pass. "It is a little quiet at work next week, so I will arrange to be off on Tuesday. I'll take you and Mum into Cheltenham."

"That would be great, Dad! Thank you. We'll make it a family adventure and I will buy lunch as well. I also want to tell you that my friends, Val, Sarah and Peg, will be living near me, so I won't be alone in my new flat."

"Well, it all sounds very exciting, Nicky," her mum added. "It will be fun to help you set up your new place and I know you will be coming home for my cooking!"

James then reached over to the sideboard and brought a small stack of mail to the table.

"This is your mail for the last month and this one arrived yesterday by special post. I think you should open it first."

Her father handed her an envelope. Nicollette saw it was from the government. She opened it very deliberately so as not to tear the contents. She pulled out the contents. There was an official letter and a check for 500 pounds. Nicollette had to catch her breath as she showed her parents the check.

"Crickey, Nicky! That is a lot of money," her father exclaimed. "What's it about?"

"The letter says this is my salary check for the last month and they have also included 200 pounds moving expenses."

Nicollette handed her father the letter.

"Lunch and dinner both are on me Tuesday!" she exclaimed.

"Hello Carol, it's me, Nicky! I just got in a couple of hours ago." Nicollette smiled as she talked to her friend on the phone.

"Welcome back, Nicky! How was your trip?"

"Great! How are things? Hard to believe I have been away for so long. You must fill me in."

"I'll do better than that! I'll call Ashley and we can get together at the Traveler tonight. I can pick you up at 8. What do you say?"

"Sounds good."

"Super! Glad you're back, Nicky, we missed you!"

As Nicollette hung up the phone, she gave thought to reuniting with her friends later. This would be the first time out in public since before her training. What would she say about her trip? How would she handle questions? Would she be believable? And deep down, how would she act if George was there? *Better rehearse*, Nicollette thought.

Nicollette grabbed her luggage and started to bring it upstairs to her room. James looked up from the cricket match on the tele.

"That's for me to do, your bags are heavy, Nicky."

"It's alright, Dad, I can do it." Nicollette picked up the large case with ease.

"Not only are you fit, but you are strong! I'll carry one anyway."

In her room, Nicollette organized her clothing. There

—321—

was plenty to wash tomorrow for sure. The training did spoil her as the laundry was done for her, but nonetheless, she would be doing her own laundry tomorrow. She looked around her room. Small by comparison to her room at Brize, but adequate for a younger person. She looked at her shelves, little items, each bringing back a memory of growing up. How much time she spent in her room. Thoughts and dreams. Good and sad times. Her room. Her area. Nicollette stood up and looked out the window. The view of the street below. She looked up and down the road. Same view since as long as she could remember. The same. Nothing ever changes. She felt a bit melancholy at the thought of leaving her room. She took a deep breath, as a tear fell down her cheek. *I'm going to miss my room.* She took another deep breath. *It's time for a change. I can do it. I can.*

"Nicky, tea's on the table," Mum yelled up the stairs.

"Coming."

Nicollette looked at her watch. It was nearly 6. She must have dozed off. In the kitchen, her mum had placed a plate of cheeses and sausage rolls on the table. She was bringing a beautiful Victoria cake with coffee icing to the table when Nicollette walked in.

"It looks great, Mum! I missed your baking for sure! I'm going to enjoy this."

At tea, Nicollette related her anxiousness about being prepared to handle questions from her friends later that evening.

"Let's talk it out," Alice said.

Nicollette had a good conversation with her parents.

They asked her a range of questions. Nicollette focused hard on her answers, and she was able to handle most of the potential questions without reservation. For the tougher questions, the ones requiring more detail, she would pause, think, then answer. *Use your training, girl!* Nicollette thought. There was one question that her parents could not help her with though. What to say and do about George?

There was a knock on the door. Carol and Ashley rushed in, and three excited young women embraced in a hug.

"We missed you! So glad you are back! Can't wait to hear all about it!"

"Let's get that first pint in you!"

They were off. Nicollette took a deep breath as they walked into the pub. She missed the familiarity of the Traveler. The smell of the stale beer and chips as well as yesterday's cigarettes. Familiar and friendly smells. There was the usual crowd in the pub that night. All the holiday decorations were long put away. The dart board was in place and music was playing. Ashley's parents had reserved a table and the girls sat down. Ashley's mum brought over a round of pints to the table.

"Welcome back, Nicollette. I hope your trip was good."

"Yes, thank you."

"I know Ashley will tell me all about it. Now enjoy!"

"A toast to our wandering traveler, Nicky! Cheers!"

Clink. There was laughter, then the questions. Nicollette talked about her training and field hockey games at Grinnell College. She explained that it was a small school in the middle of nowhere, not much to do or see.

"They don't call them 'pubs' over there, they are called bars! And they're not as nice as our pubs either. But at least it was a place to get a beer."

"What about boys?" the girls asked.

Nicollette thought for a moment.

"Well, even though it's a small college, they do allow boys!" Nicollette answered sarcastically. "Not much to tell though," she continued, "the spring classes started just last week, so not enough time to get to know anyone. I did have a few dances though." The girls had a laugh.

"Now, before you tell me what is happening with you lot, let's refill those pints. On me."

"Not much happening here since you went away," Ashley stated. "I'm working at the pub, and I have applied at Uni. Hopefully, my marks are good enough."

"I took a small job at my uncle's warehouse in Stratford." Carol added. "I'm like a bookkeeper. I keep track of orders and inventories. Trucks coming in and out and the lot. It keeps me busy and because I'm family, I get paid well."

"Not like here," Ashley added.

Laughter. The evening was going well. Nicollette missed the time with her friends. Always a laugh or two and good gossip. She was excited to talk about her new job as Sports Liaison and her flat in Cheltenham. She would invite her friends over as soon as she could. It was nearing eleven and Nicollette noticed the crowd thinning out. The night's chilly air was entering the pub through the door as patrons were leaving. The combination of the day's events and the beer were beginning to take an effect on her.

"I think I should be getting home, Carol, you alright to drive?"

"No problem! It takes more than three pints to hold me back, but for you, I will take it slow."

The friends said goodnight and Nicollette thanked Ashley's mum for the drinks. Carol drove her home and to her credit, she drove slowly.

"Glad you are back, Nicky, we missed you."

Nicollette entered a quiet house. It was nearly midnight. Her parents must have gone to bed earlier. Later, in her bed, she thought about the day. How wonderful it was to be in her own bed, in her room, in her home. She thought about how nice it was to have such good friends as Carol and Ashley, and how she did not have to deal with George tonight. By instinct, she turned to say goodnight to Val, then realized her mistake and smiled. She drifted off to a deep sleep.

Nicollette awoke with a big stretch. Sudden panic! *Had she overslept her morning exercises? Sergeant Harris would have her head!*

Her eyes focused. She was home. Panic over. Nicollette realized that this was the second time she instinctively acted. She was not at Brize anymore, she was home. A quick glance at the clock on her dresser showed it was past ten. *Oh my gosh! Half the morning is gone.*

She dressed and headed downstairs.

"Good morning, Nicky. Thought we would let you sleep. How was last night? Did all go well?" her mum asked.

"I had a great time with Carol and Ashley. I guess I may have been overly worried about questions, but it wasn't too bad really. We had some laughs."

"And George?"

"He wasn't there last night."

"I'm sure you will see him around. Now how about something to eat?"

It was a dark and damp day outside. Too cold for a run or a walk. Nicollette was thinking this would be a good time to organize her belongings to get ready for her move. In her room, she turned on the radio and started through her cabinets. She was making good progress when her father yelled up the stairs that she had a call. Nicollette went down the stairs and into the kitchen. Her Mum was cooking Sunday dinner and the kitchen smelled wonderful again. She picked up the receiver.

"Hello?"

It was Val.

"How was your first day home? Did you sleep late? How about your folks?"

Before she realized it, Nicollette had been on the phone for nearly an hour. They planned to meet up for lunch on Tuesday and include their parents.

Nicollette hung up the receiver. She looked at her mum.

"That was Val, my roommate. Her flat is in the same building as mine. She and her mum are going to join us on Tuesday for lunch. I can't wait for us to get together."

# Cheltenham

Nicollette had set her alarm for eight o'clock but had woken naturally, nearly an hour earlier. *I am still waking up for Sergeant Harris!* No lie in today, too much to do. Her mum was already in the kitchen and there was a pot of tea on the table, her father had just left for work.

"Sleep good, Nicky?" Alice asked.

"I never knew how much I missed my bed, Mum. All the lumps are in the right place!" They laughed.

"If you want, you can take your bed to the flat. Your Dad can organize transport."

"Maybe."

"What's on for today?"

"The weather doesn't look too bad, so I thought a run down the village. Must stay in shape, Mum."

The air was crisp and the sky clear as Nicollette headed down to the village. This was the first time in a month that she would be running outside. Quite a difference from the morning routine at Brize. Heading into the village, Nicollette saw that all the holiday decorations were gone. Now there were posters for the spring fete. All else looked the same. The buildings, the people, the single traffic light. Her legs felt good, and she noticed her pace was faster. Breathing was easier. She felt stronger. As she turned and headed up the village back towards home, Nicollette saw the War Memorial like she had seen hundreds of times before. Something inside her made her stop at the statue. As she looked at the memorial, she thought back at her time at Brize and the soldiers and civilians she encountered there. Any one of them could end up with their name on a memorial. They were all willing to pay the ultimate price for the protection of freedom and a way of life. She realized that in a small way, she was now going to be a part of that continuing work that these brave soldiers, now just names on a plaque, had paid their lives for. With that thought, a warm feeling arose from within her. A feeling of usefulness and purpose. Destiny. It was as if those names on the plaque were calling her. Encouraging her. Thanking her. Nicollette realized at that moment, any lingering doubts that she may have had about her future were going away. She reached out and touched the plaque bearing the names of the fallen and whispered, "Thank you!" Confident and strong, she sprinted home.

A cup of tea. Now more packing. An inventory of twenty years of life. Nicollette and her mum had some laughs and a few tears as they went through her room. Pictures, school projects, and old clothes. Her favorite doll and stuffed animals, now left for her two nieces to love. Another cup of tea, Alice started a list of essentials.

"Tomorrow will be a busy day, we must be organized and prepared, there's not a lot of time to waste if we are going to get you moved in on time," she said.

Carol called just after tea and invited Nicollette for a pint. She looked at her parents in the small living room. Her mum knitting and her father reading the Times. There was a fire in the small coal fireplace. She told Carol that she would like to spend the evening home, after all, she would be on her own in a couple of days.

Nicollette remembered a bottle of wine in the cabinet. She retrieved three glasses. Later in bed, Nicollette thought about the evening, the warm fire, the good wine, her loving parents and the safety and security of her house. Tomorrow was a big day for her. Her own flat, a new career and new challenges, but despite all the changes in her life, this house would always be home.

It was about a forty-five-minute drive to the flat in Cheltenham. Nicollette noticed a number of nondescript office buildings that were set well off the road. There was a wrought iron fence in the front and a large, guarded gateway entrance. She noticed several guards checking each car as it entered through the gate. Her father turned down the street to the address where her flat was. The street was tree lined with large oak trees that partially hid the buildings on either side. James parked the car in front of one of the buildings.

"We're here, Nicky! Let's see your new flat."

Nicollette used her ID badge to swipe the card reader mounted on the side. The front door unlocked. Her flat was on the third floor. They walked up the stairs and found the flat number. Nicollette opened the door to reveal her new home.

"Wow, Nicky! This is really nice!" her mum commented as they walked inside.

The flat was freshly painted and there was new carpeting throughout. There was a large living area and a sliding door that led to a balcony. The balcony overlooked a grassy courtyard between two other buildings. The kitchen was about the same size as the one in Brockwirth.

"Central heating, Nicky," James announced.

There was a dining area and a short hall to her bedroom.

"It's enormous!" Nicollette shouted as they walked in. "It must be five times bigger than my room in Brockwirth!"

There were two closets and a large window with curtains.

"Plenty of space for all my things," Nicollette announced.

They investigated the bathroom. It was large enough for her needs and she was pleasantly surprised to see a fitted shower above the bathtub. There were a few pieces of furniture around. There was a sofa and matching chair in the living room and a small table with four chairs in the kitchen. There was an oak dresser with a mirror and a matching bed in the bedroom. Nicollette found the keys to the flat by the kitchen sink. There was a note attached to the keys. The note welcomed her to the building and gave her some instructions for the appliances. At the bottom of the note was her new phone number and tele license number. Her father was already unloading the car bringing bags and boxes into the living room.

"Sit down, James. We need to coordinate our shopping." Alice placed her list on the table.

"What time are we meeting your friends, Nicky?"

"We decided on Pizza Hut at 12:30."

"Well, it's nearly half past ten, so we better get started." Alice took control. "Let's get the rest of your things in and then head out."

It was just half twelve when they walked into Pizza Hut. Nicollette saw Val in the corner. It felt as if they hadn't seen each other for a long time even though it was only a couple of days.

"Hey, you lot! Mind if we join you?"

"Sarah!" Nicollette exclaimed.

"It's a reunion! Great to see you! Have you heard from Peg?"

"She's coming early tomorrow," Val answered, "a bit delayed, I'm afraid."

"We'll help her out, no problem," Sarah announced.

Introductions made with the parents and pizza order-ed. Val announced that her flat was on the second floor and Sarah's on the first floor of Nicollette's building. They hoped that Peg's would be close to make the group com-plete. The young women talked of their flats and all the shopping. Nicollette told how she was able to secure a mattress and a tele in the morning. They both would be delivered at five today. Val and Sarah each had successes as well. It was nearly two. More shopping to do. Phone numbers exchanged. Catch up later. Busy afternoon. Household goods. Kitchenware. Linens, towels and gro-ceries. It was nearly five when Nicollette and her parents returned to the flat. The delivery van was already parked outside her building.

"Three deliveries here, miss," one of the delivery men said to Nicollette as she opened the door.

"Val and Peg must have gone to the same store!" She chuckled.

By six-thirty, her flat was taking shape. Her bed was

made, clothes put away, and food in the fridge. There was still the kitchen to organize and some more bits to buy, but there was tomorrow. James turned on the tele.

"Tele works, Nicky."

"Thanks, Dad."

Nicollette did an accounting of her expenses. She had spent almost 300 pounds. *Thank goodness for the allowance*, she thought.

"I noticed a pub at the end of the street," her father announced. "How about a pub dinner?"

"Sounds good to me. I could use a pint. How about you, Mum?"

"Good by me."

It was after nine when they returned to the flat. Nicollette said goodnight to her parents and asked them to call when they got back to Brockwirth. As she walked the stairs to her flat, a voice called out to her, "Time for a nightcap?"

Nicollette turned to see Val holding a pack of beer.

"Sure. Not too late though."

Val walked into Nicollette's flat.

"I love what you've done with the place, darling!" she exclaimed in a mock posh voice.

It was nearly midnight when Val left, the beer long gone. Nicollette set her alarm. Mum was coming mid-morning to help finish organizing. *I must meet her at the bus stop.*

Her own shower. Plenty of hot water. A luxury. Quick breakfast. The bus stop was a couple of blocks away. Luckily, it was a bright day. Nicollette met her mum and they walked back to the flat.

"Cup of tea, Mum?"

"Please, Nicky."

She put her new tea kettle on the stove.

"First cup of tea in my flat, Mum, and I'm glad I'm having it with you!"

A knock on the door.

"Peg! You're here. Come in, I just made a pot of tea!"

"Love to Nicky, but we are unloading. Just wanted to pop by and say hello."

"Where's your flat?"

"I'm on the second floor near Val. Here is my number. Let's get together later. Big day ahead, must dash."

"See you later, Peg."

Nicollette returned to the kitchen. Her mum was already at work organizing.

In the late afternoon, Alice was able to catch the bus to Brockwirth, about an hour's bus ride away. Her mum had worked hard, and the flat was clean and organized. Nicollette locked the door as she left the flat, her flat, her place, almost hard to believe, she thought, but true. She went down the stairs to Val's. It was good to be together with the group again. Fish and chips from around the corner. Cokes from the local. No beer tonight, big day tomorrow.

"Are you excited for our first day, ladies?" Sarah asked.

"And nervous," Peg responded. "I doubt I'll sleep tonight."

"I think we will be alright," Nicollette said. "We're still in training really. No heavy things for a while, I would imagine."

"Plus, no Sergeant Harris at 06:30 hours!" Val concluded.

It was an early evening. They would meet at Peg's flat at seven and walk to work together. There was a chat about what each would wear. The weather report was chilly but clear. A brisk couple of blocks to the gate, then the first day. *The first day*, Nicollette thought to herself as she went off to sleep. *Tomorrow is my first day.*

# The First Day

Nicollette awoke from a restless sleep before the alarm clock could do its job. A combination of excitement, anxiety, and apprehension made an interesting mixture of emotions in her mind. *My first day! A new start! My new life!* The hot shower revitalized her and helped, at least temporarily, as she poured a cup of tea and ate a piece of dry toast. While dressing, Nicollette took a hard look at herself in the mirror.

*Look at yourself, girl! You're all grown up and have accomplished so much in such a short period of time! Be proud of yourself, Nicky!* Nicollette could see a smile crossing her face in the mirror's reflection as she was applying a small amount of makeup. Her hair looked good, and the new dress fit her well. *Not bad for the first day!* As she was leaving, Nicollette looked out of the large window in the sitting room, the sun was just lifting the early morning shadows away. *Just like me, a new day.* Nicollette grabbed her coat and brolly. *Mum always said to be prepared.*

Nicollette knocked on Peg's door.

"Morning, Nicky! Big day today!"

"Good morning, Peg, and yes, it sure is!!"

Nicollette walked into the flat to see Val and Sarah standing with a cup of tea in their hands, each of them eyeing the others up and down, like sisters heading off

A NASTY BUSINESS

to the ball. "How do we look, ladies?" Val asked.

"I think we'll pass," Sarah chuckled. "It's after seven, grab your brollys, ladies."

Nicollette did not mind the walk to the Iron Gate entrance. *It's still shorter than my ride to Russell's, a lifetime ago,* she thought. The four of them tried to make small talk as a way to take their minds off of what was about to happen, but as the Iron Gate came into view, the chatter stopped, and eyes became focused. Nicollette could feel her heart starting to pound heavy in her chest as they approached the guardhouse. There were four soldiers checking passes. Nicollette reached into her case for her pass. Her hand was shaking as she tried to hold the pass steady, but to no avail.

"Good morning, miss," the soldier said to her as he examined the pass. "Lovely day today. Please wait here, Miss Beverley."

Nicollette's heart was now pounding feverishly. It felt as though it would pound right out of her chest. *What's happening? What's wrong? Why am I waiting?*

"Beverley!"

Nicollette turned to see a soldier motioning her to come to the guardhouse. As she started to walk towards him, the first soldier handed her pass back.

"Enjoy your first day, miss," he said with a smile.

The four of them were waiting in the guardhouse when a civilian arrived.

"Good morning, ladies. I've come to collect you. I'm your escort this morning."

"An escort! Wow!" Val said in excitement.

"Probably first day procedures. Don't get too excited," Sarah responded.

The four young women followed the escort. They walked across the entry road, down a path between a couple of buildings to a cement stairwell hidden in the back. The escort pressed some numbers on a dial and the door opened.

"Have a good day, misses!" the escort said as he left the women in the foyer. There was a security desk off to the side.

"Good morning, ladies. Please step over here," the man behind the desk called out. "Please let me see your passes." He read out, "Beverley, Davies, Green and Wilson." A voice from behind a corner just past the desk added, "Blankin."

"Lieutenant!" the four of them cried out simultaneously.

"Welcome to your new employer, everyone, follow me to our office."

As they were walking to their new office, Lieutenant Blankin turned to the ladies, "Don't get used to this service, it's your first day, tomorrow you will be on your own."

They came to a wooden double door. There was a sign at the side of the door.

"Group 228/157! Ladies, we are official," Nicollette exclaimed.

Inside the room, Nicollette, Val, Sarah and Peg were greeted by Major Hartwell, Captain Blasingame, and Sergeant Durban.

"Welcome, ladies! Good morning! Please take a seat," Major Hartwell instructed.

There was a conference table in the middle of the room.

"Welcome to group 228/157. This is where we will make a difference," she said emphatically. "This morning, we have some housekeeping to do and later, a tour of the facilities. Remember, you are still technically in training, so please follow all directions. Your ID badges must be worn at all times once you enter this facility, no excuses. Every morning or as duty calls, we will meet in this room for briefings and updates. We will use this room for the passing of ideas, for information and discussions. Any questions? None. Good. Ladies, let's get started. I have a feeling we are going to be put to use rather quickly. Lieutenant Blankin and Sergeant Durban will give you the tour."

Lieutenant Blankin opened the side door to reveal a large room with many desks. There was a buzzing noise permeating the room. There were a dozen or so steel desks, each with a tele screen, several phones, and a large binder. Nicollette found a desk with her name plate.

"Here's mine," she said, excited. "And here's yours, Val."

Peg and Sarah found seats. Sergeant Durban and Lieutenant Blankin pointed out where they would be sitting. Major Hartwell and Captain Blasingame had offices behind a glass wall off to the left. Nicollette noticed there were no windows in the room, just like the room at SHAPE.

Nicollette slowly sat at her desk. The chair was comfortable and just the right height, as if it was custom made just for her. *Feels a lot better than my chair at Gordon Russell's!* She reached for her nameplate. "Nicollette Beverley, Intelligence Officer." She was official! Sergeant Durban motioned for the group to follow her into the computer lab. The buzzing sound was more prominent as they entered the lab. Several offices shared the computer area and there was a lot of activity happening. Sergeant Durban then led the group down several corridors and a stairway to a set of double steel doors. There were several armed guards posted at the entrance and three military policemen sitting at their desks. One by one, the ladies showed their passes and one of the MP's opened the door for them. Once inside, Nicollette's eyes went wide open.

"Ladies, welcome to the Oval," Sergeant Durban announced.

It was a cavernous room very similar to the "eye" at SHARP. Desks and screens, phones and headsets. The large movie screen at the front. Lots of people, military and civilian, shuffling about. A buzz of activity. Nicollette's heart started pounding as she thought about her time at the "eye." The prisoner exchanges. The shootings.

She snapped out of her thoughts as Sergeant Durban announced, "You may spend some time here in the future, but for now, you just need to know that this is where our information originates. Our 'hub' so to speak."

Sergeant Durban continued the tour, bringing the ladies to a security room where they were photographed and issued new, permanent badges. Nicollette thought her picture looked better on the new badge, her hair and makeup had held up through the exciting morning. She looked more mature, more professional. They walked back towards the group room, passing the cafeteria and break room.

"The cafe is open twenty-four hours and coffee and tea are free," Sergeant Durban said. "You can eat here quite reasonably as well."

Back in the group room, Captain Blasingame went over a list of procedures and protocols. She then brought them back into the computer room and had each young lady sign in with their new IDs. Headsets were put on and notepads at the ready. Captain Blasingame instructed each of them to turn to a particular frequency and calibrate their monitors. Nicollette followed the instructions. Suddenly, there was a steady stream of signals coming across her screen. Red for incoming and green for outgoing. She could hear through her headsets the coded messages, but they were too fast for her to keep up. Lieutenant Blankin motioned for all to remove their headsets.

"This may take you some time to get up to speed, but you'll get faster with practice."

In the afternoon, Lieutenant Blankin brought the group to a meeting room on the other side of the building. She told the group that there was a briefing going on inside. As they walked into the room, Lieutenant Blankin motioned for them to be very quiet and find seats against the wall.

Seated at a large conference table were a dozen men, half-military and half-civilian. Cigarette smoke was coming off the table. Nicollette looked around the room and she noticed that they were the only women in the room. Not one woman was sitting at the table. Nicollette listened closely as the men around the table discussed a cable decoded earlier in the morning that was sent by an agent in Bulgaria. There was an intense discussion about Soviet naval activity in the Black Sea. A map was being projected onto the front wall. There were aerial photos of ships and dry docks at Sevastopol in the Crimea. Nicollette remembered from Geography class that this was the Soviet Union's warm water port on the Black Sea. She also remembered that the Dardanelles Strait was the only exit and entrance to the Black Sea for the Soviet Union. The trouble for the Soviets is that the Strait was in Turkey, a NATO ally. The discussion continued about strategies. The officer at the head of the table announced that they would keep an eye on the situation and moved on to recent information received about Iran.

Sergeant Durban motioned that it was time to leave. Back in the group room, Major Hartwell introduced the group to Mr. Peter Johnson. Mr. Johnson was a cryptanalysis expert and would be spending time with the young women. By the day's end, Nicollette felt more comfortable with the decoding and coding process. Mr. Johnson was an excellent coach, still more work to do, but well on her way.

At five o'clock in the evening, everyone was called back to the group room. Captain Blasingame reviewed the day's events. She thanked Peter Johnson and invited him back in the morning. Captain Blasingame then asked for any questions. There was a short discussion. She then dismissed the group.

"Good job on your first day. There is still a great deal to learn, and I know we are on the right track. Big day tomorrow. Get some rest. See you in the morning."

"Goodnight, Captain Blasingame," Nicollette said as she

was leaving the room. Captain Blasingame thanked her and asked her to call her and any other women officers. "Ma'am."

"I'll remember that" Nicollette responded. "Goodnight, ma'am."

It had rained during the afternoon, making it a dark, damp walk home.

"What did you think of our first day, ladies?" Val asked the group.

"It was very interesting, but I think there is a lot more that's about to happen," Sarah responded.

"I don't know about you lot, but I'm rather tired after today," Peg added.

"Me too!" Nicollette voiced as they went past the gate into the dark, damp walk to the flats.

"Hello, Mum, it's Nicky!"

"Hello, Nicky! How was your first day?"

Nicollette remembered her promise to call after work. "Very interesting and still a lot more to learn."

Nicollette knew she had to be careful about what she could say to her parents, so she shifted the conversation to her flat and what she was having for tea. Nicollette wanted to talk to her father, but he was away at Swindon for the night. They would meet up in Cheltenham on Saturday.

Later in bed, Nicollette thought through her first day. So much to take in, so much to learn. What was in store for tomorrow? She fell fast asleep.

The group met at Peg's as they had planned. The weather was dry and chilly. The cold air felt invigorating against Nicollette's face as they walked past security at the Iron Gate and down the path to their building. The group walked into the briefing room at seven twenty.

Captain Blasingame entered the room with Peter Johnson.

"Good morning, ladies. We have lots to do today. Mr. Johnson is with us, and you will be training with him this morning. We will meet here after lunch. Have a good morning."

Captain Blasingame left the room as Nicollette, Val, Peg and Sarah followed Mr. Johnson to their desks in the computer room.

"Today, we will be live," Mr. Johnson announced. "We will be monitoring signals coming from the Balkans region. Specifically, Romania, Bulgaria, Yugoslavia and Albania. It is currently quiet in that region, so primarily, just standard communication protocols will be sent and returned."

Nicollette sat at her desk, put on her headphones, and switched on the monitor. Mr. Johnson looked over her shoulder as she recorded transmissions and relayed responses. She was becoming much more adept as the morning continued. The decoding and reply to techniques she had learned from Captain Murphy at Brize were now being put to use.

At the after-lunch briefing, Captain Blasingame handed out a red binder to the group. She explained that these binders were to be kept at their desks and never to leave the facility. Captain Blasingame instructed the group to open the binders as she talked about the resources, operations, and special services available to group 228/157. As she looked through the table of contents, Nicollette was amazed at the broad variety of services the group had at their disposal. She looked at Sarah as she read about the Chemistry Laboratory section.

"You'll be right at home there, Sarah," Nicollette whispered.

There were sections in the binder about armaments and munitions, special adaptations, and one that caught Nicollette's eye and curiosity, a section called "illusions." Captain Blasingame went through the catalog in detail. She pointed out that some of the resources were located right here on campus and others were located nearby. It was nearly four-thirty when Captain Blasingame finished. Her final comments on the binder stayed with Nicollette.

"I want to remind you again that all the information we've talked about this afternoon is strictly confidential. If group 228/157 needs to access any of these resources, it must be channeled through Major Hartwell or myself. No exceptions."

Captain Blasingame paused for a moment. She then had a short review of the last two day's activities and wished the group a good weekend.

"See you Monday morning."

# Weekend

It was a dark, chilly walk back to the flats. It was decided that a pub night was in order as a celebration of the first two days. Although it was only two days, Nicollette felt mentally exhausted. So much information was being thrown at her and still, there was much more to learn. Underneath it all, however, Nicollette was getting anxious to put some of her newfound skills to work, to become a real operative of the team. There was something in the way Captain Blasingame spoke to them before they left work that made Nicollette feel that the opportunity was getting close.

Saturday morning in her own flat. What a trail she had traveled, she thought. Nicollette felt a sense of pride and accomplishment as she looked out of her big window. *My own flat!* Val and Sarah were heading home, and Peg was having a quiet day. Nicollette was shopping and having lunch with her parents, then heading back to Brockwirth for the weekend. Although it was routine, she enjoyed the family shopping trips in Cheltenham and there were still some things on her list to buy, including her own groceries.

It had only been a couple of days since she last saw them, but it seemed like a special afternoon to be with her parents this Saturday. Nicollette felt like a different person walking in and out of the shops with her mum. She would always be their daughter, but today she felt more grown up, mature. A confident young woman. It was a great feeling. Nicollette followed her father into a car parts store. He was always quite handy around the house and car. Today's purchase was wiper blades. Nicollette wandered around the store. So many parts, so much to know, so much to learn. *Just like work!* she thought.

Nothing much ever changes in Brockwirth, one Saturday afternoon turns into another. Walking down the village for sausage rolls, Nicollette knew that no matter where she was, Brockwirth would always be home. She would never be a stranger here.

There was a new park located behind the Church on High Street and Nicollette could hear children's voices as she walked past the path leading there. She took a small detour down the path to see. The park was full of children having fun. Benches were filled with adults, some with strollers by their sides. It was like a scene from a painting. It brought a smile to Nicollette's face. Her beloved village was alive with youthful energy. As she turned to head back to the high street, two figures standing by the swings caught her eye. There was a man pushing a woman sitting on a swing. Nicollette could not quite make out if she knew them, but her curiosity rose when they stepped away from the swing and embraced in a kiss. *What a spectacle for the children to see in the park*, she thought. Suddenly, the man came into focus. It was George! Nicollette turned away and quickly walked towards home with mixed emotions. Should she be sad about losing a boyfriend or relieved that she knew what was going on with him? *Was it my fault? I know I didn't return his call before I left for training. Was I too busy or subconsciously trying to disconnect with him to focus on the training? Am I really that upset? Let it go, Nicky, let it go.* She gathered herself as she walked through the front door. Her voice broke up a bit as she announced, "Sausage rolls for tea."

As she was washing for tea, Nicollette took a hard look in the mirror. It was decision time. She promised herself to be above the Georges of the world. To be strong, confident, and selective in her relationships. She would focus on herself and career. She would grow from this and live under her own terms. Nicollette wiped a few tears from her face, gave one last smile in the mirror, and headed downstairs for tea.

Carol called and mentioned some of the field hockey team members were meeting in Pershoe. Nicollette thought an evening with friends would be just the medicine for the afternoon's events. Ashley was in the car when Carol picked her up. On the way, Nicollette told her friends about George. Surprisingly, she didn't feel so upset as she described what she saw in the park. Had she moved on already?

"Sounds like a pint for you, my brave girl," Ashley joked.

"Maybe two," Carol added.

Sunday lunch was delicious. Mum had really outdone herself. Roast beef and Yorkshire pudding. Mash and sprouts. Queen of Puddings for dessert. A meal fit for royalty. Plenty of leftovers for Nicollette to take home. As they were talking over lunch, Nicollette still detected a bit of angst in her parents. The uneasiness of their conversation with her and a hesitancy not to delve too deeply into her new life.

Back in her flat that evening, Nicollette called Val. *No answer, must not be back yet.* Same with Sarah. Peg was cleaning when Nicollette called.

"Have you eaten yet?" Nicollette asked.

"No and I'm famished."

Nicollette described her leftovers and Peg was soon in the flat having dinner. Val and Sarah arrived. They finished off the leftovers. Looking at the empty plates, Nicollette asked, "Doesn't anyone ever feed you lot? That's my dinner for the next couple of days you just ate!"

"Your mum is a very good cook, my mum can't make Yorkshires like that," Peg commented as she wiped the last Yorkshire pudding across the gravy on her plate.

Small talk, a cup of tea, and a few biscuits later, it was getting late. Monday morning wasn't that far away. They would meet at Peg's in the morning. Later, as she was falling asleep, Nicollette thought back to the weekend's events. There were her parents, George, her friends, the training and career. So much was happening and yet, she felt as if something even bigger was about to happen.

# The First Mission

The briefing room was full as Nicollette entered Monday morning. Major Hartwell, Captain Blasingame, Lieutenant Blankin and Sergeant Durban were all present as well as four people she hadn't seen before. Major Hartwell asked all to be seated. She welcomed and introduced the four guests: three civilians—Mr. Robert Illington, Mr. Louis Bensour, Mr. Benjamin Stokes—and a Royal Air Force Captain, Sean Mills. Nicollette looked at the four men. With their graying hair and receding hairlines, they all looked middle-aged, maybe in their late forties or early fifties.

Major Hartwell continued, "This morning, I received instructions from Colonel Baron that Group 228/157 is to assist in a special project code named Operation Twist. We have been assigned to work with these gentlemen to learn as well as assist."

Major Hartwell paused and looked directly at Nicollette, Valerie, Peg and Sarah and spoke in a soft but stern voice. "Ladies, you have worked very hard to get to this day. It is our first mission. We will be challenged to complete this assignment timely and successfully. There are many eyes watching us. Let us prove the doubters wrong."

Major Hartwell softened her tone and raised her eyes, "Now I want your full attention, Mr. Illington will give us the details of Operation Twist."

Nicollette's heart started to pound with excitement as pads were handed out for note taking. This is it, she thought. *All the training, all the work, all the effort leading up to now, her first mission.*

Mr. Illington stood from his seat at the table. He had a stoic, business like air about him. His voice was deep and monotone. Nicollette knew from his accent that he was an American. She also thought he was speaking in a slightly condescending manner, almost as if he did not want to be here and that he certainly did not want to work with the "B" team. *Or was it because we're women! Be that as it may,* she thought, *they will still have to work together to be successful.* Nicollette listened intensely.

"Good morning. I am Mr. Illington, and I am a Senior Operations Director for Joint American and British Intelligence. With us on Operation Twist are veteran linguist Mr. Bensour, a Senior Program Analyst, Mr. Stokes, and a Logistics Specialist, Captain Mills."

Mr. Illington pulled down a projection screen and placed a slide projector on the table. The lights were dimmed as he continued. The first slide was a map of the Black Sea.

"A quick geography lesson. The Black Sea is very strategic to the Soviets. Their main warm water port is located here at Sevastopol, on the Crimean Peninsula. They also have a smaller naval operation at Kerch, on the Kerch Strait. These are vital for Soviet commerce and operations in the Mediterranean and Middle East. The Soviets export agricultural products as well as petrochemicals and machinery from these ports and receive most of their sea delivered imports there as well."

Mr. Illington pointed to Turkey on the map.

"As you can see, the only route in and out of the Black Sea is through the Bosporus and the Dardanelles. This singular route, however, is in Turkish territory, a NATO ally. By treaty, the Soviets are allowed to use these waterways, assuming protocols are followed. They have to inform the Turks and NATO about all ships passing through the straits in both directions. It goes without saying that warships are not allowed. Like I said, the naval base at Kerch is small with no heavy assets."

He went to the next slide, a picture of several cargo ships lined up in a row.

"As you can imagine, there can be significant delays entering the Bosporus. So, the Soviets have teamed up with the Bulgarians to expand and update the Bulgarian port of Varna. With Bulgaria being firmly in the Soviet camp, they have increased the facilities capacities many fold. This makes good sense for the Soviets for three major reasons. First, Varna is only about a hundred miles from the Bosporus; secondly, the Soviets can reprioritize their shipping as needed; and thirdly, the Bulgarians are a more dependable ally than their northern neighbors in Romania." He paused then continued, "There may be a fourth reason, one that we are very interested in. They may be using Varna to transfer and rearrange cargoes. Bills of lading and freight registers are issued in Sevastopol, passed through Varna and on to the Turks. The Turks are notoriously bad with cargo inspections.

Hence, a perfect recipe for deception."

Next slide, a satellite view of Varna. Mr. Illington used his pointer to show imagery of the expanded facilities.

"There are many large warehouses and oil storage facilities and heavy infrastructure in the port area including roads, railways, and power distribution."

Next slide, another satellite view of Varna with much more detail.

"As you can see, Varna has become quite busy. Notice the number and length of the trains."

He pointed to long straight black lines crisscrossing the slide. Mr. Illington then pointed to large black dots and large black squares and rectangles on the next slide.

"Here are just some of the many additional storage facilities and oil storage tanks that have sprouted up in Varna."

Mr. Illington then asked for the lights to be turned on.

"Any questions? None. Good. Now you have a background on Varna, so let's talk about what we know."

He reached into his briefcase and handed out folders to everyone at the table and he laid a large three ring binder in the center of the table.

"Please open your folders."

Nicollette opened her folder to see a large black-and-white photograph of a uniformed officer. She thought he must be high ranking with all the ribbons and decorations on his uniform. The officer in the picture had a stern face with weathered features.

"The gentleman you are looking at is General Dimitar Lukanov and he is a favorite of General Secretary Todor

Zhivkov, the Dictator of Bulgaria. General Lukanov's official title is Director of the Port of Varna, but his real occupation is to serve as liaison between Zhivkov and the Soviets. It is his job to ensure the port operates to everyone's satisfaction. He does this by providing logistical and material support to the Soviets on demand. In return, the Soviets make sure Zhivkov stays in power. They provide financial, military, and intelligence support to Zhivkov and his government. Zhivkov and Lukanov's relationship goes back a long way. The two met during World War II when they were in the Bulgarian resistance movement against the Nazis. They became very close, and we have reason to believe that at some point, Zhivnov saved Lukanov's life. The Bulgarian resistance was supported by the Soviets with arms and logistics. Zhivkov and Lukanov met with Stalin on at least one occasion and at the end of the war, Zhivkov was the Soviet's choice to lead Bulgaria. So now we have a brief background. Any questions?"

Upon receiving no replies, Mr. Illington continued.

"Now, Mr. Stokes will talk about Operation Twist."

Nicollette took a brief look at her watch. It was nearly eleven, they had been sitting for nearly four hours.

"Good morning. I think before we detail Operation Twist, a short break is in order. Let us take fifteen minutes."

Mr. Stokes was British by his London accent, Nicollette concluded. The break was just what she needed. A stretch and a coffee. Her mind was whirling with information. She felt a strong curiosity about the mission and the role she would play. Nicollette looked at Val, Peg, and

Sarah and knew they were feeling the same by the look in their eyes. She took a deep relaxing breath as Mr. Stokes resumed the meeting.

"Let's talk about Operation Twist. A couple of years ago, through private channels, we were approached by Lukanov. As surprised as we were to hear from such a 'hardcore' Communist and supporter of Zhivkov, we responded with our interest in listening to him. Lukanov described his relationship with Zhivkov not in 'rosy' terms. He told us that on the surface, the two seemed to be inseparable but behind the scenes, as Zhivkov aged, the relationship was becoming coarse and hostile. Lukanov described Zhivkov as having a condescending relationship with him, constantly reminding him of who saved his life and that he, Zhivkov, controlled, no, owned Lukanov and expected and demanded complete loyalty and obedience. Lukanov told us he was becoming angry and resentful as his relationship with Zhivkov became more and more intolerable. He wanted to protect his interests and create some sort of 'security blanket.' We were apprehensive at first and very cautious, but over time, we slowly developed the relationship. Lukanov told us that he was not alone in loathing his boss. There were others in the inner circle of the Bulgarian government who felt the same way and that he, Lukanov, had a great deal of internal support if he wanted to dispose of Zhivkov and become the next head of the Bulgarian Government. He further 'spiced up' the deal by promising that once in power, he would 'tilt' towards the West like his northern neighbor, Romania. Maybe there was some resentment at Zhivkov being chosen over him by the Soviets to lead Bulgaria. Lukanov said he felt the future for Bulgaria was to escape Soviet domination and develop the country in western fashion and perhaps even join NATO. But and this is a big but, he wanted our tacit if not outward support and money. We were very intrigued by these overtures. The idea was very risky. Supporting an internal uprising and overthrow of the Bulgarian government could bring large Soviet reprisals. We were also at a disadvantage in Intelligence. We had no real way to confirm and verify what we were being told. Establishing assets in Bulgaria is a difficult task. Zhivkov was a staunch communist and was running a 'Stalinist' state. The secret police were everywhere. The country is in 'virtual lockdown' and we had very limited assets on the ground to build on, certainly no one placed well enough to verify Lukanov's story. So, we proceeded very slowly with Lukanov as he started to feed us small amounts of information. Little tidbits at first, but gradually we started receiving useful information about Soviet activity at Varna. We slowly but steadily gained his trust and in return, furnished him with cash. This gave us the time we needed to organize a small network in Varna and in the capital of Bulgaria, Sophia. We responded to his flow of information with more and more of a commitment to him, both emotionally and financially. We even supplied him some information, quite useless really, to solidify our commitment. This effort of trust building seemed to be working. In November, we received our biggest 'payday' when Lukanov informed us that the Soviets had been secretly transferring components of the S200 surface to air missile system to Varna. He explained that the Soviets had established a sophisticated transport system from the Ukraine to Varna through Yugoslavia and Romania. The Soviets incorporated rail, river, and road transport. Components are being broken down into small sections, completely undetected by our Intelligence. Once in Varna, these small sections are carefully concealed and loaded onto large dry bulk ships and tankers. The ships were issued Bills of Lading for the transport of grain and petroleum products. In addition, just in case the Turks became suspicious, special compartments were built into the ships to hide the components. The ships are then filled with the actual identified cargoes, covering the secret compartments, making it virtually impossible to find the illicit cargo. We also believe an additional layer of secrecy for the ships has been established by Lukanov in the form of bribery. He has family in Istanbul and they, surprisingly, work for the Turkish government's shipping division. Very convenient and easily influenced. Finally, by staggering the schedule, ships can pass easily through the Bosporus and Dardanelles and in the off chance the cargo was discovered in one of the ships, others can still sail through undetected. You may ask, why all the bother?"

Mr. Stokes took another sip of his tea and continued.

"Syria is the Soviets' main ally in the Middle East and the Syrians are desperate to shore up their air defense systems after their war with Israel in 1973. The Israeli

Air Force established air superiority a few days into the conflict and inflicted a beating on the Syrians. Consequently, the Syrians have been pressuring the Soviets for more sophisticated systems and armaments. The Soviets, for their part, are interested in growing the naval base at Tartus on the Syrian coast. Arms and influence trading for a bigger Soviet footprint in the region. Not a bad deal for either side. To sum it up, the port of Varna has been set up as a conduit for advanced armaments and material that will secretly end up in Syria. Our man, Dimitar Luvkov, is essentially the man in charge of that conduit."

Mr. Stokes drank the last of his tea. He then asked the group to turn to the next series of photos in the folders.

Val slid her chair closer as Nicollette pulled several 8½ by 11 black and white photographs from the folder. Nicollette then spread the photos out to get a better look.

"As you can see, despite the coarse relationship with his boss, Luvkov seems quite the happy man. Please look at the first picture."

Nicollette placed the picture on top of the stack. The picture was of Luvkov and an elegant looking blonde-haired woman. She looked younger than Luvkov.

"The woman in the picture is his wife, Anna. Luvkov met Anna Sidorov when they were in the resistance around 1944. She was seventeen and he was twenty-three. Despite their age difference and the constant danger, they fell in love. After the war they continued their relationship and were officially married in 1951. Next picture."

The next picture showed a family of four.

"This is a picture of Luvkov's family, his wife Anna, and their daughter Rosa, born in 1955 and who currently attends Technical University in Sofia. His son Peter, born in 1957, will attend the University of National and World Economy in Sofia in the fall."

Nicollette took a long look at the picture. Luvkov's children were near her in age. She wondered what kind of father he was. *What was it like growing up in a "privileged" household?* Her thoughts were interrupted by Mr. Stokes as he asked for the next group of photos. Nicollette pulled a series of photos from the folder. The first three pictures were of Luvkov's home. A large two-story mansion with a circular driveway, beautifully kept lawn and gardens. An iron gate surrounded the property. The rear of the home showed a tennis court and an inground pool and to the side of the house, a multi-car garage.

"Rank does have its privileges in Bulgaria. Luvkov lives very well indeed. He has all the trappings of an elite bureaucrat. He also has some expensive hobbies as well."

Nicollette pulled the next group of photos from the folder.

"He is an avid skier and travels to his chalet almost every weekend."

Nicollette looked at a photo of Luvkov standing with his skis in front of his chalet. She noticed he was smiling, a happy family man. The next photo was of his chalet. A wooden structure with many windows and a double garage attached. The next photos were of his automobiles.

"Luvkov loves his automobiles. As you can see by the

photograph, he has four—three Mercedes and a Toyota. He uses the larger Mercedes sedans for his work and family travel as well as his trips to the chalet. Anna drives the smaller sedan. The Toyota and the Mercedes convertible are for pleasure. Luvkov employs two chauffeurs. He is quite protective of his automobiles and demands they are cleaned almost daily."

Nicollette looked at the cars. A far cry from the small sedan her father had. Excess for the elite, she thought.

"The next group of photos are very interesting," Mr. Stokes went on.

Nicollette looked at a picture of a dark, long-haired, shapely woman.

"This is Lyubina Sarac, Luvkov's mistress. She is thirty-three years old and lives in Sofia. Sarac is Luvkov's personal assistant and travel companion. She started working for him almost four years ago and their 'special' relationship started after about a year. We are working on getting more information on her. We do know that she was born to a working-class family in Sofia. It is not uncommon for the ruling elite to have at least one mistress. We are not sure how much the family knows about the affair. So, there you have it. Dimitar Luvkov is deeply involved with Soviet deception at the port of Varna. He is a well-placed elite bureaucrat in the Zhivkov government. He has opened a dialogue with us, and he continues to provide useful information in exchange for money and tacit support for his potential takeover of the government. He has become our highest ranking and most important contact behind the

Iron Curtain. And now, ladies," Mr. Stokes paused for effect, "we have to kill him."

# A Nasty Business

Nicollette's eyes were wide open. Her heart was beating through her chest as she tried to catch her breath. Mr. Stokes's last comment had taken the air out of her lungs. *A murder! Why would they want to kill Lukanov? All the time and effort being spent on him. All the useful information he is providing! He's a family man with children. Certainly, they could do something other than kill him! And what about the future?* These thoughts were racing through Nicollette's mind as she slowly regained her composure. She looked at Val. Val's complexion was chalky and white. Her eyes were wide open, and she did not blink.

"Breathe, Val, breathe," Nicollette whispered as she turned to the stack of pictures in front of her. She started to look through them again when Mr. Stokes addressed the group.

"Now that we have a background on our man Luvkov, let's address why we need to eliminate him."

Mr. Stokes paused to gain everyone's attention.

"On the surface, it appears that we have established a very well-placed operative at the highest levels of government in Bulgaria. Luvkov's information has been reliable and beneficial, and his intentions are believable. We know he has a rather lavish lifestyle for a poor country. How does he afford it without raising his boss's suspicions?"

Mr. Stokes reached for a paper in front of him. He held it up for all to see.

"Our payments to Luvkov are paid directly to a Swiss bank account. We monitor the account very closely and we know there have been no transactions other than our deposits. Is he hedging his bets in Bulgaria by having a fallback in Switzerland or is he planning something else?"

Mr. Stokes reached into his dossier and pulled out another small stack of papers and pictures and continued.

"We believe we have some answers. While we have been developing our relationship with Luvkov, we have also been working on establishing assets on the ground. As we have stated earlier, Bulgaria is a difficult place to work, however, we have been able to establish a modest cell."

Mr. Stokes pulled a picture from the stack of papers and passed it around the table.

"This is a picture of Teodore Popov. He is one of the two chauffeurs employed by Luvkov. He is also in charge of the maintenance and upkeep of the automobiles and general handyman around the Luvkov estate. Teodore is thirty years old, single, and lives with his mother Simone and stepfather in Sofia. His background is very interesting. He is the only child of Pavla and Ivan Popov. He is a quiet, very nondescript man and very loyal to his boss and the ruling Communist Party. So how were we able to 'flip' him? In September 1944, the Russians were about to liberate Bulgaria from the Nazis. At that time, Pavla and Ivan were married and members of the resistance. Ivan was a priest and with a small group of fellow priests, would travel with the resistance fighters. This small group was not involved with the fighting per se, but rather served as a connection between the resistance and the Bulgarian Orthodox Church. In September 1944, as the Nazis were retreating, the resistance fighters that Ivan and Pavla were traveling with captured a squad of German soldiers. That evening, a drunken massacre of the prisoners started. When Ivan and a couple of the other priests tried to stop it, they were shot too. Hearing all the noise, Pavla, who was five months pregnant at the time, rushed to see what was happening and arrived to see her husband murdered. She and another priest ran away that night. They made their way back to Sofia where she gave birth to Teodore in 1945. Fearing postwar reprisals, she changed her name to Simone and married a railroad engineer in 1948. Teodore had a normal upbringing. He went to school, served in the military, and developed an interest in automobiles. When he asked his mother about his real father, Simone would just say he died in the war. In the military, he was trained as a mechanic and when he finished his duty in 1970, he was assigned to Luvkov as personal chauffeur. Now, how did we put this together?"

Mr. Stokes took a sip of water, just as there was a knock on the door. Sergeant Durban opened the door and two uniformed men wheeled carts into the room containing sandwiches and drinks. Mr. Stokes called for a break.

Nicollette looked at her watch, it was nearly half one. The morning had flown by! She did not feel hungry, but the sight of the sandwiches on the cart soon changed that. As she was walking to the cart, she noticed the picture of Teodore on the table. She took a closer look. He was a handsome man, with dark curly hair and a firm jaw. His skin was smooth, and he had a boyish grin. Nicollette took a long look at his eyes. They were deeply set in his face. She thought they told a story of uneasiness and sadness, reaching out for some sort of stability.

It was past two when lunch was finished. Nicollette looked at her notepad. She hadn't taken notes like this in a long time. The pages were filled. Mr. Illington and Mr. Stokes's words were as clear in her notes as if she was hearing the two men all over again. Mr. Stokes stood from his chair and continued.

"Now where were we? Yes. How did we put this altogether? Here is where the story gets very interesting. Remember the priest that ran away with Pavla? Well, during all these years, he kept in touch with Pavla, now called Simone. Just before he died, he gave her a diary he kept during the war. The priest's diary was very detailed, including the night of the massacre and the post war days in Sofia. He asked that she keep it safe, but he wanted the story of his time with the resistance during the war to be made public after his death. The priest could then pass on with a clear conscience. Pavla, I mean Simone, made a plan. Because she was the wife of a now senior railroad engineer, she had some 'free' range to travel into Greece for shopping and the odd weekend away. While in Greece, she would secretly make contact with a writer she met through a local bookseller. She was nervous at first, but by her third trip, a direct connection with the writer was made. Through a series of contacts, and we have many connections in Greece, we became aware of the diary and of Simone and Teodore's relationships. We asked Simone to bring her son with her on the fourth trip. Under the guise of a 'mother and son' weekend in Athens, they left Bulgaria and we met them at a prearranged location to discuss publication of the diary. Simone introduced us as British historical writers and publishers to her son. We were able to communicate because one of the men at that meeting was our Mr. Bensour, the linguist with us today. Simone told her son about the diary and the true story about Teodore's father. She asked him to read the diary while they were in Athens. He refused. Didn't he want to know the truth about his father? At first, he was very hostile and did not believe a word of what we were saying. We pressed harder and again asked him to read the diary. He finally reluctantly agreed, and we arranged to meet the next day. When we saw him the next day, his attitude had changed. He was very inquisitive. He asked many questions. His mother painfully recalled to her son that fateful night in detail. There were tears and anger. How could his mother hide the truth from him all these years? The deception? The falsehoods? As we talked, his anger and resentment grew. You see, according to the diary, Luvkov, Teodore's boss and hero, was with the fighters on the night of the massacre and did nothing to stop it! Luvkov was involved with his father's murder! According to the diary, Luvkov could have prevented the murders, but looked the other way. Teodore, his anger and resentment now at a boiling level, could not believe that a man he had come to respect and admire both as his employer and as a leading government official, could be involved in a massacre of unarmed prisoners and the killing of several priests. Worst of all, Luvkov could have prevented the murder of his father. At this point, we identified to Simone and Teodore that we were Intelligence Officers and that we needed their assistance."

There was a deafening silence in the room. The tension in the air was as thick as pea soup. Nicollette could feel her hands and legs shake with anxiety as her emotions hung on every word of the story Mr. Stokes was telling.

Mr. Stokes took a sip of his tea and calmly continued.

"As you can imagine, Simone and Teodore were in a state of disbelief. They kept asking us questions. British Intelligence? What was going on? What did we want with the two of them? We tried to answer the questions as simply and clearly as possible. We pressed the question about their help a little harder, we did not want to appear desperate and wanted to leave a way out for them. Simone and Teodore asked to be alone. We left the room. After about twenty minutes, with tears flowing down his cheeks and his voice straining to be heard, Teodore, a fiercely loyal Communist and an employee of his father's murderer, agreed to work with us. We had our plant! We put to rest Teodore's concerns about his mother's safety. With her son's concerns about her abated, Simone agreed to work with us as well. This was nearly two years ago. We instructed Simone and Teodore to remain low key and that information was to be passed through Simone to our 'bookseller' in Athens. No one, not even her husband, was to know about this. She would take her normal trips on the train. Nothing more, nothing less. In the meantime, we were able to establish a small group of other contacts in Bulgaria. This gave us additional channels of information in the event the railroad was shut down. The information started to flow. At first, trivial bits about Luvkov's life and family, the same information we have shared with you. We found out about his relationship with Zhivkov, the Soviets, the Turks and Varna. Jackpot!"

Mr. Stokes paused for another sip of his tea. Nicollette had stopped taking detailed notes, preferring to focus all her energies on listening to Mr. Stokes. *How can Mr. Stokes be so calm? I feel like I am watching a "spy" movie except, I am actually in it!*

"Teodore passed on information about Lyubina Sarac, Luvkov's personal companion and mistress. We were now able to do deeper research on her. Sarac is not who she really is. Our people discovered she was an alcoholic prostitute in Moscow. She had some very important clients. Realizing that this could prove embarrassing to some high-ranking Soviet officials, Sarac was caught and arrested. She agreed to remain silent under penalty of death and was sent to a rehabilitation camp. When she became sober, her jail keepers realized she was an educated, well-versed women, quite unlike her fellow sex workers. They gave her administrative jobs at the camp and slowly, Sarac gained the trust of her keepers. The KGB became interested in her. She would make a useful tool, so they put her into special training. About this time the KGB wanted some insurance on Luvkov. The Soviets needed to protect their interests in Varna and Bulgaria. They knew that Luvkov had an eye for attractive women and Sarac checked all the boxes. Sarac was sent to Sofia. She would be a direct set of eyes and ears on Luvkov. With the help of the Bulgarian State Intelligence Agency, the SIA, she received a new name and background. She became Luvkov's personal assistant, a gift from his friend Zhivkov and soon thereafter, she became Luvkov's mistress. The Soviets now had their plant."

Mr. Stokes took a moment. He had been speaking for some time now. He finished his tea and sat down. Nicollette stretched in her seat. This briefing continued to feel like a spy movie. Twists and turns at every corner. Espionage and counter espionage, with one major exception, it was not a movie or book, it was real, and she was living it.

Mr. Illington continued.

"Now let us get to the core of Operation Twist, the elimination of Dimitar Luvkov. It seems Luvkov has loose lips in moments of passion. He has told Sarac about his anger with Zhivkov and his desire to have an internal coup. He believes he would make a better leader for Bulgaria. He has told her about leaving for Switzerland while the coup unfolded. If the coup were successful, they could lead Bulgaria together and if it failed, they would be very comfortable living together in Switzerland. Of course, Sarac has passed this information to the KGB and SIA. Despite his efficiency in running the port of Varna,

Luvkov is becoming very expensive in their eyes. The Soviets are keenly aware of a shipment of minor missile parts recently caught by the Turks. Even though it was only the one time, it was still very embarrassing to the Soviets and could have ruined their whole operation in Varna. But it seems Luvkov still has some value to the Soviets. The Soviets are always looking to strengthen their ties to the leaders of their satellite nations, and they want to cover all possibilities. If they are unable to stop a Luvkov coup, the Soviets want to maintain a firm relationship with Luvkov and Bulgaria. Varna and Bulgaria are very important to them. We know the KGB is evaluating the information they receive from Sarac and it is just a matter of time before they discover our involvement. Then the whole house of cards will fall, and we will become the embarrassed party! Our credibility in the region will be shot and there will be serious repercussions. The Soviets could use this discovery to endanger our operations elsewhere, putting years of work at risk, or even worse. Therefore, Luvkov must go."

Mr. Illington sat down. Nicollette finished her now cold tea. Her mouth had felt as if she was eating cotton balls. She never liked cold tea, after all, tea was meant to be swallowed hot. Nicollette eyed the tea urn on the cart. She would love a hot cup of tea but dared not to be the first to get up. Nicollette wasn't even sure if she could get out of her chair. Her legs were numb from sitting. Lieutenant Blankin came to the rescue as she left the table and helped herself to a cup. Nicollette followed and soon it was an undeclared tea break. Sarah, Peg and

Val all joined Nicollette.

"It's like a spy movie," Sarah said to the group.

"And we are the spies!" Val responded.

Nicollette had that same thought earlier and was glad her friends were feeling the same. Peg, however, was very quiet, almost still trying to digest what was happening around her. She was drinking her tea very deliberately and Nicollette noticed a slight shaking of her cup as she raised it to drink. *Nerves. We're all a bundle of nerves!* Nicollette thought as Mr. Stokes asked everyone to return to their seats. *I guess we all will soon get used to it!* Once everyone was seated, Mr. Stokes continued the briefing.

"So, there we have it. We need to eliminate Luvkov. Our Intelligence estimates we have about a week before the KGB and SIA discover our involvement and the pro-verbial dung hits the fan. So, our challenge is to make the death of Luvkov look like an accident, not a delib-erate hit. And we must beat the Soviets to it. We need to be creative with no possible trail back to us. We are already working on extricating Simone and Teodore out of Bulgaria. Let us see what we can come up with in a hurry. Captain Mills is here with any logistical concerns and Mr. Bensour can help with any linguistic issues. Let's get to work, ladies. The table is open for discussion."

With that, Mr. Stokes sat down. Major Hartwell walked around the table. She placed a hand on Nicollette's shoul-der and spoke to her team.

"Let's get this done, ladies. We have the resources, and you have the talent. Think 'outside the box.' Let us talk it out."

It was a serious discussion. The usual ideas—poison, explosives, shooting and the like. Nicollette kept being drawn back to the photos of Luvkov and his family. The houses and his cars. It was well past six when the major asked all to go home and get a good rest for a fresh start tomorrow.

"It's time to leave, Nicky," Val whispered in her ear.

"You lot go on. I want to look at these pictures some more. I won't be long, I promise."

"Ok, not too long, it's dark outside. Check in with me when you get home."

Nicollette focused on the pictures again. *The answer is here waiting for me*, she thought. *I just need to look harder. Concentrate, Nicky!* The family. The homes. The life. She kept shifting the photos. Focus.

A hand on her shoulder broke her concentration.

"You really do need to go home now, Miss Beverley."

It was Captain Blasingame.

"I have been watching you since your friends left nearly thirty minutes ago. Give it a rest, we will pick it up tomorrow. I'll drive you home."

Nicollette looked at her watch. It was half past six. "I guess it's time. Thank you for the ride."

In her flat, Nicollette made herself comfortable. She put on the gas stove to make some soup. There was that slight lingering sulfur smell that always happens when the gas stove first ignited. *Nuisance*, Nicollette thought, *maybe an electric range next time.*

She lit a scented candle she kept in the kitchen to mask the remains of the sulphuric smell of the gas. She toasted a couple of slices of bread, poured her soup and sat in front of the tele. Tomato soup, her favorite, with hot crusty bread. Perfect. A cold Vento to wash it down. She liked the flavor of the Vento and the bubbles tickled her throat as she swallowed.

She was staring at the tele, watching but not seeing. Her thoughts kept going back to the pictures of Luvkov. When she finally did focus, an advertisement was playing showing the virtues of using a weed killer that was packaged in a container that had an attached wand. The user could then feel safe using the wand to avoid contact with the poison. Not for her though. She lived in a flat, no garden to attend to. It was nearly half ten. She had dozed off. She dragged herself to bed.

The alarm went off as usual. Nicollette readied herself. She checked the mirror as she was leaving. Her make-up was a little uneven, so she went back to her room to finish it. On top of her dresser was a tray of scent. She forgot that as well. A little splash and a little cotton wool and she was ready to go. Val, Sarah, and Peg were waiting for her. The walk was brisk. It was a cold February day. There were flurries coming down.

"How'd you lot sleep last night?" Sarah asked.

"Like a baby," Peg responded, "I was tired."

"Me too," Val added. "You, Nicky?"

"I fell asleep in front of the tele."

Inside the meeting room, Major Hartwell asked if everyone was rested and ready for work. There was no tea this morning, so Nicollette poured a coffee. She was not much of a coffee fan, but the smell enticed her. The discussion started and ideas were shared. Lieutenant Blankin made notes on large pieces of paper attached to an easel. Nicollette asked for the photos again. She remembered how particular Luvkov was with his cars, how clean and tidy they had to be. She thought of Teodore and the pressure he must face. She looked at the photo of the large Mercedes, the traveling car. She asked for a magnifying glass. Nothing unusual there. She looked at the Mercedes photo again. At second glance, something in the back window caught her eye. She stared intently at the object. It looked like a crown-shaped air freshener, just like the one she saw in the auto parts store when she was with her father. Nicollette remembered how distinctive the crown looked and how the scent would freshen any car. Her mind started to race. She wrote feverishly on her notepad. The gas from the stove. The candle. The weed killer advertisement. The Vento bubbles tickling her throat. Her splash of scent this morning. The Mercedes. Luvkov's weekend trips to the ski chalet. Teodore. All the pieces of the puzzle were there right in front of her. She just needed to put them together. *Think, Nicky, think*, she thought to herself.

Major Hartwell could not help but notice how intense Nicollette was working. She watched her writing notes and drawing lines on her pad, occasionally looking up at the ceiling to think. The Major walked over to Nicollette and sat down next to her.

"What are you working on, Nicollette?"

Nicollette turned to the major. "I have put together my

notes. I believe there is a plan right here in these notes. Like a puzzle, I just need to put the pieces together." She looked back at the pad, then at the major, then back at the pad. "I think I have solved the puzzle!" Nicollette exclaimed. "I have an idea."

"Tell me about your idea," the major asked.

Nicollette briefly explained her plan to the major. The Major then called for Captain Mills.

"Do we have a map of the route that Luvkov takes to get to his Chalet?"

"I believe so, Major."

"Good, bring it here, Nicollette has a plan."

Captain Mills contacted his office and within ten minutes, a civilian laid the maps across the table. Major Hartwell continued her conversation with Nicollette. The plan was becoming more crystalized as Nicollette, and the major talked.

"I think it's time we offer your plan up for discussion," Major Hartwell whispered to Nicollette.

Major Hartwell stood up and announced to the group that Nicollette had a plan to share. Nicollette was nervous and her heart was racing. Her idea was creative to say the least and now she had to talk about it in front of the seasoned professionals around her. *What if they laughed at her? Would they think she had a big imagination, maybe too creative? Even overstepping her position. Too young?*

Val patted Nicky's back and Sarah gave her some words of encouragement. Nicollette took a deep breath.

"My idea came to me this morning. As Mr. Illington explained yesterday, Mr. Luvkov loves his cars and is very demanding about their cleanliness and appearance. I noticed in the photo of the Mercedes that he uses for travel, there was a crowned-shaped air freshener in the rear shelf of the car. This air freshener is just like the ones I saw in town when I went to the auto parts store with my father. Maybe we can use that air freshener to deliver some sort of poison that could be mixed into the scent. Luvkov and his driver would succumb to the poison by breathing it. They would quickly be eliminated. The car would crash and explode, leaving no trace of the poison. It would be an accident. Driver error. No evidence and an autopsy would be fruitless."

Nicollette paused for a moment and thought about what she had just said. The word "eliminated." Was it just a sterile word for murder? Was she getting cold and callused? She took a breath. No time for that kind of thinking now. She was doing her job.

"All the pieces are in place. We use Teodore to place the crown in the Mercedes. It must be a time when he is not the driver, of course. He waves goodbye to Luvkov. The deed is done. We then extricate Teodore and his mother."

Nicollette stopped and looked at the faces around the room for reactions. Nothing, just blank stares. A chill ran up her back. *They are about to laugh at me,* she thought. The silence was deafening. Major Hartwell glanced at Nicollette then at the group around the table.

"I like it!" she exclaimed. "It's a simple idea. It will take some work. But simple. I think we can pull it off. Let us look at that map."

The civilian who brought the maps to the room showed

the group the route Luvkov would travel from his home in Sofia to his chalet in Bansko. He explained the trip was about 170 kilometers and would take a little less than three hours. He pointed out the most treacherous part of the trip would be about an hour from his home in Sophia.

"That is where the road is winding with steep ascents and descents," he explained.

"So, we have about an hour," Major Hartwell announced. "Now for the crown. Sergeant Durban, go with one of the guards to the auto parts store in town to pick up at least a dozen of those crown air fresheners. Captain Mills will issue a requisition. Mr. Stokes, I need a poison expert and a chemist here by 13:00 hours. We will also need a meteorologist and a seven-day weather forecast for Sofia and Bansko. Mr. Bensour, we need to send a 'standby' message to Teodore."

The room was in motion. Activity.

"Miss Davies, please attend to the notepad." Major Hartwell commanded, "Ladies, let's get to work."

Nicollette retold her idea in detail to her group.

"We need to use some sort of deadly poison, one that is fast and effective, and integrate it with the scent in the crown. We start by having Teodore do his normal preparation of the Mercedes. He would place the poisoned crown air freshener in the rear window. To ensure the car would burn, we could also have Teodore put a pinhole in the gas tank. The gas smell from the leaking fuel would be covered up by the scent. Luvkov and his driver set off. The poison does its job. The car crashes and burns. Teodore and Simone leave Bulgaria."

Val was writing notes on the pad when there was a shout.

"VX poison!"

Everyone looked at Sarah.

"VX poison. We studied poison gases at school and VX would work. It comes in liquid or gas form, so it is versatile. It has no odor and is colorless and is very deadly."

"Heat," Captain Blasingame added. "Gas expands with heat." Everyone turned to the captain.

"If we integrate the gas form of the VX into the contents of the crown, and seal it, the heat from the rear window would cause the gas to expand and burst through a sealant. The gas would then expand throughout the cabin of the car."

Val was writing the notes on the big tablet. Nicollette remembered the bubbles in the Vento.

"Like carbonation," she added.

"Yes," responded the captain.

"Wax melts with heat," Sarah spoke up. "Could we mix the poison in its gas form with a wax product? Then as the wax melts from the heat, it would release the poison gas."

"Carbonated wax!" Nicollette exclaimed.

The door opened and Mr. Stokes walked in, followed by four men. Mr. Stokes introduced Ian Clarke, senior chemist; Randy Horn, a poison expert; Stuart Michaels, a meteorologist; and Kenneth Troughton, a production engineer. The major invited the guests to sit down.

"Miss Beverley has put forth an idea and we have been discussing it. I believe it has merit and will work, but we need your help gentlemen. Miss Beverley, this is your idea. Why don't you catch up with our guests on what we have been talking about?"

Nicollette stood from her chair. She noticed the room was getting rather crowded. *More old men*, she thought. As she started to speak, the earlier nervousness disappeared and was replaced by a rush of enthusiasm. This was her idea, and it had the endorsement of Major Hartwell! Nicollette described the poisoned crown and how it would work. She reviewed the logistics and the goal. When she was finished, all eyes were upon her. Again, there was that unnerving silence while the guests digested the plan.

Major Hartwell broke the silence. "Can we make this work?"

Mr. Horn spoke up. "With all due respect, Major, you realize that VX is a banned substance. We will need authority to obtain the VX."

"I can arrange that," the major replied confidently.

"Where can I get some of those crowns?" Mr. Troughton asked.

"Already handled. They will be here shortly," the major answered. "This is the bottom line. We need to build this poison crown and be confident of its success. The crown must be packaged and sent to our contact in Bulgaria. It must be easy enough for the contact to safely use and here's the best part." She paused for effect. "We have thirty-six hours to get it done!"

The major paused again to let her words penetrate.

"If there are no further questions gentlemen, I suggest we get started. We will meet back here at thirteen thirty hours and I expect answers. Let's get this finished."

The room emptied. The major asked Mr. Michaels to stay for a moment. As the room was clearing out, Nicollette noticed that Mr. Stokes and Mr. Illington were in deep conversation as they left the room. She wondered what they must be talking about as she turned to the table where Major Hartwell and Mr. Michaels were gesturing over the map. Val and Sarah were listening intently as the major instructed Mr. Michaels as to the importance of the weather forecast down to the smallest detail. Major Hartwell would forward him the timing of Luvkov's trip. Mr. Michaels rolled up the maps and left the room.

"What did I miss?" Peg asked.

"Where have you been?" Sarah added.

"Personal business, all the tea was catching up to me. But never mind that! I need to tell you lot something very interesting."

Nicollette, Val, and Sarah drew near to Peg as she whispered a bit of a conversation she overheard when she was coming back into the room. "It appears our Mr. Illington doesn't believe your plan has merit. I overheard him talking to Mr. Stokes about developing a plan 'B.' Evidently, he resents having to work with us novices and doesn't want to be outdone by 'young women.'"

"What do you want to do?" Val asked the group.

"Nothing," Nicollette responded. "I know the plan will work. Then we'll see about our Mr. Illington."

Captain Blasingame and Lieutenant Blankin walked over to the group.

"How about lunch, ladies? We have a busy afternoon ahead of us."

It was nearly 13:15 hours when the group arrived back from lunch. Major Hartwell was already at the table looking through a stack of papers in front of her. The room was soon filled.

"Let's get started," the major announced. "Mr. Michaels, how are we with the weather forecast?"

"Good news, Major," he replied as he laid a map across the table. Our indicators show a high-pressure system over the area through Sunday with higher-than-normal temperatures. We estimate Friday's midday temperature at about 6 degrees with a clear sky."

"Thank you, Mr. Michaels. Mr. Horn, I have word that your VX will arrive by 14:30 hours. Mr. Troughton, did you receive your crowns?"

"Yes, Major Hartwell, your Sergeant Durban brought us two dozen about an hour ago. Mr. Clarke, Mr. Horn, and I are coordinating our efforts. We have instructed the lab on what needs to be done and work is proceeding as we speak."

"Good," replied the major. "Miss Wilson, Miss Green and Miss Davies will be returning with you to the lab. Miss Wilson and Miss Green have backgrounds in physics and chemistry and our Miss Davies has a background in engineering. This will be an excellent experience for them. Mr. Bensour, did the communications go out to Teodore?"

"Yes, Major. We sent a code to him nearly two hours ago. We received confirmation about twenty minutes ago. He is standing by."

"Excellent." Major Hartwell turned to Captain Michaels.

"Captain Michaels. Once we build our 'crown,' we will need to get it to Teodore by Friday morning. Have you any thoughts?"

"Yes, Major. We are working on transport now and we should have the logistics arranged shortly."

"Fine," replied Major Hartwell. "Are there any other concerns or questions?" There was a short pause. "Good. We will reconvene here at 17:30 hours. Thank you."

Val, Sarah, and Peg passed Nicollette as they were leaving the room.

"Good luck, ladies," she exclaimed.

"And good luck to you, Nicky, whatever it is you are going to do," Val responded.

The room soon emptied leaving only Nicollette, Sergeant Durbin, Lieutenant Blankin, Captain Blasingame and Major Hartwell. The major approached Nicollette.

"I guess you wondered why I left you behind, Miss Beverley?"

Nicollette looked at Major Hartwell and nodded her head.

"I want you to accompany us as we visit each of the areas involved with Operation Twist. You will get a close-up view of what we can do here and see your plan in action."

The five of them left the room. Captain Blasingame led the group to the communication room where they were met by Mr. Bensour. Mr. Bensour escorted the group to an area of desks and screens. Nicollette noticed two clocks on the wall. One was London time, and the second clock displayed a sign: Sophia, Bulgaria. She noticed a two-hour time difference. Two men were wearing headphones and viewing the monitors.

"We are expecting a contact from Simone in fifteen minutes. Teodore will be arriving home from work around that time."

"How are we communicating with them?" Nicollette asked.

"Good question," Mr. Bensour answered.

"We know that Bulgaria is virtually shut down. There is heavy government monitoring of the communication systems. We are going to use that monitoring to our advantage. We are going to monitor the monitors! The authorities know that Simone communicates with her husband regularly each day. We have supplied Simone with key words to use in normal conversation with her husband. The conversations between Simone and her husband are very mundane, 'How's your day going? When are you coming home? What's for dinner?' That sort of chatter. The monitors also know that she has permission to travel to Greece. They know she makes purchases there. Therefore, some communications between Simone and Greece are expected. We use those conversations to communicate with her. We have been doing this for a couple of months now. So far, no problems. We have one other 'ace in the hole,' if you will. Because he is trusted by Luvkov, Teodore is allowed to use the private home line in Luvkov's garage to order supplies. We have also given him key words to use and because he is normally alone in the garage, he has some degree of privacy."

"Sir, Simone is contacting her husband," announced one of the men.

"Let's have a listen in, shall we."

Mr. Bensour handed out headphones.

"You may want to watch the monitors as the conversation will be in Bulgarian."

Nicollette listened as the conversation began. Simone's voice came across quite clear and she sounded very nice. Her husband's voice was rather deep and raspy, like a heavy smoker's voice. The monitor displayed the conversation and the translation. Nicollette noticed that certain words were highlighted in different colors as they flowed across the screen. These highlighted words were listed on the second monitor. It was a brief conversation; everything was good at work and home. Dinner would be a stew and served around seven. Teodore would be at home this evening, not going out. The phone call ended, and the headphones returned. *Very normal and mundane conversation,* Nicollette thought. She looked at the second monitor where there was a list of maybe twenty words in different colors. Mr. Bensour pointed to the list of words on the screen.

"According to the coded words she used, Simone is letting us know that Teodore is on schedule Friday. He is not driving Luvkov to Bansko but is responsible for the preparation of the car. Simone also tells us that Luvkov is scheduled to leave for Bansko at 11 a.m. and that she, Simone, is home alone all day tomorrow for further communications."

Nicollette was amazed that Mr. Bensour could decipher

all that information out of just a few words.

"It's not only the words, but sentence structure and word placements as well," he responded.

There was small talk. The major summoned the group to leave. "Next, we'll visit the lab."

Mr. Clarke greeted the group in front of two large steel doors leading into the lab. Eye protection was issued as they entered the lab. It was a large well-lit room with lots of activity. Mr. Clarke led the group to a corner area where a mock automobile rear window was being constructed.

"Nicky." Nicollette heard her name called. It was Val.

"Look at you, all scientific with your eyewear and white lab coat," Nicollette exclaimed.

"You should see Sarah and Peg," Val responded and announced.

"Hey, ladies, look who's here." Sarah and Peg appeared from behind the mock upped automobile.

"Nicky! Welcome to the lab! Glad to see you! Come see! We're building you a car, or at least the rear end of one!" Peg chuckled.

Nicollette was amazed at what was constructed in such a short time. Peg showed her around the model.

"Mr. Troughton's team brought in an actual rear window from a Mercedes, and we put together a rear shelf just like the real car."

Peg showed how they used a sofa and chairs to imitate the seating. There was tape on the floor to show accurate placement of the seats and where the driver and passenger would sit.

"And we are even using the photo of Mr. Luvkov's car

to place the crown in the exact spot."

Nicollette noticed several crown air fresheners on a table nearby. They were broken apart into different pieces. Peg noticed Nicollette looking at the table.

"And this is where we've dissected some of our lovely crowns," Peg commented in a satirical manner, "after all, we need to know how to build our devious device. Now, we're just waiting for the chemists to bring us some samples, but that's Sarah's department."

Nicollette noticed several men on ladders above the model.

"That's the electricians hanging special lights," Sarah said. "We are going to shine lights on the crown to imitate the sun. We are calculating the sun's angle in the sky at various times, and we have placed a thermometer on the rear shelf so we can get an accurate temperature reading. Once we get the samples, we can assemble the crowns and start testing."

Nicollette could hear the excitement in Sarah's normally subdued voice. Major Hartwell and Captain Blasingame approached the four young women. The major looked towards Mr. Troughton and then at Sarah, Val, and Peg.

"Captain Blasingame and I couldn't help but overhear your explanation, ladies. Very impressive. Mr. Troughton, you and your team are doing a splendid job. Well done, all. Now let us get it finished."

Major Hartwell reached for Nicollette's arm,

"Let's let them finish, Miss Beverley. We have another stop. Miss Green will be joining us."

Mr. Clarke led the group to a far section of the lab.

"This is my section of the lab," he announced as he pulled back a curtain to reveal a large functioning laboratory. "This is where real science happens. Sort of a lab within a lab." He chuckled proudly. "Follow me."

Mr. Clarke led the group to a large table. He showed the group a long series of beakers with contents of different colors. Men in lab coats were making notes and continually checking thermometers in the beakers.

"Ah, Mr. Horn. Our guests are here."

Mr. Horn walked over to the table.

"Good afternoon, everyone, and welcome to our laboratory. At this station, we are checking the melting points of various substances. We are looking for a 'coating' to contain the poison. It must be strong enough to hold together and yet sensitive enough to melt using only the heat in the rear shelf of the car. As for the poison itself, let me show you what we are doing."

He led the group to another station table. On the table were a series of clear globes with tubes coming out from the top of the globes. At the end of the tubes, what looked like small balloons were attached. Dishes containing different colored substances were underneath the globes. There were large lamps over each globe. The scene reminded Nicollette of a botany class she had a couple of years ago when the class was experimenting with growing plants indoors using sunlamps. Unfortunately, she remembered, her plants died. *Isn't that the objective,* she thought to herself. *Interesting coincidence.* She grinned as Mr. Horn explained how this experiment would determine the speed of the poison dispersion. He demonstrated the experiment by turning on one of the sunlamps. As the inside of the globe heated, the substance changed into a gaseous form and expanded throughout the globe. Soon the balloon expanded until it was nearly full. A timer attached to the balloon started to ring. Mr. Horn turned the timer off.

"Two minutes seventeen seconds. Not bad," he stated as he made a note on a pad.

He then pulled the balloon out of the tube and released the gas. Nicollette gasped.

"Don't worry. We are not using actual VX gas. We are using substances and gasses that have similar characteristics to the VX poison. We will use the real stuff later under different circumstances, of course."

"Very impressive," Major Hartwell announced. "We'll leave you so you can continue. Miss Green will stay here with you, Mr. Horne, and act as a liaison between the two labs. She has a chemistry background, so put her to good use."

The Major gave a wink to Sarah as she turned to leave. "We have another visit to make."

The group entered the office through a plain white door.

"Welcome, Major," Mr. Michael's voice coming from the back of the room.

Nicollette looked around the room. It reminded her of the antique bookstore in Brockwirth. Rows of shelves full of books. Another cabinet of maps and charts in wooden bins. The distinct musty smell of old books permeating the room.

The major asked Mr. Michaels one question. "Any updates on the weather?"

Mr. Michaels brought a map over to a small table. The map had many lines and circles of varying colors drawn on it. To Nicollette, it looked like a bunch of scribbles, like a child would do with crayons and a coloring book. Mr. Michaels explained that there was a high-pressure system over the Adriatic Sea. The system was moving slowly west, and the Balkan area should have clear weather for at least the next seventy-two hours. "Good, thank you, Mr. Michaels."

Back in the conference room, Nicollette found herself alone at the table. The room was quiet and calm, quite in contrast to all the activity going on in the lab and communications rooms. Nicollette reached for the photo of Luvkov and his family. She stared at the images in the picture. The thought kept racing through her mind that in seventy-two hours, this whole picture will change. Luvkov's wife and mother to their children will be a widow. The two children, almost the same age as Nicollette, will be fatherless. *Aren't they innocent to their father's activities? Aren't they going to suffer as well? What is their future? What is going to happen to them?* Nicollette put the picture down. She drew a deep breath and looked through the window at Major Hartwell sitting in her office on the phone. *The major was right. This is a nasty business!*

# Collateral Damage

The evening meeting started promptly. Major Hartwell stood from the table and asked each section for a status report. Mr. Clarke was first. He told the group that the Mercedes simulator was completed and ready to receive the poison models. He also stated that they were working on several possible devices that would insure an explosion. Mr. Clarke was confident that all would be ready by tomorrow afternoon. He also thanked the major for Miss Davies's, Miss Wilson's, and Miss Green's assistance. Mr. Horne spoke next. The shipment of VX arrived just after the group had left this afternoon. He explained that there was still some work to be done involving the exact formula of the poison but that they had made significant progress in building the final design of the crown.

"What does significant progress mean?" Major Hartwell asked.

"We will have it ready for testing tomorrow morning," Mr. Horne responded.

"Thank you, Mr. Horne. Mr. Michaels, any weather updates?"

"Everything is holding steady. The weather should be fine for the operation."

Mr. Bensour announced that communications were open with Teodore and Simone. He added that the contacts in Greece had been fully briefed and were standing by.

Mr. Bensour then asked the major about communications with the British and American Embassies in Sofia. Colonel Baron and Mr. Illington are handling that, she responded. "Captain Mills. Logistics?" the major asked.

"All is in order, ma'am," he replied.

"We are exploring several delivery ideas. Logistics can be a bit tricky in Bulgaria, but we'll have a final plan in place when we have a better idea of the packaging. We should be ready to go tomorrow afternoon."

"Good. It seems that Operation Twist is in full motion, and we are on schedule for a final plan in twenty-four hours. Thank you, ladies and gentlemen. We will reconvene tomorrow at 16:00 hours. The meeting is over."

As the room emptied, Captain Blasingame approached Nicollette and asked her to stay. She did the same for Val, Peg, and Sarah. Sergeant Durban asked the young women to have a seat. Nicollette looked around the table. It was the core of group 228/157. All women. Eight people, few in number compared to the many people involved with the operation. Lieutenant Blankin was seated when she directed a question to the young women. Her voice was soft and calm when she spoke.

"Are you alright, Miss Beverley, Miss Davies, Miss Green, and Miss Wilson?"

She paused. Silence. The lieutenant continued.

"We know there is a lot going on here and it can be a bit overwhelming. Operation Twist is just the first step in your careers, and we want to make sure you are OK. We have been given a very important operation and a lot of people are depending on this group to get it done.

So far, the four of you are holding your own, but if at any time you need to talk to one of us, please do not hesitate. We have all been here before. Now I suggest a good night's rest. Tomorrow is going to be a big day. Goodnight."

The cold night air nipped at her face as Nicollette and the group walked to their flats. The landscape was covered by a light snow that had fallen in the afternoon. It seemed unusually calm and quiet for the walk home. The group decided to eat together that night, hoping each other's company might reduce the underlying stress. A big pot of soup was waiting at Sarah's flat. It was an early night for the group and Nicollette was soon in bed. The fatigue of her body overwhelmed the feeling of stress from the day. It was a deep sleep.

Major Hartwell was not present at the morning briefing. Captain Blasingame offered the major's apologies and spelled out the day's activities. Val, Peg, and Sarah would return to the lab and Nicollette would begin her day in the communications room. She reminded the group of the important meeting at 16:00 hours. There were no questions, and the captain dismissed the group. Nicollette walked into the communications room with Lieutenant Blankin. Mr. Bensour motioned them over to a cluster of desks.

"We are in communication with Simone now."

There was a message scrolling across the screen and the data clerk was typing a return message.

"Simone is telling us that Teodore left for work at the usual time and that he would be home for lunch around noon. We are responding to her to stand by."

Mr. Bensour looked at Nicollette.

"We must be careful not to have too much contact with Simone in a short time period. We do not want to raise any suspicions if her phone is being monitored. So, each contact we make with her must have a logical and consistent conversation. We have set up Simone to contact an agent in Greece. The cover conversations are about a couple of dresses she bought in Greece that are being altered for her. Our timing is good with this story. Bulgarian liberation day is March 3rd, and the government celebratory ball is March 6th. So, our ruse about dresses makes perfect sense and shouldn't raise any questions."

Mr. Bensour then asked the lieutenant and Nicollette to follow him to a door in the far corner of the communications room. He opened the door for the two women, revealing a cluster of desks.

"This is our official contact room. This is where we make direct contacts to embassies throughout the world. Captain Mills asked us to make the embassy in Sofia aware of what we are planning."

Nicollette noticed that the screen showed an endless flow of numbers, letters, and symbols. Quite different then the simple messages they were getting from Simone. Here is where the cryptanalysis training she had at Brize would be put to use. Nicollette was amazed at the speed and efficiency the analysts had in deciphering and returning the messages. Mr. Bensour asked if Nicollette would like to sit in.

"Don't worry, nothing happening at this moment."

Lieutenant Blankin left as Nicollette sat down and put

her headphones on. It was a fascinating morning.

The conference room was being prepared for the meeting at 16:00 hours when Nicollette walked in from the communications room. Two large white boards were set up and the table was expanded for more seating. There were name plates and dossiers at each seat. Nicollette found her seat. When she saw her name plate, Miss N. Beverley, a sense of pride swelled up in her. *Miss N. Beverley has a nice tone to it,* she thought.

Val, Sarah, and Peg arrived a few minutes later and were seated at either side. By 15:45 hours, the room was full. Nicollette knew many of the people from earlier meetings, but there were a handful of new faces at this meeting. At 16:00 hours, Major Hartwell walked in, followed by Charles Thompson and Colonel Baron. The sense of pride Nicollette felt earlier suddenly turned into a sense of anxiousness. Her palms were sweaty, her heart pounding, and her leg twitching. Colonel Baron sat at the head of the table and removed his hat. Sergeant Durbin stood by the whiteboards. Major Hartwell asked for everyone's attention and called the meeting to order.

"We are here to finalize the plans for Operation Twist. Mr. Clarke and Mr. Troughton, your report please."

Mr. Clarke reached into his satchel and produced two crowns. Slowly and deliberately, he took one apart. He stood from his chair and explained how the crown air freshener worked.

"Simple, really. The actual crown is merely a piece of molded plastic covering a small bottle of scent. At the top of the bottle is a cap."

He raised the bottle and unscrewed the cap.

"When the cap is unscrewed and removed, the opening of the bottle is covered by a thin plastic screen. The holes in the screen allow the scent to evaporate naturally. We are going to use the same simple formula to deliver the poison, with a few modifications, of course. First, we are going to replace the small screen on the top of the bottle with a thin layer of soy wax. We know soy wax will melt at a temperature between 105 and 110 degrees.

"We have conducted multiple simulations and with a bit of sun, the temperature in the rear shelf area of the Mercedes can approach 110 degrees. We know we want between fifty and seventy-five minutes to release the gas. After using multiple scenarios, we are confident we have the right thickness to ensure the wax top melts at the appropriate time. In addition, to ensure the gas release, we are adding an effervescent pill to the mix. Like what my American friends call a 'fizzy.' This small pill will have a thin hard surface. When placing the crown in place, the operative must just tap the pill against the side of the bottle once or twice. This will create cracks in the pill. The effervescence material is slowly released through those cracks. The gas pressure builds up inside the bottle. As the wax seal melts, the built-up pressure is released, accelerating the distribution of the poison. We have conducted multiple tests and are confident we have the right combinations of effervescence and VX poison."

Mr. Troughton stood from his chair as Mr. Clarke sat down.

"We were also faced with the challenge of making sure

the Mercedes would catch fire upon impact."

Mr. Troughton opened his closed fist to reveal a round steel object, a little smaller than a digestive biscuit. He took the object from his hand and laid it on the table.

"This, ladies and gentlemen, is what little jokers call a 'joy buzzer.' It's a simple novelty device that gives a small electrical shock to whoever is shaking the hand of the person wearing it. Let me demonstrate. First, we wind the device up then place it in my palm."

Mr. Troughton reached for Mr. Clarke's hand. They shook hands. Mr. Clarke quickly withdrew, shouting, "Ouch." Mr. Troughton reached into his pocket and pulled out a similar device, laid it on the table, and continued.

"We modified the device to create a side-to-side motion. We then added a diamond tipped pin to the spring mechanism. Finally, we added a light magnet to the upward face of the device."

Holding the device up, Mr. Troughton continued, "Our Mr. Teodore merely winds the device up and attaches it under the gas tank of the Mercedes. We have run multiple tests on the device and adjusted the tensions of the springs so that our little friend here will penetrate the fuel tank in about thirty-five minutes. Upon impact, the device will slide along the tank creating sparks. Boom! Our Mr. Luvkov will find no joy in our 'joy buzzer.'"

There was a small chuckle at Mr. Troughton's last comment.

"Thank you, Mr. Clarke and Mr. Troughton." The Major tried very hard to keep a straight face.

"Mr. Horne, your report please."

Mr. Horne rose from his seat and held up the scent bottle.

"We were faced with two major problems. First, how to place the VX gas into the bottle and secondly, how to ship the deadly crown. We know that we need about twenty-five milligrams of poison gas to do the job. We felt that this is a case, where pardon the pun, overkill is in order. We built a completely sealed small incubator with internal arm attachments. We then reduced by half the amount of scent fluid in the bottle, leaving us plenty of room for the gas. Then a needle attached to a pressure line from the gas canister was used to inject fifty milligrams of VX into the bottle. We quickly resealed the bottle, then evacuated the air inside the incubator in the event any VX was accidently released. We allowed the bottle to rest inside the incubator as we monitored the bottle for any leakage. We were successful, no leakage. We built three working bottles. Our second problem was shipping. Mr. Troughton came up with a rather simple idea of placing the crowns inside one- and one-half liter liquor bottles. We designed the bottles to resemble Jack Daniel's Whiskey bottles. The bottles unscrew in the center."

Mr. Horne reached under his chair and produced a normal looking Jack Daniel's bottle. He demonstrated how the bottle would unscrew in the center.

"We fill the bottle with Styrofoam peas and then bury the poison container in the peas. Finally, we fill the whiskey bottle with a brown syrupy liquid."

Mr. Horne reached under his chair and produced a second Jack Daniel's bottle.

"Hard to spot the difference," he stated proudly.

"Thank you, Mr. Horne."

The Major then turned to Captain Mills.

"Your report please."

Captain Mills stood from his chair and placed a brief-case on the table.

"We know that the British Embassy in Sofia receives a courier once a week. The courier arrives either on Thursdays or Fridays. This Thursday, the courier will deliver the poison bottles to our people at the Embassy."

He then opened the case to reveal three Jack Daniel's bottles encapsulated by a gray spongy material.

"And this is how he will deliver them! Since the courier is normal protocol, we should not raise any suspicions from the SIA. I also want to mention that our courier for this operation will be Mr. Charles Thompson." Captain Mills paused for a moment.

"Once in Bulgaria, we will get the poison bottles to our operative very simply. There is a central fueling station in Sofia for the use of embassies and government officials. We know that Luvkov's driver, in this case Teodore, always fills the Mercedes the day before Luvkov travels out of the city. One of our Bulgarian drivers will take an embassy vehicle to the fueling station at the same time. They will meet and quietly exchange 'lunch bags' or wine or in this case, Jack Daniel's bottles. These 'exchanges' between Bulgarian and Embassy drivers happen fairly frequently, so no suspicion should be aroused.

Teodore now has the bottles and the device. Friday morning, he will replace the scent bottle in the Mercedes with one of the poison bottles. The plastic crown is easily removed and reattached to the scent bottle. Teodore will then attach the 'joy buzzer' device to the fuel tank. During his normal trip home for lunch, he will dispose of the remaining poison bottles in a small river nearby. The deed is set."

"Thank you, Captain Mills. Mr. Bensour, your report."

Mr. Bensour stood from his chair.

"I am pleased to report that all communications are in order. We have been in contact with the Embassy, and they are proceeding accordingly. We are also signaling Simone with specific instructions about her 'dress.' We are instructing her to place a return call on Friday at 4 p.m. local time.

"Mr. Michaels, your report."

"The weather should cooperate. There should be plenty of sunshine and temperatures between two and five degrees."

"Thank you, Mr. Michaels."

"Mr. Thompson, are your arrangements made?" Major Hartwell asked.

"Yes ma'am. I leave on a diplomatic flight in time to arrive at the Embassy in Sofia at noon local time on Thursday."

The major thanked everyone for their efforts. She announced that there would be another briefing tomorrow at 16:00 hours. Colonel Baron then stood and thanked everyone as well. He wished the group good luck then dismissed the room.

Nicollette stood and stretched her legs. She glanced

at her watch. It was nearly seven.

"Long meeting," Val stated as the group came together.

"I'm knackered," Sarah offered.

"Me too," Peg added.

Nicollette looked at her friends.

"No wonder you're tired! You worked your bums off. What a job you did! I mean working down to the smallest details. I'm impressed!"

"It was a lot of work that's for sure, but I also learned an awful lot," Peg answered.

"That Mr. Troughton is an absolute genius, in fact, the people in the lab refer to him as 'Doctor Gadget.'"


The air was thick with anticipation in the Thursday morning briefing. For the second day in a row, Major Hartwell was absent. Captain Blasingame announced that Mr. Thompson was enroute to Sofia and would arrive around noon local time. She then reviewed the day's schedule. Nicollette would be in the communications room accompanied by Val. Peg and Sarah would enjoy the day in the lab. Captain Blasingame reminded the four young women that while Operation Twist was active, the world continues to move.

"I know this is your first mission and I know it will be hard to put the mission out of your minds, but our world never stops or sleeps. You must remain sharp and focused, diligent in your jobs."

Captain Blasingame announced a short briefing at 13:00 hundred hours, just after lunch. She dismissed the room.

The morning seemed to drag on. Nicollette and Val were assigned communications from Southeast Asia. Nicollette tried hard to focus, but the mission was first on her mind. She kept thinking of Mr. Thompson in the airplane, then transporting the case to the Embassy. *What would happen if there was an accident? What if he were caught? What about Coach T?* She tried desperately to clear her mind and focus on the messages coming from Thailand. She closed her eyes and took a deep breath.

There was a tap on Nicollette's shoulder. It was lunchtime. Her relief was here. The group met up in the cafeteria. Sergeant Durbin joined them.

"Hungry?"

"Not so much, I have butterflies in my stomach," Val answered.

"Me too," Nicollette added.

Looking at Sarah and Peg, Val asked, "What did you two do this morning?"

"Mostly clean up and restocking," Sarah replied. "You should see the size of the warehouse, it's huge!"

"And you wouldn't believe all the material stored there!" Peg added.

Major Hartwell was waiting in the briefing room when the group arrived. "This will be very brief," she announced. "We have received word that Mr. Thompson has arrived at the embassy in Sofia. All is in order. Arrangements have been made to meet with Teodore at 15:00 hours local time." The major looked at her watch and continued, "Or any time now. We will reconvene here at 16:00 hours. You may go back to your morning assignments."

Nicollette and Val went back to the communications room. There were more communications coming from Thailand. "Drug Lord is starting to receive captured American weapons from the Vietnamese. Weapons are being transported through Laos to northern Thailand ending up an area near the China border. Mostly small arms but a couple of armored vehicles in the mix. Awaiting instructions," the signal read.

Nicollette gave the decoded message to Mr. Bensour. "Any reply?" she asked.

"Send a signal, standby."

Nicollette sent the reply. Seeing the word "received" on her screen, Nicollette realized that she had just been involved in a live communication. *This was definitely a week of firsts*, she thought.

Major Hartwell held several pieces of paper in her hand as she addressed group 228/157 at the evening meeting.

"We have received word from our Embassy in Sofia that the drop off was successful. Contact was made at 15:15 hundred hours local time and an exchange of American whiskey and local wine took place. Both drivers left unceremoniously. Our Mr. Thompson will be leaving Sofia at 09:00 local time tomorrow. We have just received communications from Simone that Teodore has arrived home and will return to work tomorrow at his normal time to prepare the car for Luvkov's weekend travel. She also states that he understands the instructions and will proceed accordingly."

The major paused.

"Well now, it seems everything is in place. I suggest an early night, tomorrow will be a long day. Goodnight."

The Major returned to her office and closed the door.

The alarm ring shattered the morning stillness. Half asleep, Nicollette stumbled out of bed. It was a restless night. Thoughts of the upcoming mission kept rolling across her mind. Today would be a day to remember.

The group was waiting for her for the short walk to work. Nicollette was rarely pleased with chilly weather, but today was different. The cold air felt good against her cheek and quickly snapped the sleepless stupor out of her. Major Hartwell was sipping a cup of tea with Captain Blasingame and Lieutenant Blankin when the group arrived. The room was unusually calm and relaxed.

"What's going on?" Val whispered.

"Very odd indeed," Peg whispered as they walked to their seats.

"Of all days, today?" Nicollette questioned.

Captain Blasingame looked at Nicollette and the group. "Please, before we start our morning briefing, help yourselves to some tea and fresh muffins. They're in the corner."

Major Hartwell summoned everyone to the table.

"Good morning, ladies. I trust you had a good rest last night. This small breakfast is with our compliments on group 228/ 157 completing their first week of duty. Well done, ladies!"

Uncharacteristically, the major gave a big smile.

"I am proud of you all! Now for today's roster."

Nicollette felt puzzled. *Wasn't today Friday? What*

*about Operation Twist? All the work! All the planning! All the angst! Was it just another day? But it is not just another day! It is a very important day! It is a mission day!*

Still confused, Nicollette listened as the major assigned her to the Embassy communications room. Val, Sarah, and Peg were assigned to the lab. Then, out of nowhere, the major made an announcement, "It is 09:45 in Sofia 07:45 our time, we will reconvene here at 09:00 hours. Thank you."

It was hard to concentrate as the signals were crossing the screen. There were more messages coming from Bangkok. The first load of weapons from Laos were getting closer to the Thai border. Maybe a week or two away.

Nicollette deciphered each message and coded the responses as Mr. Bensour instructed: "Stand by for instructions," "further evaluation," and "planning underway." Nicollette looked at her watch. It was nearly nine. There was a tap on her back. She handed the headset off to her relief and walked into the briefing room.

Captain Blasingame and Lieutenant Blankin were already in the room as Nicollette took her seat. There was a large map of Bulgaria on the easel stand. Val, Sarah and Peg arrived along with Misters Clarke, Horn, Troughton and Michaels. At exactly 09:00 hours, Major Hartwell walked in followed by Misters Stokes and Illington and Sergeant Durban. The atmosphere was quite different in the room as compared to just over an hour earlier. There was a growing sense of uneasiness in the air as Major Hartwell addressed the group.

"It is 11:00 hours in Sofia, Bulgaria. Operation Twist is

now fully activated."

Major Hartwell had a stern face as she looked around the table. "Mr. Michaels, is the weather cooperating?"

"Yes ma'am, everything is how we forecasted."

"Thank you. Mr. Bensour, all lines open and functioning with our contacts in Greece and the Embassy?"

"Yes ma'am, all in order."

"Thank you. Mr. Stokes, are we set for satellite surveillance?"

"Yes ma'am. All positioned and ready."

"Thank you." Major Hartwell faced the group and took a deep breath. "Thank you all for your hard work and diligence. It is now 09:20 hours, 11:20 hours in Bulgaria. We should be receiving communications shortly."

The major sat down and had a quiet conversation with Mr. Illington. Nicollette looked at her friends then at the clock on the wall. 09:21 hours. Her heart started to beat faster. This was it, she thought. The mission she helped orchestrate was now in full motion. Her mind started to race through different scenarios. *Would Teodore complete his task? Would the poison work? Would there be a crash? Would the device make a spark igniting the car? Would this? Would that? What if?* Nicollette placed her hand on her chest, pretending to scratch an itch. Her heart was now racing fast and pounding out of her chest. Pearls of perspiration were forming on her forehead and under her arms. 09:30 hundred hours. Time seemed to stand still. 09:33 hundred hours. She took a quick look at Sarah. Sarah was staring directly down at the table focusing on her fidgeting hands. Nicollette glanced at Peg. Her eyes were closed, and her breathing was very deliberate. Val seemed to be the calmest of all, at least on the surface, just sitting quietly, arms crossed upon the table. Her face was expressionless. Across the table, small talk continued among the men. They appeared far more relaxed with the situation. *How could they be so relaxed?* she asked herself. 09:37 hours. *Calm, Nicollette, calm. Breathe, just breathe.* 09:40 hours. *Close your eyes and relax, she kept telling herself. Breathe.* 09:42 hours. *Breathe.* 09:44 hours. Her heart now pounding so hard, Nicollette was sure everyone in the room could hear it.

Suddenly, a communications specialist quickly entered the room and approached Mr. Bensour. He handed him a paper. Mr. Bensour walked over to Major Hartwell and showed her the paper. He whispered in her ear. The Major rose from her seat.

"We have received a signal from our contact in Greece. Mr. Bensour will read it to us."

*Here we go,* Nicollette thought to herself. *This is it!* Her heart was pounding like a hammer on an anvil, her palms were roiled in moisture, and she could feel drips of sweat falling from her chest.

Mr. Bensour announced that a call was made from Simone to the dress shop in Greece. She asked if the alterations were going along well. This tells us that Teodore has completed the swap of the poison bottle and installed the device as instructed. "We responded to her question affirmatively and that we should have a final fitting date for her later this afternoon. She responded, 'That's fine,' which tells us it is safe to call her later. Then

Simone asked another question, which caught us a bit by surprise. Was it still possible to add three more buttons to the two already on the dress? Again, we responded affirmatively and cordially ended the conversation."

Mr. Bensour put the piece of paper down. A very serious look spread across his face as he looked around the table.

"The buttons on the dress that Simone is referring to are passengers in the Mercedes."

He paused to let his words sink in.

"We were planning the operation around Luvkov and his driver traveling to Bansko. It appears that Luvkov is traveling with his wife and two children for the weekend trip."

Mr. Bensour paused again.

"Ladies and gentlemen, we could have collateral damage in Operation Twist."

The room was silent. Nicollette could hardly breathe. She closed her eyes and envisioned the Mercedes. Luvkov was traveling in the back seat. On one side, his wife and the other side, his daughter. His son was riding in the front seat with the driver. The family would be traveling together for a weekend of skiing, laughing and reconnecting. A happy family. Nicollette's mind then envisioned a crash. A massive fire engulfed the car. No survivors. She felt a lump in her throat. Mixed emotions gathered in her. What did she want the mission to do, fail or be a success? Save the family or complete the objective. At what cost? She remembered the shootings during the prisoner swap in Germany, but this was different. She was not directly involved in the swap, to her it felt more like watching a show on the tele, but now, she was an active participant in this operation. She wanted to scream out loud.

Major Hartwell broke the silence. Nicollette refocused and gathered in a deep breath. Hearing the major's voice brought about a certain calm from within her, like a feeling of not to worry, everything will be alright. Nicollette's heart stopped pounding so hard. Her breathing was easier, and she was not perspiring as much. She turned to look at Sarah and Peg. Sarah was covering her eyes. Maybe she was tearful and did not want anyone to notice or maybe in her mind she was revisiting the poison bottle, wondering if it would work. There was little color in Peg's face. Her eyes stared straight ahead. She wasn't blinking. Nicollette turned to look at Val. She was expressionless, deep in thought. Her hands were still lying on the table. Nicollette noticed a bit of blood on Val's hand. She must have pinched herself very hard so as to draw blood. She may not have even realized what she had done to herself.

The Major announced that it was just after 12:00 hours in Bulgaria and assuming Luvkov left Sofia around 11:30 hours, the next hour or so would be critical to the mission.

"All we can do now is wait."

A tea cart was wheeled into the room. Some of the men stood and stretched and there was quiet talk. Nicollette wanted to stand and stretch but her right leg had fallen asleep. Sarah approached her. Nicollette could see she had been crying.

"I am going to freshen up. How about you?"

Using the table as support, Nicollette stood from her chair. The numbness was slowly leaving her leg. She looked at her friend.

Nicollette noticed Peg was still sitting. She walked behind Peg's chair and placed a hand on her shoulder. Peg turned around and looked at Nicollette.

"I had no idea this was going to be so hard. Bulgaria is so far away. It was so distant to me when we planned the operation, but his children, they're our age." Peg stood up from her chair.

"I know, Peg, I know."

Nicollette did not have the stomach for food, there was still hurt inside of her. She poured a cup of tea and glanced at the wall clock, 12:10 hours. She took a sip of tea. The warmth of the liquid felt good in her throat, it had a calming effect and helped her gain some composure. Nicollette began to think. If everything were to go perfectly, the poison would start dispersing in about twenty minutes. Luvkov, his family and the driver would quickly succumb to the deadly air. The vehicle would veer off the road, hit a barrier, another vehicle or even run off a steep hill. The device would create a spark and the vehicle would explode. The whole thing would be over in only a couple of minutes. Nicollette looked at the clock on the wall. 12:15 hours. 12:20 hours. Tick tock, tick tock. Val and Sarah returned to the room. Sarah had reapplied her makeup.

"Any news?"

"Still a little early yet," Nicollette answered softly.

"I'm going to try and eat something," Val announced. "It may be a long afternoon. You lot should try as well."

Nicollette sat down in her chair, her hands wrapped around the warm cup of tea. Captain Blasingame sat down next to her.

"How are you holding up, Miss Beverley?"

"I had my moments, especially when we heard that the family was in the car."

"I was watching you and I could see the angst in your face. Nicollette, the first time is always difficult. We must be prepared for the unexpected. Most of the surprises we face in our business are not very pleasant. I am not saying you shouldn't be sensitive or emotional, but these situations are part of our job, a job that we expect big things from you in the future. If this mission is successful and I believe it will be, you should be proud of your contribution. The sting you feel for the family will never leave you, but over time, it will become less painful. Trust me. I've been there."

Nicollette looked back at the captain. Their eyes locked. Although she was still hurting inside, she knew there was wisdom in what the captain had said.

"Thank you, ma'am. Thank you."

Nicollette looked at the clock. 12:30 hours. She still felt anxious, but not to the degree she felt earlier. The captain's little chat with her hit right to the point. This was her job! Bad things do happen. It will be hard, it will always be hard, but she must be strong, Nicollette thought as she looked at the clock again. *Anytime now! Anytime now!* Nicollette closed her eyes and waited.

# Success or Failure

A sudden stir in the office brought Nicollette out of her trance. She took a quick glance at the clock on the wall. 12:55 hours. A soldier was talking to Mr. Stokes. By the look of the uniform, he appeared to be an airman with the RAF. Mr. Stokes walked over to Mr. Illington. The two of them approached Major Hartwell. Nicollette observed the three of them in a soft conversation. Mr. Stokes handed a folder to the major. She glanced at it and walked to the head of the table.

"I need everyone's attention. Please take your seats."

Nicollette looked around the table. Everyone was focused on the major. *Was this the message everyone was waiting for?* Her heart started to race again. It came down to one question. Was the mission going to be a success or failure? The major looked over the table.

"Mr. Stokes has satellite pictures of the area that Luvkov was travelling."

Mr. Stokes rolled the overhead projector to the head of the table and asked for the lights to be dimmed. An image appeared on the wall. Nicollette tried hard to understand the picture. It looked like something her young niece would draw with crayons. Mr. Stokes used a pointer to identify images on the slide. Now it was becoming clearer to Nicollette. He pointed to a squiggly line.

"This is the road that Luvkov was traveling on. There

are some steep slopes and curves on the side that Luvkov's car would be on. The other side is relatively flat. Now I want you to focus on this spot."

Mr. Stokes enlarged the image. He pointed to what Nicollette thought looked like a piece of cotton wool.

"We have checked the coordinates and the timing. We are very certain that this is an image of a plume of smoke caused by a large fire." The lights were turned on. There was small talk around the table as Mr. Stokes rolled the projector away. The room became very quiet as Major Hartwell addressed the group.

"It appears from the satellite imagery that we have completed a successful mission. We are working on confirmation now, bearing in mind that we have limited resources in Bulgaria. We will keep you informed as information is received."

The room cleared out. Sergeant Durban walked over to Nicollette, Val, Sarah and Peg.

"The major would like to meet with you after everyone has left."

"I wonder what this is all about?" Val whispered to her friends.

"We're going to find out shortly," Sarah whispered back.

The room was empty except for group 228/157. Major Hartwell asked everyone to move closer, this would be an informal discussion.

"First off, I want you to take a deep breath." She paused then continued, "I want to thank each of you on what appears to be a successful mission. Your hard work was a big contributing factor to the outcome." She paused again.

"You will always remember your first mission, the hard work, anxiety, and emotions. Take it with you on your journey. Our work continues. So, we will go back to our areas and finish the day. We will have a briefing at 16:00 hours."

Nicollette walked to the door with her friends. "It's like another day at the office for this lot," she whispered to her friends.

"It may be for them, but I'm still shaking inside," Sarah responded.

"Me as well," Peg added.

"We'll catch up later, ladies," Val said as she walked through the door.

Nicollette sat down at her communications station. Nothing new coming from Bangkok. A large storm was firmly over the area, halting any progress of the arms movement. The signals coming and going were just filling the airtime. *How boring,* Nicollette thought, *especially after all the excitement earlier in the afternoon, but the work is important, it must continue.*

A tap on her shoulder meant her relief had come and Nicollette entered the briefing room. Val, Sarah, and Peg were already seated.

"This has been a long afternoon," Sarah told the group. "I'm shattered!"

Captain Blasingame was the first officer to enter the room. By 16:00 hours, the room was filled with the mission group. Mr. Bensour accompanied Major Hartwell as she walked into the room. The major asked all to be seated.

"We have communications with Simone. Mr. Bensour

will read the message."

Mr. Bensour stood and read from a small stack of papers.

"At 5:45 local Bulgarian time, our 'dressmaker' in Greece received a call from Simone. The coded conversation told us that Teadore arrived at the Luvkov home at his usual time. Teadore told her that the housekeeper came to him around 4 p.m. and looked visibly shaken as she stated to Teadore that staff at the Bansko chalet were still waiting for Luvkov and his family. They were very concerned because it was very unusual for Luvkov to be late, he was always punctual. Teadore also told Simone before he left for home that he had seen people he did not recognize coming in and out of Luvkov's home. Simone told Teadore not to worry and just come home. Simone then said she was sorry for the 'additional button work.' We responded by saying the dress looked fine and should be completed tomorrow."

Mr. Bensour sat down, and Major Hartwell looked around the table. "It appears we have success. We should have final confirmation in the next twenty-four hours."

There was a buzz of chatter as the major left the room. Nicollette felt a bit empty inside. The emotional roller coaster she had experienced throughout the day left her feeling numb and physically exhausted. She knew she needed a break.

"Anything going on this weekend?" Nicollette asked Sarah as they left through the main gate,

"Peg and I are headed to London for an overnight. Do you and Val want to join us?"

"Thanks for the invite," Nicollette responded, "but I think I'll go home to Brockwirth for a quiet weekend. I need to relax."

"How about you, Val?" Peg continued.

"I was just going to stay here and relax alone," Val responded.

"That's no good," Nicollette answered. "You can't be alone! Why don't you come to Brockwirth with me? It will be fun! We can relax and you know how my mum can cook a Sunday lunch!"

"Are you sure I'm not imposing?"

"Never! It's settled! Peg and Sarah will go off to London and you and I off to Brockwirth!"

It was lunchtime when Nicollette's father and mum picked up the two young ladies. First, Pizza Hut for lunch then home. Val had never been to the small village before. She knew about the Cotswolds but had never had the chance to visit. Nicollette settled her into the spare room, and they decided to walk down to the village. The sun was full in the sky, and it was warm for a February day. The village was alive with people taking advantage of the weather. As they walked, Nicollette looked around at the people in the village. She wondered if they knew what went on just a few kilometers away or that she was part of it.

Val and Nicollette enjoyed visiting the shops; it temporarily took their minds off the past week. Val especially enjoyed the old bookstore, leaving with more than a few books.

As they passed the War Memorial, Nicollette paused.

"What's up, Nicky?"

"This is a special place for me, Val, I always stop when I pass it. This memorial reminds me about what these brave men from my hometown did for England. We're a small village in the center of the country, and yet when called for, the men of Brockwirth responded. I get inspiration from their courage and sacrifice."

Nicollette turned to her friend.

"To me, Val, this is what it's all about. I want to give to my, I mean, our country. It's my call of duty, my destiny."

Before she went to bed later, Nicollette noticed an envelope on her nightstand. Next to it was a note her mum left. The note said the envelope was delivered by a government man while she was in the village. "The messenger said it was some tickets or something that you forgot on Friday but will need on Monday. He asked me to make sure you received it, so I left it here." Nicollette was curious. Tickets, what tickets? She looked at the envelope. There was nothing to identify who had sent it and it was sealed only by a wax plug.

Nicollette broke the wax seal and slowly removed the letter. It was a handwritten note.

"Miss Beverley,

We received confirmation of the success of Operation Twist this evening. The mission went as planned. We heard from Simone that Teodore did not arrive home from work Saturday afternoon as per his usual routine. Later in the evening, he was found dead by a lake near their home of an apparent suicide. A note he left asked for forgiveness from his mother. Simone has asked us about leaving Bulgaria. We know Miss Davies is with you and we thought you two should know. Our briefing meeting is at 07:00 Monday morning."

The letter was signed by Captain Blasingame.

Nicollette clutched the letter and read it again. She was stunned and in disbelief, full of conflicting emotions. The mission was a success. The poison crown did its job. It was her idea. She was both a hero and an accomplice. Because of her, innocent people had died, but also because of her, a serious mission was completed that could save many more lives.

In bed, Nicollette tossed and turned, unable to get the pictures of Luvkov's family or Teadore's fate out of her mind.

Finally, out of sheer exhaustion, Nicollette managed to fall asleep. She dreamt of being in a car with her mum and dad, traveling along a Cotswold Lane. It was a happy ride with plenty of sunshine and birds flying overhead. Nicollette was looking out the window and the smell of fresh flowers filled her nose. She turned to look out the rear window and saw a crown air freshener. Immediately, Nicollette turned to see her father slumped at the wheel and the car heading straight for a tree. *Wake up, Dad! Wake up, Dad!* she yelled, but to no avail. Nicollette was panicking. The car doors were locked, and she could not get away. *No!* she yelled.

Nicollette sat up in her bed and opened her eyes. She was wet from perspiration. Her watch said it was nearly 7 a.m. It was no use trying to sleep. She needed some air and to be alone with her thoughts.

It was still dark when she looked out of the window, and it looked to be a typical chilly February morning. She dressed warmly, grabbed the note, and quietly went down the stairs. She was careful not to disturb anyone as she left the house. The air was cold as it hit her face. The village was very still and quiet this early Sunday morning. Nicollette started to walk at a modest pace out from her street and onto Upper High Street. She looked down at the village. Nothing stirring, just the constant yellow flashing light of the traffic signal breaking the darkness. She picked up her pace as she climbed onto the path that leads to Brockwirth Tower. Nicollette sat down at the old picnic table on the Tower grounds. Many times, she had come here with her family to enjoy a packed lunch and enjoy the wonderful view of the village below. Now it was reflecting time. She pulled out the note and read it over and over. At first, she wanted to cry, then she wanted to scream. Her mind drifted to the War Memorial in the village. Those heroes may have cried, but they did their job. They were human just like her. Her new job really was a nasty business! There would be emotional ups and downs. Nicollette closed her eyes. She recalled the last two months of her life. The excitement of being accepted into the program. The cover story. Leaving home for the first time. Her new friends. The rigorous demands of physical and mental training. The late nights and early mornings. The prisoner exchange in Germany. The Bridge. The shootings. The first mission. The collateral deaths in Bulgaria. The emotional ups and downs. The teamwork and the success. The feeling of being significant and part of the team.

All these thoughts roared through her head like a freight train, her hands covering her ears as she tried to quiet the internal noise.

The tension shattered as an early morning walker asked, "You alright, miss?"

"Yes, fine thank you," Nicollette answered in a forced voice.

As the walker left, Nicollette could see the sun coming through the clouds, illuminating the village below. She always loved this view, the whole Vale of Evesham spread out in front of her. It brought a sense of calm and a sense of well-being to her. Today, however, it reinforced a much deeper sense, that of purpose.

Nicollette took a glance at her watch. It was nearly half past eight. Her mum would be preparing breakfast. It was time to leave the serenity of the Tower grounds and head home. She stood from the table and headed down the path towards Brockwirth. Her pace quickened as she thought to herself how much she had grown. How strong and confident she had become. How she had entered the group as a fresh-faced young lady and now, well, watch out world!

She was only twenty years old.

A light rain started to fall. "Damn rain," she thought. "Damn English rain!"

# Reunion

"Come on, Nicky! It's time to leave! We don't want to be late!"

"Ok Val, let me grab my coat."

It was one year to the day that Nicollette Beverley started in Cheltenham as an Officer of British Intelligence. *February 3rd, 1978! Has it really been a whole year?* Nicollette thought as she picked her coat off the back of the chair. Before she turned off the light, she had a quick look around her new office. It was very small, not much bigger than a closet. The office consisted of a small government issue steel desk, a few folding chairs, and a four-drawer gray file cabinet. Nicollette had received permission to bring her own soft leather desk chair into the office. A Union Jack was perched on a pole in the corner and the latest portrait of the Queen hung on the wall above her desk. It was small, but it was hers. *Still no window. Maybe next promotion.*

It was a short walk to the large conference room where the reception was being held to celebrate the first-year anniversary of Group 228/157.

"This year has certainly gone by fast, Nicky. I still can't believe it! It seems like just last week when we were in training. Remember Sergeant Harris and those early exercises?"

"Who could forget that and the long nights studying,"

Nicollette responded as the two of them entered the conference room building.

"Nicky! Val!" Sarah exclaimed as she rushed to greet her two friends. "So good to see you both."

It was six months ago when Sarah was temporarily assigned up North. What was supposed to be a short stay ended up being much longer. She had cut her red hair to shoulder length and changed her glasses.

"Are you back with us now?" Nicollette asked, excited.

"Moving back into my old flat later today. Received my papers on Wednesday and here I am. Did you miss me?"

"Of course we did." Val answered. "The lab was just not the same without you!"

"Have you heard from Peg?"

"Last I talked to her she was still in London. It's been since December. It would be great if we were all together again!" Nicollette added.

"Sure would!" came a voice from behind the group hugging trio.

"Peg!" Nicollette, Val, and Sarah screamed.

"Is there room for one more?" Peg asked as she jumped into the frenzied friends' embrace. "I'm back. My instructions came yesterday, and I moved back into my flat this morning."

"The crew is back together again. I can't wait to get caught up!" Nicollette exclaimed as the four of them found a table.

The door was shutting as Major Hartwell and Major Blasingame walked into the room, Major Blasingame having just recently been awarded her new rank.

Lieutenant Blankin, Sergeant Durban, and Charles Thompson were also present as well as the staff from the lab and "Professor Gadget" Kenneth Troughton. Mr. Peter Johnson from the communications room and Mr. Bensour, the linguist, sat at a table across the room. Nicollette noticed several new faces in the gathering. She knew about Mr. Stokes and Mr. Illington's recent retirements but had yet to meet their replacements.

Major Hartwell tapped a knife against a glass and called for everyone's attention.

"Good afternoon, everyone! Today is a very special day! We're here to celebrate two special occasions. First, the well-deserved rank promotion for our now Major Blasingame and secondly, to celebrate the first anniversary of service for Group 228/157."

Major Hartwell's words were followed by a round of applause and a standing ovation. She continued, "Group 228/157 was established under the instructions of the Ministry of Defense to attract young women to the Intelligence Community. The training was hard, and many were against us, but here we are today, one year later, a strong, energetic and capable family of professional women." Applause. "I remember and I'm sure you do as well our first task, Operation Twist. I remember pleading with then Colonel Baron, now General Baron, to let our women assist in the planning and execution of the mission. And did we ever." More applause.

Major Hartwell opened a box from her table and raised a wooden plaque to show everyone.

"I received this award from General Baron last week

along with this note:

'To Special Group of Operations 228/157. Congratulations on reaching this special milestone of your one-year anniversary. I know there have been many who doubted you. You have worked very hard to overcome these and other barriers. I commend the leadership of Group 228/157 for forming and maintaining a strong, cohesive and determined team. Group 228/157 has grown into a valuable asset for British Intelligence, and we are the stronger for it. Keep up the good work, ladies.' And it's signed by General Nigel Baron. I shall hang this plaque in Group 228's briefing room with pride."

Major Hartwell passed the plaque to Nicollette's table and continued, "And now, it is with great pleasure that I recognize our own Major Blasingame!"

Major Blasingame stood from her seat and thanked the group for everything they had accomplished together. She credited her promotion to hard work and determination and having the best staff to work with. As the major continued, Nicollette thought about how much she liked her. Hard work and determination. Now I work with two Majors, and they are both women! That's the stuff!

The weekend was quiet. Nicollette enjoyed reminiscing with her friends. They shared stories and more than a few laughs, but as much as she enjoyed the reunion, a deep, troubling thought kept surfacing in her mind. *There must be a reason we are all together again. Something big must be happening, something very serious.*

Little did she know just how big or how serious it was, or how soon she would find out.

# Abraham's Tent

The Monday morning briefing started at seven just like it always did. In addition to Group 228/157, Charles Thompson, Mr. Bensour, Mr. Johnson and Mr. Troughton were also in attendance. Major Hartwell addressed the group.

"Good morning! I suspect you may be wondering why the full house this morning. It will become clear in a few minutes. Welcome back, Miss Green and Miss Wilson. We have a lot to cover so let us get to it."

*Here it comes,* Nicollette thought. Unlike the mission briefings on Operation Twist, she felt more excitement flowing through her than apprehension. Maybe it was because of the tedium of the last few months or maybe it was because she was anxious to be part of something bigger, or some combination of both.

Major Blasingame stood from her chair and an orderly rolled a screen projector to the front of the room. Notepads were handed out as the lights were dimmed.

"Good morning!" Major Blasingame started.

The first slide was flashed on the screen.

"First, a little geography lesson. This is a map of the Persian Gulf. Most of the world's oil is produced and shipped from this region. You see this narrow point in the Gulf. This is the Straits of Hormuz. All the oil from the Gulf area has to travel through this narrow point.

The navigable water in the Strait is about four miles wide and the entire Strait is only twenty-one miles across. Next slide please. This is a political map of the region. As you can imagine, it is very important for the West to maintain good political relations with the countries surrounding the Straits. The southern shores of the Strait are controlled by Oman and the United Arab Emirates, and the northern shore is controlled by Iran. The British and Americans currently have good relations with all three leaders of these three countries. However, these three countries may not have the best relations with each other. In 1971, Iran invaded three little islands right in the middle of the Persian Gulf shipping lanes. At that time, these little islands were under the control of the United Arab Emirates which was still a British Protectorate. So indirectly, we, the British, were responsible for allowing the invasion. Now, our Persian Gulf allies may look at our security arrangements with them with some suspicion. They seem to have long memories. Next slide please. These are the leaders of the three counties. First, this is Qaboos, President of Oman. He is British educated and served in the British military for a short period of time. We feel stable with Qaboos. He works closely with the West on matters of security and has allowed a small presence of British Military on his soil. The leader of the United Arab Emirates or better known as the U A E, is Sultan Al Nahyan. Again, we feel stable with him as well although we believe he still may have some bitterness over the loss of those little islands in the Gulf. Again, the British have a very small military presence in the UAE. The last leader and the one we are going to focus on is Mohammed Reza Pahlavi, better known as the Shah of Iran. Next slide please. The Shah may be the weak link in our security arrangements around the Straits of Hormuz. This is a slide of his family. They live like aristocracy and have tremendous wealth. The Shah runs a very strict country. Despite his massive oil revenues, his country remains poor. His controlling arm is the military, and his secret police are known as Savak. He spends a great deal of money on his military, buying primarily American and British arms including purchases of the F-14 Tomcat at the rate of six a month. He buys so much equipment that his military cannot be trained fast enough on how to use it. All the latest military hardware from tanks to helicopters and air to surface missiles are in his armory. The Shah is spending on his military like a drunken sailor on shore leave. He told the *Times* a few years ago that his ambition was to make Iran the strongest non-atomic power in the world. We could talk about this for hours but let us move on. Next slide please."

The next slide showed a turban-wearing, white-bearded man. Nicollette was drawn closely to his eyes. They were recessed and capped by deep, black eyebrows. His facial expression was hard and unforgiving. His glance was making Nicollette feel uncomfortable inside. There was something about this man that made her think that he was dangerous.

"This is Ayatollah Ruhollah Khomeini. We will just call him Khomeini. He is currently living in Paris. You may have read about him in the papers recently. He is the one directing all the current unrest in Iran. He is loved by the young people wanting a change in government. His followers are fiercely loyal and dedicated to him. His followers protest almost daily and are not afraid to use violence. They see Khomeini as the savior from the Shah's harsh rule. As for Khomeini, he wants to gain power and turn Iran into an Islamic Republic where the country is ruled by clerics. We feel that the Shah is in trouble. His opposition are fanatics. Our Intelligence is showing daily defections from the Armed Forces of Iran and even SAVAK is having trouble containing the protests. The Shah did visit Washington in December and received a message of support from President Carter, however, our people in Washington say America is nervous as well. Plus, one last little detail, our Intelligence in Iran is reporting that the Shah is not well, and they believe he has terminal cancer. Lights, please."

Major Blasingame took her seat as the projector was rolled away. Major Hartwell stood from her chair and walked around the room as she spoke.

"As you can see, this is a very dangerous situation. On the one hand, Iran controls the Northern Shore of the Straits of Hormuz, and we know just how important that is. On the other hand, the Shah spends a lot of money buying the latest military hardware from Britain and America. He has built a strong and powerful armed force. Now add to the mix his, as we see it, tenuous position as leader of Iran. Whether he is removed because of health or by coup, you can see the problem. Plus, can you imagine Cleric Khomeini, with all his fanatical followers, controlling all this latest military hardware and the Straits?

Bad medicine."

Major Hartwell paused.

"Now we have simplified a very complicated situation. The Shah is still in power and as much as we can tell will continue to be for the foreseeable future. There are over 50,000 American and British contractors and military advisors in Iran. And we operate a full embassy in Tehran. The Americans have Khomeini blanketed, so good there. But and this is a big one, we have become aware of some glaring holes in our secure communication lines. We believe that our lines of intelligence are being monitored by both Savak, the Iranian secret police, and Khomeini supporters. There could also be a mole in the Embassy as there are several local employed workers in the compound. Sort of a triple jeopardy. We cannot make any abrupt changes. We don't want to tip off anyone or raise any suspicions. So, it's business as usual in Tehran. Now for the big question, where does Group 228/157 fit in?"

Major Hartwell looked at her watch.

"I think we need a break. How about fifteen minutes everyone?"

It was nearly ten. Nicollette had been sitting in the briefing for three hours and she felt it as she stood from her chair. Her left leg was numb, and she tried to hide it as she went to the tea cart.

"This is very interesting," Val whispered into Nicollette's ear.

Nicollette could see that her friend was uneasy. Val was having a hard time standing still. Sarah and Peg approached.

"I'm dying for the loo. Anyone else?" Peg asked.

"I need a splash," Val answered.

"Don't be long, you two," Sarah said as she turned towards Nicollette. "What do you think, Nicky?"

"I'm not too sure. This is a long briefing and there's been a lot of information passed and—" Nicollette paused as she turned her head towards the door.

"Look what we have here, Sarah."

Three Royal Navy Officers walked into the room and went straight to Majors Hartwell and Blasingame. Nicollette instantly knew they were Royal Navy by their dark blue double-breasted jackets. Each was carrying their white officers cap under their arm. Two of the officers were carrying attaché cases. Nicollette could see that one of the three was a woman. The tight hair bun of black hair was a giveaway.

Major Hartwell called everyone to their seats. Nicollette looked at Val. Some of her makeup had washed away from the water she had splashed on her face. *Too late to do anything about it now*, Nicollette thought, *and besides, I don't think anyone will care after what's happening here.*

"We left off with the question 'where does Group 228/157 fit in' regarding all the information you received this morning. Here to explain a bit more is Captain Avery of Royal Navy Intelligence. Captain Avery."

"Good morning. I am sure the major's impressed upon you the importance of the Persian Gulf to you earlier. It is imperative that oil is continually free flowing without any obstruction. We also have a political narrative in that we are allied with Iran, the UAE, and Oman. All active players.

We also have resentment between Iran and the UAE and Oman. Add into this mix the unrest in Iran and we have a real problem on our hands."

Captain Avery paused. He placed his attaché case on the table and pulled out a carousel of slides and a short stack of papers. He asked for an orderly to set the screen up again.

"As you may have guessed, there are any number of British registered oil tankers in the Gulf at any one time. They must all pass through the Strait of Hormuz. Unfortunately, we at present do not have a permanent naval presence in the Gulf. We do, however, have some air assets in the region. So, let's get to the point. Lieutenant Amin will hand out a briefing report on several communications Naval Intelligence has been monitoring."

Captain Avery handed the lieutenant the briefing papers to distribute. Nicollette watched as she approached. She was of medium build with dark eyebrows and hair. Her eyes were deep brown set against an olive tan complexion. She had a firm, no-nonsense facial expression, probably in her early thirties. As she handed the briefing report to her, Nicollette noticed her short, plain fingernails. *This one is all business*, Nicollette thought as she turned to read the briefing report. Her attention was diverted back to the front of the room as Captain Avery continued.

"A couple of weeks ago, Naval Intelligence began to pick up some curious communications within Iran. As we began to decode each message, our interest increased. As best as we can tell, someone is organizing some sort of attack on Persian Gulf shipping. Now we don't know who is sending these messages or who is receiving them. From what we can gather, this plot is still in its organizing phase. If so, then we are right on top of it. If not, well we are behind and need to catch up in a hurry. This is where we need Group 228/157."

Captain Avery paused for a moment and looked around the room. Multiple sets of eyes returning his look. Nicollette's throat suddenly became very dry, and swallowing was impossible. Her stomach felt like a big knot and her eyes wouldn't blink. *This is it! This is big! Naval Intelligence wants our help! Are you kidding me?* She wiped her now wet palms on her skirt. *Focus, Nicky! Focus, Nicky!*

Captain Avery took a sip of water and continued.

"This is a very delicate situation. We are eavesdropping on an ally. The Shah is our friend and is very important both geopolitically and financially to Britain and the West. We can't afford to be seen as undermining that friendship, even more so with this Khomeini character pledging revolution against the Shah as well. The Shah could easily turn towards the Soviets in repercussion for our actions and even play havoc with oil shipments through the Strait of Hormuz. And, he has the military equipment to be reckoned with. No, this operation needs to be totally clandestine with no chance of exposure. We approached the Admiralty for assistance. They in turn directed us to General Baron. In discussions with General Baron, he suggested that we needed a small, agile, and effective group. People who could 'fly under the radar,' pardon the pun. He pointed out your group's success with

Operation Twist and your experience in communications. At first, we balked, but as our discussions increased, we were swayed to his side. Your Major Hartwell is a very strong advocate. So, there you have it, Group 228/157 will be working with Naval Intelligence. We have named this Operation Abraham's Tent."

# Field Trip

Nicollette was finally able to swallow and blink her eyes. Her mind was still digesting the information her ears had channeled into her brain. Her palms were no longer wet, but a strange tingling sensation was going up her spine. She looked at her friends. Sarah and Peg were whispering to each other. Sarah kept lightly tapping her hand against the table as if to add emphasis to what she was saying. Peg seemed to be miles away. As Nicollette looked at Val, she could see the excitement Val was trying to hide behind her concerned smile.

"You were right, Nicky! This is something big! You think we are up to it whatever it is?"

"We talked this weekend about our training days, you know Sergeant Harris, late nights studying and the lot. Well, Valerie Davis, I think we're going to remember what we learned then and since then and...need every bit of it!"

Val reached her right hand along the table and grabbed Nicollette's left. They squeezed their hands together. Friends.

A lunch cart was wheeled into the room. Major Blasingame announced a forty-five-minute break. The briefing would continue after lunch. Nicollette was glad for the break. The morning had been very intense to say the least. Her knotted stomach had uncurled enough to suggest she was hungry. Val walked over to the cart with Nicollette. Peg and Sarah followed.

"Any ideas, ladies?" Peg started the conversation.

"Not the foggiest, however, this is some serious cow stuff," Sarah added, too proper and polite to use the word "shite."

"You're not kidding. Who knows what or where we'll be or even what we'll be doing?" Val added in an apprehensive tone.

"I think this afternoon is going to be very interesting for sure," Nicollette spoke as she looked over at the Royal Navy Officers in the corner. "And I think we're going to get to know that lot well."

Sergeant Durban wandered over to the group. She reached for a napkin and a plate.

"Ladies, quite a morning, wasn't it?" she asked, putting a sandwich on her plate. "It's going to get even more interesting this afternoon."

Major Hartwell called out that the briefing would resume in ten minutes. Nicollette put a couple of biscuits on a napkin and poured a cup of tea. She and Val went back to their seats. Val's seat was to her left like it was every day, but the seat on the right, normally used by Sergeant Durban, was empty. Major Hartwell called for everyone's attention. Nicollette noticed Sergeant Durban sitting at the rear of the room. As Nicollette turned her head towards the front of the table, Lieutenant Amin sat down in the chair next to her. Captain Avery stood at the head of the table and reopened his attaché case.

"Let us see where we left off. Yes, Operation Abraham's

Tent and Group 228/157. These recent intercepted communications we have talked about have shown us some glaring holes in our ability to unilaterally act on any threats to British shipping in the Gulf. We have become complacent and reliant on the Americans and our Gulf Allies for protection. In short, we have left ourselves vulnerable."

Captain Avery paused and took a sip of his tea. He asked for the lights to be dimmed and switched on the slide projector. A map of the Persian Gulf appeared.

"Here is the Persian Gulf. Let us focus on the Straits of Hormuz. As we stated earlier, most of the world's oil is transported through here. The actual shipping lanes are relatively narrow, so any attack on British shipping is likely to happen between these points."

Captain Avery used a small flashlight to identify the areas of concern.

"Let me, in simple terms for now, describe our objectives in Abraham's Tent. The first step is to establish a secure, local, on-the-ground communications network. We are already in Tehran, Baghdad, and Kuwait. All these points are farther away from the Straits than we would like to be. We need eyes and ears near the Straits. Step two is to establish a quick response force near the Straits. A very low-profile, agile force to compliment the small air assets we have nearby. The Admiralty and Ministry of Defense are currently working on this. We believe this coordinated effort will give British shipping far more security and certainly enhance our ability to handle any short- and long-term threats. Group 228/157's role is in the first step. This group will be vital in establishing coordinated communications during Abraham's Tent."

Captain Avery asked for the lights to be turned on and returned to his seat. Major Hartwell stood from her chair. Nicollette noticed an unusual deliberateness in the major's steps as she approached the front of the room. It reminded her of a doctor walking towards a family to give news about a patient. A sudden shiver climbed up her spine. *This is real, Nicky!* Her left leg started to shake automatically. Nicollette instinctively looked at her friends. They were all intensely looking at the major. Sarah took a quick glance back at Nicollette. Her eyelids were blinking uncontrollably. Nicollette looked to her right. Lieutenant Amin was expressionless, eyes forward, stoic in her stature. *Not her first "big game,"* Nicollette thought, trying to hide the up and down motion of her left leg.

"Ladies and gentlemen, Group 228/157 is going on a Field Trip," Major Hartwell announced. She paused and unrolled a piece of paper. "I have instructions that Captain Avery and Lieutenants Simons and Amin will be temporarily joining our group and under my command. Now for the details. We will be leaving here tomorrow morning at 07:00 hours for RAF Brize-Norton where we will depart at 09:00 hours. Lieutenant Blankin is going to hand out a list of items to pack. The weather in the Gulf is very comfortable with daily highs around 25 Celsius and lows around 17 Celsius. Please abide by this list to the letter."

Major Hartwell motioned Lieutenant Blankin to distribute the information paper. As the lieutenant circulated around the room, Major Hartwell continued.

"Now to more immediate matters. You will notice on your information sheet a brief synopsis of your cover story. Miss Beverley, Miss Davies, Miss Green and Miss Wilson, your current cover will not change. Your circle of influence, family, friends, etc., understands that you are working as sports liaisons for Her Majesty's Government. Your story is that there are invitations from some countries in the Middle East for football, cricket, and or rugby exhibition matches later this summer, and your presence is needed for the negotiations. We know there are these types of tours and such annually, so this practice is not uncommon. Since no sport or country is mentioned, you should not get caught up in any details and as of now, there is no defined return date. Are there any questions?"

Major Hartwell looked around the room. All eyes were upon her. Without moving, Nicollette's eyes glanced across the table and around the room. No one was moving, even the most senior people in the room were motionless. *A field trip! A mission! I guess even the most experienced never get used to a trip away from home.* Nicollette's left leg had calmed down, but her palms were getting wet. She was worried about what to say to her parents and friends, but she realized that her story was all laid out for her. No big deal. Maybe deep down, she was apprehensive about where she was going or what she may be doing. The unknown. *Yeah, that's it,* she thought, *but that will be laid out for me soon. Calm down, Nicky!*

Major Hartwell continued, "No questions for now then; good. It is 14:00 hours. We all have personal business to attend to. Should you need to reach me, my contact information is listed on the bottom of your information sheet. We will meet back here at 06:30 tomorrow morning. Misses Beverley, Davies, Green and Wilson, Major Blasingame, Lieutenant Blankin and Sergeant Durban and Mr. Charles Thompson, please remain. This briefing is adjourned!

# The Papers

The meeting room emptied quickly, and Major Hartwell announced a short break for those who remained behind. Nicollette stood from her chair. Her palms were still a bit wet, so she subtly wiped them on the sides of her skirt. She extended her arms above her head and stretched her back. That felt good! A lot of sitting! Need to get the blood flowing! Val and Peg were still sitting when Nicollette put her hands on their shoulders.

"I think you two should stand and stretch, otherwise you may become glued to the chair!"

"Very funny, Nicky!" Peg responded rather sarcastically. "But you're probably right. Come on, Val, up we get!"

Sarah walked over from chatting with Sergeant Durban. Nicollette noticed a serious troubled expression on her face.

"What's up, Sarah? You look like something's really bothering you," she asked.

"Yeah, Sarah. You look like you've seen a ghost!" Val added.

Sarah looked at each of her friends and motioned them towards the tea cart. Nicollette could see Sarah's hand shaking slightly as she held the paper cup to accept the tea being poured. Sarah took a sip of the hot beverage.

"That's better, girl. Now take a breath and tell us what's going on?" Val asked as she placed her hand on

Sarah's shoulder.

"Well, you lot are my friends, so please keep this among us."

"Sure, Sarah, it stays here with us."

"I was talking with Sergeant Durban earlier about today's briefing and suddenly, it hit me. We're leaving here to go to who knows where to do who knows what. This is not like being a guest in Belgium or even working on Operation Twist. At least we were here, together, away from the deed. Even when I was up North, I was in England. Now I know I've been trained and prepared, but I must admit, I'm scared, and I shouldn't be!"

Tears were welling up in her eyes as she took another sip of tea.

"And then Sergeant Durban says that we should be prepared to have our group split up on this mission. So, the only stability I know out of all this is being taken away! And then Sergeant Durban mentioned the papers!"

"What papers, Sarah?" Peg whispered softly. "What papers?"

"Sergeant Durban says this little meeting we are about to have will include some paperwork and that we should pay attention to what we are signing."

"Did she say what the papers were about?"

"No, she didn't. It wasn't about what she was saying to me, but how she said it. The tone and manner of her voice made my body feel numb. I'm feeling 'little' and I don't know what to do?"

Nicollette looked at Sarah. "Well, the first thing we're going to do, Sarah is get you some air."

Nicollette softly grabbed Sarah's hand and gently pulled her towards the door. She turned towards Val and Peg.

"We're going for a walk. We should be back before the meeting, but just in case…"

"We know, Nicky. Don't worry."

"Thanks, you two."

Nicollette and Sarah walked down the hallway arm-in-arm.

"The first thing we're going to do is get some water on that face of yours, Sarah," Nicollette announced as they entered the ladies' room. Sarah splashed some water on her face as Nicollette handed her a towel. Sarah fixed her hair.

"That's better, Nicky. Thank you! I'm feeling better just talking about it. You're a good friend. Thanks!"

As they were leaving the ladies' room, Nicollette suddenly turned back at Sarah and blocked the door.

"What's this, Nicky?"

Nicollette looked sternly at Sarah and in a calm but firm voice, "We're not done yet, Sarah! I want to talk with you. There is no one else in here. Just you and me. Now Sarah, I want you to hear this and hear it good."

"Nicky, you're scaring me!"

Nicollette knew what she wanted to say. The strength and the words were coming to her easy.

"Good, I want you to be scared, Sarah, because in fear, strength and courage arise. No one, I mean no one, had to work as hard as you to pass the training. I know you're not the physical type, but you put a man twice your size on the mat in Krav Maga class. Yes, I could see you were visibly upset when we witnessed the murders in Germany. I know it hit you hard. It hit us all hard. But I also remember Operation Twist. You were the catalyst in the science lab, and we got the job done! And you, Sarah, yes you, were a big part of that success! You are the brains of the group, girl, smartest one of the bunch! Sure, you are sensitive, we all are! But this type of work requires you to put that sensitivity away sometimes."

Nicollette stared directly into Sarah's eyes.

"Scared, yes, we all are! I am just a girl from a small village in the middle of nowhere. Damn right I'm scared and right now, I am really scared, but I know no matter where I am or what I'm doing, I know these things. First, I have been well trained and prepared. Secondly, I know this is the job I want to do, and I know I am going to be good at it. There is no alternative! Thirdly, I know I'm working with a great team and good friends who are supportive and strong, and lastly, I know deep down that what I am doing is right and for a good cause! So, Sarah, knuckle down! Pull yourself together. You are part of this team and I'm glad you are!"

Nothing was said for almost a minute. They just looked into each other's eyes. Sarah whispered, "Thank you, Nicky! I'll be better, I promise!"

"I know you are strong, Sarah," Nicollette whispered into Sarah's ear as the two hugged.

As the two walked down the hall back to the briefing room, Nicollette thought about what just happened. She normally was not one to give "pep talks." That was usually reserved for parents, coaches, and bosses. But something inside of her said this was the right thing to do for her friend. As they entered the briefing room, Nicollette thought, *Was that little talk only for Sarah's benefit or was it really meant for me too? Maybe I needed to hear it as well.*

Major Hartwell welcomed the two back to the room. "Good, now let us get started."

Sarah chose to sit next to Nicollette in the seat that Lieutenant Amin had used. She turned to Nicollette and smiled.

"Lieutenant Blankin is going to distribute a folio of papers for you to look over. These are very important, so we will take our time and review them with you."

Major Hartwell asked the four young women to open the portfolio. The cover sheet was printed on heavy stock paper and had the Ministry of Defense symbol embossed on the top.

"The first page is a letter from the Ministry acknowledging that you are under the service of Her Majesty in protection of the Realm. If you read further, the letter talks about certain risks associated with your position."

Major Hartwell paused to allow time for the women to read the official document.

"Now that you've read the letter, are there any questions? None? Good."

Major Hartwell walked behind the four. She leaned in between Nicollette and Val and whispered, "Read these documents carefully. Everyone in this room but you four has read and signed them. This is your first operation abroad, read them carefully. I will be here if you have any questions. Take your time."

Major Hartwell walked back to her seat where she was in quiet conversation with Major Blasingame and Lieutenant Blankin.

Nicollette read the cover letter again. *Fairly official letter really, recognizing our work could be dangerous and carries risk.* There was a spot for an initial in the lower corner. NB. Next page. The second page was written on a thinner paper. It was a letter explaining proper behavior and decorum in a Foreign Nation, reminding everyone that they were guests of the host country, and that local laws and customs must be adhered too. Violation of this policy may result in local prosecution, recall, and/or termination. Nicollette reread the letter, located the initial area, and signed.

The next page talked about the use, importing, exporting or simply being in possession of illegal contraband and banned materials. The letter talked about harsh consequences including termination and imprisonment. *Not for me!* Nicollette thought as she wrote her initials in the prescribed box.

The next page talked about currency. The letter gave specific instructions as to how much money and what kind of transactions were allowed. It was stated not to use credit cards or checks. Cash only. The instructions pointed out that cash "leaves no trails to any specific individual." All cash would be obtained and distributed by supervisors. *Easy enough,* Nicollette thought, *I don't even have a credit card!* Initialed.

Last page. The last page was very official like the first

page. The Ministry of Defense symbol was embossed at the top and the letter was written on heavier stock. As Nicollette started to read the contents, a knot quickly formed in her stomach. Her palms started to sweat, and her heart began to pound heavily. *This is the paper of all papers!* Nicollette thought as she read it and reread it. She had a sudden urge to stand up but found herself staring at the ceiling instead. The letter described what the government's responsibility would be "in the event of any injury or disability occurring in the Line of Duty." But the next paragraph is the one that caught Nicollette off guard: "In the event your death should occur in the 'Line of Duty.'" *Death! Death! I'm twenty-one years old! Death! I guess deep down I knew it was possible, but to see it in black and white in this letter! Death!* Nicollette closed her eyes and imagined her parents' reaction to the official letter they would receive. Her family, her friends Carol and Ashley, the village! Her heart was still pounding as these thoughts raced through her mind, making tears swell up in her eyes. She opened her eyes hoping the letter would go away, but it was still there. She wiped her hands against her skirt and carefully ticked the box stating religious preference. Nicollette tried to hold her hand steady as she listed the beneficiaries of her estate. Her parents, Edward and Sying, Mae and Sue. It was all she could do to list her family, but when she finished writing her nieces' names, that was it. Nicollette put her pen down and quietly sobbed into her hands. A firm hand rested on her shoulder.

"It's all right, Miss Beverley. It is a normal reaction. I

have seen it many times before, but this is the business we are in and anything is possible. We must be prepared."

Nicollette put her hands down and turned to see Major Blasingame's reassuring smile.

"Thank you, Major."

"You're welcome, Nicollette," Major Blasingame whispered back as she handed Nicollette a tissue.

Nicollette found the area marked for her signature and signed her name. As the pen was moving across the line, she thought, *You are going to be careful, Nicky. Good and careful! You are going to die of old age!*

# Ash Sha'am

It was after three when Nicollette, Val, Peg and Sarah left the briefing room. There was an unusual silence among them as they walked through the main gate. Normally there would be small talk, maybe even a joke or two, but not now. About a block from their flats, Nicollette stopped abruptly and looked at her three friends.

"Alright you lot! I know what you are thinking because we all are thinking the same. This afternoon was like a poke in the stomach. The mission, the travel and the papers. Those damn papers! Well, ladies, we knew this day was going to happen. We knew it a year ago as much as we know it today! This is the business we chose to get in and that is the way it is! So, it seems we have two choices. The first is we pitch everything away we have worked so hard for and be miserable or we take a deep breath and proceed with strength and determination."

Nicollette looked at her friends. Val raised her head. She was followed by Sarah and Peg. A slight smile crossed Nicollette's face. *My second pep talk of the day! I may be getting good at this!* She reached into her pocket and pulled out the list of items for the trip.

"Here's how I see it! I need to do some shopping and the shops close soon. Let's get that done and pick up fish and chips for dinner. Then, you lot, we will make the calls we need to do, pack and an early night. Tomorrow, we start a new adventure! How 'bout it, ladies?"

It was a small list of items to pack and most everything Nicollette and her friends needed was obtained at Woolies and Mark's. The chippy wasn't busy, and the group found themselves at Nicollette's flat.

"Not much to pack, Nicky," Peg stated as she sipped her Coca Cola. "Maybe we're not going for too long. What do you think, Val?"

"We might not even be leaving the country if you think about it. Maybe just a couple of days, I reckon."

Nicollette listened to her friends as she dipped a chip into the blob of ketchup on her plate. Something was telling her that this was no easy jaunt. *Why would they include the RAF if it were just a short trip, maybe not even leaving England? I know the packing is light, but that may not mean anything. Plus, they really have not said much to us either!*

Although she was suspicious, Nicollette did not want to raise any angst among her friends. Everyone, including naturally quiet Sarah, seemed to be over their earlier anxiety but there were still calls to make. That task would be hard enough to do, let alone with any mission apprehension.

It was nearly seven when the group left Nicollette's flat. It was agreed they would meet up at 6:30 to walk to work together as usual. After letting her friends out, Nicollette leaned her back against the door to gather her thoughts before calling her parents. *Keep it nice and casual, she thought. No need to get anyone excited. They know this is part of my job, so easy it goes, Nicky.*

Nicollette picked up the receiver and dialed home. It was half seven. Her parents would just be settling down after tea. The tele would be on and maybe glasses of wine would be on the little table.

"Hello, Mum!"

"Hello, Nicky!" Nicollette could hear her mum hold the receiver and call to her dad, "James, it's Nicky!" She put the receiver back to her ear. "How are you? Everything alright?"

"Everything's fine, Mum."

Nicollette paused a moment to gather her thoughts. Light and easy. Her mum broke the silent pause.

"You sure everything is alright, Nicollette?"

Her mum only used her full name when she was angry with her or when she was digging for information.

"Yes, everything is fine, just clearing my throat. Anyways, I wanted to let you know that I am leaving tomorrow on a trip for work. My group is needed to assist the government in planning tours of several sports clubs. We are headed to the Middle East to help in the negotiations and do background work. Not too sure where or for how long, but I wanted to let you know. No need to worry."

There was a pause on the line. Nicollette could just imagine her mum looking at her father, motioning him to the phone, all the while an anxiousness building up inside her. Nicollette could hear her mum breathing just a little bit heavier as she responded.

"Sounds exciting, Nicky! You be careful! Have a safe trip! Love you! Your father wants a word."

"Hello, Nicky! What's the exciting news?"

"Hi Dad! We were told today that my group is leaving for the Middle East tomorrow. We are needed for talks and planning regarding several English sports tours in the region. Should be fun. Not too sure how long I will be, but I'll stay in touch. Didn't want you two to worry."

There was a short pause on the line.

"That does sound exciting. Are you packed?"

Nicollette could hear her father's angst by the forced excitement in his voice about her news.

"I wanted to speak to you and Mum first."

"Well, glad you did. Nicky, you take care and work hard on your trip. Stay in touch. We love you! Be safe!"

"Love you too, Dad! And don't worry! This is a fun trip! Talk soon! Bye!"

"Bye-bye!"

Nicollette hung up the phone. *That was it! I did it! Not too bad really. I sure hope they believed me and do not worry too much!*

Later, in bed, Nicollette revisited the day. A lot had gone on, but she kept thinking about the call to her parents and the papers she had to sign. She tried to put it all out of her mind. Mercifully, she fell into a deep sleep.

The group met at the appointed time at Peg's flat.

"All packed and ready, are we?" Sarah asked.

"It wasn't that bad actually. Not too much to pack really," Val answered.

"We'd better be off. Let's go."

It was the normal walk to work, past the security gate and into their building. Nicollette noticed a luxury coach parked away from the building.

"Look, ladies! Our carriage awaits!" she exclaimed.

The briefing room was full at 07:00. There was Group 228/157 as well as the three Royal Navy officers, Captain Avery, and Lieutenants Simons and Amin. Mr. Bensour, Mr. Johnson and Mr. Troughton were there as well. Fourteen in all. Nicollette did not see Charles Thompson. *Odd, he was here yesterday*, she thought, *maybe he is coming later.*

"Good morning!" Major Hartwell announced. "I trust everyone had a good evening. In just a few minutes, we will be off to Brize. Once we have boarded and are in the air, I will brief you on specifically where we are going. Any questions? None? Good. Let's go."

The coach was warmed up and ready when the group boarded. Nicollette and Val found their seats, and Val turned towards Nicollette,

"I could get quite used to this. It seems everywhere our group goes; we ride in style."

"Don't speak too soon, Val," Nicollette whispered back. "We're not there yet."

The two laughed nervously.

The airplane was waiting at the hanger for them. A ladder step was put in place for the passengers to climb and enter the plane. Instructions were given to leave the luggage in the loading area. Nicollette noticed several military vehicles nearby. They had the distinctive drab gray color and dark green canvas roofs. There was a dozen or more soldiers standing around the trucks.

The plane was like the one they flew to Belgium a year ago. The interior was more like a hotel lobby. The four young ladies found a couple of sofas and made themselves comfortable. Major Hartwell announced they would be leaving shortly and to buckle in. Take off was smooth and easy. Hot drinks and biscuits were served. Nicollette eyed the refreshments with a bit of suspicion. She turned to Val.

"Last time we were drugged, remember," she whispered to her friend.

"I don't think we have to worry this time, Nicky," Val whispered back.

They were in the air about an hour when Major Hartwell walked into the center of the seating area.

"I think now's a good time to fill you in on our destination. We are headed to Abu Dhabi, the capital of the United Arab Emirates, you may know it as the UAE. Once there, we will be transported to Ash Sha'am. We should arrive there around 17:00 hours local time so make yourselves comfortable."

"Now I wish they drugged us, Nicky," Val whispered back to Nicollette.

Nicollette just chuckled under her breath.

Both Majors Hartwell and Blasingame had come over to chat with the young women. Sergeant Durban produced a deck of cards and a lively game of Snap ensued. Even Lieutenant Blankin joined in. Lunch was off a printed menu and there were plenty of beverage choices. Nicollette was lucky to grab a nap after lunch and was awakened by the wheels of the plane touching down. She looked at her watch, it was nearly 4 p.m., 7 p.m. local time.

Major Hartwell addressed the group as the plane

slowed towards its final parking spot. "We will disembark directly to waiting vehicles. The officers will ride in the first two vehicles and everyone else in the next two. We have about a three-hour ride to our next destination, Ash Sha'am, so I suggest you take care of personal business now. We speak to nobody on the ground here or enroute to Ash Sha'am. Understood?"

"Ash Sha'am? I've never heard of it," Peg exclaimed as they rose from the sofa.

"Neither have any of us, I can assure you," Val replied.

"I need a stretch. How about you lot?" Nicollette announced as she placed her arms over her head and then bent from her waist to the floor.

"No cracking noises. Nicky! You must still be in pretty good shape!" Val laughed.

Major Hartwell motioned for the officers to exit the plane. About ten minutes later, Sergeant Durban guided the rest to leave the plane. Nicollette was first in the group to leave. As she stepped onto the descending stairs, all she could see were the multi-colored lights illuminating the airport. The sun had set, and it was still very warm compared to Cheltenham. As she reached the bottom of the stairs, an RAF airman directed her to a tan-colored Range Rover. She was joined by Val, Peg, and Sarah. Another RAF airman held the door open and Nicollette, along with Val, climbed into the rear third seat. The inside of the Range Rover was very warm and Nicollette could feel sweat forming on her body. Sarah and Peg took the middle two seats and the two airmen sat in the front.

The airman in the front passenger seat turned around

and looked at the four young women.

"Welcome to Abu Dhabi! You may find it a bit warm here, but good news, it only gets warmer in the daytime!" he added sarcastically. "We will be leaving here shortly so open your windows for some air. We have several canteens of chilled water up front, so please help yourself. Ash Sha'am is about 280 kilometers away, so about three hours. Make yourselves comfortable and enjoy the scenery."

"Look at us! The posh travelers!" Val exclaimed as the Range Rover lurched forward.

The cool breeze coming through the windows helped moderate the heat inside the vehicle. They were soon away from the airport on a paved two-lane highway. There was a steady flow of traffic on the road despite it being after dark. The caravan of vehicles seemed to be moving at a quick pace. There was not much to see outside the window, only the lights of the oncoming traffic. The further away they traveled from the airport, the more the full moon illuminated the land. From her window, Nicollette could just make out what seemed to be a great extent of wasteland. Every now and then, a building would appear. Sometimes, the moonlight would highlight mountains way off in the distance. Nicollette looked out of the rear window. She could see the trailing Range Rovers and several military type vehicles bringing up the rear. *Are those the same trucks from Brize? Did they fly those vehicles in? What kind of cargo are they carrying, I wonder?*

After a little over an hour, there was a lit road sign

announcing in Arabic and English that they were nearing Dubai. Traffic was increasing and the pace was slowed. For the next thirty minutes, they drove through urban traffic. The driver announced they were about halfway there and asked if anyone wanted anything. Once past the urban areas, the road narrowed to a single lane each way. Nicollette could see what looked like an ocean on her left as moonlight reflected off the water. It seemed the road was hugging the shore. Maybe it was boredom or the tediousness of the road trip, but Nicollette soon found herself closing her eyes. The vehicle turned left and started down a bumpy path, bringing Nicollette back from her nap. The smoothness of the paved roads was now replaced by a rutted, bumpy ride. Nicollette was bouncing hard and thought she might even hit her head against the ceiling of the Range Rover. The headlights were now on bright, and the vehicle was crawling along. Nicollette could see the headlights of the trailing vehicles moving up and down, showing just how bumpy the road had become. There was nothing but darkness on either side. The Range Rover made several sharp turns and stopped. Nicollette could see a brightly lit area in front of the convoy. The road was suddenly smoother as they approached the lighted area. The Range Rover in front moved forward and stopped. A khaki-uniformed guard saluted the passengers and motioned them through a wired gate. The guard turned towards Nicollette's vehicle and directed it forward. The airman driver stopped and showed the guard some papers. The guard walked around the vehicle and peered into Sarah's window.

"Hello, misses, and welcome to Ash Sha'am."

He then directed the vehicle to a staging area with the other Range Rovers. The airmen in front opened the doors for the women. Nicollette could immediately feel the coolness of the night. She had been sweating three hours ago and now she was chilly. The sky was clear, and the moon and stars seemed to illuminate the darkness. Val asked one of the airmen about the facilities. He laughed a bit and pointed to a series of tents off to the right.

"Anyone else?" Val asked the group.

"Good idea."

The four of them wandered over to the tents. A small sign outside one of them said, "Women's Latrine."

"It's sure not the Savoy," Peg exclaimed sarcastically as they walked into the tent, "but it will have to do!"

Sergeant Durban met the four women as they were leaving the latrine. She instructed them to head back to the vehicle and wait for instructions.

After about five minutes, Major Hartwell asked the group to follow her. They walked about a block on a hardened sand path to a big tent. Sergeant Durban held the flap open as the group followed the major inside. There were several large steel tables and stacks of folding chairs along the side. Nicollette, Val, Sarah and Peg grabbed chairs from the stack and sat at the table in front. Major Hartwell addressed the group.

"Good evening and welcome to Ash Sha'am. It has been quite a day. A long one as well. You may want to set your watches ahead three hours. I have 20:30 hours. Ash Sha'am is going to be our home for a while. As you can tell, the Royal Marines and Royal Navy are here, and I think you will be surprised as to what they have accomplished in such a short time. I want to remind everyone that this is a military base so military rules extend to everyone, civilian and service alike. We are guests, so best behavior please. We are on the twenty-four-hour system here. Wake up horn is 06:00 hours and flag raising is at 06:30. There are morning exercises for those who want to join in at 06:45. For our group, there will be a briefing in this tent at 07:15 hours. Now, after this meeting, we have been invited to the mess tent for a meal. I imagine you might be a little hungry. From there, you will be escorted to your sleeping quarters. I suggest an early night, tomorrow will be a busy day. Sergeant Durban will hand out a map of the base for reference as we leave. Any questions? None? Good."

Major Hartwell led the procession out of the tent to the mess hall. The mess tent was bigger than the briefing tent. On one side, there were several glass cabinets with shelves of sodas and drinks. There was a separate case with bottled beer and wine. There was a coffee and tea cart next to the refrigerated cases. Directly in front of them was what looked to be a buffet area. Nicollette followed the others as they lined up for food.

"Now I know this isn't the Savoy!" Peg whispered to her three friends.

"What, you mean no linen napkins?" Val responded in a sarcastic tone.

"We'd better get used to it, ladies. The major implied we're going to be here a while." Nicollette whispered back.

The four of them found an empty table. Nicollette found herself rather hungry. They hadn't eaten for quite a while. The shepherd's pie on her plate wasn't nearly as good as the one's her mum would make, but it would suffice. A cold Coke to wash it down and some biscuits for after. As they were finishing, Lieutenant Blankin sat down next to Nicollette.

"Enjoying your meal?" she asked with a smile on her face.

"My compliments to the chef," Val responded trying hard not to laugh in front of the lieutenant, but it was too late. There was a quiet laugh at the table.

"If you are ready, let me take you to your quarters," Lieutenant Blankin announced.

"If you want to grab something to take with you, it's all right to do so." She motioned with her eyes towards the cooling cabinets.

Nicollette and Val grabbed a couple bottles of beer and Peg grabbed some packages of crisps and biscuits. Lieutenant Blankin used a small flashlight as she escorted them down a partially lit path to a series of tents. There was a small sign in front of the tent.

Their names, "Beverley N, Davies V, Green S, Wilson M," were listed on a sheet of paper tacked to the sign.

"Here it is, ladies, home for a while," Lieutenant Blankin exclaimed as she turned on a gas lantern hanging from the center of the tent.

There were two steel military issue cots on either side of the tent. There was a metal cubby next to each cot and a steel trunk at the foot of the bed. There were bed linens and a blanket at the foot of the bed. A pillow rested at the front of the bare mattress.

A folded-up net hung over each bed.

"That's for the flies," Lieutenant Blankin spoke as Val reached for the net over her bed. "Sometimes they get pretty bad here."

"Thanks for the warning, Lieutenant," Sarah responded.

"Lovely!" Peg whispered under her breath.

"Well, if you lot are good, I'll leave you to it. The latrine is on this path about fifty yards to your left. There is a flashlight in your cubbies. See you in the morning. Sleep well. Good night!"

As Lieutenant Blankin left the tent, she closed the flap at the front. The four friends looked at each other.

*What have I got myself into?* Nicollette thought as she passed out the bottles of beer.

"I don't think 'room service' is coming anytime soon, ladies, so I guess we should make our beds," Val laughed as she unfolded her linens.

"Remind me to ring for a 'wake up' call," Peg added.

Jokes and rhetorical comments were passed the rest of the evening. They all had a laugh, but later in bed, Nicollette's mind was racing. *Would all the joking about this place come back to haunt them? What was going to happen here? What was she expected to do? Should I worry?* Sheer exhaustion brought a restful, deep sleep.

# Morning Briefing

The wake-up horn brought Nicollette out of her slumber. She automatically reached over for her alarm clock to shut the alarm off. She banged her hand against the steel cubby. *Ouch!* The horn continued, as she sat up in the cot. *Damn! I forgot we're in Ash Sha'am, wherever that is!*

It was dark inside the tent as Nicollette climbed out of bed to turn on the gas lamp. Val was stirring in her cot.

"Morning, Nicky," Peg said softly as she rolled out of bed.

"Morning, Peg! Sleep all right?"

"I guess. I was exhausted!"

"Come on, Val! Rise and shine, girl!" Nicollette scolded her friend.

"I hate you all," Val grunted as she put her feet on the floor.

"Where's Sarah?" Peg asked.

"Don't know. She must have gotten up earlier, but I didn't hear her," Nicollette responded.

"Did we leave her in England?" Val commented as she put on a pair of jeans.

"No, I'm sure she was with us! You are cheeky this morning, Val!"

"Poppycock! I'm never cheeky!" Val responded in a posh voice. "Look, here comes room service!"

A light was shining in from the front of the tent. The

flap opened and Sarah walked in, turning off her flashlight.

"Good morning, ladies! Glad to see you are all awake. Good news, I looked all over and for the life of me, I couldn't find Sergeant Harris!"

"Now who's being cheeky!" Val exclaimed in between snickers.

The four of them left the tent as the sun was just starting to light up the landscape. As they walked towards the mess tent, they came across the ceremonial raising of the Union Jack. Nicollette stopped and watched as the flag climbed the flagpole. She started to think of the War Memorial at home in Brockwirth. *How many times did those brave men and women experience the flag hoisting? How many times was it their last time?*

"God Save the Queen" was played by a small group of soldiers as the flag reached the top of the flagpole. Nicollette just stood as she watched the wind unfurl the Union Jack.

The four friends found seats in the mess tent. The buffet included powdered eggs and half-toasted bread pieces. There was also porridge, cereals, canned fruit and something that passed as bangers.

"First class fare, ladies," Val added sarcastically as they sat.

"It's really not too bad," Sarah reacted as she raised a spoon of porridge.

"I guess we'll have to get used to it anyways."

"We've got about fifteen minutes, ladies, then we have the morning briefing," Nicollette reminded her friends.

"I wonder about this morning's briefing," Peg offered.

"I think our job here will become much clearer," Nicollette responded. "At least we're not worried about the cold and damp here!"

"That's for sure!" Sarah concluded.

Major Hartwell greeted everyone as they arrived for the briefing. There was a sense of urgency as she spoke. *Something has happened,* Nicollette thought as the major retrieved a display easel from the corner.

"Good morning again. We have a lot to get through, so let us get to it. Major Blasingame will bring us up to date. Major."

Major Blasingame stood from her chair.

"At the Senior Officer's 06:00 briefing this morning, we were given new information about our mission. Our timetable has been advanced considerably. New communications intercepted have given us a new sense of urgency. It appears the interception and capture of a British Flagged tanker is much closer than we originally thought. We now believe the attack will occur during Rabi Al-Awwal. Rabi Al-Awwal is the Muslim holiday celebrating the first day of spring and ladies and gentlemen," Major Blasingame paused and took a breath, "it takes place this Thursday! As you can see, time is of the utmost importance."

Major Blasingame paused again as she started to walk around the room. Nicollette's heart started to race as she realized that no matter what, the next seventy-two hours were vital, and she was going to be a part of that. *But what is my role? What do they want me to do?* Her mind was racing with a multitude of questions.

"Our mission here is to set up distinct lines of secure communications between this base and our Royal Navy base of operations in Aden. There will also be a direct link to London, but most importantly, we are instructed to set up a forward communications base in the Gulf waters. Preferably somewhere in the shipping lanes of the Strait."

Major Blasingame rolled out a large map and tacked it to the easel. "Here is where we are in Ash Sha'am, on the tip of the UAE. Additional information this morning suggests that the interception will take place in this area, just west of the Straits of Hormuz. Our nearest Royal Navy base is here, in Aden, nearly 1,600 kilometers away, not very convenient at this point. So here we are. We have been able to piece together what the plan is once the tanker is intercepted. It will be taken to the Iranian port of Bandar Abbas. This is the closest port capable of handling a large tanker and is located strategically at the western entrance to the Strait. It is approximately 100 kilometers from the main shipping lanes. The city is in an area of Iran that is sympathetic to Khomeini. We are still not sure if the Khomeini followers are carrying out the attack or if it is the Shah. In the meantime, we have increased our aerial reconnaissance in the area around Bandar Abbas. We are also monitoring the shipping lanes. We should have more information in our afternoon briefing at 13:00 hours. Now I will give you back to Major Hartwell."

"Thank you, Major. So, there you have it. As Major Blasingame says, time is critical at this point. When we dismiss here, we will look at what we are doing to get ready. I think you will be impressed. Royal Navy Lieutenant

Simons will be escorting the group. Any questions? None? Good. Again, we will meet back here at 13:00 hours."

Lieutenant Simons stood and motioned the group to follow him. Nicollette, Val, Sarah and Peg followed along.

As they started walking, Val turned towards Nicollette. "I wonder what Lieutenant Simons does. He looks to be about our age."

Overhearing the question, Lieutenant Amin responded. "Our Lieutenant Simons is an engineer and quite a good one at that."

Nicollette turned around to see Lieutenant Amin. This was the first time that she or anyone else in the group heard the lieutenant speak. *She does have a voice*, Nicollette thought as Lieutenant Amin continued.

"He specializes in building specialized equipment almost like your Mr. Troughton."

Val looked at Lieutenant Amin and asked, "How do you know about Mr. Troughton?"

Lieutenant Amin gave a smug smile as she responded, "We have been thoroughly briefed on your group, including you, Miss Davies and Miss Beverley."

*Well, that is something!* Nicollette thought as the group turned left to reveal a sight that nearly took her breath away. There, just a hundred or so meters down an embankment, was a good-sized lagoon and several piers. There were five odd-looking vessels tied to the piers and maybe fifty or so workers actively at work on the boats. As the group reached the bottom of the embankment, Lieutenant Simmons stopped the group. He turned and pointed to the odd-looking boats.

"These funny looking boats are called dhows. They are very common in the Gulf and are typically used for fishing and the transport of goods in the Gulf."

Lieutenant Simmons guided the group to the two larger dhows.

"These large dhows are called sambuks and the two medium sized dhows over here are called jalibuts." He pointed to the jalibuts and continued. "The smallest dhow is called a barijah. We have one on the far end of the dock. Now we really do not expect you to remember the names of the dhows, but they are going to play an important role in our mission. As the phrase goes, 'never judge a book by its cover,' so too these dhows. Do not let the outside condition of these boats confuse you. We are expediting the retrofit of each dhow with advanced engines and technical equipment. A complete armament package is also being installed."

Lieutenant Simmons motioned the group to follow him as they boarded one of the sambuks. Once the group was on board, he pointed to three heavy poles on either side of the deck.

"These poles are seemingly harmless, nothing to raise suspicion from any passersby. However, these poles are not just poles, but mounts for fifty caliber machine guns!"

Lieutenant Simmons reached down to a small steel ring on the deck. He twisted the ring and pulled it straight up to reveal the fifty-caliber machine gun.

"We have the three you see here on either side of the sambuk and two more in the aft, I mean rear of the boat. Now look at this mast." He pointed to the large main mast in the center of the deck. "Although some dhows have engines, most are wind driven using sails. Our mast here has been converted to a radio antenna."

Lieutenant Simmons motioned the group to follow him into the main cabin. Nicollette turned to Val.

"This is like a miniature Destroyer," she whispered. "I've never seen anything like it!"

"I'm sure glad it's on our side!" Val responded.

Inside the main cabin, the lieutenant showed the control area. He pointed out the navigation and radar equipment. Then he showed a row of night vision binoculars hanging to one side of the large front window. Lieutenant Simmons opened a small side hatch and asked the group to crawl through. Inside the hidden small room was the communication center.

Nicollette recognized the equipment. "It's like a much smaller version of our space in Cheltenham."

There were three chairs although the space could hardly accommodate two. *Whoever is in here is going to be very cramped*, she thought.

Lieutenant Simmons continued his tour. He showed the group the storage area and sleeping quarters below the deck. As they were leaving the boat, a lot of noise was coming from the rear of the boat. Lieutenant Simmons explained that the engines were being fitted and unfortunately, it was a noisy process. As the group was walking up the embankment back towards the main camp, Majors Hartwell and Blasingame and Captain Avery made their apologies and headed off in a different direction. Lieutenant Blankin asked Sergeant Durban, Nicollette,

Val, Sarah and Peg to follow her. She excused the rest of the group but not before reminding everyone of the afternoon briefing at 13:00 hours.

"I wonder where we're going," Sarah asked Peg.

"How can I guess where we are going when I'm not sure where we are," Peg responded.

Lieutenant Blankin, having overheard the question, stopped and turned towards the young women.

"We're going shopping, ladies," she announced.

"What the devil is she talking about?" Val asked as the group continued to walk.

"Just wait and see," Sergeant Durban replied with a smile.

The group arrived at a large tent that was hidden behind several large trucks and military vehicles.

"Welcome to Marks and Spencer's in Ash Sha'am, ladies," Lieutenant Blankin announced jokingly as she held open a flap for all to enter.

Inside, the tent was filled with boxes and crates from floor to ceiling. Soldiers were coming in and out with supplies. The Lieutenant brought the group over to a table in the rear of the tent. A soldier behind the table saluted and asked Lieutenant Blankin what he could do for the group.

"This is group 228/157 from Cheltenham. I believe you have packages for us."

"Let me check, ma'am."

The soldier pulled out a clipboard and turned a few pages. "There you are. Group 228/157. We have several crates for you." He pulled a walkie talkie from his belt and barked instructions. "We'll have them up in no time, ma'am."

After about ten minutes, three soldiers, each using a cart, brought six large boxes to the table.

"Here you are, ma'am. Would you like us to bring these somewhere for you?"

"That would be fine, Corporal, just follow us."

Lieutenant Blankin led the group to the tent where Nicollette, Val, Peg and Sarah were staying. She asked the soldiers to leave the boxes in the center of the tent and then dismissed them. The lieutenant closed the flap of the tent and walked next to the boxes.

"Ladies, here is your new wardrobe!" she announced. "Let's separate and open the boxes."

Nicollette opened the first one.

"It's tops, ladies," she exclaimed as she pulled one from the box and held it up for all to see. It was a tan-colored, dual-pocketed top complete with epaulettes on the shoulders.

"More like camp shirts," Val responded, "And that color does not suit you, Nicky!"

"Cheeky girl! What is in your box, Val?"

"Shorts! And they match your shirts!"

"Fancy that!" Sarah added as she held up a pair of socks in one and a pair of low-cut utility boots in the other.

"I've got belts and hats here," Peg announced.

Lieutenant Blankin called for everyone's attention.

"Ladies, as we are guests here at Ash Sha'am, we've been asked to dress appropriately. Plus, I think these outfits are more comfortable for the weather. Each of you is to get three of each item. Two belts each and one hat and pair of boots. You are required to wear this outfit while we are here. You should be able to find your size as everything is either small, medium, or large. We have your shoe sizes on record; however, we have added half a size because of the heat here. Sergeant Durban and I will take our outfits and meet you back here in twenty minutes."

Lieutenant Blankin reached into one of the boxes and pulled out a manila envelope.

"And ladies, you must wear these badges at all times while we are here. Civilian badges are in green, and military are in black."

The Lieutenant handed out the badges as she and Sergeant Durban organized their clothes.

"See you in twenty minutes," she announced as she and Sergeant Durban left the tent.

Nicollette found her size and laid out the clothing on her cot. She changed into the khaki tan outfit. *Oddly enough, this fits fairly well, and I do feel more comfortable with the heat,* Nicollette thought as she laced up her low-cut boots. She stood up and used her hands to rub out the small creases in the shorts. There was no mirror in the tent, so Nicollette looked to her friends for an opinion.

"What do you think, ladies?"

"I think we look like right wallys," Val replied.

"It's like we are in Bermuda or Australia in these outfits," Peg added. "And I do love the hat!"

"Well, I for one think we look very official." Sarah put her name tag on above her right pocket.

"Sarah may have something, you lot," Nicollette exclaimed as she sat down on the cot.

"What do you mean, Nicky?" Val asked as she sat down next to Nicollette.

Peg and Sarah joined on Nicollette's cot.

"Seriously, Nicky, what's up? We're just having a bit of fun," Val stated as she reached for Nicollette's hand.

Nicollette took a breath. A strange and uncomfortable feeling rushed up her spine as she responded.

"Listen, I'm going to tell you something I'm worried about. It started when we boarded the plane yesterday and has continued as we put on these clothes. Then it hit me. I am concerned we may have been treating this operation too lightly. We have been joking about everything from the food to these tents to even our clothes! Are we failing to take what is happening here seriously? Remember the papers we signed and having to make the calls? Now we are here on the front lines, away from the safety of home! Did you see those guns on the boats?"

Nicollette paused as she let the rhetorical question settle.

"There's a lot going on here and we're an integral part of this. Are we just afraid and covering up the fear with 'light-heartedness'? And when do we wake up and realize where we are? Well, you asked me 'what's up'? I think I am a little scared and I have been using our laughter as a 'plaster' to cover my fear and I do not want it to affect my ability to do my job. So, there it is. Now you know."

There was a silence as Val, Peg, and Sarah let Nicky's words sink in. Sarah reached for Nicollette's other hand

and squeezed it as she whispered to Nicollette, "Remember that little talk we had in the ladies on Monday? Well, you were right then, and you are right now. We all are a bit afraid and overwhelmed here. But as you said to me, we've been trained and now have experience."

"We'll be just fine, you lot!" Val added.

Peg nodded her head in agreement, unable to find the words to reply.

"Let's have a look at you!" Sergeant Durban announced as she walked into the quiet tent.

Nicollette stood from the cot and put on her hat. Val, Peg and Sarah followed suit.

"You four look like seasoned veterans, I must say. I think you will find this dress more comfortable in the heat. Now do not forget your badges. Lieutenant Blankin suggests we eat something now." Sergeant Durban took a quick glance at her watch and continued, "It is nearly 11:30 hours and the briefing is at 13:00. So, let's head out."

As Sergeant Durban led the group out of the tent, she stopped and commented, "Just a reminder, hats are only for outdoors, always remove them when you enter a facility."

Nicollette followed along to the mess tent. She felt as though she should eat something, but her stomach was still churning. She forced down a sandwich and a Coke, her stomach quieting just a bit. The normal banter with Val, Sarah, and Peg was subdued. Nicollette looked into each of her friend's eyes. *They must be thinking like me. I have a feeling this afternoon is going to be very serious.* Nicollette took a bite from her cookie. *Very serious indeed!*

# Dress Code

*Damn, it is hot outside!* Nicollette thought as the group entered the briefing tent. Just the walk from the mess to the meeting had created beads of sweat on her forehead. Inside the tent, several large fans were humming along.

"At least we'll bake slowly," Val whispered to Nicollette as they took seats in the front row.

Three easel stands had been placed in front. Nicollette could see that each easel had a map displayed. She could make out that the first map was of the Persian Gulf. The other two maps looked strange to her. Nicollette did not want to leave her seat for a closer look, she had a feeling that all would become clear shortly.

Major Hartwell entered the tent through the back carrying a brown satchel. At exactly 13:00 hours, she asked for everyone's attention. Nicollette looked around the room. There was Group 228/157 and at least ten people she had not seen before. Major Hartwell opened her satchel and produced a short stack of papers.

"Major Blasingame, Lieutenant Blankin, and I have just come from a two-hour briefing. We have been given the latest updates and now time is of the utmost importance."

Nicollette could see in the major's expression and hear in her tone of voice that the pressure was on.

"Our Intelligence estimates that an attack on a British

tanker is to happen within the next twenty-four to forty-eight hours. Major Blasingame and Captain Avery will now give you the details of our plan of action."

Major Hartwell took a seat next to Sarah as Captain Avery addressed the group.

"Here's what we know," he stated as he pulled out a pointer and walked over to the first easel. "Aerial reconnaissance has spotted an uptick of activity at the Iranian port of Bandar-e Abbas. A large area, big enough to accept a full-size tanker, has just recently been cleared in the port. Most of the minor vessels in the area have moved away, and curiously, the small detachment of Iranian Naval ships stationed there, have also been moved. We've tracked them heading west, away from the Strait of Hormuz."

Captain Avery relinquished to Major Blasingame.

"Communications monitors have also detected a significant uptick in messages in the area. We have deciphered many of the messages, but one seems to give us a strong clue of the impending attack."

Major Blasingame reached for a paper from the satchel.

"The decoded message reads, 'The big brother always takes care of the little brother, especially in the beginning.'"

Major Blasingame paused for a moment as Captain Avery walked back to the map of the Persian Gulf, then continued, "There are two strategic islands located just west of the Strait of Hormuz. All westbound shipping coming through the Straits into the Gulf travel just north of these islands and those leaving the Gulf and heading east into the Straits of Hormuz, just south. In other words, these islands are right in the middle of the major shipping lanes."

Captain Avery identified the two islands on the Gulf map.

"This is where the message gets interesting. The larger, eastern island is called Greater Tunb and the smaller, western island is called Lesser Tunb. They are about twelve kilometers apart. We believe the message is referring to these two islands. The Iranians seized control of both islands in 1971. Let us talk about Greater Tunb. The island is about ten square kilometers in area and has a population around 300. Since gaining control, the Iranians have made a small fortress out of the island. They have built several hard large gun emplacements throughout the island and have built a cement runway capable of handling a mid-sized aircraft. There are several areas around the island the Iranians have dredged to create small docking areas. Intelligence suggests a normal military presence of around thirty. For the past week, we have been including Greater Tunb Island in our twice daily aerial reconnaissance. Along with the usual dhow traffic, we spotted three Iranian patrol boats at the southern part of the island. A fourth and fifth patrol boat were seen this morning leaving Bandar-e Abbas, heading towards Greater Tunb. We believe any interception of a British tanker will take place near Greater Tunb Island."

Major Blasingame paused a moment and asked if there were any questions. Hearing none, she took a sip of water as Captain Avery moved to the third map. The major continued.

"Now a little about the other island: the Lesser Tunb. This island is about two square kilometers in land area and has no permanent population. There is no source of fresh water on the island. It is used primarily as a rest area for fishermen from the mainland and rarely used or patrolled by the Iranian Navy. However, Iran has built a very small runway on the western part of the island and a permanent, albeit unmanned, communications station at the eastern end of the Island. Aerial photographs show three small buildings and a tower at the site. There are limited areas around the island where dhows can dock. Any questions?"

Major Blasingame and Captain Avery stepped aside. Nicollette's leg started to fidget, and her hand was shaking slightly. She looked at Val. Her arms were crossed, and her expression was blank as they looked at each other. Nicollette turned towards Peg and Sarah. Same blank expression each. Sarah's eyes were twitching.

A man Nicollette had never seen before walked to the front.

"Good afternoon, I'm Lieutenant O'Malley. My group monitors British shipping arriving in and leaving the Persian Gulf. We have been tasked with identifying potential targets, those tankers or cargo ships that may be in the area in the next twenty-four to forty-eight hours. We first looked at westbound traffic passing through the Strait. There are several tankers in the Indian Ocean, but they are several days away. We then checked for tankers heading east towards the Strait of Hormuz. There are tankers currently loading or waiting to be loaded in Kuwait and

Saudi Arabia. So, nothing there, however, there is one tanker, the 'British Engineer,' that has loaded up at Kharg Island and is heading east. Kharg Island is Iran's main oil terminal in the Gulf. The British Engineer is an older tanker that is scheduled to be decommissioned in the fall. It is currently about 350 miles away and with an average cruising speed of fifteen knots, we estimate the British Engineer would be in this area between 08:00 and 12:00 hours tomorrow morning."

Lieutenant O' Malley took his seat in the back. Major Hartwell walked very deliberately to the front. "Now for the details and your assignments in Operation Abraham's Tent."

Major Hartwell reached into the satchel for more papers. Nicollette's heart started to pound harder and faster. Her hands were suddenly wet with perspiration and her mouth felt like it was full of sand. Her leg continued to twitch. *This is it! The mission!*

Major Hartwell took a sip of water, cleared her throat, and organized the papers in her hand. "We believe we have put together the outline of a potential attack on one of our tankers in the Gulf. First, our intercepted messages indicate a plan to seize a British tanker in the Gulf. Secondly, we think the hijacking will occur around the Greater Tunb Island. Thirdly, the tanker the British Engineer will be in the area we deem as 'hot' tomorrow. Finally, the Muslim holiday, Rabi Al-Awwal, celebrating the first month of spring, begins tomorrow, making the argument that this action has a religious tie-in. So, there we are. We have the time and the target. We must get to work and fast. Time is critical. Now here is our plan and your assignments."

Major Hartwell paused, took another look at her sheet, and continued.

"A small detachment of Royal Marines will leave here after the briefing and head to Lesser Tunb Island. They will arrive at dusk and quickly secure the Island. Mr. Johnson, Mr. Troughton, Miss Beverley and Lieutenant Amin will be accompanied by additional marines and arrive on the island after it is secured. They will be transported by the large dhow and immediately set up the communications equipment and establish radio contact with this base and the 'British Engineer.' You will be our eyes, ears, and voice on the Island. At the same time, another detachment of Royal Marines will take the second large dhow to meet the 'British Engineer.' They will rendezvous with the tanker about 200 miles away. Miss Davies and Mr. Bensour, as well as the necessary equipment, will be taken by helicopter to the British Engineer in advance of the marines. At 22:00 hours, the three remaining dhows will leave here and head to various locations in the east bound shipping lanes. Each dhow will have Royal Marines on board. Miss Wilson will handle the communications from the lead dhow. Miss Green will remain here with Sergeant Durban, Lieutenant Blankin, Major Blasingame and myself. We will be in the communications tent."

Major Hartwell took a breath and continued.

"Our plan is to stop a potential hijacking of our tanker by either terrorist or Iranian government forces. We will do this by preparation, monitoring transmissions, including setting up lines of communications and deploying assets. If and when an attack is determined to be eminent, we will use the assets in place to secure the tanker. A word of caution, we want to avoid casualties and loss of property and we certainly do not want to get involved in politics. We are still not clear if this hijacking is government or terrorist led. The politicians will sort that out. Understood? Good. Ladies and gentlemen, we have a mission to do, let's get the job done! Dismissed and good luck!"

*Casualties? What? Like shooting! Me!* Nicollette's mind was racing along with her heart. She could feel the perspiration dripping down her sides and her left leg was shaking. A sudden tap on her shoulder quickly brought Nicollette out of her trance. She turned to see Val.

"You alright, Nicky?"

"I'm ok. How about you?"

"I'm going on a bloody helicopter! Can you believe it! You know how I am with heights!"

"You'll be just fine, Val. No problem."

"No problem is right, ladies!" Sarah interrupted, forcing her voice to be calm, "We'll do our job, and everything will be fine."

"I will buy the first round when we come back here," Peg announced.

A Royal Marine interrupted the group.

"Miss Davies and Miss Wilson. Please come with me."

"This is it, Nicky! Good luck, you two," Peg said as she turned towards the marine.

"Yes, good luck, Nicky and Sarah!" Val added as she joined up with Peg.

"And good luck to you two," Nicollette and Sarah

responded.

"Miss Beverley."

Nicollette turned around to see Lieutenant Amin.

"Follow me, please."

Nicollette turned back to Sarah. "Good luck!"

"Good luck to you, Nicky."

Nicollette followed Lieutenant Amin to a corner of the tent where Mr. Johnson and Mr. Troughton were already standing. A Royal Marine Officer approached the small group.

"I'm Captain McQuinn. I oversee this operation. We will be leaving very shortly, but before we leave, we have a stop to make." His deep Scottish brogue bellowed from his mouth.

Captain McQuinn was a big man in stature, standing over six feet. His face was weather worn, and his red hair was cut short. Nicollette guessed him to be in his early forties. There was something about him that made Nicollette feel far less anxious, more secure, safe. She did not know if it was his size or the deepness of his voice, but there was something.

Captain McQuinn motioned for the group to follow him to an area behind the supply tent that Nicollette had visited earlier. He opened a flap, revealing a small table. The soldier sitting behind the table rose to attention.

"Good afternoon, sir."

"We need to dress this group," Captain McQuinn instructed.

The soldier walked from behind the table and glanced at Nicollette and Lieutenant Amin. He then asked Mr.

Johnson and Mr. Troughton about sizes, then made some notes on a pad. Walking behind the table, he turned to Captain McQuinn.

"Just be a minute, sir."

"Be quick about it, man," the captain barked in reply.

The supply soldier returned with three boxes. He placed a box on the table, "These are for you misses." He then handed a box each to Mr. Johnson and Mr. Troughton.

"Now I want you to change, take care of any personal business and meet at the dhow in fifteen minutes. Understand?"

Nicollette acknowledged the captain with a head nod and picked up the box.

"My tent is nearby, Miss Beverley. Why don't we change there?"

Nicollette looked at Lieutenant Amin. It was only the third time she had heard her speak. "Sure."

They entered the lieutenant's tent and placed the boxes on the cot. Nicollette opened her box and pulled out what looked like a very large black pillowcase. She noticed a slot towards the top.

"It's called a burqa," Lieutenant Amin announced as she placed the garment over her head.

"Go on, put yours on."

Nicollette unraveled the burqa and placed it over her head and let it drape down over her body. The slot was at eye level. She turned to Lieutenant Amin. "Not very flattering, is it."

"That is the whole point of it, Miss Beverley. Most devout Muslim women wear the burqa when in the presence of non-related males. As for us, this is part of our disguise. We want to blend in to look like a group of fishermen or traders using the island as a resting area. We don't know if the Lesser Tunb is watched or not, so this is a precaution. Just think how much we'd stand out in our khaki outfits. And those hats."

Nicollette went back to the box and pulled out a pair of dark brown sandals.

"Yes, even our footwear is part of the disguise. You wouldn't find the women we're trying to look like wearing military boots, would you?"

Nicollette removed her boots and socks. "Where do you want these?"

"Put them by the cot please."

As Nicollette put her boots down, she happened to notice a picture on Lieutenant Amin's nightstand. "Your family?"

"Yes. I think we should leave now," Lieutenant Amin added, hurried, as she walked out of the tent.

*Lieutenant Amin is sure a quiet one*, Nicollette thought, *very private as well. We must work together, and I don't even know her first name!* Nicollette followed the lieutenant down the hill to the pier. At the pier, they were greeted by Captain McQuinn.

"Follow me," he instructed.

The three of them walked to the edge of the pier where several military supply trucks were parked. Nicollette had noticed them earlier but did not think anything about them. The captain motioned them to go to a truck in the back. At the side of the truck, a small table was set up.

When the soldier behind the table saw Captain McQuinn, he stood and saluted.

Captain McQuinn saluted back and gave his instructions.

"We need to equip these two, corporal. Standard supplies."

"Yes sir."

Nicollette watched as the corporal disappeared behind the truck. *I wonder what standard supplies means. I'm already in this disguise. The marines are bringing the gear. What else is there?*

Within minutes, the corporal returned with two boxes. He looked at Nicollette as he opened the first box.

"This is for you, miss," he stated as he pulled out a large torch followed by a small first aid kit, but what he pulled out next nearly sent Nicollette's heart out of her body. The corporal raised a side arm holster out of the box and placed it on the table. He unsnapped the leather strap that held the gun in place and handed the weapon to Nicollette.

"I understand you're familiar with the Browning pistol, miss," Captain McQuinn said as Nicollette gingerly held the weapon.

"Yes sir," she whispered a response, trying hard not to show her shaking hand. "We used these in training."

"Good. It is required for personal protection on our expedition. Hopefully, you will not have to use it. Now go ahead and put it on, miss."

*Yes, I do know how to use it, but I hope I don't have to!* Nicollette thought.

Nicollette removed her burqa and wrapped the holster belt around her waist. It was surprisingly lighter than she expected. The corporal handed her two cartridges and loaded a third into the pistol. Nicollette found the spots on the belt for the spare cartridges and the torch. She checked the safety on the pistol and placed it in the holster. She felt almost numb as she pulled the burqa over her head.

"Now you're set, miss," the corporal stated as he handed her a clipboard with a pen attached to it with a piece of string.

As calmly as she could with her sweaty hands, Nicollette signed the spot by her name.

Her mind was racing so much, she did not have time to think about how hot she was getting with all the clothes she was wearing and the afternoon heat. Nicollette followed Captain McQuinn and Lieutenant Amin down the pier to the waiting sambuk. She was greeted on board by Mr. Johnson and Mr. Troughton. At first, she did not recognize them. They were dressed in shabby, color-worn pants and very loose-fitting odd shirts. Bandanas were tied around their heads and sandals on their feet. Nicollette quickly noticed that they were also wearing sidearms.

"We look a right bunch!" Mr. Troughton exclaimed. "But then, this whole boat does."

Nicollette looked at the Royal Marines moving about on the deck. Everyone was dressed like pirates, just like the ones she had seen in the movies. She could never tell that these were highly trained, highly skilled Royal Marines. *Hopefully, the bad guys will feel the same!* Nicollette thought as she, Mr. Troughton, and Mr. Johnson found a bench to sit on. After a few minutes, Captain McQuinn appeared on deck, completely changed into his disguise. He ordered the crew to gather around him. Nicollette counted fifteen marines.

She tried to conceal her amusement hearing the Scottish captain give orders in his deep, brogue voice all the while dressed as a poor Persian fisherman. For just a moment, some of her anxiety left her mind and a sense of calm returned.

"We are shoving off here in two minutes," he barked. "I want to review our plan, so everyone is on the same page. The first dhow has left and will arrive at the island just after dark. They will secure the island and signal us to arrive. We will then proceed to the communications area about 500 meters from where we disembark. Then, with the assistance of Mr. Johnson and Mr. Troughton, we will set up the equipment. Miss Beverley and Lieutenant Amin will follow to set up and work communications." Captain McQuinn pointed out four marines. "You four will proceed to eastern side of the island and set up a visual post." He then pointed at four other marines. "You four will do the same on the south side. The remainder stay with me. Any questions? Good. Now let me remind you, we do not know who is watching us, so act like fishermen. Move about, play with ropes and nets. Look lively! Dismissed!"

The dhow moved away from the pier and ten minutes later, they were in the Gulf heading northwest. Nicollette found a spot in the shade as the mid-afternoon sun beat down relentlessly on the deck of the dhow. There was a cooling breeze that she could feel through the eye and mouth slots of her burqa, but it offered little relief.

"Would you like something to drink, miss?" a marine asked her.

"Thank you, please."

The cold water tasted good as Nicollette nursed it down. She stood up and looked over the side. She could see what looked like a big ship. *A tanker maybe? They are big!* A noise in the distance became louder and louder. Nicollette looked up at the sky to see a helicopter heading west. *I wonder if Val is on that. Good luck, my friend!*

# Lesser Tunb

The sun was mercifully setting in the western sky, cooling the afternoon heat. Nicollette pulled the burqa off her arm to look at her watch. It was nearly six. *The first group of marines will be landing soon and then it will be us!* As she was rolling the burqa back over her arm, she looked at her watch again. It was not a fancy new digital type, just a simple basic watch with a green face. Nicollette closed her eyes and recalled her 13th birthday when she received it as a present from her brother. She was so excited because it was waterproof and included the day and date on the face. *That was over eight years ago!* The band had been changed a few times over the years and the crystal was replaced just last year. Still, the watch worked fine. Her mind drifted back to her home in Brockwirth. *What was going on in the village? What were her parents doing? What would they think if they knew she was on a boat, surrounded by Royal Marines? In a burqa and carrying a sidearm?*

The dhow slowed down to a stop. The noise of the engine now down to a gentle purr. Mr. Johnson walked over to Nicollette.

"The captain wants us on the bridge, Miss Beverley."

As she stood up, Nicollette realized she had been sitting for a while and a short stretch was in order. As she raised her arms over her head, she could feel the holster on her side. *It's still there.*

The bridge was small and crowded. Captain McQuinn walked over to the three civilians.

"Won't be long now. The first group should be landing in about twenty minutes, and we should get the all-clear around 19:00 hours. We will then get in as close as we can and disembark. You two may get a little wet. You will be escorted to the communications area. We have a full moon tonight so there is natural light. Our men will help you set up the equipment. Any questions? None. Good."

Captain McQuinn turned and looked out of the front window.

"There she is, the Lesser Tunb Island."

Nicollette could just make out the outline of the island in the fading dusk. It still seemed rather far away to her. Maybe they were keeping a safe distance till the island was secure.

"We're looking for a yellow flash. That's the signal they've landed. Once the island is secure, we will get a green flash. Excuse me now, must get the crew organized and ready. Watch for those flashes!"

The captain excused himself from the Bridge. Mr. Johnson and Mr. Troughton announced they wanted to look over the equipment and followed the captain onto the deck. Nicollette was left on the bridge with two marines, a navigator, and a radioman. The radioman removed his headphones and turned to Nicollette.

"Not as fancy as your stuff," he said as he smiled and pointed to the radio imbedded in the control panel.

"No, I guess not." She smiled back. "But yours works

just fine, I bet."

The radioman smiled back at Nicollette and put his headphones back over his ears.

"There it is!" the navigator exclaimed. "They're on the island!"

Nicollette could see the yellow flash in the now dark distance. *Will not be long now,* she thought as her heart started to pound. The captain walked into the bridge and instructed the three civilians to leave. The cool night air felt good as Nicollette looked over the side of the dhow. The sky was clear and illuminated by the full moon. The water was calm, a surreal peacefulness seemed to be settling in. In the distance she could see small specks of light. *Maybe other boats, maybe land, maybe both.* A moment of tranquility. Nicollette took a deep breath, savoring the moment.

The engines started up and the dhow began to move. A Royal Marine walked past Nicollette. "Green flash, we're good to go, miss. Should be there in twenty minutes."

Nicollette looked around. There was a lot of activity around her. Several large crates were being broken down and their contents organized in separate areas. She could see Mr. Troughton and Mr. Johnson inspecting equipment. Oddly, she could not see Lieutenant Amin on the deck. *Wonder where she is? Just a few minutes from the island. She could not have gone anywhere,* Nicollette thought as a smile crossed her face.

The engines were cut off and the dhow drifted towards the island. Nicollette could see silhouettes of the Royal Marines waiting for them in the moonlight. The area they were porting was relatively flat with a sandy beach. Captain McQuinn ordered the small lifeboats to be filled with equipment and lowered. He motioned for Mr. Johnson and Mr. Troughton to board the first small boat carrying the equipment. Two more lifeboats were lowered away.

"We're next, Miss Beverley."

Nicollette turned around to see Lieutenant Amin. She thought better of asking her where she had been, knowing full well there would be no answer. They were directed to the other side of the deck where a rope ladder descended into the water below. A lifeboat was waiting for them as they made the short climb down the rope ladder. A marine manned the small electric motor and brought the boat to the beach. He held his hand out for Nicollette to assist her.

"Thank you," she said as she stepped into the water and walked onto the beach.

"This way, misses," a marine sergeant commanded. "Be careful, lots of rocks on the trail."

They walked across a flat area and Nicollette could see clear across the island. *This must be the airstrip we saw on the map.* The terrain became rockier and hillier, as they moved towards the center of the Island. Beyond some large rocks, Nicollette could make out what looked like torches moving around. She saw the three buildings, *Not much more than shacks really.* There were several oil lamps hanging about illuminating the activity. Mr. Johnson saw Nicollette and Lieutenant Amin and directed them to the middle building. Inside, Mr. Troughton and two marines were busy assembling the equipment. It was a small building with open windows on either side. A table had been set up for the communications equipment and a quiet whirr from a generator permeated the room.

"Ready to give it a go, Miss Beverley?" Mr. Troughton asked as he handed her the binder containing the codes.

"Yes. Ready."

"Lieutenant Amin, you're here," he continued as he pulled out a chair for the lieutenant.

Nicollette turned on her screen and adjusted the radio. She opened her code book and sent an initial message back to Ash Sha'am. It was to be sent three times, two minutes apart per the instructions in the codebook. A return confirmation would be sent three minutes after the last transmission. Nicollette rolled up the burqa and looked at her watch. She synchronized to the clock on the screen. In exactly three minutes, a return message appeared. *Sarah is up and ready,* she thought, *now for Val and Peg.* Nicollette sent out the initial signals to the others. Same procedure as before. Same results. The network was complete. Nicollette was now on standby mode. She took off her headset and looked at Lieutenant Amin. She was busy adjusting frequencies on her radio. The Lieutenant had not plugged in her headset yet so the crackling noises from her radio were easily heard in the room. Once she found a live frequency, she put on her headset, but not before Nicollette could hear a strange language coming from the radio, one she had never heard before.

"It's Persian, Miss Beverley. The Lieutenant is a linguist."

Nicollette turned around to see Mr. Johnson standing

behind her. He smiled at Nicollette. "And so am I."

"I thought you were a cryptanalysis and communications expert. Now you're telling me you translate Persian as well?"

"And Spanish and French too."

Nicollette looked at Mr. Johnson as he spoke. *I believe I am in the presence of a genius*, Nicollette thought.

"That's impressive, Mr. Johnson." Nicollette responded not knowing exactly what to say to a man nearly her father's age.

"While we are here, you can call me Pete, Miss Beverley, after all, we are civilians," he added with a smile.

"You can call me Nicky."

"Well Nicky, I'm glad you were chosen for this operation. This mission is dangerous and demanding and I think you will own up to the task very well."

"Thank you, Mr. Johnson, I mean Pete."

Mr. Johnson winked and smiled as he left the hut. "Oh, and by the way, you two can take your burqas off whilst you are in here but be sure to put them on when you leave."

Nicollette felt flattered by the comments of the middle-aged man. *That genius of a man wanted me on this mission. Me! Better not let him down.* Nicollette took off her burqa and folded it over her chair and went back to her screen.

For the next two hours, communications were very light. *Not much happening tonight*, Nicollette thought. *Maybe this is just a false alarm or something.* She looked over at Lieutenant Amin. She was listening intensely and watching her screen all the while writing notes on a pad.

When she was finished, she called for Mr. Johnson.

Mr. Johnson walked in from the neighboring hut.

"I've just overheard some chatter that sounds interesting. What do you think, sir?"

Lieutenant Amin handed Mr. Johnson her pad. He examined her notes and sat down between the lieutenant and Nicollette. He read the notes a second time and looked back at Lieutenant Amin.

"Maybe something, maybe not. I'd like Major Hartwell's thoughts." He turned to Nicollette. "Miss Beverley, please send this to her straight away."

Nicollette quickly coded the notes and sent them to Sarah. *Something about an unusual amount of traffic for this hour around the bigger island. Could be just fishermen taking advantage of the full moon's light. Not uncommon in the Gulf.*

As they waited for a reply, Mr. Johnson asked Nicollette and Lieutenant Amin if they would like a break. Nicollette checked her monitor, it was nearly ten. She had been sitting for well over two hours. Mr. Johnson said the marines had set up some food in another hut and spoke. that he would monitor communications while they were away. Nicollette stood and stretched and slid into her burqa. She looked at Lieutenant Amin who stood as well. Outside the hut, the air was clear and cool. The few trees blocked the light from the full moon, so the oil lamps provided just enough light. Inside the next hut, there was a folding table with sandwiches, crisp packages, and wrapped cookies. A large cauldron of tea was next to a jerry can filled with chilled water. Nicollette grabbed a sandwich and sat in a folding chair. It had been some time since she had eaten, and she did not realize how hungry she was. Mr. Troughton walked in for a cuppa. He looked at the two women.

"Everything working alright?"

"Yes, mine is working fine, Mr. Troughton," Nicollette responded after swallowing some tea.

"Mine as well, sir," Lieutenant Amin added. "Had to calibrate a bit, but the signals are strong and clear."

"Good, glad to hear. If you need me, I'll be with the captain down at the boats."

"Mr. Johnson says you're a linguist and that you specialize in Persian," Nicollette said, hoping to start some sort of dialogue.

Lieutenant Amin looked at Nicollette. Her disinterested expression spoke volumes.

"Yes, I speak Persian and I work as a linguist," the lieutenant responded as she turned back to her sandwich.

*What is with her!* Nicollette thought. *We're working together and I can't get anything out of her. A couple of sentences over the last three days and I still don't know her first name! I guess that is the way she wants it. Then that's the way it will be. Shame.*

# Nazrine

Nicollette walked back into the communications hut to find Mr. Johnson sitting in Lieutenant Amin's chair.

"Glad you two are back. Nothing really going on currently. We did get a response from Major Hartwell regarding our earlier signal though. It seems they are of the same opinion that the increase in dhow activity is rather normal during the full moon here in the Gulf. So not to worry. Nicollette, they want you to continue sending a clearing signal to your three contacts every thirty minutes at seven minutes and thirty-seven minutes after the hour. You will receive a staggered response every two minutes from the three. Use the signal guide on page six of the code book. Lieutenant Amin, your instructions are to continue to monitor chat on the airways. It is 10:25 or 22:25 hours, I will be back at 1 a.m. or 01:00 hours to give you two a break."

Mr. Johnson headed out of the hut. Just before he reached the door, he turned to the women. "The major sends you a 'well done' for what you've done so far, and she says for you to keep up the good work."

With that, he was gone. Nicollette took off her burqa and resumed her seat. *Do women actually wear this thing all day? It can be really annoying, but I guess to each her own!* She looked over at Lieutenant Amin, her headphones were firmly on her head, and she was focused on moving the radio dial. *She must be highly skilled; I can tell by just how she is so gentle with the tuning dial. A talker, however, she is not! She is quieter than a church mouse!*

Nicollette checked the clock on her screen and reached for the code book. *It's nearly 10:37, I must get ready to send.* Nicollette sent the necessary signals and by 10:45, she had received the responses. *All is in order,* she thought as she removed her headset. She took a quick glance over at the lieutenant who was still engrossed with the radio dial. The hut was very quiet, only the soft whirr of the generator and the occasional crackle of Lieutenant Amin's radio broke the silence. Nicollette stood and stretched. *This is going to be a long night! They trained us well at Brize, but not on monotony! I must stay alert!*

Nicollette sat down and put her headphones on. She began to think about how Val was getting along on the tanker and how Peg was doing on the big sambuk. Then there was Sarah, smartest one of the bunch, and how was she faring with Majors Hartwell and Blasingame looking over her shoulder? Nicollette looked forward to sharing stories about this adventure with her friends over a cold pint, but that was later, she knew she had to remain in the now. *Seven minutes past eleven, same signal, same responses. All good!* Stand and stretch. Drink some cool water. Check the equipment. Breathe!

"I just picked this up, Miss Beverley, I think we need to send it to Ash Sha'am," Lieutenant Amin announced as she handed Nicollette two sheets of paper.

*She speaks!* Nicollette thought as she looked over the handwritten notes. The top page was written in what looked like cursive, with scribbly lines, dots, and dashes. *Must be Persian.* The second page was written in English. Nicollette read through the paragraph.

"Just send it, Miss Beverley!" Lieutenant Amin commanded impatiently.

Nicollette put her headset on, coded the message, and sent it off to Sarah in Ash Sha'am.

*Nothing too unusual about the information,* Nicollette thought, *just some chatter about a couple of good fishing locations in the Gulf.* She looked over at Lieutenant Amin. *She must have thought it was important though. Just send it, Miss Beverley, from the woman of few words!* Nicollette waited for the response from Sarah in Ash Sha'am. It was almost time for the next clearing message. At 11:07 the communications went out and by 11:15, all was clear. *Still no response about the lieutenant's message. What could be taking so long?* Nicollette wondered. Thirty more minutes, same routine. Send the clearing message, wait for the response. All good. *And still nothing on the lieutenant's message!*

"Miss Beverley, anything yet?" the lieutenant asked.

It was almost midnight.

"Nothing yet, Lieutenant, sorry. I can send it again if you'd like?"

"That will not be necessary, thank you. Just let me know when you get a response."

"Absolutely."

*Wow! A conversation, albeit all business, but a conversation nonetheless!*

It was after midnight, another round of clearing

messages, another round of responses. Same results; all clear. Nicollette stood for another stretch and a drink of cool water. She was starting to feel the effects of the long day. *Must stay alert*, Nicky, she kept telling herself, *only a few minutes till a break, the fresh air will help.*

At 12:50, Mr. Johnson walked into the hut.

"How are you two doing? Ready for a break?"

"Sounds good to me, I could use some fresh air and use the necessary."

Nicollette stood from her chair, pulled the burqa over her head, and handed Mr. Johnson Lieutenant Amin's communication notes.

"Lieutenant Amin asked me to send this to Ash Sha'am. We still haven't received a reply."

Mr. Johnson accepted the notes as Nicollette left the hut.

"Take as much as an hour, Miss Beverley, it's quiet now."

Outside, the air was cooler than during her last break, making the burqa more comfortable. On the way back from the latrine, she stopped at the food hut for a snack and cup of tea. *It's such a beautiful night, I think I'll find a quiet place and relax*, she thought.

Nicollette carefully walked behind the group of huts and ended up in a small clearing past a group of trees. The ground was uneven, littered with small stones and the exposed roots of the trees. *No need to spill any tea.* She found a perfect spot, sat against some small rocks, and marveled at the view. From where she sat, the land gradually sloped to the Gulf, just a couple of hundred meters away. She was close enough to hear the gentle sound of the small waves lapping against the rocks. The moon cast a shadow on the water. It was very calm, almost surreal.

The tea and biscuit were soon finished. Nicollette checked her watch, she had another thirty minutes or so for break. She closed her eyes for a short kip. The rhythmic sound of the waves and the feel of the slight breeze off the water soon had her in a sleep.

Nicollette dozed into a dream about the High Street in Brockwirth. It was evening and there was traffic up and down the road. The headlights from the cars illuminated the shops on either side. She was standing at the crosswalk, the crossing signal flashing its familiar yellow light. As she crossed the street, the lights from the stopped vehicles shone brightly on her. The light of the signal began to flash at a quickened pace. She saw herself standing in the middle of the crosswalk. People were yelling at her, but she could not understand what they were saying. She could not move. The lights became brighter and more intense! The yelling became louder! She still could not move and felt trapped in the crosswalk. The lights and the yelling grew more and more intense! She tried desperately to move, but she was stuck. The bright lights were swirling around her. The voices screaming in her ears. She started to spin. Faster and faster! Too much for her, Nicollette raised her hands to her ears. *Enough!* She yelled waking her from the dream.

As Nicollette regained consciousness, she rubbed her eyes with her hands. *That was some dream!* She looked down at the Gulf and took a deep breath of the refreshing air. The moon was still illuminating the calm waters. Off to her right, near the water, Nicollette noticed two large white lights bouncing around. At first, she thought the lights were from the torches carried by the four marines stationed in the area, the bouncing caused by the marines climbing over rocks. But, then a third, fourth, and fifth light appeared, in fact, Nicollette counted twelve lights. She rubbed her eyes again. *Am I seeing double?* The lights from the torches were shining all around her and someone started yelling. Nicollette could not understand what was being said, but the language sounded like the radio signal Lieutenant Amin had been listening to. *Persian?* A light glanced over her and soon the area around her was being lit up by the strong torches. The yelling was becoming louder as the lights seemed to move closer. Nicollette quickly and instinctively dropped to the ground, her heart racing and pounding against the inside walls of her chest. *This is not good,* she thought, *something is terribly wrong! Must stay composed.* The lights were coming even closer now, maybe 100 meters or so. It seemed everyone was yelling. Then she heard a sound that brought her reality home. Pop, pop, pop! Like the sound of popcorn popping in a pot. Automatic weapons fire!

Nicollette recognized the sound from her weapons training at Brize. Pop, pop, pop, again! She turned and started to crawl back to the relative safety of a group of trees about twenty meters behind her. *Must get out of this clearing!* The lights from the torches were shining just above her. The bullets whizzed and pinged as they bounced off the rocks around her. She was sweating profusely. The ground was hard, and her body seemed to feel every stone and rock she crawled over. Pop, pop, pop! The lights were still following her. *Stay down, girl! Must keep moving!* The burqa was being torn apart by the jagged edges of the stones. Nicollette could feel blood rolling down her right leg. A tree branch fell in front of her, a victim of the automatic weapons fire. She crawled another few meters. Pop, pop, pop! She could see tracer bullets flying in the air. Using all her strength, she continued to crawl, the adrenaline kicking in. Every ounce of energy she had was being expended as fast as her body could find it!

Then, out of nowhere, she heard her name.

"Miss Beverley, over here!"

Nicollette kept crawling, the whiz of tracer bullets flying over her. She heard it again. "Miss Beverley, over here!"

Wiping the perspiration from her eyes, Nicollette looked to where she thought the voice was coming from. Off to her left, she could see Lieutenant Amin. The Lieutenant was kneeling on top of a small mound above a natural ditch just a few meters away. The lights were getting brighter, indicating the attackers were getting closer. Pop, pop, pop! *Must get to the lieutenant!*

With everything she had, Nicollette crawled towards the ditch. Blood and sweat seemed to be pouring from every pore on her body. She could see the lieutenant's left hand reaching for her as she crawled closer to the ditch. In the lieutenant's right hand, she held a gun.

"Gotcha," Lieutenant Amin exclaimed as she grabbed Nicollette's left arm.

Just then, the lights focused on the two of them. Immediately there was the popping sound of more shooting. Pop, pop, pop! Tracer bullets everywhere. Lieutenant Amin's grip opened as she fell back into the ditch. Nicollette rolled into the hole and saw the lieutenant slouched in the back of the ditch.

"You've been hit!" Nicollette yelled.

Nicollette crawled to the lieutenant and yelled into her ear over the sound of the whizzing bullets.

"Where are you hit!" she screamed.

The Lieutenant was struggling to keep her eyes open. Nicollette raised the burqa and could see a stream of blood flowing down her leg and a large patch of blood staining her khaki shirt. Nicollette quickly ripped off what remained of her burqa and pulled up the lieutenant's top. There was a bloody hole on her side just below her rib cage. Nicollette lifted the limp torso and wrapped the burqa over the wound and around her body. The wound on her leg was just above the knee and bleeding fast. Nicollette ripped off another piece of the black material and made a tourniquet for the leg. She pulled it tight. The lights were now all directed to the top of the mound. More and more weapon fire was flying above their heads. Leaves and branches were everywhere. *They're getting close!*

In a small window of consciousness, Lieutenant Amin spoke in a whisper to Nicollette, "Fire back at them. Give some resistance."

Nicollette leaned in to hear as the lieutenant whispered and repeated her instructions. "Fire back at them now before it is too late. Aim at where the lights and tracer bullets are coming from. Do it now!"

Nicollette could see the lieutenant's gun against the front of the ditch. She picked it up and released the safety. Nicollette looked back at the lieutenant. Her eyes were closed, and she was breathing heavily. The shooting was becoming more intense and Nicollette could hear voices coming closer.

"FIRE THE DAMN GUN, MISS BEVERLEY!" Lieutenant Amin yelled before falling unconscious.

Nicollette turned towards the front of the ditch. She found an opening between two rocks that would afford her some protection from the incoming fire. Another tree branch fell behind her as she aimed at a group of lights and pulled the trigger. Pop, pop, pop! Three shots off. Pop, pop, pop! Another three shots off. The return fire was intense, tracer bullets everywhere. Using her left hand to fire the lieutenant's gun, she used her right hand to un-hook and remove her weapon. She emptied the cartridge in the lieutenant's gun and immediately started shooting with hers. Pop, pop, pop! Nicollette aimed at a different set of lights just a few meters away. She quickly emptied that cartridge and reached for her two spares. She reloaded and continued to shoot. The return fire continued in intensity. She took a quick glance back at Lieutenant Amin. She was unconscious. The blood flowing down her leg seemed to have stopped and the stain on her shirt had not got any bigger. Nicollette loaded her last cartridge. She knew the lieutenant had spares but did not know if there was enough time to get them. *Make this count, Nicky!* she said to herself as she aimed at the closest group of lights. Pop, pop, pop! *Three shots off, nine left!* Pop, pop, pop! *Six left!* Bullets were flying! Branches, leaves and dust were everywhere. Nicollette aimed at another group of lights. Pop, pop, pop! *Three left! Make 'em count, Nicky!* She aimed at the closest group again. Pop, pop, pop! *That's it! Better get the lieutenant's spare cartridges.* As Nicollette turned around to get to the lieutenant, the gunfire became more intense than ever. Tracer bullets and automatic weapon fire everywhere. Nicollette reached for the lieutenant's belt and retrieved the two spares. The bullets were flying directly overhead as she crouched down to reload.

"Stay down, misses! Stay the bloody down!"

Nicollette went flat on her belly, holding the loaded gun close to her chest. The gunfire gradually slowed in intensity. As she looked up, it appeared that the bullets were coming from behind her.

In what seemed like an eternity, the shooting finally stopped. There was quiet. Nicollette, hesitant at first and very cautious, rolled over to the lieutenant. She could see she was still breathing. *Thank God for that!* A large shadow appeared over the ditch. Nicollette readied her gun and rose to her knees.

As she turned, she yelled, "Who goes there?!"

"It's Captain McQuinn, lass. You can put your weapon down. Everything is under control."

*That wonderful Scottish accent! How beautiful it sounds!*

"Lieutenant Amin has been hit twice, once in the side and once in the leg. She needs attention now!"

Captain McQuinn called for a medic.

Nicolette dropped her weapon and put her hands to her face. She wanted to sob tears of joy, but the tears didn't come. Instead, a sense of self pride flowed through her. She'd been challenged to the extreme and had acted bravely. *I survived! I survived!*

The medic called for a stretcher. He looked up at Captain McQuinn. "We need transport for the lieutenant."

"Aye." The captain called into a walkie talkie, "On its way, take her down to the beach head."

The medic tuned to Nicollette. "You did good, miss."

Nicollette took her hands away from her face. "Thank you. Take good care of her."

"We will, miss."

Nicollette watched as the stretcher was lifted from the ditch. Lieutenant Amin opened her eyes and looked at Nicollette.

"Nazrine, my name is Nazrine," she whispered.

Nicollette smiled at the lieutenant. "Nice to meet you, Nazrine. My name is Nicollette, but my friends call me Nicky."

"Nice to meet you, Nicky." Nazrine smiled back.

Nicollette reached for Nazrine's hand. She squeezed it gently. "Take care, Nazrine."

Nicollette watched as the stretcher was carried into the darkness.

"Miss Beverley. Lass." Captain McQuinn spoke in a calming voice.

Nicollette turned and looked up at the captain. She put her weapon back in the holster and reached for his hand. He had a firm grip as he helped her to her feet and out of the ditch. She took a deep breath as she looked back towards the clearing.

She could see a group of men sitting on the ground with their hands in the air being watched over by five marines. Several large tree branches had fallen around the ditch and a putrid smell of sulfur permeated the dusty air.

"Don't look, lass," Captain McQuinn told her in a quiet voice. "We'll talk about it later."

Nicollette acknowledged the captain as she pulled the torch out of her holster belt. He pointed the way back to the small buildings. As she walked, her legs started to feel like they were encased in cement and the scratches on her body felt like deep knife cuts. She felt like she was in a trance, her mind in a daze. *One step in front of another,* she told herself.

The whirring from the generator was a welcome sound as Nicollette walked past some large rocks. The hut area was dimly illuminated, but there was just enough light to reveal several pock marks on the outside wall of the communications hut. She entered the hut to find Mr. Johnson sitting in her chair, headphones on, busily typing a message. His left arm was wrapped in a bloody white bandage, supported by a makeshift sling. She leaned against the door, trying to imagine what must have happened.

Mr. Johnson sensed her presence. He finished his communications, took the headset off, and turned around. His face lit up and a big smile crossed his face with the sight of Nicollette.

"Nicollette! You're ok! Thank God!" he exclaimed

enthusiastically as he rushed to help her to her chair. "Where is the lieutenant?"

Nicollette sat down and looked around the room. There were bullet holes in the walls. She turned to Mr. Johnson, his expression becoming more serious waiting for her response.

"Nazrine, I mean the lieutenant, was hit in the chest and leg. She was pretty bad off. They took her to the landing area."

Nicollette paused, wanting to change the subject. "What happened here? What happened to you?"

"Here, let me get you some water." He brought a canteen to Nicollette, and she took a swallow. He leaned forward in his chair, trying hard to hide his reaction to the news about Lieutenant Amin. He took a slow, fluttered breath and started very deliberately to explain the series of events. "Remember just before you went on break, you handed me some papers that Lieutenant Amin asked you to transmit but were still waiting for a response?"

"Yes, something about fishing."

"Well, not long after you left, we received a reply. Ash Sha'am believed that the 'good fishing area' the message was talking about was the staging area for the attack on the tanker! It is just off the southern coast of this island. To make matters worse, the bandits were going to assemble here to coordinate the attack. Nicollette, this island was going to serve as the base for the attack! Even worse, the attackers were already here, too late for any help from Ash Sha'am! We were on our own!"

Mr. Johnson reached out for Nicollette's hands as he

continued. "We had to find you and bring you back here. Someone saw you leaving the supply hut and said you were walking northeast behind the huts. Lieutenant Amin went to find you while I secured the communications hut. I heard gunfire in the distance. Then there was a shot through the door, followed by more shooting. The two marines in the supply hut quickly set up outside and we held them off until Captain McQuinn arrived with some more men."

"What happened to your arm?" Nicollette asked.

"Oh this." Mr. Johnson chuckled as he pointed to the sling. "It's really nothing. A bullet hit the wall by the door and a shred of cement landed in my arm. I guess you could call it a shrapnel wound. Now tell me what happened out there."

Nicollette reached for the words, but nothing was formulating. "I'm still playing it over in my mind and I'm just not ready to talk about it yet, sorry."

Mr. Johnson squeezed her hand gently and reached for a notepad on the table.

"This is the message we received from Ash Sha'am as you were walking in the door. They want us to come back to base. You, me, and Mr. Troughton will head back to Ash Sha'am at that time. That about sums it up, Miss Beverley. I suspect things will be a bit quiet for a while, so just relax if you can."

As Mr. Johnson left the hut, he turned towards Nicollette. "You did very well out there. I'm proud of you!"

Nicollette watched as he disappeared outside. *Relax? Really! After what just happened! I've too much adrenaline to relax!* She took another sip of water from the canteen and focused on calming herself down.

As she leaned back in her chair and closed her eyes, a voice broke the silence. "Miss Beverley, Miss Beverley."

Nicollette turned around to see a marine, his automatic weapon hanging off his shoulder. "Yes."

"Captain McQuinn wanted you to have these until the island is completely secure."

The soldier handed Nicollette three cartridges for her gun. She placed them on the table.

"Captain McQuinn's orders are to make sure your gun is loaded before we leave. Please, miss."

Nicollette reached for the gun in her holster. She unsnapped the leather strap and pulled the gun from the holster and laid it on the table. She checked the safety and removed the spent cartridge and replaced it with a fresh one.

"Thank you, miss. We'll be checking up on you."

As Nicollette picked up the gun to return it to her holster, something caught her eye. On the handle was a large red smudge. *Blood! Was it hers or Nazrine's? Does it matter? Blood!* She put the gun back in the holster and brought her hands in front of her face. Her eyes pouring over each finger, each knuckle and each bend as she turned her hands slowly. They were covered with a combination of dirt, sweat, and blood. Her fingernails were caked with a blackish brown mud that had hardened. *These hands! My hands!* Nicollette looked at her arms. They were also caked with dirt and blood. *I must be a real sight!* She saw her watch, the one she was given to as a teenager, now covered in dirt. She rubbed the face, it was nearly 3:30. *Two hours! 120 minutes I will never forget!* She leaned back in the chair again, closed her eyes and tried to rest.

"Miss Beverley?" a husky voice called. "I'm here to relieve you. Didn't they tell you? You're going back to Ash Sha'am."

Nicollette opened her eyes and slowly turned towards the voice. Her hand instinctively moved towards her holstered weapon. She saw the voice belonged to the marine radio operator she met on the sambuk.

Another marine entered the supply hut. "Miss Beverley? Are you Miss Beverley?" he asked as he looked at Nicollette.

"Yes, that's me."

"I'm here to take you to the beach head, miss."

"This way, miss," the marine commanded as the two left the hut.

The sun's light was just starting to chase the night's darkness away. The marine's torch lit the path as they crossed the airplane runway. Nicollette could make out the beach head just a few hundred meters away. As they got closer to the water, Nicollette noticed a large circle of men sitting on the ground surrounded by Royal Marines with automatic weapons. Prisoners, I suspect. *There must be twenty or thirty of them and there was only a dozen or so of us!* Curiosity taking over, she asked her marine escort, "Prisoners?"

"Yes, miss. This is most of them."

At the beach head, Nicollette was greeted by Captain McQuinn.

"Aye, Miss Beverley. Feeling better, lass?"

"Yes sir. Thank you."

"That's good. You are going back on the first boat. The dinghy is waiting for you. Mind your step."

Nicollette stepped into the cool water and boarded the very small craft. As she turned to sit down, she noticed the sun reflecting off several large blue tarps on the beach. The engine started and the marine steered the craft towards the waiting boat. Again, Nicollette's curiosity got the better of her and she asked about the tarps she saw on the sand.

"The tarps are covering the bodies, miss."

"You mean the dead? Ours?"

"No, miss, theirs."

The dhow was smaller than the one she arrived on and there was hardly anyone aboard. A small area was set aside with a tea cauldron and some packaged biscuits. The sun was now shimmering over the water and the air was warming. Nicollette was enjoying the strong tea and the quiet serenity of the voyage. Her mind kept drifting back to the events of just a few hours earlier. *I will never forget these last twelve hours! I am strong! I survived!*

A voice awakened her from her thoughts. "Miss. Miss Beverley."

Nicollette looked up at the tall, stocky marine.

"Hello. I'm her."

"We just received a message from a Miss Davies aboard

the tanker, the British Engineer. She asked for you to look southeast. I brought you these."

The marine handed her a set of binoculars and guided her to face southeast.

"I don't see anything."

"Keep looking. You should see something very shortly."

Nicollette kept searching the horizon.

"I see it!" Nicollette exclaimed as she turned to the marine. But he had left without her realizing it.

She refocused the binoculars on the object, now more clearly in view. *It's the tanker!* As Nicollette watched, two green flares were shot into the air. *That's the signal. All good. All safe. Well done, Val!* Nicollette watched as the tanker disappeared from view. She took a deep breath of the clear, salty air. *Well done, me too!*

The dhow slowly sailed into the docking area at Ash Sha'am. A Royal Marine escorted Nicollette off the boat. Sarah and Sergeant Durban were waiting for her on the dock.

"Nicky! So glad to see you!" Sarah exclaimed as she rushed to her friend. "We were worried about you!"

"Welcome back, Miss Beverley," Sergeant Durban said. "We're glad you're safe."

Sergeant Durban looked Nicollette over.

"Besides getting you cleaned up, I think we should have a medic look at your legs," the sergeant continued.

Nicollette looked at her legs. There were exposed scratches and cuts from her ankles to her knees. *I guess the water must have cleaned my legs when I boarded the dinghy.* The upper part of her legs was still caked with a combination of mud, sweat, and blood. As they walked off the pier, Sergeant Durban motioned for Nicollette to go to the supply truck, the same truck where Nicollette had checked out her gear a little more than twelve hours ago. They approached the table in front of the truck and the same soldier from yesterday greeted them. As per instructions, Nicollette removed her torch and holster belt. She released the strap on the holster and laid her gun on the table.

"There's blood on that gun, Nicky," Sarah pointed out. "What the hell happened last night?"

Nicollette heard the concern in Sarah's voice. She knew she would be asked about last night many times. *I'm just not ready to address it yet.* Trying not to be rude to Sarah but still avoiding her question, Nicollette slowly and deliberately removed the cartridge from the weapon and laid out the six empty cartridges from the holster belt. She turned to Sarah and Sergeant Durban. Sarah's eyes and mouth were wide open, and she had turned pale white, like she had seen a ghost.

"Those cartridges are empty, Nicky."

"Yes, they are Sarah. It was some night."

Sarah placed her hand on Nicollette's shoulder. She could feel the tension flowing inside Nicollette's body.

"When you are ready then, alright, Nicky."

"Thanks, Sarah."

The shower felt wonderful as the remains of the last night were washed away from her body. The resulting mind numbness she was feeling from the events she had experienced just a few hours ago seemed to subside. She started to feel normal again. Nicollette felt like she could stay in the shower all day, but unfortunately, the water also made the open sores and cuts on her legs and arms sting. Still, it was good to feel clean. *I will never complain about a lukewarm shower again!* Nicollette promised herself.

The medical officer checked Nicollette over. He gave her some creams for the cuts and suggested a rest. Nicollette asked the medical officer about Lieutenant Amin and Mr. Johnson.

"We stabilized the lieutenant in the helicopter when we left the island, and we flew directly to HMS Sheffield in the Arabian Sea. They have a full medical staff on board. Her wounds were well beyond our abilities to deal with them here. The wound in her leg was severe enough that she could have lost her leg and her chest wound was, well, let us just say, critical. We've been told that she is stable, but she still has a way to go yet. Whoever applied the aid to her saved her leg and probably her life. The lieutenant is very lucky."

The medical officer paused and took a deep breath and then looked directly into Nicollette's eyes.

"Mr. Johnson's wound was not nearly as bad as the lieutenant's. He had a couple shards of cement imbedded in his arm that needed to come out, so we sent him along with the lieutenant to be treated. It must have been very interesting on that island last night, Miss Beverley. Yes, an interesting night to be sure."

Nicollette stood from the examining table and started towards the tent entrance. "Thank you, sir."

"You're welcome, Miss Beverley, be sure to get some rest."

Nicollette walked out into the late morning heat. *I wonder if he knew I was the one who helped Nazrine. I wonder.* She turned the corner and headed to her tent.

# A Final Briefing

A hand was gently shaking her shoulder.

"Nicky, Nicky. Wake up, sleepyhead."

Nicollette sleepily opened her eyes as she rolled over. "Val! Val!" Nicollette exclaimed, "What are you doing here?"

"Aren't you glad to see me, Nicky?" Val responded sarcastically.

"Of course I am! Don't be silly! When did you get in? What's going on?"

"I just got in from the tanker."

Nicollette looked at her friend. It was good to be safe and back at Ash Sha'am. She was starting to feel comfortable; the rest had done her good.

"What time is it? What's going on?" Nicollette rolled out of her cot.

"It's nearly five, Nicky," Val responded, "and we have a briefing at six!"

"I must have dozed off. I've been asleep for almost six hours," Nicollette exclaimed.

"I'd say you earned it after what I heard from some of the marines. What happened last night, Nicky?" Val asked.

There was a silence. A pause allowing the inquisitive tension among the two friends to abate a little. Again, Nicollette knew she would be asked about her experience. She did not want to hide anything from her friends, but she just wasn't completely comfortable talking yet.

"I'm still putting it all together in my head. Give me just a little more time." Nicollette smiled at Val. Her internal numbness was abating, but she still did not feel ready to tell her story. "Besides, I'm a bit peckish and we have a meeting soon. How about heading over to the mess?"

Sarah entered the tent as Nicollette, and Val were leaving.

"Where are you two going?" she asked quietly.

"Off to the mess to eat something before the briefing."

Sarah looked at her two friends and agreed to join them.

At the table, Nicollette could see that Sarah was struggling, hardly touching her food, eyes facing down. She excused herself and left the mess tent.

"I wonder what's up with Sarah?" Val asked. "She's been like this since I got back."

"I don't know, I'm concerned as well. I'm sure she will tell us when she's ready. Val, have you heard anything about Peg? She was supposed to relieve me at the Island but did not show up. They said it was a change of plans."

"She's probably still on the dhow. When they brought me in, I saw a couple of boats missing so I assume she is still out in the Gulf."

Nicollette and Val entered the briefing tent at 17:45. The tent was filled with more chairs than yesterday. The maps of the Tunb Islands were still displayed on the easels at the front. As more people entered the room, Nicollette recognized some of them as the Royal Marines who were with her on the Island. Captain McQuinn walked in as well as the radioman from the dhow and

Val recognized some crew members from the tanker. Sarah walked in and sat down next to Nicollette. Her expression was blank, and she stared straight forward.

"Hello, Miss Beverley."

Nicollette turned to see Charles Thompson. He was in a suit and tie, quite unusual for a man to be dressed that way in such heat like Ash Sha'am.

"Hello Mr. Thompson," Nicollette replied with subdued excitement given her surroundings. "What are you doing here?"

"I'm here for the briefing. There is a lot to cover this evening. A lot has happened." Charles Thompson turned to the front where Majors Hartwell and Blasingame had arrived as well as some other official looking people, including some men attired in full Arab dress. "Looks like we are going to start, Miss Beverley." He leaned in and whispered into Nicollette's ear, "I'm very proud of you."

Nicollette watched as Mr. Thompson walked to the front and sat down next to the men in Arab dress. *I wonder what he meant when he said he was "proud of me?" How does he even know about last night?*

Major Hartwell opened the briefing.

"Good evening. Early this morning, an attack on the British petroleum tanker, the British Engineer, was thwarted on the Lesser Tunb Island. This was the result of a coordinated effort of Intelligence, Communications, and the Royal Marines. As we talked about at yesterday's briefing, our Intelligence has been monitoring signals in the area for some time regarding the potential hijacking of a petroleum tanker. Our readiness was accelerated Monday when analysis suggested an attack was possible as early as today. It was determined that the timing for such an operation would be ideal during this time. Our naval strength in the Gulf is currently rather diminished. The HMS Sheffield was in port at Aden and the Americans were preoccupied off the coast of Kuwait. In addition, today is the Muslim holiday of Rabi Al-Awwal, a time of new beginnings, in this case, the start of spring. Couple this holiday with the current political situation in Tehran between the Shah's government and the Khomeini revolutionaries and there you have it. Timing. Now, Major Blasingame will review what actions we took in preparation in the event of an attack. Major Blasingame."

Major Blasingame walked to the front, cleared her throat, and started to speak. "Good evening. Our preparations began about a week ago. We have all heard about 'towns springing up overnight,' well, welcome to Ash Sha'am. With the assistance of our Emirate allies, we were able to construct our base here at Ash Sha'am in 96 hours. Everything you see here had to be flown into Dubai and transported to this area. Our local friends helped with the heavy equipment and logistics."

Major Blasingame pointed to the group of men dressed in Arab attire and continued.

"It was quite a task. Most of the logistics were carried out at night as we wanted to keep the scope of this base relatively small and indiscreet. No need to raise any suspicions as to our presence here. The Royal Marines finished the project, and we were up and running by Saturday. We obtained the dhows and immediately went to work modifying them to meet our needs. Our plans finalized Monday morning. Under the recommendation of the M O D, Communications group 228/157, Major Hartwell's and my group was assigned to handle the communications and were flown in from Cheltenham on Tuesday. In total, an attachment of one hundred Royal Marines, under the command of Captain McQuinn, was assigned to Ash Sha'am."

Major Blasingame returned to her seat. Major Hartwell moved back to the front of the room.

"So, this is where we were just twenty-four hours ago. Captain McQuinn will now review our strategy and the events of last night. Captain McQuinn." The marine captain addressed the group.

"Aye. Our plan was to deploy a small force, fifteen marines, three civilians, a naval linguist and myself, on the Lesser Tunb Island and establish a communications outpost. We would also deploy about fifty marines on three dhows and place them near the route of the British Engineer tanker. Communications specialists would be airlifted to the tanker and a communications center established here at Ash Sha'am. Now everyone could talk to each other. We landed at the Lesser Tunbs at approximately 19:15 hours and were operational by 20:00 hours. Just after 22:00 hours, our Naval linguist, Lieutenant Amin, overheard a concerning message and had it forwarded to Ash Sha'am for analysis. Upon review at Ash Sha'am, it was determined to call an all-out alert. An attack was imminent on the tanker and the staging point was determined to be the Lesser Tunb Island. We immediately called for reinforcements from the marines escorting the tanker. At approximately 01:30 hours, a firefight started on the northern face of the island."

Captain McQuinn used a pointer to show on the map of the island the location of the firefight. He then explained that most of his marines were pinned down on the southern side of the Island.

"Our position was tenuous at best. We were facing a force of at least fifty and there were fifteen of us. Reinforcements were still an hour away. We established a defensive perimeter. Meanwhile on the northern side, the naval linguist, Lieutenant Amin, and one of the civilians, Miss Nicollette Beverley, found themselves facing a force of nearly twenty. If they failed to stop the advance, we on the southern side would be surrounded. The mission would fail."

Nicollette closed her eyes as Captain McQuinn described the situation on the island, her heart racing in her chest as her mind relived the events of the last night over and over. Pow, pow, pow! Her ears could still hear the gun fire. She could smell the sulfur in her nose. Sweat was now forming under her arms as Nicollette envisioned Lieutenant Amin crunched up in the back of the ditch, bleeding severely. *Fire the damn gun, Miss Beverley!* Nicollette opened her eyes and looked at the captain.

"We were able to contain the situation on the southern side of the Island until the reinforcements arrived. A group of us went to the northern side where the firefight was continuing. When we arrived, we found the naval linguist, Lieutenant Amin, severely wounded and the civilian, Miss Nicollette Beverley, firing into the assailants. We quickly finished the firefight and were able to remove the lieutenant to receive treatment. The island was secure by 03:30 hours. Our casualties were two dead and eight wounded, one officer, six marines and one civilian injured. Latest reports say that all are stable. Of the seventy-five or so attackers, there were twelve dead on the southern side and ten dead on the northern side. There were another twenty attackers wounded on the Island. We took over thirty prisoners including the officers in charge. They are currently under interrogation. The tanker, the British Engineer, went past the Lesser Tunb Island at 08:00 hours, unharmed. We received orders to evacuate our position at 13:00 hours this afternoon."

The captain sat down as Major Hartwell stood at the front again. There was a hand on Nicollette's knee as Val whispered into her ear. "Omigosh! What a night you had! What a night!"

The thoughts in Nicollette's head now turned to the number ten. *Ten dead! Perhaps it was me or maybe it was the marines! Either way, I was there! I was shooting! It was self-defense, but still, I killed another, maybe several!* A sudden numbness filled her body, her hands and feet felt heavy, and all the moisture left her mouth. Her breathing became more pronounced, she could not get enough air. *Calm down, Nicky*, she thought. She forced a deep breath, then another and another. Nicollette recalled Captain McQuinn saying to her, *Don't look, lass. Do not look.* Nicollette turned to Val. Tears were flowing out of her friend's eyes and her complexion had turned pale. Nicollette took another deep breath and reached for Val's hand.

"I'm alright, Val! I am here. I did what I had to do!" she whispered. "And you would have done the same."

Another Royal Marine officer stood up in front of the group. Nicollette did not recognize him. His protruding jaw emphasized his expressionless face. He started to read from a paper he was holding.

"At approximately 13:00 this afternoon, communications with our command dhow went silent. We immediately went into critical mode but were unable to reestablish communications. We called for aerial reconnaissance and dispatched two dhows to investigate. At approximately 14:00, we received word that debris was seen floating in the last reported area of the command vessel. Air recon is looking for survivors and the dhows should be arriving shortly. We will pass on information as we receive it."

The room was silent. Nicollette, still holding Val's hand, turned to Sarah. Their eyes met.

"Peg?" Nicollette whispered.

All Sarah could do was nod her head. She raised her hands to cover her face. Nicollette turned to see Val quietly staring at the floor, tears flowing down her cheek. Nicollette went numb. *Peg, our poor Peg. Maybe she's alright. Please let her be alright!*

Charles Thompson was now addressing the group about the political aspects of the early morning action. Nicollette could hear but her mind kept thinking of Peg.

"We interrogated the prisoners, including officers of the raiding party. For the most part, they have been surprisingly cooperative, and we now have a better idea of the full scope of the operation. In brief, we have learned that the attack on the British Engineer was orchestrated by senior officials of SAVAK, the secret police in Iran, and approved by the Shah himself. Evidently, the situation in Tehran is becoming more hostile towards the Shah and the Khomeini followers are gaining strength. I can tell you firsthand, having been in Tehran the last few days, that the protests are getting larger and more violent. A plan was devised to reverse the momentum of Khomeini and galvanize Iran and support around the Shah. Hence the attack on the British Engineer. The attack would be blamed on Khomeini, discredit his intentions and cast doubt on his 'revolution.' All in the hopes of rallying the Iranian people around the Shah."

Charles Thompson paused, drew a breath and peered out at the group.

"Our operation here was a success, however, there will be no victory parades or recognition. In fact, no one outside of the people involved will ever know anything about what took place these last few days. We must remember how important the Shah and his country are to England and the west. We do not want to embarrass him. Our ambassador in Tehran has met with Iranian officials to discuss the situation and arrangements were made to release the prisoners back to Iran. This was accomplished just before this briefing. I will note that several prisoners asked for asylum. I will be going back to Tehran in the morning. Thank you."

Charles Thompson returned to his place. Nicollette

could feel the strength coming back to her body. Her numbness was now being replaced by a sense of calm and the hopeful feeling that Peg was alright. She could breathe. She felt thirsty.

Major Blasingame concluded the briefing by thanking everyone for their efforts. She announced that the HMS Sheffield would be in Dubai tomorrow and that further instructions would be announced in the next day or so. The briefing was adjourned. There was quiet chatter as the tent emptied. Nicollette stood from her chair, her legs still shaking and heavy.

# The Year

Major Hartwell was standing with Captain McQuinn, Mr. Thompson, and Lieutenant Blankin. She looked directly at the three women. Her mouth was flat and her eyes firm.

"Miss Beverley, Miss Davies, Miss Green. I know you, like all of us, are deeply concerned about Miss Wilson and the crew of the dhow. Please be assured that every effort is being made to find any survivors. I know it is hard but all we can do is wait. You are welcome to accompany Lieutenant Blankin to the communications hut if you wish, but I would suggest a quiet time instead. I will personally keep you updated as information becomes available."

As the four of them left the tent, Sergeant Durban approached Nicollette and pulled her aside.

"Major Blasingame would like to talk with you for just a minute, Miss Beverley."

Nicollette turned to Sarah, Val and Lieutenant Blankin. "I'll catch up with you later."

She saw Major Blasingame standing alone in the back of the tent. Forcing a smile, she approached her. "Major, you wanted to see me?"

Major Blasingame looked at Nicollette and put her hand on her shoulder. "Miss Beverley. I know this is a difficult time for you and for all of us as well, but there are some important people who want to talk with you. Could you be up to it?"

Nicollette looked back at Major Blasingame. *How can she ask me to do this after everything that has happened to me last night and now with Peg? I'm human and I have feelings!* Charles Thompson walked over and placed his hand on Nicollette's other shoulder.

"Nicollette, this is rather important, so, if you could."

*After all he has done for me, it is the least I can do. I need to gather myself and do what they ask. It must be very important.*

She looked at Major Blasingame and said, "Yes ma'am."

"Splendid, thank you. Go and freshen up and meet back here in ten minutes. Does that work?"

When she returned, Major Blasingame met her at the tent opening.

"Feeling a little better, Miss Beverley?"

"Yes ma'am, thank you."

"Good. I just want to remind you of where we are, and that this society is very male dominated. The people you are about to meet are very important to us, so I know you will act accordingly."

Nicollette nodded as Major Blasingame brought her to meet four men wearing full Arab dress. She held out her arm as if to usher Nicollette into the group.

"Ah, Miss Beverley. I want to introduce you to Sheik Yousef bin Ibraham. He is the local leader in this part of the UAE and is the personal representative of the government in Abu Dhabi and this is his translator, Ahmed."

Nicollette extended her right hand to shake hands but was not met with a counter hand from either man. *Must be tradition or something.* She withdrew her hand.

Ahmed said something to the sheik, and he looked at Nicollette. Ahmed replied in his heavily Arab-accented English.

"The sheik was informed about the heroic efforts last night and when he found out that one of the heroes was a woman, he wanted to see her."

*Me! A hero!* Nicollette's heart started to pound at a rapid rate. She did not feel like a hero. She did not feel deserving. *Peg is the hero! How can I be a hero when Peg is...well?* Nicollette could not finish her thought. Her stomach was churning, and her heart continued to pound. She felt like she wanted to run away, be alone, and avoid the recognition. *I do know how important this is, after all, the major asked me directly.*

The sheik spoke to his translator while looking at Nicollette. Ahmed nodded his head.

"In this country, women are not allowed to be heroes, only men. There are few women heroes if any, but you are not from here. The sheik says he is surprised how young you are to be so brave."

Nicollette could feel herself blush at the compliment and yet she could feel herself standing a little bit straighter and taller. She gathered her thoughts and responded politely. "Tell the sheik thank you from me and that this is the first time I've met a sheik."

Ahmed said something to the sheik, and he gave a slight grin. There was more conversation between the two men. The translator turned to Nicollette and began to speak, all the while under the grin of the sheik.

"The sheik wants to tell you he has four daughters, and he hopes that when they grow up, they will have a chance to be heroes and to be as brave as you. He also wants to give you a token of appreciation for your bravery here in the Emirates."

Nicollette could feel a hand on her shoulder. She took a quick look to see Mr. Thompson standing behind her as Ahmed reached into a pocket and handed Nicollette a small purse. Nicollette looked at the major for permission to accept the gift. The major nodded her head in approval. Nicollette opened the purse and removed an object that was wrapped in tan silk. She gingerly unwrapped a medal that was about the size of a fifty pence coin. It was gold with four stones embedded. One green, one black, one red and one white. There was Arabic writing around the edges. Nicollette's eyes were wide open, and her hands were shaking as she showed the medal to the major, Mr. Thompson, and Captain McQuinn. It was the most beautiful piece of jewelry she had ever held. Nicollette looked back at the sheik, holding back tears from all her mixed emotions. She forced a big smile as Ahmed described the medal.

"Miss Beverley, the sheik wanted me to present to you this medal. He says it is his first time to present this award to a woman. The four stones, a red ruby, a green emerald, a black onyx and a white diamond represent the four colors of the Emirate flag and the writing says, 'For Bravery in Action. United Arab Emirates.'"

Nicollette looked at Ahmed and then the sheik. She fought harder to hold back her tears. She did not know what to say or do. She remembered how she felt when she received the field hockey championship trophy, but this was way more exciting and on a much different level. Nicollette gathered a breath and, doing her best to hide her emotions, responded politely, "Thank you. I am very honored by this." She smiled at the sheik and gave a slight bow.

With that remark, the sheik walked away. Ahmed said goodbyes and followed him out of the tent. Nicollette watched the two men leave. She turned to Major Blasingame, Mr. Thompson, and Captain McQuinn.

"That was some honor they gave me. I feel very humbled."

"Well lass, you were very brave last eve. By holding off the attackers, you helped save the day and you certainly saved Lieutenant Amin."

In all the excitement, Nicollette had almost forgotten about the lieutenant. She looked at the major.

"Have you heard anything about Nazrine, Mr. Troughton, or Peg, sorry, I mean Margaret?"

"Lieutenant Amin is out of surgery and is stable and Mr. Troughton will be here tomorrow." The major's expression turned serious. "As for Miss Wilson, the search and rescue mission should be underway, and we will be hearing from them soon." The major surprised Nicollette when she reached for her left hand. "Nicollette, I know you are going through a wave of emotions right now. I also know that you will work through them at your time. You were trained to handle situations physically and mentally. The emotional part, well, that is an individual experience. We are here if you need us. What you just did, accepting the sheik's gift, will go a long way politically. Thank you. What you do with the medal is up to you; however, not a word of your actions should ever be spoken beyond this organization. Believe me, it's for the better." Major Blasingame's expression softened, and she smiled. "We are very proud of you, Miss Beverley. Well done."

The major extended her hand and Nicollette obliged. As they shook hands, a deep desire to embrace her overcame Nicollette. Major Blasingame received her. A few tears rolled down Nicollette's cheeks as they clutched, her pent-up emotion now surfacing from deep inside her. They embraced for what seemed like an hour, but it was just a minute or so when Mr. Thompson put his hand on Nicollette's back and she stepped away from the major.

"I'm sorry, Major. I know that wasn't protocol."

"That is quite alright, Miss Beverley. We bend the rules sometimes," Major Blasingame responded with a smile. "Now if you three will excuse me, I'm going to the communications tent. You are welcome to join me."

"Thank you, Major, but I have to finish my report first," Captain McQuinn replied.

"Maybe later, Major. I have to get ready to leave," Charles Thompson added.

"And you, Miss Beverley?"

"Thank you, Major, I'll probably see you later."

The major left the tent leaving Nicollette alone with Charles Thompson.

"I wanted to talk with you, Nicollette. First, I am very proud of you and how you handled yourself early this morning. I also know firsthand about what you are feeling now, the emotional and physical toll of this job can be overwhelming, but you must remain strong. I remember my first experience like it was yesterday. We learn and grow and get even better at our positions. You will be just fine, I promise. Anyways, I just wanted to say, well done, girl."

Charles Thompson smiled at Nicollette. They embraced and smiled at each other.

"Thank you, Mr. Thompson. Thank you for everything."

"You're welcome, Nicollette Beverley. Very welcome."

Nicollette wrapped her medal back in the silk and put it into the small purse. She had been clutching it in her hand the whole time. The purse went into her front pocket.

The sun's last rays were dimly lighting the camp as the two of them exited the tent into the cooler evening air.

"I must get ready to leave, Nicollette. We'll catch up later in Cheltenham."

"I hope so."

Val and Sarah were leaving as Nicollette approached her tent.

"Everything alright, Nicky?" Val asked.

"Everything is fine," Nicollette responded with a purposeful smile, trying to avoid eye contact.

"We're headed to the communication tent. There's got to be some word by now," Val said, anxious.

Sarah appeared totally drained of energy. Her normally fair complexion was now absent of any color and her long red hair was in need of a brush. She looked at Nicollette and in a raspy voice asked if she wanted to join them.

"Yes, but I need to do something first," Nicollette said. "I'll be there shortly."

As Nicollette entered the tent, she noticed her clothes from the night before lying bunched up at the side of her bed. The dried blood stains on her shirt and shorts caught her eyes. She looked at her dirty clothing and felt the medal in her pocket. She sat on Peg's bed, Peg's belongings and clothing in the same neat order as they were when the four of them left the tent yesterday. *But now, there are only three back in this tent. Oh Peg, please be alright,* Nicollette pleaded silently.

She turned her attention back to the bloodied clothes on the floor. She closed her eyes. She could hear Lieutenant Amin, Nazrine, yelling, *Fire the damn gun, Miss Beverley,* over and over in her head. Nicollette started to feel anxious. Her mind and body demanded some fresh air.

There was music wafting from the mess area as Nicollette left the tent. The sun had set, and the lights were on in the camp. There was another full moon out as she found herself wandering towards the docking area. The music from the mess slowly faded away as she reached the hill above the docks; now all she could hear was the gentle lapping of the water against the shore. The sky was filled with stars and the moon cast brilliantly against the water. She sat down and drew in breaths of the cool, calm air. Nicollette pulled the small purse from her pocket and gingerly unwrapped the medal. She held it up to the moonlight and the stones sparkled. It was truly beautiful. Magnificent. Hers. She stared at the medal for a few minutes then wrapped it and put it back in her pocket.

Nicollette's eyes closed, trying to enjoy this moment of calm, working hard to push out thoughts of the last night's events and of her friend Peg. Instead, she focused her mind on recapturing moments of the last fourteen months of her life. She had come a long way, from the field hockey team to working at Russell's, to the letter, the training, the bridge, Bulgaria, communications and now to Ash Sha'am. *What a journey it has been! And I am just getting started!* Her mind now drifted to Brockwirth, home, her parents and friends on the outside. She thought about her time spent reflecting at the tower and at the war memorial. Nicollette felt she should be emotional as she thought about her journey, but the emotions were not coming. She was drained. She had spent most of her emotional currency in the past few hours; instead, she felt a sense of pride and accomplishment rising throughout her being. She had been through so much and grown well beyond her years. She had experienced highs and lows and participated in events that others only read about or see on tele. But for her, Nicollette, this was real! This was her life! She worked hard for it, and deep down, she loved it! She was only twenty-one years old, so much more waiting for her.

Nicollette opened her eyes and took a deep breath of the salty air. She would be ok, and everything would be alright. She stood up and dusted the sand from her shorts, wiped her eyes, and headed back to the communications tent. Cheers!